He's The One

Katie Price is one of the UK's most famous women. She is a successful businesswoman and a bestselling author, having published nine novels and five autobiographies. Katie is a patron of Vision Charity which supports blind and visually impaired children, a role inspired by caring for her disabled son Harvey. Katie lives in Sussex with her new husband and four children. She is a keen horsewoman.

Praise for Katie Price's novels:

'A page-turner… it is brilliant. Genuinely amusing and readable. This summer, every beach in Spain will be polka-dotted with its neon pink covers'
Evening Standard

'The perfect post-modern fairy tale' *Glamour*

'*Angel* is the perfect sexy summer read' *New Woman*

'A perfect book for the beach' *Sun*

'Glam, glitz, gorgeous people… so Jordan!' *Woman*

'A real insight into the celebrity world' *OK!*

'Brilliantly bitchy' *New!*

'Celebrity fans, want the perfect night in? Flick back those hair extensions, pull on the Juicy Couture trackie, then join Angel on her rocky ride to WAG central' *Scottish Daily*

'*Crystal* is charming. Gloriously infectious' *Evening Standard*

'Passion-filled' *heat*

'Peppered with cutting asides and a directness you can only imagine coming from Katie Price, it's a fun, blisteringly paced yet fluffy novel.'
Cosmopolitan

'An incredibly addictive read' *heat*

Also available by Katie Price

Fiction
Angel
Angel Uncovered
Paradise
Crystal
Sapphire
The Comeback Girl
In the Name of Love
Santa Baby

Non-Fiction
Being Jordan
Jordan: A Whole New World
Jordan: Pushed to the Limit
Standing Out
You Only Live Once
Love, Lipstick and Lies

Katie Price x

He's
The One

arrow books

Published by Arrow Books 2014

2 4 6 8 10 9 7 5 3

First published in Great Britain in 2013 by Century

Arrow Books
Random House, 20 Vauxhall Bridge Road,
London SW1V 2SA

www.randomhouse.co.uk

Addresses for companies within The Random House Group Limited can
be found at: www.randomhouse.co.uk/offices.htm

The Random House Group Limited Reg. No. 954009

A CIP catalogue record for this book
is available from the British Library

ISBN 9780099564744

The Random House Group Limited supports the Forest Stewardship
Council® (FSC®), the leading international forest-certification
organisation. Our books carrying the FSC label are printed on FSC®-
certified paper. FSC is the only forest-certification scheme supported
by the leading environmental organisations, including Greenpeace.
Our paper procurement policy can be found at:
www.randomhouse.co.uk/environment

Typeset by SX Composing DTP Ltd, Rayleigh, Essex
Printed and bound by CPI Group (UK) Ltd, Croydon, CR0 4YY

Part 1

Chapter 1

June 1999

Liberty was not having a good day. Her daughter Brooke had been up all the night before with a raging temperature, which meant Liberty barely had an hour's sleep. She had started her shift at the restaurant – a popular Italian in Brighton – feeling like a zombie and no doubt looking like one too. And of all nights it would be a Saturday – the busiest of the week. She wouldn't finish until after midnight.

She plastered on her best, *Hi, I'm your waitress, can I help you?* smile, which felt more like a grimace, and went over to the table by the window. There were six twenty-somethings sitting there, a mix of young men and women all out to enjoy themselves. Most likely they were going on to a club afterwards, or a film, or a party. Lucky, lucky them . . . Liberty tried not to let it get to her, but it had been a very long time since she'd been anywhere other than to her friend Em's with a cheap bottle of wine and a video from Blockbusters. She was only twenty-one and sometimes felt that her mum, who was in her early-forties, had a far better social life than she did. Plus she had a boyfriend, which was more than Liberty did. She may as well be wearing a sign round her neck that said, *Single, loser, game over*, because that was pretty much how she felt.

'Hi, are you all ready to order?' She was obviously wearing her invisibility cloak as they continued chatting, oblivious to her standing there. She was used to this as a waitress: you were either ignored or leered at. Very occasionally someone was actually polite.

She sighed and pulled the notepad out of the pocket of her black apron. If they didn't get on with it she was likely to fall asleep standing up. She'd have to down a Red Bull to try and wake herself up, or a double espresso, or both.

Finally a young man noticed her.

'Guys, we should order. Sorry to keep you waiting.' His accent was American. He smiled at Liberty and, even feeling like one of the living dead she registered how strikingly handsome he was, with blue, blue eyes and dark blond hair. He had the look of a twenty-something Brad Pitt in *Thelma and Louise* – a film which she and Em had watched many times, rewinding a particular scene involving Mr Pitt. He was boyishly handsome and radiated confidence, his smile a reminder that life didn't have to be so grim.

'No problem at all.' She smiled back, the most genuine smile she had managed all day. But hang on, she didn't have a pen. She patted her pocket and felt around the neckline of her t-shirt. Bollocks! She was for ever losing pens. It drove Marco the manager absolutely crazy.

Good-looking gestured to his own face. What was he on about? Did she have a mark on her? Knowing her luck it would be a glob of Playdough courtesy of her daughter. She had once worked an entire shift with half a breadstick in her hair, which Brooke had stuck there without her realizing. Not her best look. He tapped his ear. Oh, so that's where her pen was. Nice of him to notice.

Liberty took down their orders for garlic bread – the men; green salad, no dressing – the three women; various pastas, pizzas, beers and wine and stifled a yawn. Shit, she ought to look more alert. At this rate she would end up with zero tips and she relied on the money from those to boost her low wages.

'How many hours have you got to go?' Good-looking asked her sympathetically. Nice of him to ask. Ninety-nine point nine per cent of her customers wouldn't have.

'Oh, I'll finish about midnight.' God, that was hours away!

'Unlucky. And Saturday night as well.'

Liberty shrugged. Yeah, like she had so many other exciting places to be. She always worked on Saturday nights. The blonde girl next to Good-looking was listening intently to their conversation; she was probably wondering why her boyfriend was talking to a mere waitress.

'Cory, can you order me a bottle of sparkling mineral water?' the blonde asked in a cut-glass accent. She had beautiful tanned skin and glossy honey-blonde hair. Everything about her looked expensive. She drummed immaculately manicured nails on the table as she spoke. Liberty curled her fingers round her notepad. She had intended to paint her nails today but, when she'd finally sat down, Brooke had wanted to make cats out of Playdough and so Liberty was still wearing chipped pink nail varnish. She had at least managed to wash her hair, but with no time to dry it had tied it back in a messy ponytail. She thought she might have put some mascara on, when she was on autopilot getting ready for her shift, but that was it, bar some lip balm.

He grinned at Liberty. 'I guess you heard that. A bottle of sparkling mineral water, please.'

Cory . . . that was an unusual name, Liberty mused as she rushed back to the pass with the orders. She rather liked it. Though it hardly mattered what she thought. Good-looking Cory had a girlfriend.

But when she took the drinks over, and was pouring out glasses of wine, he again made a point of talking to her.

'So do you work here all the time . . .' he read her name badge . . . 'Liberty? Cool name. Unusual.'

Embarrassing actually. Her mum Nina had wanted something striking for her daughter, but Liberty didn't think the name suited her at all. It seemed a big name for someone with such a small life. And, ironically, her mum and lots of her friends had ended up calling her Libs.

'Part-time.'

'So what else do you do?'

Blondie was giving her the evil eye.

'Well, I want to be an actress and I sometimes get modelling jobs.' She tried not to think about how long ago it was since she had done any modelling . . . or how long since she'd had an audition.

'Is this the Sauvignon Blanc we ordered?' the blonde interrupted, holding up her glass. 'It tastes funny.'

Liberty steeled herself for an argument. She knew there was nothing wrong with the wine, it was one of the most expensive ones on the list, but probably not good enough for high-maintenance Blondie.

Cory picked up her glass and took a sip. 'It's fine, Zara. You had that glass of champagne earlier, so it's

6

probably the contrast.' He looked at Liberty again. 'So you're an actress and a model?' he continued. 'I just knew it with your looks.' He lowered his voice slightly. 'You really do have the most incredible eyes I have ever seen.'

Liberty frowned. He was handsome and charming, and she appreciated the nice things he'd said – God knows they had been thin on the ground lately – but it was completely out of order for him to be saying those things when his girlfriend could hear everything.

'Thanks, but maybe you'd better save your compliments for your girlfriend.'

And before he could reply Liberty whisked away to serve another table. Wanker! Coming on to her with the girl sitting right next to him. Unbelievable! She should be used to it by now – only last week some sleaze bag had written down his phone number on the receipt, while his wife was sitting there entertaining their toddler with a picture book.

She didn't even look at Cory when she returned to their table with the garlic bread and salads and he didn't say anything. He must have realised that he'd overstepped the mark. But when she was on her way to the bar to collect a drinks order he caught up with her.

'Hey, I really didn't mean to offend you.'

'Don't worry about me.' Liberty folded her arms defensively. 'What about your girlfriend?'

Cory shook his head. 'I don't have one. That's Zara, she's my ex-girlfriend. We're just friends now.'

He might think that, but Liberty doubted Zara felt the same. He slid his hands into his pockets, and gazed at her. 'And I don't usually do this, but you're the most beautiful girl I've ever seen.'

He sounded completely genuine and Liberty

wasn't easily taken in. Wow! Suddenly all the noise surrounding them – the chatter of the diners, the clinking of glasses, Celine Dion singing that her heart would go on – seemed to recede, until it was just the two of them, looking at each other. She was lost for words.

'Look, I know you're working, but a friend of mine is having a party and it will still be going on when you finish. I'd really like it if you came,' he was saying.

She couldn't even remember the last time she'd gone to a party. Well, one that wasn't a children's party, that didn't involve Pass the Parcel, Musical Bumps, and at least two toddler tantrums plus all of the guests having a major sugar rush. Her mum would be cool with her staying out, Brooke was better and Liberty wasn't due back at work until twelve the following day. Why not go to the party? She never did anything impulsive any more, her whole life revolved around her daughter and work.

'I'd really like it if you came,' Cory repeated. 'Who am I kidding? I'd love it.'

She smiled at him. How could she resist that? 'Okay, sure.'

She got a smile right back. 'You've just made my night.' He took a piece of paper out of his wallet and scribbled down the address and his phone number.

'Liberty! Can you go and sort out table six? They're saying they didn't order the Puttanesca . . . one of them is allergic to anchovies apparently,' Marco cut across their conversation. And just like that the moment was gone. Cory returned to his table and Liberty went back to work, but she felt a spark of excitement at the thought of seeing him later. She hadn't felt like this for ages, and though the customers at table six were grumpy, her good mood seemed to calm them down.

Her friend Em, who also worked at the restaurant, insisted that Liberty come round to her place later on to borrow something to wear for the party. Liberty had known her since the age of three when they'd gone to the same nursery school. Em wanted to be a photographer and lived with her boyfriend Noah, an Aussie doing the travelling thing. Liberty kept dreading that Em was going to say she was moving to Australia with him. Em was her best, best friend; she had been such an incredible support when Liberty had found out she was pregnant with Brooke, and had always been there for her. Life without her was unimaginable.

While Em rifled through her wardrobe, pulling out various garments, Liberty sat cross-legged on the bed and looked at the note from Cory again. 'The party's on Portland Place. That's one of those really posh roads off Marine Drive, isn't it? Those houses are massive. They'll probably think I'm staff when I turn up and expect that I'm going to do the washing up.'

An eye roll from Em. 'No, they won't, not by the time I've finished with you. Right, I reckon it's got to be between these two.'

Liberty looked at the dresses Em was holding up. She lived in combats, jeans and trainers, and couldn't wait to dress up for a change. Before she'd had Brooke she'd loved getting dressed up for a night out, but nowadays she never really had the chance. This night was already turning into the best she'd had in ages and she hadn't even got to the party yet.

Em chucked both dresses on the bed. 'Go on, girl. I know you can't wait to get them on.'

Grinning, Liberty pulled off her waitress uniform of black trousers and white shirt. Thank God she had shaved her legs yesterday. She picked up the first dress – a tight red Lycra off-the-shoulder mini dress.

She slipped it on and looked in the mirror. The colour suited her dark brown hair and green eyes, and her figure didn't look too bad either.

Em came back into the room holding two glasses, one of which she handed to Liberty. 'Vodka and Coke, get that down you.'

She took a sip, and instantly felt a warm glow envelop her.

'Liking that dress,' Em said, casting a critical eye over it. 'Classy *and* sexy. They definitely won't mistake you for staff in that. Let's see you in the other one.'

It was a baby pink halterneck that suited Em with her blonde hair but made Liberty look washed out, so the red it was, along with a pair of gold strappy sandals that killed her feet, but what the heck! A bit of make up, a spritz of Em's Obsession perfume, her hair out of the ponytail, and she was ready. It had to be the quickest-ever makeover . . . but seeing as she usually got dressed in five minutes flat, she felt like she'd had a full on pamper session.

Getting ready had been fun, but now as she stood outside Em's flat waiting for the taxi to turn up, Liberty felt jittery with nerves.

'Can't you come with me?' she asked her friend, who had joined her to smoke a sneaky roll up – Noah strongly disapproved of her smoking and Em was supposed to have given up. Liberty shivered in the thin party dress. It was a cool June night and she regretted not having a jacket.

'Nope, he didn't ask me. Stop stressing, this is meant to be a bit of fun. Remember what that was?' She smiled at her friend. 'That guy is gorgeous. And he obviously really likes you.'

Liberty fiddled with her hair. 'I think I've lost my flirting mojo.'

'I'm not surprised – it's been so long since Eddie.'

Eddie was a friend of Noah's, and Liberty had gone out with him for five months, a year ago. He had been the first guy she had seen since Luke – Brooke's dad. Nice enough, fit enough, she had almost begun to fantasise about them falling in love and creating a happy family for her daughter, when he had said he wasn't ready for that commitment – even though she hadn't mentioned it – and buggered off back to Australia. Liberty wasn't so much heart-broken as extremely wary of getting involved with anyone again, for her daughter's sake.

Her heart had been broken once before by Luke, who hadn't wanted to know when she fell pregnant at eighteen. He'd harboured his own ambitions of being an actor, and fathering a child at the age of nineteen didn't figure in them. He had seen Brooke twice since she was born and didn't give Liberty any money for her maintenance. She dreaded her daughter asking questions about him as she got older. What did you say? How could she soften the blow when she had to reveal the fact that her dad was never interested in her and didn't want to see her?

Em blew out a perfect smoke ring. 'Libs, you'll be fine. It's like riding a bike. It'll come back.'

And then there was no more time to worry as the taxi drew up and Em gave her a quick hug. By now it was half-past twelve and a big part of Liberty wanted to go home, to tiptoe into her daughter's bedroom and watch her sleeping, to kiss her goodnight and shut out the rest of the world. But then she thought of Cory's blue eyes, the way he had looked at her, the way he'd smiled at her. She couldn't deny to herself how much she wanted to see him again.

Chapter 2

Liberty doubted that whoever lived at the house on Portland Place had ever worked as a waitress. No, they would be more used to people waiting on them. When she stepped out of the taxi she froze for a moment looking up at the grand four-storey Regency-style house, painted cream and with huge bow windows. She was tempted to get back in the car but at that moment the front door swung open and Cory stepped out. He was holding two champagne flutes and raised one towards her invitingly.

She walked up the stone steps, feeling awkward and slightly shy. Cory kissed her lightly on the cheek. She caught the scent of some delicious spicy aftershave and again felt that spark of excitement.

'You came. I wasn't sure that you would. I've been looking out for you.' He handed her the glass and clinked his against hers. 'Sorry, does that make me sound desperate? I should warn you now, I'm no good at playing it cool.'

She took a sip and felt the bubbles explode and fizz in her mouth. This was the real deal, not the supermarket Cava she and Em would occasionally treat themselves to when it was on special offer.

'I wasn't sure I would come either.'

He was gazing at her with his blue eyes, and that combined with the champagne made Liberty feel reckless. Her flirting mojo had definitely reawakened . . .

'But then I thought, what the hell?'

A stunning girl in a gold dress appeared in the doorway. 'Cory, come in and shut the door, for God's sake! It's fucking freezing and I don't want to piss the neighbours off with the noise. Daddy will go ape if I do.' She was slurring her words, which made her posh voice into even more of a drawl. Liberty had to swallow back a grin. The drunk girl looked her up and down. 'And you are?'

At least that was what Liberty thought she asked – her words all ran into one another.

'This is Liberty, the friend I told you about. Liberty, this is Olivia.'

'Hiya,' Liberty said politely. 'Pleased to meet you.'

'Hi. Is that a Gucci dress?'

Not unless Gucci dresses retailed for £15.99 . . . 'No, it's House of River Island.'

Olivia wrinkled her nose. 'Don't know it.'

'Oh, it's very exclusive.' Liberty couldn't resist coming out with that.

One of the guests called for Olivia then and she swept away.

Cory grinned. 'Come on, we'd better go inside, we don't want Daddy to go ape.'

He took Liberty's hand and led her in. She felt overwhelmed by the size of the house and its luxurious interior. The vast hallway that was large enough to have a sofa in it where several guests lounged; the glittering chandeliers; the abstract art on the walls; the designer clothes everyone else was wearing; the upper-class accents cutting through the music; the air that was heady with expensive perfume and scented candles. There was a bar in one of the huge living rooms, a DJ set up in the other. Chill-out music was playing, which gave the party a dreamy, late-night club feel, and revolving lights turned the rooms alternating shades of midnight blue and mauve. How the other half lived . . .

They sat down on one of the black velvet sofas. It was after one a.m. now but Liberty felt wide awake.

'Do you always go to parties like this?' she asked, sipping her champagne – it was going down very quickly, probably too quickly, she would slow down in a minute.

Cory smiled. 'No, but Olivia is going out with one of my best friends so that's why I'm here. She's nicer than she sounds, by the way. She can't help being so incredibly filthy rich that she doesn't actually bother to speak properly.'

'Poor her, what a tragedy.'

'I really don't care about her. It's you, with your mesmerising green eyes, I want to know about,' he said, moving closer.

She was aware of his arm behind her on the sofa, his thigh inches away from hers.

Liberty shrugged. 'There's not much to tell that you don't already know – I live in Brighton, I want to be an actress, I work as a waitress.' She didn't want to talk about Brooke – not because she was in any way ashamed of being a single mum, but because she wanted to be an irresponsible twenty-one-year-old just for tonight, and if she mentioned her daughter that would change everything.

'See, not very exciting. What about you? You're American, right?'

'Yep, I'm from San Francisco originally. I'm taking time out from college to travel.'

'And what do you want to do eventually?'

'It might sound pretentious but I want to be a painter.' He reached out and lightly ran a finger along her jawline. 'In fact, I'd love to paint you.'

There was a beat while they gazed at each other in silence.

'So are you at art school?' she asked.

A shadow seemed to fall across Cory's face as he replied, 'No, I'm studying law. My parents weren't keen on me going to art school . . . not academic enough for them. Too risky a future. But I just passed the first year at law school and the deal was that I could have a year out before going back.'

'It doesn't exactly sound as if your heart's in it.'

'Yep, well, we'll see.'

He clearly came from a very different background from hers, with his wealthy friends and a mummy and daddy who wanted him to study law. Liberty's mum and dad had divorced when she was eight – her dad now lived in Manchester and had remarried and had two more children. Her mum had just started going to college because she wanted to be a counsellor, and meanwhile worked part-time as a hairdresser. Neither of them had ever held strong views about what Liberty should or shouldn't do with her life; they just wanted her to be happy.

'So where have you been travelling?' she asked Cory.

'India, Thailand, Australia, various parts of Europe. I'm in the UK for the summer and then I'm supposed to go back to college in the States. But we'll see. At the moment I'm loving Brighton. I've got a flat just along the road from here.' He grinned. 'Who knows? I might stay here for ever. It's got everything

I love . . . the sea, an artistic vibe, a beautiful girl.'

She groaned, 'Please, that was *so* cheesy.'

'I'm sorry, there's something about you that makes me come out with these things. You know, like when I stopped you in the restaurant? I never normally do stuff like that – I'm a shy and reclusive artist. I hardly dare to talk to women. But I think you could be my muse, the woman I've been waiting for.'

'I really think you're taking the piss now.' But Liberty wasn't annoyed – on the contrary she was enjoying, the banter, which had been very much missing from her life recently. She'd thought she'd had an easygoing, fun relationship with Eddie, but then he'd left . . .

'Okay, sorry, I can't help it. I'm fantastically happy that you came to the party. And now you're here I just can't stop looking at you, especially in that House of River Island dress. You're so beautiful, Liberty, and I don't think you realise it, which makes you even more special.'

He was so open and direct about his feelings, it gave her an incredible buzz just to be with him. So far she felt as if she had been stumbling through her life, making the best of things, trying to be a good mum, but always aware that something was missing. Meeting Cory made her feel as if a light had been switched on inside her.

She forgot all about how late it was as they talked, flirted and drank champagne; forgot about being in this wildly expensive house; forgot about how she had work the next day. She was oblivious to everything except Cory. Something drew her to him, she couldn't keep her eyes off him. He made her feel so alive, fizzing with excitement and joy. She felt some of the weight of these last three years fall away from her: the worry, the loneliness, the feeling that she was never going to get

16

a break as an actress, that she'd be a waitress for ever, that she would never be able to give her daughter the sort of life she wanted for her. They covered exes – well, Liberty did a bit of careful censoring – and Cory had apparently ended a two-year relationship with a girl just before he went travelling. Zara, the blonde girl from the restaurant, had been a three-month rebound. Then music – he was into Massive Attack and U2, she liked Robbie Williams and Madonna – and films. He was into movies like *Lock, Stock and Two Smoking Barrels*, while she admitted she loved *Titanic*, that she and Em had been to see it twice at the cinema when it came out the year before and watched it on video at least three times since. They thought it was the most romantic film they had ever seen. He teased her about this. She felt as if they were cramming a month's worth of dates into one night. She wanted to drink it all in. Relish every single second. If this night was going to be all they had, then she wanted to make it one to remember . . .

That was until Zara wandered into the room and made a slightly unsteady bee-line for Cory. She was very drunk. Ignoring Liberty she flopped down on the sofa next to him and rested her head on his shoulder. 'Cory darling, will you take me home now?'

He looked less than impressed. 'I can call you a taxi. I'm not going yet and I'm not taking you home.'

Zara raised her head and squinted at Liberty. She herself was not looking quite so glossy and immaculate now. Her mascara had smudged, her hair was tousled and she was having difficulty focusing.

'Oh, it's your waitress girl. You are *so* predictable.'

'Her name's Liberty,' Cory muttered, sounding annoyed.

Zara didn't bother to say hello.

'And the week before, what was that other girl

17

called? Tash something? And the week before that?'
She leaned forward to speak to Liberty. 'The point is,
Waitress Girl, you're not so special. Cory is always doing
this. He'll have forgotten who you are by tomorrow.'

'Go away, Zara, you're drunk. Again. It's becoming
boring.' There was a hard edge to his voice.

On the verge of tears, she exclaimed, 'Why do you
keep doing this to me? Cory, please . . .'

'You're doing it to yourself.'

For a second Zara remained where she was, as if she
couldn't believe that Cory wasn't going to give in to her.
When it became apparent that he was not, she gave a
strangled sob and rushed out of the room, colliding
with another guest as she did and causing them to spill
their drink.

'Just a friend?' Liberty commented, feeling angry.
Had she fallen for some smooth act from Cory after
all? Was she just his Waitress Girl for one night only?
She had thought he was genuine. God, she was easily
taken in. So out of practice that she fell for the first
good-looking guy who took any interest in her.

'Just a friend now,' he said firmly. 'I'm sorry. She's
off her face . . . doesn't know what she's talking about.
It's all bullshit. I don't want to be with her, and she
can't handle it. I know I might have seemed harsh
with her, but it's time she moved on.'

'You're being cruel to be kind, are you?' For a
fleeting second Liberty felt some sympathy for Zara.
She knew what it felt like when someone didn't want
you any more. 'I should probably go now,' she said.

He stood up. 'Let's get out of here – I can see that
Zara has upset you. How about coming to my flat for
a drink? It's up the road from here.' He held out his
hand to her.

For a moment Liberty hesitated. Would it just be for

a drink? Did she want it to be anything else? The fact was she was enjoying herself more than she had done in such a long time, she wasn't ready for the night to end, even if Cory turned out to be a player . . .

'Please, forget about what Zara said.'

Liberty took his hand and again thought, Why not?

Outside she shivered in the cool breeze coming off the sea. Instantly Cory slipped off his jacket and put it round her shoulders. It was warm with the heat from his body. She loved the gentlemanly gesture, and thought then of Luke, who wouldn't have noticed if she'd been turning blue from hypothermia.

They didn't have far to walk – thank God, as Em's shoes were crippling. Cory was renting a first-floor flat on an elegant crescent overlooking the sea.

'How come you can afford to live here?' asked Liberty as they walked up the wide staircase leading to his front door. It didn't exactly seem the kind of flat a student could normally afford.

He shrugged. 'My parents are paying for it.' He seemed slightly embarrassed to admit it.

Inside it was beautiful, all high ceilings and full-length windows, but phenomenally messy. There were paint brushes, tubes of oil paint, half-empty coffee mugs and wineglasses on every available surface in the living room. CDs were scattered across the floor, and canvases stacked haphazardly against the entire length of one wall. Clearly Cory was not a fan of cleaning.

'Sorry, I would have tidied up if I'd known you were coming. I'm usually much tidier than this,' he said, sweeping a pile of newspapers and magazines off the sofa and on to the floor. Liberty had a feeling that he wasn't – maybe he was too used to people tidying up after him . . .

He opened a bottle of white wine and poured her a glass, and switched the stereo on. Massive Attack's 'Teardrop' pumped out. It felt as if he was setting the scene. Maybe he had done all this the other week with Tash or whatever her name was. Still wearing his jacket, Liberty slipped off her heels and walked around the room, taking it all in, biding her time. She paused in front of a huge painting of a man playing the saxophone. The colours were so vibrant that they seemed to bounce off the canvas and it had an energy that drew her in, so that it felt as if she was there in the picture. Liberty knew absolutely nothing about art but to her Cory's work seemed very impressive.

'This is great,' she told him.

He shrugged. 'I'm not sure it works.' He seemed reluctant to talk more about it. She remembered how Luke used to boast at any opportunity about what a good actor he was.

'Well, for what it's worth coming from me, it's obvious you're really talented.'

'I don't think I am, but thanks anyway. So, are you going to come and sit down?'

The nerves, the sense of anticipation, returned as Liberty sat down next to him on the sofa. She was so out of practice at flirting, completely rusty. She didn't know what to do with her hands or her legs, crossing them then uncrossing them, fiddling with her hair, picking her wineglass up and taking a sip, putting it down again, and all the while wondering what was going to happen next . . . She babbled away with a funny story about how she and Em had dyed their hair red for Comic Relief . . . except Em used permanent dye and it had cost a fortune afterwards to get themselves sorted out at the hairdresser's.

'You'd look beautiful whatever colour your hair was,' Cory said. And, moving closer, lightly kissed her. Liberty felt her heart beating so hard, she was surprised he couldn't hear it. She shivered with longing at the feeling of his lips against hers. At first she was shy and self-conscious. Could she even remember how to kiss properly after so long? He would think she was useless . . . But at the feel of his mouth on hers, and the probing of his tongue, desire overtook her and she kissed him back.

He trailed his fingertips along the side of her neck; she slipped her hand under the back of his shirt, feeling the heat of his skin, longing to feel more. They lay back on the sofa. His hands were on her waist, her breasts. She wanted him so badly her legs turned liquid, and she felt a burning need throbbing between them . . . his body was solid against hers . . . she didn't want this to stop. She tugged at his t-shirt longing to feel his skin against hers. He peeled it off in one fluid motion then unzipped her dress, pausing to gaze at her as she lay there before him.

'God, you're even more beautiful like this,' he murmured, unfastening her bra and kissing her breasts, sucking her nipples until she could feel herself melting at his touch, and burning, and when his fingers reached between her legs, she almost came, it was so intense. She gasped as his caresses quickened, building up whirls of exquisite pleasure within her. She unfastened his jeans, longing to feel him inside her. His cock was ready, perfect. He paused for a moment, and she groaned.

'Sorry, I just need to . . .' He reached into his jeans pocket and pulled out a condom. For a moment she was shocked that she hadn't even thought of it. But then she grabbed it from him, tore the wrapper open

21

and rolled it down his long, hard length. She couldn't wait any longer. 'Now. Hurry,' she gasped.

He plunged into her, and their kisses became harder, deeper, as they fell into a rhythm, and she was going to come and it was breathtaking, dizzying, mind-blowing, and then an orgasm was rippling through her and he was reaching his own climax and arching his back, holding her tightly as he came, burying his face against her shoulder.

There was a moment when they held each other tightly, hardly able to believe the intensity of what they had shared. Then he looked up at her. 'That was incredible,' he murmured

It *was* incredible. She had never slept with someone on the first night she had met them, but with Cory it had felt so completely right. It would have felt wrong not to.

They lay together, bathed in the soft orange glow of the streetlight outside the window. She didn't want to go, she wanted to stay with him, feel his skin against hers. She felt blissed out, relaxed, and couldn't even remember when she had last felt like this – or if she had ever felt like this.

He kissed her and said, 'I've got such a good feeling about you, Liberty.'

'So will you still remember my name tomorrow?' she teased. 'Or will I be that waitress girl you met in Brighton?'

He shook his head. 'I would never forget you.'

Somehow she believed him. She didn't think she would ever forget him either.

He made them both cups of tea and thick slices of toast – he had Marmite on his and she had jam on hers and she refused to kiss him afterwards until he had cleaned his teeth, protesting that she hated the taste of Marmite.

'I'll throw it away and never have it again,' he promised.

They talked some more. She wanted to hear about his travelling: his descriptions of the places he had been; the people he had met. It was all fascinating to her. He couldn't believe that she had only ever been to Spain and France. And France had only been a day trip to Dieppe with the school, where they had gone round a *supermarché* and watched their teachers stock up on cheese and duty-free wine, then walked aimlessly round the old town in the rain before boarding the ferry back to Newhaven. She felt as if she hadn't lived compared to Cory.

'I never seem able to afford to go abroad,' Liberty told him. As a single mother, foreign holidays had been out of the question so far. She could barely even afford to take time off and go camping for a week. She changed the subject after that.

'So will you let me draw you now?' asked Cory, reaching for his sketchpad and a pencil.

'But I'm such a mess!' she exclaimed, aware that her make up must have rubbed off, that her hair was cascading wildly over her shoulders, that she was naked except for a white t-shirt of his that she had slipped on.

'You're perfect. Except the t-shirt has to go.' When she didn't make a move, he added, 'I dare you.'

Usually she would have felt self-conscious about being completely naked in front of someone, even someone she'd just slept with, but again she had that reckless feeling. Why not?

Holding his gaze, she sat up and slowly pulled off the garment, then lay on the sofa, reclining on her side, propping her head up on one hand.

'Will this do?'

He nodded and began drawing. She felt as if every part of her was being observed, and instead of feeling awkward as a result, she felt powerful, sexy and desired. He drew with intense concentration for half an hour, without saying a word. Then he closed the sketchpad and threw it on to the floor.

'Hey, can't I see the picture?' Liberty demanded, sitting up and wincing as she rubbed an arm that had gone numb from being too long in the same position.

'I never show off my work until I've finished,' he replied. 'It's a superstition of mine.'

'But I want to see it!' Liberty protested. 'I've been lying here for ages! It was so boring. And then I nearly got the giggles because I remembered that scene in *Titanic* when Leo paints Kate Winslet and she's naked except for a huge blue-diamond necklace.'

'Poor baby, I'll make it up to you, though I can't promise the necklace,' he teased. And, ducking down, he kissed her lightly on the lips then moved lower to kiss her breasts, her stomach, and came to rest between her legs, teasing her deliciously with his tongue, circling, probing, licking, sending stabs of intense pleasure through her body until she found herself on the brink of yet another earth-shattering orgasm.

When she opened her eyes he was smiling at her. 'I hope that wasn't too boring for you.'

'That was amazing,' she murmured, sitting up. 'And there's only one thing that would make it even better.' She put her arms round his neck and pulled him towards her.

'My thoughts exactly,' he whispered, slipping off his boxers.

It was getting light by the time Liberty carefully

24

extricated herself from Cory's embrace. He had fallen asleep and looked adorable stretched out on his side, hair flopping over his forehead. He woke up as she was tiptoeing round the living room, gathering her things. She didn't feel as if she was doing the walk of shame. Her only regret was that she couldn't stay.

'Hey, what are you doing? Let's go to bed,' he suggested.

She thought of waking up next to him, seeing those blue eyes and feeling his body entwined with hers. It was so tempting. And impossible.

Liberty shook her head. 'I have to go. I've work today and I need to sleep first or it will be a disaster.' She quickly got dressed as he called her a taxi. She had spent nearly all her tip money on last night's and she was usually so careful with every penny. As she was about to leave he once more put his jacket round her shoulders.

'Won't you need it?' she asked.

'I'll get it back from you tomorrow . . . I mean today. You'll see me tonight when you've finished work, won't you?'

She said yes, even though she had no idea if she would be able to.

Back home she crept into her daughter's room. Brooke had flung off the duvet and was sleeping on her back, limbs spread out like a starfish. Liberty gently pulled the cover over her and bent down and kissed her forehead.

Chapter 3

'Mummy, Mummy! Can we go to the park?'

Liberty opened her eyes and saw her daughter just inches away: bright-eyed, bushy-tailed, ready for the day. She felt as if she had only been asleep for five minutes, and her head was pounding from all the champagne and wine she'd drunk. 'Hi, baby,' she murmured. 'Come and give Mummy a cuddle.' She raised the duvet to let Brooke scoot inside. With any luck her daughter might be persuaded to go back to sleep.

Or not, as Brooke wriggled round, tickling Liberty with her long blonde hair and digging pointy elbows into her every time she turned over. Sleep was clearly not an option. Sighing, Liberty hauled herself out of bed and into the shower. And half an hour later she and Brooke were at the park, and Liberty was trying to wake herself up with a coffee while Brooke fearlessly scaled the climbing frame. It was only half-past nine. Liberty reckoned she'd had about three hours' sleep. Still, it was worth it . . . *he* was worth it. Every time she thought about Cory she couldn't stop herself from smiling. She had forgotten what it felt like to be so close to someone, to feel a connection. She had told herself that she was perfectly happy, that she didn't need anyone else. Last night had blown that theory out of the water. She couldn't wait to see Cory again.

Back home Liberty's mum Nina was up and making Brooke a snack in the kitchen. She was wearing jeans, a purple t-shirt and flip-flops, and she had tied her long auburn hair into a ponytail. She looked tanned, healthy and a good ten years younger than her actual age of forty-four. Liberty was convinced that it was her mother's spirit and zest for life that kept her looking so young. Nina had always supported her, and helped with Brooke. When Liberty had told her that she was pregnant and was going to keep the baby, Nina was there for her in every way, never once doubting her daughter's decision. Liberty had always had a strong relationship with her mum, and told her everything . . . well, nearly everything. Last night she'd called her from the restaurant and said she'd met a handsome man who wanted to take her to a party.

'Good night?' Nina asked with a smile. 'I didn't hear you come in so I'm guessing it was late.'

Liberty stifled a yawn. 'It was. Very. Morning actually.'

'So, how was the party?'

'It was good.' She couldn't stop a smile from spreading across her face. 'And Cory is gorgeous. He's American and he wants to be an artist.'

'Sounds interesting.' Nina stopped chopping up apple and glanced at her daughter. 'Did you tell him about Brooke?'

At this reality check, Liberty's sense of excitement fizzled out. She was not single and carefree, living for the moment, able to do whatever she wanted whenever she wanted. She was a mum with zero prospects and a lot of responsibility.

She shook her head. 'I wanted to see how it went first. Do you think I should have?'

'I think you should do whatever feels right for you.'

Liberty rolled her eyes. Since her mum had started her course there had been many comments like this one. 'That's a classic counsellor comment!' she protested.

'What do you want me to say then?'

What she'd wanted her mum to say was that everything would be okay. No, that everything would be brilliant, and that Cory would have absolutely no problem accepting that Liberty had a child. And that he would live in Brighton . . . and . . . oh, bugger it, she didn't believe in fairy stories. So instead she settled for the practical, 'Do you think you could babysit Brooke again tonight so I can see Cory? I'll bath her and put her to bed.'

'No problem. It's about time you went out and had some fun. And I'm away on that course next week so I won't be able to babysit then.'

Liberty's shift at the restaurant seemed to pass even more painfully slowly than usual. She kept checking her watch, willing the time away. Only the snatched conversations with Em made it bearable.

Back home she had a long soak in the bath and spent longer than usual on her make up. She thought of the immaculate rich girls at the party last night with their designer outfits – there was no way she could compete with them – so it was a little black dress from TopShop for her. Brooke sensed that she was going out in that way children always do and took ages to settle. She was still awake and crying when Liberty went downstairs. She felt awful as she heard her daughter calling out, '*Mummy!*' No one could twist her heartstrings in the way her daughter could. She hesitated at the front door; maybe she should stay. She could see Cory another night.

'She'll be fine in a minute, she's trying it on,' Nina told her. 'I'll pop up in a bit. Now go!'

Liberty couldn't afford to get another taxi, and there wasn't a bus for half an hour, so she ended up walking the two miles to Cory's flat, arriving late.

'I was beginning to think you weren't coming,' he said when he opened the door to her. He put his arms round her waist and drew her to him, and instantly she felt a flash of lust as he kissed her. And then there was no need to talk as he led her into the bedroom and they tumbled on to the bed together, and the little black dress was soon thrown to the floor . . .

'Are you hungry?' he said, some time later. 'I've made dinner, though it's probably ruined by now.'

'Starving.' She hadn't eaten all day. Her tummy rumbled as if to underline the point.

He pulled on his jeans. 'I should warn you, I'm not the greatest cook.'

'You have other qualities,' she teased, admiring his half-naked body.

Liberty slipped on one of his shirts and followed him into the kitchen where there was a strong smell of burning. Cory had taken the lid off a saucepan and was frowning at its contents. She looked over his shoulder, and saw what looked like congealed brown gunk, stuck to the bottom of the pan.

She wrinkled her nose. 'What exactly is that?'

'It's supposed to be bolognese sauce. It's one of the

few things I can cook – except not tonight apparently. It wasn't part of my plan to poison you. How would you feel about pizza?'

She laughed, charmed that any man would cook for her, even if it had turned out to be a complete disaster. Neither Luke nor Eddie ever had.

They sat on the living-room floor, leaning against the sofa, and ate pizza straight from the boxes and drank red wine. He showed her more of his pictures and she was bowled over by his talent, but still he refused to show her the picture he had drawn of her, however much she pleaded with him.

Time seemed to be on fast forward and all too soon it was half past two. Liberty just couldn't have another day when she was too exhausted to look after her daughter.

'I'd better go,' she said reluctantly.

'Why don't you stay? I want to wake up with you next to me.'

What did she say to that?

'I really need to go. I have to get up early tomorrow for a casting.' She felt terrible about lying to him but didn't know what else to say. Maybe she should have told him about Brooke right at the beginning.

'You can wake up early here.'

'I'm sorry, I really do have to go. All my stuff's at home.'

He put his arms around her and kissed her. 'Okay. Well, good luck with the casting. What's it for?'

'Some kind of moisturiser, I think,' she mumbled. 'I probably won't get it. I hardly ever do.'

'You'll be brilliant. How could they not hire you on the spot?'

Because I will be looking after my daughter all day . . . 'You should be my agent, you've definitely got more

30

faith in me than she has,' Liberty told him, kissing him goodbye.

She felt like the worst mother in the world when her alarm woke her up at seven a.m. She was still half asleep as she gave Brooke her breakfast and got her ready for nursery. After dropping her daughter off she came straight home and went back to bed for two hours, which made her feel even worse when she woke up again, as if she had jet lag – well, she guessed that was what jet lag felt like, never actually having flown long haul. But there was an instant pick-me-up when she saw the green light flashing on the answerphone and played back a message from Cory, asking if she was free to go for dinner that night. She must have slept through the phone ringing.

If only . . . She picked up the phone and punched in his number and was disappointed when she only got his voicemail.

'Sorry, I can't make tonight, busy few days. I could do Thursday?'

God, it sounded as if she was playing it cool and giving him the brush off, which was the last thing she wanted to do. But there was no more time to obsess about it as she dashed out to collect her daughter from nursery.

Em came round in the evening, with a bottle of wine and bag of Doritos. So much for Liberty trying to eat healthily . . . pizza yesterday and now these. Even if she landed a casting, at this rate she wouldn't be in shape for it.

'So come on then, I want to hear all about it,' Em declared, pouring Liberty a large glass of white wine. She tucked her long blonde hair behind her ears and looked at her friend expectantly.

Liberty curled up on the sofa. 'I really like him, Em. It's the first time I've felt like this – ever. I mean, I thought Luke was the one, but this is completely different.'

'No one else ever thought that about Luke,' straight-talking Em muttered, ripping open the bag of crisps. She had never made any secret of the fact that she thought Luke was an arrogant bastard, who only cared about himself. Liberty had been too much in love to see it until it was too late . . . and he had trampled all over her heart and abandoned her to cope with Brooke alone.

'But there's something about Cory . . . I don't know, I just feel we connect.'

Em grinned cheekily. 'You mean he's a great shag?'

'He's a fucking brilliant shag!' And then Liberty paused, because that didn't even begin to cover the powerful emotions Cory aroused in her. It wasn't just about sex, although that was mind-blowing.

Em raised her glass. 'Well, it's about time you saw some action. So when are you going to see him again?'

'Mum's away this week, so it's going to be hard, but I wondered if you might be able to babysit on Thursday? I haven't told him about Brooke. And I don't know if I want to yet, it's too soon. I vowed I wouldn't let her get close to anyone after Eddie left.'

Brooke had adored Eddie and, to be fair to him, he had given her a lot of attention and genuinely seemed to enjoy being with her. Until he didn't, and Brooke had spent the following month asking Liberty constantly where he was.

She sighed. 'But then again, it feels like I'm keeping back such an important part of myself. And I hate lying.'

Em gave her a searching look. 'It is 1999, not 1899.

32

You don't have to be ashamed of being a single mum. And you know I'll babysit, but I think you should tell Cory. If he's worth anything at all, he'll understand.'

'Yeah, exactly like Eddie, you mean?'

'I like Eddie but he can be an immature dickhead, and he probably always will be.'

'I don't know, Em. And anyway, Cory'll be going back to the States soon. I shouldn't read too much into any of this. Maybe I should just see it as a summer fling.'

But after Em had gone, Liberty lay in bed listening to Massive Attack and 'Teardrop' to remind her of him.

Chapter 4

'So what have you been up to?' Cory asked over dinner. He had taken Liberty to a French restaurant she had always wanted to go to, but never been able to afford, overlooking the sea. The location was perfect, the food was perfect, it was perfect being there with him, everything was perfect except for this question.

How could she answer it without coming out with too many lies? The real answer would be work, looking after Brooke, trips to nursery, to the park, making cakes and pretending to be a fairy . . . Brooke's current obsession.

'Um . . . just working double shifts. The restaurant's been really short-staffed this week.' She couldn't meet Cory's eye as she spoke. For all her acting ability, she was the world's worst liar when it came to her own life. She blamed her mum for that – always drumming into her how important it was to be honest. 'How about you?'

'Oh, you know – painting, swimming, thinking of you, painting, swimming, thinking of you.'

She smiled; it was sweet of him to admit it. And

just as she was thinking she'd got away with the lie, Cory said quietly, 'I went into the restaurant yesterday because I really wanted to see you, but they said you weren't working there.'

Fuck! 'Oh, yeah, I had another casting. I don't think it went very well, though. I've tried to blank it out. It's so depressing thinking about it.' She just hated this. Why did everything have to be so complicated?

'Well, it's their loss. So . . . any auditions coming up?'

She shook her head. The brutal truth was that there hadn't been any auditions since she was pregnant with Brooke. Then she had landed a part in an ITV crime drama, which would have been a huge break for her. But the pregnancy had ruled it out entirely. When she had broken the news to her acting agent, after he had hammered out a good deal for her, the bastard had said that she should get rid of the baby rather than lose the role. When she'd told him what she thought of that idea, and what she thought of him, he had dropped her. Looking back, Liberty wished she had contacted the director herself and asked if there was any way she could have taken the part – actresses got pregnant all the time and directors had to film round them. But she had been too young and inexperienced, and being pregnant was a big enough event for her to deal with.

'I'm sure you'll get something soon.' Cory reached out for her hand. 'Someone as beautiful and talented as you.'

Liberty didn't share his conviction. She looked out to sea. It was still light, the sky streaked with red and pink from the sunset. The crumbling but still elegant West Pier stood out starkly against the silky-calm water. For ages she had been telling herself that something would happen with her acting career, and so far nothing had.

But she was determined to keep going. There was so much she wanted to achieve – not just for herself, but for her daughter. She wanted to show Brooke that you could be who you wanted to be, do what you wanted to do. She wanted to seize life, take hold of it, rather than feeling it pass her by.

'Don't look so down, you have the rest of your life to concentrate on your career.' Cory paused thoughtfully, then he said, 'You might think that this sounds crazy, but how about coming travelling with me for a couple of months? I was thinking of going to Australia for Christmas and hanging out on the Gold Coast. The surfing there is fantastic. And I have friends we could stay with – it would be awesome. I think you'd love it. Acting will still be here when you come back.'

She had a sudden image of the pair of them, hand in hand on some beautiful white sand beach. It was tantalizing, but impossible. Brooke needed stability, and Liberty couldn't give up on her dreams. She gazed at him. He was so sexy, but sometimes she felt a hundred years older than him.

Not wanting to hurt his feelings, though, she leaned over and kissed him. 'You are adorable – and completely mad. Don't you know how much that sort of trip would cost? I'd have to work all day, every day at the restaurant for a year, just to pay for the flight.'

He smiled. 'I have enough money for both of us. Just think about us on the beach, in the sun, drinking beer, going surfing . . .'

Liberty slapped him playfully on the arm. 'Hey, isn't Brighton Beach good enough for you?'

He grabbed her hand across the table, his face suddenly serious. 'Ah, Liberty, as long as you're there, any beach will do for me.' She smiled as he kissed her hand, but inside she couldn't help worrying that their lives were so different. Would it pull them apart one day?

After dinner they walked hand-in-hand back to his flat. Brighton Pier was lit up and the lights were flashing on and off. It was kitsch and pretty and always reminded her of being twelve years old and going on the amusements with Em, after they had begged and borrowed the money from their parents, for spins on the dodgems and rides on the rollercoaster and then gorging themselves on doughnuts and feeling sick afterwards . . . but it had never stopped them from wanting to do it all over again the next time. Life had seemed so straightforward to Liberty then.

'I love it here,' Cory told her. 'I either want to live by the sea or in the countryside; I have to have space. Back in San Francisco my parents' house overlooks the Bay. When I wake up there the first thing I do every day is look at the sea. However crazy everything else is, that always calms me down.'

'What do your parents do?'

He grimaced. 'They're both lawyers, and so is my brother, and my sister is a doctor so that's as good as in their eyes. Dinnertimes were always about everyone arguing their point of view. It drove me crazy – all those egos competing with each other, each trying to be the centre of attention.'

'So where do you get your artistic talent from?'

'Not my parents, that's for sure – they only appreciate art as an investment. They don't care what's hanging on their walls so long as it's expensive and increases in value. My grandfather Henry – my dad's dad – is the artistic one. I'd spend my summers hanging out with him – he lives in the hippy part of San Fran. He'd love to paint you. He loves a beautiful woman . . . or beautiful women, I should say, which is why he split up from my grandmother and now lives with someone half his age. It's the great scandal in our family.' He turned to her, 'So what about yours. You've only mentioned your mom.'

'She's all I have – I'm an only child. I have a dad, but he and Mum split up when I was young and I hardly see him now. He doesn't really figure in my life.'

'That's sad.'

Liberty shrugged. 'Not really, it's just how it is. And my mum's brilliant.' Was this the moment she should tell him about Brooke?

'But families fuck you up, don't they? I can't imagine going for the whole married thing, with two kids and a home loan and one vacation a year. It would feel like being trapped, closing off all your options. Or, worse, having kids and spending your whole time working, which is what my parents do. I really don't get why they bothered to have us.'

'Do you think you'll ever want kids?' It felt like torture to ask this, but she had to know.

'Not sure. Maybe, but not for a long while. There's so much else I want to do. So many places I want to see.'

What else could she expect of someone who was only twenty-one? Fortunately he didn't ask her if she wanted children.

The discussion about families put a downer on the rest of the night for Liberty. Not even the fantastic sex that followed could entirely shift her feeling of sadness and the conviction that she and Cory belonged in different worlds. After they'd made love she wriggled out of his arms and slipped from the bed. It was past midnight.

'Hey! You're not going, are you?'

She looked at him. His body seemed even more tanned against the white duvet cover, and she wanted nothing more than for him to hold her all night, to feel him next to her. It was like a physical pain having to leave.

'I have to get back. I have an early start, and I know I won't sleep if I stay here.' She reached for her clothes.

'Are you seeing someone else, Liberty?'

The question blindsided her completely. She spun round to face Cory, midway through buttoning up her dress. 'Of course not! Why would you think that?'

'You never want to stay. You weren't at work when you said you were. I can't help thinking there's something you're hiding, and I can only imagine that there's someone else.'

Now was surely the time for her to tell him about Brooke, but she just couldn't, not like this. It would look like she had been ashamed of her own daughter.

'I'm not seeing anyone else, I swear. You do believe me, don't you?'

Cory didn't answer. He remained in bed, staring at the ceiling, arms behind his head, looking thoroughly pissed off. When she let herself out of the flat he didn't even say goodbye.

Liberty picked up the phone and keyed in Cory's number, then hung up before it rang. It was the third time she had done this. He hadn't called her. She had blown it, spoiled the one good thing to have happened to her in ages. She tried to tell herself that he would have left at the end of the summer anyway, off for another adventure in Australia. He would be on that white sand beach, just not with her. He would forget her long before she could ever forget him.

39

She was even more depressed the next day when Em showed her the latest edition of *OK!* and there was none other than Angel Summer on the front of it. Em and Liberty had been at school with her, and she had gone on to be an incredibly successful glamour model. True enough, she'd had her ups and downs; there had been a disastrous relationship with a boy-band singer, a spell in rehab, but now she was with the gorgeous Premiership footballer Cal Bailey, and it couldn't hurt that he was filthy rich.

'God, I miss Angel. She called a couple of weeks ago, and I knew she was doing well but I didn't realise how well. What a glittering success her life is compared to mine. Mind you, anyone's life is a glittering success compared to mine,' Liberty said gloomily as the two girls grabbed a break outside in the back yard of the restaurant, next to the bins so Em could have a fag. The concrete was littered with cigarette ends, and the bins needed emptying.

Overhead the seagulls squawked noisily and Liberty narrowly missed being showered with bird shit. That really would have rounded off her day. She felt like shoving the magazine in with the rubbish. Much as she loved Angel, she didn't want to look at her radiant face a second longer. The cover should carry a warning: looking at this picture will seriously damage your self-esteem.

'Forget about Angel. Call Cory and tell him about Brooke,' Em urged her. 'You've got nothing to lose. If he doesn't want to know then at least you can get out now.'

She handed Liberty her mobile, a chunky black Nokia that she was enormously proud of. Liberty couldn't afford to get a phone on her wages. 'Go on, you've got five more minutes.' Em threw down her roll up and ground it out under her heel before she went back inside the restaurant.

Liberty keyed in Cory's number, but when it went to voicemail she yet again chickened out of leaving a message, and hung up.

It was late-afternoon when she finished work and still a beautiful day. Liberty changed into her shorts and bikini and picked up Brooke from the childminder she sometimes used, heading straight to her daughter's favourite playground by the sea after that. She relished the feeling of the warm sun on her skin after being cooped up inside all day. She was determined to put Cory from her mind and enjoy this time with her daughter. So what if it was just the two of them? She was lucky to have Brooke. She splashed about with her daughter in the paddling pool, and tried to tell herself that it didn't matter, that she was all Brooke needed, that they would be all right. But it was hard watching dads playing with their children, messing about with them in the water or carrying them on their shoulders. Not that for a second she wanted to be back with Luke. Better to be alone and struggling than trapped in an unhappy relationship.

By six o'clock Brooke was getting tired and Liberty settled her in her buggy for the walk home. She was annoyed with herself for feeling lonely as she strolled past the lively bars that lined the seafront. Loud music blasted out of them and people kicked back there after work with jugs of beer and Pimm's, chatting and laughing. She had no plans for tonight; Em was going out with Noah and so wouldn't be able to come over. Once Brooke was in bed it would be just Liberty and the remote control. Before she'd met Cory she'd never minded being on her own. Now she

41

craved the feeling of excitement she got only when she was with him.

A burst of laughter from one of the tables nearby attracted her attention and, looking over, she saw him. Cory was sitting at a table with a group of friends, including Zara. His blond hair caught the last rays of the sun, which turned it golden. He had never looked more handsome to Liberty, or more out of reach. Her heart started racing. Should she go and say hi? Or should she pretend she hadn't seen him and carry on? It seemed crazy to be feeling so insecure when they had slept together, but the truth was she didn't know where she stood with him or what he would think when he saw she had a daughter.

The decision was taken out of her hands when he glanced up and noticed her. Immediately he stood up and came over. She stood there awkwardly, clutching the handles of the buggy for reassurance. She was aware of what a mess she must look, her hair tangled by the sea breeze, her white vest splattered with the chocolate ice cream her daughter had spilled on her.

'Hey, I thought you were going to call me?'

Just having him close again made her feel almost overwhelmed by the strength of her emotions. But he made no move to kiss her.

'I know, I did try, but I kept getting your voicemail.'

'Well, you could have left a message, that's what those things are for.' He was gazing at her, but then registered Brooke and quickly kneeled down. 'And who's this gorgeous girl? Hi, sweetie, what's your name?'

Brooke was sucking her thumb and ignored him.

'Well, isn't she a sweet thing? She looks exactly like you.' Zara had sauntered over to them. 'Is she your baby sister?' She gave Liberty a sly smile. Zara was once again looking groomed and glossy in a white sundress that showed off her tan to perfection.

'I didn't know you had a sister, Liberty?' Cory looked perplexed.

'Oh, haven't you got round to swapping stories about your families yet?' Zara's voice was smug. Liberty could tell immediately that she'd guessed this wasn't her sister, and was taking great delight in making her feel uncomfortable.

'No, I . . .' Liberty began.

'No,' Zara wouldn't let her continue, 'I'm sure I've heard you say that you're an only child. So that can only mean . . .' She opened her eyes wide. 'Oh, you must be one of those single mothers the government's always talking about? How brave of you to have her so young. Don't you think she's brave, Cory? And so good of you too, darling, not to mind. You really are a sweetheart. Isn't he, Liberty? There can't be many men happy to have someone else's child foisted on them.'

Zara gave Liberty a hard stare before turning to look at Cory. 'Oh, dear, didn't you know? What a surprise for you. I can't imagine why Liberty wouldn't trust you enough to tell you her little secret. I thought you two were so close?' She turned back to Liberty with a triumphant smile on her face.

She felt anger rise in her. What a bitch Zara was! Well, Liberty wasn't going to be made to feel ashamed of having had a child so young. She needed to come clean, she had nothing to feel ashamed of, although the expression of shock on Cory's face almost made her lose her nerve. But then she straightened her shoulders and looked him squarely in the face.

'Zara's right. Brooke is my daughter. How clever of her to guess.' She was looking only at Cory as she spoke, though, trying to show with her eyes that she was sorry she hadn't told him.

Cory either didn't notice her look or chose to ignore it. He seemed lost for words. 'I . . . um . . . I mean . . . Jesus, Liberty, why didn't you tell me?' The words burst from him angrily.

She was silent for a moment, not sure what to say. But when he just stared at Brooke with an expression of total shock on his face, her patience snapped. Bastard!

'Because I'm used to insensitive, immature little fuckers like you running a mile when they find out,' she said venomously. 'I'm sorry I didn't tell you, I was going to and I had hoped you'd be different from all the others, but I can see you're not. Now, if you'll excuse me, I need to get Brooke home. See you around, Cory. Hopefully I won't see you, Zara.'

Head held high, Liberty marched off, anxious to get away from them. She could just imagine them staring after her, judging her to be some feckless single mother who only had herself to blame. She could feel tears of humiliation and anger stinging her eyes: anger with herself for caring so much, and anger with Cory and Zara too. Fuck them. Rich, spoiled, over-privileged twats, what did they know about life?

It was only when she was giving Brooke her bath later on that she calmed down. She watched her daughter play happily with her toy whale, taking great delight in squirting Liberty with water. She would never for a second regret having Brooke. She loved her with a fierce, proud determination; she would do anything for her. It didn't matter what anyone else thought. Her daughter was all that mattered.

The doorbell rang when Liberty had finally flopped on to the living-room sofa, too exhausted to make herself anything to eat. She wasn't expecting anyone; it was bound to be someone trying to sell something. She ignored it, hoping that whoever it was would go away. But the bell rang again. Wearily she hauled herself up. She swung open the front door with her 'don't bother me' face on, only to be confronted by Cory.

'What are *you* doing here?' she muttered, still smarting from their earlier encounter. 'Shouldn't you be drinking Pimm's with all your ra-ra friends? Planning your next round-the-world trip?' She knew she sounded bitter, but she couldn't help it. She felt vulnerable and raw.

'I got your address from Em. I had to see you. Can I come in?' he said.

When she didn't reply, he tried again. 'I know I must have seemed shocked when I saw you with Brooke, but it took me by surprise. I had no idea you had a daughter. But I swear, it makes no difference to how I feel about you.'

She shrugged as if it wasn't important to her. But as soon as Cory had shut the door he took her in his arms and hugged her. 'I'm sorry, Liberty. Sorry for being an idiot and thinking you had a boyfriend, and sorry for not saying the right things when I saw Brooke.'

His body against hers; the delicious clean smell of him mixed with his spicy aftershave and the scent of sun cream. She wanted him so much, but he'd hurt her badly. She didn't feel she could trust him, his life was too different from hers. Things would never work out for them.

Liberty pulled away. 'Yeah, well, you really were an idiot, and you and Zara made me feel like shit. I don't need that in my life or my daughter's.'

'I know, and I'm sorry. I fucked up. Please will you give me a second chance? I swear it won't happen again.'

45

Cory sounded so heartfelt and looked so sincere that she felt her resistance weakening.

'We have this connection between us . . . I know you feel it too. I've never felt like this about anyone else before,' he told her.

'Not about what's her name . . . Tash? And Zara? How do I know I can trust you?'

'Because, as I think you know, this is something different.'

From the living room Liberty could hear the sound of the TV. She should tell him to leave and never see him again. She should shut the door on him, and go back to watching TV, and getting up in the morning and going to work, and doing the same things over and over again. Or she could take a chance. She could end up getting hurt again. Really hurt. It was a risk. But Liberty knew she had to take it.

She hesitated then said quietly, 'Okay. A second chance. So long as you understand that my daughter will always, *always* come first.'

She didn't know if she was making the right decision, she only knew that she couldn't be without Cory.

Chapter 5

A brilliant month followed when Liberty saw Cory every day and even managed to stay over with him several nights a week. It was like being in a dream, a wonderful, happy dream. And forming the perfect backdrop to their romance, summer had taken hold, with days of glorious sunshine and bright blue skies and nights that were warm enough for them to drink wine and have barbecues on the beach. Even completely caught up in the moment, Liberty still had the feeling that this was going to be the summer of her life, the one she would always look back on . . .

They were at that can't-keep-their-hands-off-each-other stage, where they longed for each other, and whenever they could tumbled into Cory's big double bed that creaked appallingly and gave them the giggles, or else made love on the battered leather sofa, slowly in the moonlight. And each time was more intense and brought them closer.

It was still early days but Liberty felt as if she had found her soulmate, someone she could be herself with. But . . . and there was a but . . . at the back of her mind was always the nagging thought that this surely couldn't last, that it was all too good to be true, that he would soon be gone. She felt that she had to keep back a part of herself and not entirely let down her guard. Cory would catch her looking wistful sometimes. He always asked her what was wrong and what she was thinking. She would make up an excuse; say she was worrying about never getting any acting work. Not entirely a lie, but not entirely the truth.

One Saturday night six weeks after their first meeting Cory met her after work. He seemed particularly keyed up and excited about something, but he wouldn't tell her what it was about until they reached his flat. As soon as they were inside he raced into the kitchen and came back into the living room brandishing a bottle of champagne. 'I'll tell you once I've opened it. This moment deserves to be toasted, and remembered, because this moment is going to be a turning point, I just know it.'

She watched as he quickly ripped the gold foil from the bottle of Bollinger and expertly popped the cork. That was the thing about Cory – he constantly came out with declarations like that, which she couldn't imagine any other man saying. He wore his heart on his sleeve, and there was an openness about him that Liberty found daily more irresistible. He handed her a glass of champagne.

'Come on, Cory! Tell me now!' she begged him, unable to bear the suspense any longer.

He grinned. 'I've told my parents that I'm not going back to law school, that I'm staying in the UK and going to art school here. I've got an interview at Camberwell next week.'

'Really? Are you sure?' It was what she'd wanted, but

it seemed such a huge step for him. 'And what about travelling? And going to Australia?'

'I've done a load of travelling.' He put his arms round her. 'And I'm one hundred per cent certain about this. I've never been so certain of anything before. And there's something else I have to say . . . and I don't care if you think it's too soon, and I'm being too over the top, I have to tell you this. I love you. What do you say to that, Liberty Evans?' He sounded confident but she could see the anxiety in his eyes.

She didn't even have to think about it. 'I'd say that I love you too.'

It was an amazing, incredible moment. They drank champagne, made love in the creaky bed, held each other all night. Liberty woke up feeling slightly hungover but blissfully happy, and for the first time ever in her life she felt lucky.

At home there was more good news when Nina told Liberty that her agent had called and she had a casting in London that afternoon for a new perfume. It was a high-profile campaign, and last-minute because the model the company had originally chosen had pulled out. Liberty was so buoyed up with happiness about Cory that, instead of feeling paralysed with nerves as she had so many times in the past, she breezed into reception feeling confident and looking forward to showing the casting director what she could do. Cory loved her and she loved him! That was all that mattered.

'Hi, I'm here to see Luke Jones for a casting, I'm Liberty Evans,' she told the young man behind reception. There was a dark-haired man already standing there, drumming his fingers on the desk top impatiently. He glanced at Liberty and then seemed to do a double take.

'So what are you?' the man addressed her. 'A model or an actress?'

She smiled back, not oblivious to the fact that he was very striking-looking, with a handsome, rugged face.

'An actress who has to model.' No need to tell him that she hadn't acted in ages and that she currently waited tables.

He glanced at his watch. 'I have a bit of time before my next meeting. The guy I was supposed to be seeing here is held up in traffic. How about grabbing a coffee?'

He was American, with possibly a Californian accent, she thought, and the watch he wore looked expensive.

'I'm in the TV industry and know a fair bit about the acting world. You never know, it might be helpful to you.'

For a while now Liberty had recognised that it wasn't simply talent that got you ahead in acting, it was who you knew as well. And she had no connections whatsoever. This looked like an ideal networking opportunity. The guy exuded an air of wealth and confidence.

'Well, my casting is now and I guess it will only take about twenty minutes, if that. I could meet you afterwards?' she said.

'Sure, great idea. I'll be waiting. I'm Zac, by the way.' He reached out and they shook hands. All the while he was gazing at her, as if he liked what he saw very much. 'And you're Liberty?' he continued. 'Great name. It suits you.'

She was still smiling as she was called into the studio to meet the director and photographer. They did all the introductions and the director asked her to get into position in front of the white screen, opposite the camera.

She posed for a series of shots pulling a range of

expressions, dreamy, happy, pensive, sultry, all of which she found came naturally. She really felt a connection with the camera, and believed she could give the photographer and director exactly what they wanted.

'Just a few more to go now,' Dave the photographer called out. But suddenly Liberty was distracted by the door opening, and to her surprise Zac walked in.

'Is it okay if I watch?' he asked Luke.

'No problem, Mr Keller,' he replied, seeming in awe of the newcomer.

Liberty was surprised by Luke's reaction. Zac really must be a big cheese in TV if he had that effect on people . . .

'Okay give me your best "I know I'm sexy and I know you want me" face,' Dave called out. Liberty tried to forget that Zac was standing there, looking at her intently, as she pouted, and narrowed her eyes, and shook back her hair. It was a little disconcerting having an audience but she knew she had done well this far and didn't want to blow it.

Afterwards, when Luke told her they would be in touch later that day to let her know, for once she believed that he meant it. And, even better, that the news might well be positive.

'Seriously? You want hot chocolate here? The place that serves the best coffee in London? I dream of this coffee when I'm in LA,' Zac teased her while they waited to order at the cosy Italian café round the corner.

'I'm too keyed up to drink coffee,' she replied.

'And I'm guessing you haven't eaten anything? Go and sit down and I'll bring everything over.'

She took a seat at one of the Formica-topped tables. It was funny, she hadn't imagined that Zac would want to go somewhere like this. She'd imagined him in a swanky hotel – say the Sanderson, which she had read about in *Grazia* – all striking architectural features and ultra-stylish furniture. Her seat here was pocked with cigarette burns.

'Oh, wow! You didn't have to get me anything to eat!' she exclaimed as Zac put down a tray with a plate on it containing a pain au chocolat, a pain au raisin and an enormous chocolate-chip muffin. And he had asked for cream in the hot chocolate! If she ate all that she might have to give up on the perfume ad job, unless they wanted a plus size model.

He shrugged. 'I didn't know what you wanted, so I got a selection. Now tell me all about yourself. How long have you wanted to be an actor? What have you been in? Where do you live?'

He caught sight of Liberty's slightly bemused expression at having so many questions put to her at once. 'Sorry, it's a terrible habit, comes of working in TV. I want to know everything instantly,' he said.

She smiled and ran through an edited version of her life story, omitting to mention Brooke. 'I haven't done much,' she finished up by saying.

'Well, I can see a great future ahead of you. You really are a beautiful woman. Incredible eyes.' He gazed directly at her. It was slightly unnerving, but also exciting to have attracted the attention of this man.

'Who's your agent?' he asked.

Liberty reeled off Lizzie's name.

'Never heard of her, but that's okay.'

He looked at the plate of uneaten pastries. Liberty had just nibbled the end of a pain au chocolat.

'So how about we have a late lunch? I could push my meeting back further.'

For a moment she wondered if lunch was all he had

52

in mind, but maybe she was reading too much into his show of attention. Either way, she was longing to get back to Brighton and see Cory.

'I'm really sorry but I have to get home.'

'Husband waiting for you? Boyfriend?'

'Boyfriend. I promised I'd see him tonight.'

'Lucky guy,' Zac replied, sounding regretful. He reached in his pocket and handed her his card. 'I'm flying back to LA tomorrow morning, but who knows? Maybe I'll see you there. I've a feeling I will.'

Chapter 6

Zac had been quite intense, Liberty thought afterwards as she dashed through Soho Square on her way to Oxford Circus tube. But very charismatic as well. The kind of man who was used to getting what he wanted, which was sort of scxy. But by the time she boarded the train at Victoria, she was only thinking of one man and that was Cory. For the hundredth time she wished she had a mobile phone so she could call him and tell him how it had gone. If she got the perfume ad that was the first thing she was going to treat herself to.

The phone rang almost as soon as she walked through the front door. It was Lizzie, telling her that she'd got the modelling job and that there was something else really exciting to tell her. Liberty wondered what on earth that could be when landing the modelling job was exciting enough.

'I've had a call from Zac Keller, who was very impressed with you today.'

'Oh?' He hadn't wastcd any time then.

'Do you realise who he is?' Lizzie went on, excitement breaking through in her usual measured tones.

Blimey! If Lizzie sounded happy then it really must be significant. Her agent usually sounded supremely bored.

'He's only one of Hollywood's hottest TV directors right now. Two Golden Globes under his belt for his last series. He wants me to send him your show reel. God, Liberty! Do you realise, this could be your big break? He absolutely raved about you. Went on about your spirit, and how there was this intriguing air of vulnerability about you. How you had the most amazing green eyes he had ever seen, the most radiant smile. How unspoiled and fresh you were. And on and on. I couldn't get a word in edgeways!'

'Wow!' Liberty was taken aback by the interest and all the praise.

'So sweetie, I'm getting that show reel off to him ASAP. And then who knows?'

What a difference a day could make, Liberty thought as she put down the phone. It was like going from 0 to 100 m.p.h. Out of nowhere there were so many possibilities ahead of her, real life-changing possibilities – though she decided not to tell anyone about Zac's interest, in case it proved to be a lot of hot air. But she could tell them about landing the modelling job and the two grand fee Lizzie had mentioned. A celebration was definitely in order.

Everyone was thrilled by her news when she told them over dinner. Cory insisted on ordering a bottle of champagne, even though they were having an Indian and it didn't exactly go with the spicy food.

'To my beautiful model girlfriend!' he declared, holding up his glass, and everyone toasted Liberty, pleased for her success.

'Now that's enough about my daughter, her head

will get too big. And she mustn't get above herself – it's her turn to take out the bin tonight. I'm not having any airs and graces,' Nina teased. But Liberty knew how pleased her mum was for her.

'How have your parents taken the news that you're dropping out of law school?' Nina asked Cory.

For a moment Liberty thought that he seemed annoyed by the question. He ran one hand through his hair and looked down for an instant, but then his natural charm took over. 'They're okay about it. Well, actually, my mom freaked, but my dad is good at calming her down. I can't do law if my heart's not in it.'

'Of course you can't,' Liberty backed him up.

'No.' Nina smiled. 'And Libs tells me you're a very talented artist. And, for what it's worth, I always think you should follow your heart and not worry about what other people think. There are probably enough lawyers in the world as it is.'

Sometimes Liberty thought she had the coolest mum ever.

'So are you going to tell them our news?' Noah asked suddenly, looking at Em. Instantly Liberty's heart sank, and the shine was wiped right off her day. This was the moment she had been dreading. She knew she was right when Em looked awkward, and said, 'This is supposed to be a celebration for Libs, let's leave it for now.'

'It's okay, Em, I think I know what you're going to say.'

Cory looked at the two girls. 'Is this some kind of code I'm not getting?'

'I'm going to Australia with Noah,' Em said quietly. 'And I really, really want to, only I'm going to really, really miss you, Libs.'

'How long are you going for?' she asked. Maybe it would just be for a year. That wouldn't be so bad, would it? Twelve months. She could deal with that.

'We don't have a set time in mind,' Noah put in. 'You guys should come out and see us. You know you'd be welcome any time, and you could stay as long as you want.'

Liberty had always got on well with Noah, who was easygoing and basically one of the loveliest guys you could ever meet. But right now she was struggling to say anything positive back to him. She couldn't help wishing that he had never met her best friend, because it felt like he was taking Em away.

'We mean it, Libs, any time you want to come over. And we can email and phone every week. We'll have a girls' night in when we call each other.'

'Except it will be morning for me, and night time for you,' Liberty replied in a quiet voice. 'When do you go?'

'Three weeks' time. Noah's got a job at a garden design company in Sydney.'

In just three weeks she would be saying goodbye to Em? Liberty's eyes welled up with tears. Unable to keep up the pretence of being happy a second longer, she got to her feet abruptly and rushed off to the loo. She was crying now. She knew she should be happy for her friend, and she was, but she was also desperately sad. If she felt like this now, how on earth was she going to feel when Em left?

She was just trying to rub away the smudges of mascara when her friend walked in and hugged her. 'You know I'm going to miss you so much, I can't really bear to think about it,' Em said, struggling to hold back her own tears.

'I know, and I know how much you want to do this

57

and I hope it'll be brilliant for you, but I'll miss you so much. *Promise* you'll stay in touch?' Liberty begged.

'You know I will, but you're going to be okay. You've got Cory and Brooke and that new modelling job. I really think things are looking up for you,' Em hugged her again. 'I'm too old to be saying this, but you're my best friend for ever.'

Liberty managed a smile. 'And you're mine.'

Chapter 7

At least Liberty had the advert to distract her from Em's big news, and the hope that Zac might get in touch with an audition. Though it had been over a week and she hadn't heard anything so far. She found shooting the advert a complete dream from the moment she arrived at the studio and Flo the make-up artist got to work on her, calling her *darling* in every sentence and generally making her feel relaxed. They were going for an ultra-natural look, which seemed to take even more make up than if she was going for full on slap. Primer, foundation, brightener, powder . . . Liberty only usually wore foundation on a night out, so the number of products seemed mind-boggling to her.

'You look beautiful, darling,' Flo told her when she'd finished. 'Absolutely stunning.'

'It's down to you,' Liberty answered, as she looked at the unfamiliar woman in the mirror, with her smoky eyes and flawless skin. Her hair had been given the star treatment as well, and blow dried straight so that it fell down her back in a silky mane.

'I think you're going to go far,' Flo said. 'Remember me when you're a famous super-model!'

Liberty laughed; this was all so unexpected. 'Actually I want to be an actress.'

'*Darling*, with your looks you could do anything you wanted, absolutely anything!'

This definitely beat getting people their orders of garlic bread and spag bol.

Liberty loved performing for the camera, taking on the persona of a sultry, beautiful, enigmatic woman. Greg the celebrity photographer was full of compliments as he got her to pose this way and that, shouting out orders and encouragement. Apparently he had photographed all the top models, and Liberty couldn't believe he meant half of what he said to her.

'Lovely . . . bit more of a smile . . . shake back your head. Gorgeous! Beautiful! Yeah, baby, that's the one. Wow! Now give me your sexy face. The you-know-you-want-to-sleep-with-me look. But you can't because I'm a princess and out of reach.'

She had to giggle at that comment, but then she did her best to compose herself and smoulder for the camera.

Liberty was still on a high some four hours later when she arrived back in Brighton. After checking with her mum that it was okay if she had Brooke, she jumped in a taxi and went to Cory's. She couldn't wait to see him and tell him about her day.

'Hi!' she exclaimed, throwing her arms round him the second he opened the door. Then, seductively, 'Do you want to see me do my sexy face? It's very good apparently, and will soon be on a billboard near you!'

She'd expected him to banter back, but instead he seemed serious. 'Actually my mom and dad are here. They arrived this afternoon.'

That was unexpected! 'Did you know they were coming?'

He shook his head. 'Nope. They must have jumped on a plane as soon as I told them about quitting law school. What devoted parents they are,' he said bitterly, and took her hand. 'Come on in, you'd better meet the Wicked Witch of the North and Toto.'

'Toto's cute.' Liberty was trying to think positively.

'Yeah, and he doesn't ever say or do anything, if you remember, because he's a dog. Cute but useless.'

Surely his parents couldn't be so bad if they'd had a son like Cory? But as she walked into the living room with him, Liberty instantly got a bad vibe from Cory's mum Melissa. She was stunningly beautiful, and had Cory's bluer-than-blue eyes. But whereas his were full of warmth and passion, Melissa's were cold and watchful. She smiled at Liberty and told her it was '*so* good to meet you', but not for a second did Liberty think that she meant it. She was painfully aware of Melissa constantly weighing her up. Cory's dad Jacob seemed a lot nicer, but Liberty guessed that it was Melissa who had the upper hand in that relationship.

'I'm sorry we arrived unannounced,' his mother said as Cory poured everyone a glass of wine. Liberty noticed that he poured himself an extra large one. 'But we were missing our son so very much. And I hope you didn't have plans for tonight, Liberty, because we thought we could take you and Cory out to dinner. I'd love to get to know the girl who's had such an effect on my son.'

'You don't have jet lag?' Liberty enquired politely, thinking she *really* didn't want to spend an evening with this woman. She wanted to celebrate her good news alone with Cory.

'First class always makes air travel so much more

tolerable,' she replied, as if that was a no-brainer. She turned to Cory then. 'So where's good to eat in Brighton? I'm guessing it doesn't exactly have the choice we're used to in San Francisco?' She sighed as if the thought was a terrible bore.

Yeah, we've barely emerged from caves back in England . . . God! Melissa was such a snob! Clearly her son had not got his easygoing nature from her.

Cory was about to reply when she went on, 'Oh, Liberty, you work in a restaurant. Maybe we should go there?'

'Liberty is only waitressing while she tries to get acting roles – not that there is anything wrong with being a waitress.' Cory looked mutinous. 'And, no, I don't think we should go there. Isn't Italian food out because of your wheat allergy?'

'Yes, you're right, Cory, my nutritionist wouldn't be very happy with me. So where is it to be?' She glanced at Liberty. 'And obviously dinner will be on us, since we've hijacked your evening.'

And because you know perfectly well I couldn't afford to pay my way in the kind of restaurant you want to go to, Liberty thought.

'Apparently there's a very good fish restaurant in the Laines.' Jacob finally spoke up. 'Perhaps we could all go there? I'll phone them and book a table. Cory tells us that you've just landed a major modelling contract, Liberty, and that does sound like something to celebrate.'

'Thank you, yes, I'm really pleased,' Liberty smiled at him. Jacob was sweet, and nothing like his scary wife.

Melissa sighed and twisted the diamond bracelet on her wrist. 'Of course, modelling is even more precarious than acting, so entirely dependent on your looks – not that acting isn't.'

'I don't think Liberty has got anything to worry about on that score,' Jacob replied, clearly trying to lighten the mood.

'And it must be even harder now you're a mother?'

Oh, so she knew about Brooke too. Liberty could just imagine how she felt about *that*.

'Well, it is hard sometimes, but luckily my mum helps out as much as she can.'

'And your father?'

'My parents are divorced and my dad lives in Manchester. I don't see him very often.'

Disapproval seemed to be coming off Melissa in waves. Liberty could feel the beginnings of a headache. She looked over at Cory, hoping he would come up with something supportive, but he just rolled his eyes as if to say, *That's my mom*. And over dinner things only got worse.

Cory seemed completely different from his usual confident, extrovert self. He was monosyllabic and subdued, hardly saying a word as Melissa continued to interrogate Liberty. It was as if her sexy, twenty-one-year-old lover had morphed into a moody adolescent, more interested in knocking back the wine than supporting his girlfriend.

And so Liberty had to face the constant stream of questions without Cory's help. She imagined Melissa must be a force to be reckoned with in court. *What did her mother do? Her father? How old was her daughter? Where was Brooke's father? Was she in touch with him? What did he do?* With every question Liberty felt as if Melissa was further confirming her worst suspicions: that this was a feckless single mother who was never going to amount to anything. And, worst of all, that Cory was way out of her league and Liberty had no right getting involved with him in the first place.

'I'd love to meet your daughter,' Melissa finally said. 'Perhaps you have time tomorrow?'

'Er, sure,' Liberty replied, looking over at Cory and hoping that he would come up with an excuse, but he just shrugged.

'I adore babies and toddlers,' Melissa continued. 'Cory was the most gorgeous baby, and so good, always smiling and happy, and so advanced for his age.'

'I'm surprised you can remember, you were always working,' he commented. 'I saw more of the nanny than I did of you.'

Melissa looked hurt and Liberty almost felt sorry for her until she said, 'Well, I wanted to be able to give you and your brother and sister the best possible start in life, the best education, the best opportunities, so I had to work.' She glanced at Liberty. 'I'm sure you feel exactly the same about your daughter.'

'Yes, but I also want to be there for Brooke as much as I can. My mum's always saying that you can never get back that time when they're little. And I love being with her and miss her when I'm not.'

'And you're so young that you've got plenty of time to get ahead in whatever career you choose,' Jacob put in.

Now please let me off the hook! Liberty wanted to exclaim. She'd never enjoyed a meal less in her life. Although the food had been lovely, she'd barely had any appetite. The only thing she'd felt like doing was drinking wine, but because no doubt Melissa would notice and have another thing to hold against her, she'd only had one glass before switching to water.

Neither Melissa nor Jacob mentioned the fact that Cory was planning to stay in the UK and go to art school, and Liberty had the feeling that Melissa was biding her time. She was certain that Cory's mother hadn't just come over here because she missed her son. She was definitely a woman with an agenda.

After the meal Melissa and Jacob went off to their hotel, leaving Cory and Liberty alone at last.

'Fuck!' he exclaimed, running a hand through his hair. 'Fuck, fuck, fuck! Why have they come over here? Why can't they leave me alone!' He stormed ahead, forcing Liberty to break into a jog to keep up with him.

'Hey, don't let them get to you! It doesn't matter what they think, you're free to do whatever you want,' she told him.

He slowed down. 'I'm sorry, you're right. Only my mom has the unique ability to push all my fucking buttons!'

Liberty linked her arm through his. 'Let's go home.' She needed to take Cory back to their own blissful world, the place where no one mattered but themselves . . .

'Yeah, sounds good to me.'

Chapter 8

Fortunately Liberty was spared an encounter with Melissa the following day when she and Jacob travelled to London, to catch up with some old friends, and stay overnight. With any luck, they would use up all their time in England this way, and she wouldn't have to see them again. But even though his parents weren't around, Cory was still distracted and on edge. He had been working on a large canvas – an ambitious study of a group of skateboarders – but with the arrival of his family, he abandoned it. When Liberty was at work the next day he spent his time lying on the beach, drinking beer, and by the time she met up with him he was already drunk and only interested in carrying on drinking, ignoring her suggestion that he stop.

She had picked up Brooke on her way over to meet him, as she couldn't expect her mum to have her again and in any case wanted to spend some time with her daughter. Brooke was usually one of the most easygoing of children, but she was grizzly when they got to the beach, and nothing seemed to pacify her. Liberty sensed that Cory was irritated. He was used to only seeing her daughter when she was being adorable.

She saw him glance over enviously at the couple lying next to them on the beach – a girl of around Liberty's age in a bikini, chilling out with her boyfriend. There wasn't going to be much chilling out with Brooke in this mood.

'Come on, Brooke baby! What's so bad?' Cory asked the little girl, picking her up and swinging her round, a gesture which was usually guaranteed to make her laugh but this time made her burst into noisy sobs. He pulled a face and handed her back to Liberty, taking a swig of beer instead. 'See – even your daughter hates me today. I can't paint. I've got the mom from hell. Everything's shit.'

Liberty was scarcely paying attention to him as she put her hand on her daughter's forehead. 'She feels really hot.'

'It's a warm afternoon; she'll be fine. Hey, shall I buy her an ice cream?' He looked at Brooke. 'Do you want an ice cream, honey? A big whirly one with a chocolate flake? Ice cream makes everything better.'

'Actually, she hasn't had tea yet. Maybe it's not a good idea.'

'Don't be such a killjoy! What difference can one ice cream make?'

It would mean Brooke wouldn't eat her tea, but Cory didn't seem in the kind of mood where she could explain that to him and Liberty didn't want to sound like a nag. By then Brooke had stopped crying and was chanting, 'I scream, I scream,' in the cute way she did, and Liberty knew from experience that if she put her foot down now and said no, her daughter would have a complete meltdown.

'Okay,' she sighed, not at all happy about it.

But by the time Cory returned with the ice cream for Brooke, she was out of sorts again. She took one lick of it, then screwed up her face and dropped it on to the pebbles.

'Hey! What did you do that for?' he said sharply, causing Brooke to cry.

'Don't speak to her like that!' Liberty shot back, picking up her daughter. She really didn't seem well at all. Her cheeks were flushed, and her hair was sticky with sweat. Liberty started gathering up her things.

'What are you doing now?'

'Going home, I need to take her temperature.'

'But I haven't seen you all day! I thought we could hang out on the beach. She probably just needs some fresh air.'

Liberty suddenly felt the distance between them. Brooke wasn't Cory's daughter and he would never understand how it felt to be her parent. Liberty tried not to reveal how hurt she was.

'I really don't think she's well.'

And finally Cory seemed to realise that she was genuinely worried. Getting up, he helped her carry the buggy over the pebbles.

'Do you want me to come with you?'

She shook her head. 'That's fine. It's probably best if it's just me.'

And that's what she thought until she arrived home, expecting to find her mum, only to discover an empty house. Brooke had cried all the way back in the buggy, but once at the house she seemed to go floppy and lethargic, which made Liberty even more anxious. She laid her on her bed and stripped off her t-shirt, bathing her face and tummy with a flannel, trying to get her temperature down. But nothing she did seemed to make any difference and Liberty's anxiety levels rocketed. What was wrong with Brooke? Was it something serious? Something like meningitis? She desperately tried to remember the symptoms – high temperature, sensitivity to light, a rash.

There was no rash, but suddenly Brooke seemed to suffer some kind of fit. Her whole body contorted and she shook uncontrollably, foaming at the mouth. Terrified, Liberty reached out to try and comfort her. 'It's okay, baby. Mummy's here.' After what seemed like ages but was probably only a few seconds the child seemed to come out of it, but thoroughly panicked now and feeling desperate, Liberty dialled 999.

It was a nerve-wracking wait for the ambulance to arrive, during which time Liberty convinced herself that Brooke was going to die, as her daughter came out of the fit only to lose consciousness. She calmed down enough when the paramedics arrived to be able to answer their questions and comfort her daughter as they travelled to the hospital, but she wished she had her mum with her, so that she didn't have to face this on her own. She held it together until they saw the doctor who said that Brooke had suffered a febrile convulsion because her temperature was so high. She would be okay once she'd cooled off. As soon as she heard that Liberty burst into tears of relief.

'Is there someone you can call to come and get you?' a nurse asked her kindly an hour later as she sat by her daughter's bedside. Brooke was calm now and her temperature had come right down.

'Yes, my mum.' She didn't even think of Cory.

When she arrived home, Liberty found that he had left a message but she felt too exhausted and strung out to phone him. Besides, there was nothing he could do now. Brooke was asleep and all she wanted to do was crash out in bed.

'You should call him,' Nina commented, handing

her daughter a cup of tea. 'He's bound to be worried.'

Liberty wrinkled her nose as she took a sip and realised that her mum had put sugar in the tea.

'Good for shock,' Nina said. 'Drink it, it'll make you feel better.'

'He's probably still pissed. Honestly, Mum, he's been behaving like a little boy, since his parents have been here. So what if they want him to do law? He's an adult, he should be able to do what he wants and tell them so.'

'Other people's families are always different, you don't know exactly what's going on in his.'

Liberty sighed. 'I know. It's just that it's made me realise how differently we view life. Everything is about *him*. Cory doesn't get what it's like to be a parent, and he won't until he is one.'

'Don't be too hard on him, Libs. Cory's a very caring, loving young man, and he will get what it's like eventually, but you can't expect him to be there straight away.'

'I suppose,' Liberty conceded. 'And his mum is a bit of a witch.'

'She probably has insecurities of her own.'

'God, Mum, stop being so reasonable! You wouldn't think that if you met Melissa. She's probably on her way back to Brighton now – by broomstick.'

Liberty checked on her daughter again, who was sleeping soundly and didn't have a temperature any more, then crashed out on the sofa, aimlessly flicking through the TV channels, unable to concentrate on anything else, while her mum worked on an assignment for college. Liberty couldn't help thinking that her inner conviction that it was all too good to be true with Cory had been right all along. Maybe she should try and see less of him, make things more casual. But even as she thought that she felt a twist of pain. She couldn't do it . . . whatever they had between them, it wasn't casual.

At ten the doorbell rang.

'Can you answer that?' her mum called out from the kitchen. 'I'm at a crucial point in my essay.'

Wearily Liberty got up from the sofa and padded out to the hallway. She opened the door to find Cory on the step.

'Hey, I've been so worried about Brooke, why didn't you call me?' He seemed to have sobered up and looked fresh from the shower.

'I don't know. I thought you had other things on your mind and we had to go to the hospital and—'

'I was an asshole, I know. I'm so sorry, baby.' He stepped forward and took Liberty in his arms. 'I wasn't there for you when you needed me, but I promise it won't ever happen again.'

She leaned against him, letting herself be comforted, but even then she wondered if this was a promise he would be able to keep.

He stayed over, holding her all night as she slept. In the morning Brooke woke them both up as she bounded into the bedroom and jumped on to the bed. She was delighted to discover Cory and immediately started chanting, 'I scream, I scream!'

'Someone seems better,' he commented sleepily

'Yeah, thank God,' Liberty replied, instantly rolling out of bed.

'Hey, where are you going?' Cory asked.

'To make breakfast for Brooke. What would you like? We've got porridge or toast.'

She'd expected him to stay in bed – he was terrible at getting up early – but he sat up, and rubbed his face. 'Give me a minute and I'll come down and make

pancakes. Would you like pancakes, sweetie?' he asked
the little girl.

'Yes, yes, yes, pancakes!' Brooke exclaimed.

Cory had to rush off and see his parents after that
and Liberty decided to take Brooke to the park –
her daughter seemed completely back to her usual
self again. Once there Brooke discovered one of her
friends from nursery and the two girls played in the
sandpit – something involving making special cakes
for the fairies who lived there . . . Liberty bought a
latte from the small café and sat on one of the benches
nearby, which had a prime view of the sandpit. For a
few minutes she felt perfectly relaxed in the sunshine
as she watched Brooke playing happily. Yesterday felt
like a bad dream, but everything was okay now.

She happened to glance away from the girls and
noticed Melissa opening the little wooden gate that led
into the play area. Fuck! What was she doing here?
Liberty had a sudden urge to run away and hide,
but too late. Melissa had spotted her. She waved and
walked purposefully over. There was no getting away.

'Hi, Liberty, I called round to your house and your
mom told me you'd be here. I really wanted to talk to
you.'

Not for the first time Liberty bitterly regretted not
being able to afford a mobile phone – then at least her
mum could have warned her that the Wicked Witch
was en route, and she could have legged it.

She managed to mutter 'hello', and realised she
knew exactly how Cory felt around his mother.

'I'm going to get a coffee, can I get you one?' Melissa
offered.

Liberty shook her head, trying to work out how
she could make a quick getaway, but Brooke was still

playing with her friend and if she tried to extricate her that might well lead to a tantrum, and she didn't want Melissa watching that and judging her to be a bad mother. She watched Cory's mother walk over to the café. She stood out a mile in her designer clothes. God, what Liberty wouldn't give for a toddler to plant his or her grubby hands on those perfectly white Capri pants . . .

Melissa returned with her drink and sat next to Liberty. 'I had to get a herbal tea, they didn't have any decaff coffee.'

And Liberty longed to come back with a sarcastic comment, along the lines of, 'We have only just discovered coffee in this country.'

'So, I'm guessing that's your daughter there?' Melissa pointed at Brooke.

Liberty nodded. She wanted Melissa to get to the point and then leave her alone.

'She's absolutely beautiful, I can see that she gets her looks from you.'

Hah! This was probably her playing good cop before she shoved the boot in.

'And she's better now? Cory told us that she had been unwell?'

'Yes, thank you.'

'It's so upsetting when your child is sick, but also amazing how quickly they can bounce back. Cory had asthma as a child – did he tell you? At times he was very unwell. It was frightening, but he's over it now – though that fear you have about them being okay never really leaves you. And when they get older you worry about them choosing the right path in life. You'll find that with Brooke.'

Was Melissa now going for the sympathy vote? She didn't seem to need any response from Liberty as she

73

continued, 'Cory seems to have such a bright future. Jacob and I looked through his paintings this morning. I hadn't quite appreciated how much progress he had made. Some of the pieces are quite stunning.'

'He's brilliant,' Liberty replied, wondering where exactly this conversation was going.

'So now we're thinking that we should support him in his ambition to follow art as his career, rather than law. He clearly has a gift.'

'But that's great news! He must be so pleased you understand that now.' Maybe she had been wrong to write Melissa off as an unfeeling witch. Liberty actually managed a smile for her. But Melissa didn't return it. Instead she twisted her diamond bracelet round her wrist. 'Actually, we haven't told him yet. We are willing to finance his place at college, but only if he goes to New York to study art. We've looked into it and really it is the best place for him.'

'Oh.' Liberty suddenly felt deflated.

'I know that Cory had the notion of studying in London but the truth is, he has no money to do that with and we're not willing to fund him if he stays in the UK. His grandmother left him some money in trust that he can access when he's twenty-five. But that's six years away.'

What was she on about? Cory was twenty-one already. 'Surely it's only four years away?'

Melissa shook her head. 'Cory is only just nineteen, whatever he might have told you. In many ways he is old for his years. He is very loving and in touch with his emotions, but he's also very naïve. He doesn't, for instance, know what it is like to be a parent. He's far too young to take on board the responsibility of being a father to someone else's child.'

And so here it came – bad cop.

'He might say that he's not too young, but he is, he really is. And he needs space and time to develop as an artist. It would be a tragedy for him not to reach his full potential, don't you think?'

'I don't expect him to be a father to Brooke,' Liberty said defensively. 'And I know it's early days, but we love each other.'

Melissa gave her a patronising smile. 'I know you feel like that, but it's only been two months. Cory has always been one to fall in love quickly. It's exactly what happened with his last girlfriend in the States. He was with her for nearly two years, and was heartbroken when she ended things with him. It's why he needed to get away. But he's over her now and it's time for him to come home. You and he have had a magical summer. Please accept, for his sake, Liberty, that it has to end now.'

The revelation that Cory was getting over a broken heart hit Liberty hard, but she wasn't yet ready to admit defeat, still clinging on to her belief in Cory. 'I really don't think it's for you to say what's right for your son any more. He's an adult.'

'Of course he is, but do you really want him to squander his talent by having to work and being unable to go to art college and fulfil his dream? At the moment everything seems golden to him because he's never had to struggle. Do you think he could do what you do, for instance? Work in a restaurant and put his dream on hold? Because I don't. He needs to be free to be an artist, and I'm afraid to say we've always rather spoiled him.'

Liberty had a feeling of walls closing in on her, of all hope being squeezed out. 'But why won't you let him study in London?' She already knew the answer – because Melissa wanted her out of Cory's life. A clean break, a fresh slate. Brooke and Liberty wiped away as if they had never been there. They weren't good enough for him.

'There are better colleges in the States and Cory needs the support of his family,' Melissa said evasively.

Every word from her was like another puncture to Liberty's dream, but she wasn't ready to give up yet. 'What about if I came over to New York with him?' she said defiantly. 'I've had some modelling success, I could get work out there too.' She wanted to add that a major TV director was interested in her, but she still hadn't heard anything from Zac, so maybe his interest had just been a whim.

Melissa looked at her as if she was unbelievably stupid. 'Cory will have enough money to pay for a room in a student dorm, which he'll most likely have to share. They don't provide space for families. And, honey, a word of advice: the streets of New York are lined with beautiful girls who want to make it as a model, actress or whatever. Beautiful girls who don't come with a small daughter in tow.'

Brooke chose that moment to approach them.

'Mummy, I'm hungry.' The little girl had taken off her shoes and socks and her legs were covered in sand.

'Oh, aren't you beautiful?' Melissa exclaimed over her as Liberty rifled through her bag to find Brooke some rice cakes. She was still reeling from the onslaught, and trying to work out what to say, when the other woman got up from the bench.

'Well, I'm glad we've had this conversation, Liberty. I'll be telling Cory of our decision this afternoon. We fly back tonight. Goodbye.' And without waiting for a response, she turned on her designer heel and walked briskly out of the playground.

Chapter 9

Liberty's first thought after Melissa left was that she had to see Cory. But she couldn't because he would be with his parents. Her next was that she had to see Em. Praying that her friend would be in, she managed to entice Brooke out of the park and practically jogged with the buggy all the way to Em's flat. To her dismay she discovered that her friend was already packing up, and the sight of her possessions being put away in boxes was like a slap in the face to Liberty. She really was losing her best friend.

'Hey, Brooke, do you want to see if *The Tweenies* is on?' Em asked the little girl, realising that Liberty needed to talk. They settled her in the living room in front of the TV, and went into the bedroom. Em had taken down all her film posters, photographs and the fairy lights that had hung round the mirror, and now the room seemed very bare. Liberty sat cross-legged on the bed and relayed what Melissa had said, very aware that there might not be many more occasions when she could do this. So often before she had sat in this very place, chatting to Em, asking advice, giving advice, giggling, swapping stories, and the thought of not being able to was almost unbearable to her. Talking on the phone and writing letters would never compensate for not being with her best friend.

'What do you think I should do? I mean, Melissa's right, Cory is too young to be a parent. And I didn't even know he was only nineteen, or about the girl in the States who broke his heart. Maybe I'm just a complete rebound for him.' Liberty chewed at her nails, a habit she'd thought she'd got out of months ago.

'First of all, calm down. Melissa has her own agenda – you thought that right from the start. But Cory's not like her, not in any way. When his parents have gone, you can talk to him and work something out. You don't have to look so desperate, I'm sure it's going to be okay.'

Liberty didn't share Em's conviction, though. She could feel the happiness she'd had with Cory slipping through her fingers, slipping away.

He had left several messages asking her to call him when she returned home. She dialled his number and he picked up after one ring.

'Can you come over? I have to talk to you?' There was an urgent note in his voice.

'Have your parents gone?'

'They have, thank God! And if they hadn't, I would have told them to. Please, come now. Get a taxi, I'll pay.'

Should she tell him that she knew about the place at art school in America? No, she couldn't do it over the phone; she had to see him.

As soon as she arrived Cory pulled her into his arms and kissed her, and kissed her, and she felt the familiar tingle of desire, which ignited whenever she was with him.

'I've missed you so much,' he murmured, smoothing back her hair and gazing at her as if he couldn't quite believe she was here in person. 'I need to tell you about the little bombshell my mom dropped.'

'I know all about it, she met me in the park this morning.'

Cory shook his head in disbelief. 'She's a piece of work.'

They sat together on the sofa and, as with Em earlier, Liberty had the feeling that this might be one of the last times she did this and was trying hard to stay strong and keep it together.

'So you know that they've promised to pay for me to go to art college, but only if I go in the States?'

She nodded.

'I'm sure my mom thinks that I'm just going to roll over and accept whatever she says, just like my dad. Well, I'm not going to, Liberty. I want to study in England so that I can be with you.'

'But how will you afford to? Your mum said they wouldn't pay.'

He shrugged. 'Then I'll get a job like you.' He reached for her hand. 'The point is, I'm not leaving. I want to be with you. I *have* to be with you. That's all that matters.'

He was saying everything she had hoped he would, and she wanted to let the happiness in, but there was something stopping it. 'Cory, you're only nineteen, why did you lie to me?'

'I thought you'd take me more seriously if I said I was twenty-one. And that's only two years out.'

'And what about this girl you broke up with – your mum pretty much said that you were on the rebound from a broken heart.'

'Oh, she did, did she? Yeah, I was cut up when she

dumped me, but I don't suppose my mom told you that she dumped me for my best friend? I think *his* betrayal hurt more. My mom is saying all these things to undermine you and make you think that what we have isn't real. But we know it is, don't we?'

He looked and sounded so convincing and she so wanted to believe him, to believe in the dream that he could stay in the UK and they could be together . . .

'Yes,' she murmured, pressing her lips to his. 'Yes, it is real.'

Melissa was as good as her word. When Cory met Liberty after work the next day he revealed that his parents had stopped his regular allowance. He wouldn't have enough to cover his rent. She really was a witch, Liberty thought. How could someone do that to their own son?

'I'm going to have to get a job,' he said, as they sat on the grass in the Pavilion gardens, catching the last rays of the September sun.

'I should be getting paid from that modelling job soon. How about I lend you some money, just to tide you over?'

He shook his head. 'No way are you doing that. You need that for you and Brooke. And I want to prove to my parents that they don't have to bankroll me, that I can make it on my own. It'll be good for me.' Cory grinned at her, 'I know you think I have been a bit spoiled, admit it, so now comes the reality check.'

'But what about your painting?'

'I can do that whenever. That's what other artists have had to do.'

A day later Cory got himself a job at a popular bar along the seafront. His shifts started at six p.m. and didn't end until after midnight. Liberty couldn't imagine when she would ever see him. But Cory was upbeat and didn't seem to share her concern.

'It'll be cool – I'll give you a key and you can call by when your shift finishes at the restaurant, whenever your mum can babysit, or I can come to yours. This doesn't have to change anything.'

Liberty didn't want to tell him that she wouldn't be able to do that all the time. She didn't want to point out that she had other responsibilities, that she had to get up at half-past seven every morning without fail so as to see to Brooke. She didn't want to put a downer on everything as she could see how much getting the job meant to Cory. But as soon as he started work, it was like the unravelling of their brilliant summer together. His first shift didn't finish until one-thirty a.m. Liberty had done as he'd suggested and let herself into his flat. She stayed up until half-past midnight, taking a long bath, listening to music, planning to surprise him by lying on the sofa in her sexiest underwear. But the evenings were getting cool, and after lying there shivering for a few minutes, she retreated into the bedroom and under the duvet.

She must have fallen asleep because the next thing she knew Cory was sliding into bed next to her, and kissing her neck. Sleepily she turned round to kiss him.

'This is the best thing ever, getting into bed with you already there,' he murmured, sliding his hands over her body. Sleepy as she was, she instantly responded to his touch and soon she was gasping with pleasure.

She expected to fall asleep after that, with his arms round her as they always did. Instead he sat up. 'D'you want a drink? I can't sleep yet, I'm totally wired.'

She stifled a yawn. 'Okay, but I'll just have a cup of tea.' She pulled on one of his t-shirts and followed him into the kitchen, where he poured himself a large measure of Jack Daniel's, topped up with a small amount of Coke, and made her a cup of tea.

'So how was it then?' Liberty asked, folding her arms to try and keep warm.

He shrugged. 'Okay, better than I thought. The time seemed to go quickly and the other bar staff are all really friendly. It felt more like a night out than work.' He kissed her. 'It's all going to be cool, don't look so worried.'

Yes, it probably did seem like fun on the first night as it was all new to him . . . She wondered what his answer would be in a couple of weeks' time, when the novelty had worn off.

Chapter 10

Sometimes Liberty hated being right. Cory's working hours meant that they hardly saw each other in the weeks that followed. When they could snatch some time together she had to stay up late, so inevitably she was exhausted the next day, snappy with her daughter and the most sullen waitress at work. Everyone commented on it, from her mum, who told her she had to slow down, to Marco, who insisted that her attitude had to improve. She felt as if she was being torn in too many directions, wanting to be a good mum and wanting to see Cory. And on top of everything Em was leaving at the end of September.

They had a special week where they crammed in all the activities that they had loved doing together over the years: rollerblading along the seafront, swimming in the sea, having fish and chips on the beach, going on the amusements on the Pier, and having one last ride on the dodgems and the Waltzer, and afterwards making themselves feel sick by eating too many doughnuts. They rounded everything off with a girls' night out together on Em's last Friday, calling in at some of their favourite haunts.

First stop was the pub in one of the roads off the seafront where they'd both scored their first Malibu and Coke aged fifteen, effortlessly conning the barman into believing they were eighteen.

'D'you remember how furious your mum was when we pitched up drunk at your house? We pretended that we'd gone to see a film but then you threw up on the sofa,' Liberty said, as they ordered Malibu and Cokes for old times' sake. She was determined that this night would be all about having fun. She would be sad when Em left, not before.

'God, yeah. She grounded me for the next month, which I wouldn't have minded except I know what a complete tearaway *she* was when she was a teenager. I wonder if you'll be that strict with Brooke? Nah, I reckon you're too much of a softie. She'll be able to wrap you round her little finger.'

Em's blue eyes filled with tears then. 'God, Libs, I'm going to miss you and Brooke so much! You will send me loads of letters and pictures, won't you? I want to hear all your news.'

'No, no, don't get upset!' Liberty exclaimed, blinking tears away herself. 'I know this is what you really want to do, and even though I wish I could make you stay here for ever and ever, I know you have to go. And one day we'll be able to come out and see you, and you'll be some gorgeous brown surfer girl.'

One Malibu and Coke became two, and then they were off to the next bar, where they went for cocktails, a Strawberry Daiquiri for Em and a Cosmopolitan for Liberty.

'So how's Cory liking his new job?' Em asked, plucking the pink paper umbrella out of her drink.

'He's been very positive about it.' Worryingly positive actually, acting as if it was temporary and that soon he'd have money again, though from where Liberty didn't know.

'That's good, isn't it?'

'The trouble is, I don't know if he's doing any painting. And he has no idea how to economise.'

'Oh?'

'When I went round the other night, he'd bought a bottle of champagne and some oysters because I'd never had them and he wanted me to try them.'

'Just as well you didn't say caviar then,' Em commented. 'But that's so sweet.'

'Yeah, but there was nothing else to eat in the flat, and I don't think he had any money to buy proper food. He came round to mine last night before he went to work, and Mum had made chilli and he had three helpings.'

'Oh, bless! He'll get used to having to budget. You did. And maybe the Wicked Witch of the USA will take pity on the son she claims to love so much and give him the money to go to college.'

Liberty doubted that very much. Melissa seemed like a woman with an iron will, who didn't change her mind once it was made up.

They managed two more pubs after that and wound up at Cory's bar, slightly the worse for wear. The place was heaving but Em found them two stools at the bar, so they could be close to Cory. He was rushing around serving people, but still managed a smile for them.

'Hey, ladies, what can I get you?' he asked, leaning over the bar and planting a kiss on Liberty's lips.

'Well, we're working through all the drinks we used to be into, so I'll have a vodka and lime and, Libs, you've got to have a Piña Colada.' By now Em was slightly slurring her words.

Liberty grimaced. She'd been mixing her drinks all night and knew that at this rate she'd end up with an evil hangover – and hangovers and small children, as she knew from bitter experience, did not go well together. 'Actually, I'll have a Diet Coke.'

'Wimp! Lightweight!' Em declared, nearly falling off her stool.

Cory smiled. 'Are you sure you haven't had enough already, Em?'

'No way. In fact, make mine a double.'

'Liking your style! Coming right up!'

They watched Cory as he competently mixed their drinks. He seemed perfectly content but Liberty felt a pang of sadness to see him behind the bar. He should be painting. This was such a massive waste of his talent. She glanced across and noticed a familiar blonde girl, sitting at a table with a group of friends. Zara. Liberty had seen her a few times before when she had been out with Cory and some of his friends, and while Zara had been considerably nicer to her than she once had and never given any sign that she wanted to get back with Cory, Liberty still didn't trust her. She remembered the girl's attitude the first time they had met, when Zara had looked at her with such disdain and seemed desperate for Cory's attention. What was she doing here? Was it just coincidence? Or did she know that Cory worked here? Liberty couldn't help feeling insecure.

He returned with their drinks and Liberty decided to come straight out with it, rather than sit there worrying.

'Did you know Zara was over there?'

'Oh, yeah, she often comes in with some of my other friends.'

He seemed completely matter-of-fact about it, no

hint that he particularly cared whether she was there or not. 'In fact, she's come up with a great idea for me to save money.'

'Oh?' Liberty didn't like the idea of Zara coming up with anything to do with Cory. She was bound to have an ulterior motive.

'Yep, there's a room going in her house – a large double, big enough for me to paint in, and it's cheap. It's getting that I can't afford my flat any more. What do you reckon?'

All she could think of was Cory spending more time with Zara, with beautiful, rich Zara who had no responsibilities and no ties. Who would be there whenever Liberty went round to see Cory, and would still be there with him when Liberty went home.

'Wouldn't it be weird, sharing with your ex?'

'No way! I told you, I don't see her like that. We're strictly friends. And this means I'll be able to save more money and I can be one step closer to going to college.' He smiled at her, so open and happy that she didn't feel able to ask him how he would feel if she was sharing with her ex-boyfriend. And then there was no time to talk further as he had to go and serve some more customers.

Em had been silent during the exchange, but she spoke now. 'He can't afford that flat, can he? So maybe it is a good idea. And it won't be for ever, Libs, just until he goes to college.'

Liberty was about to reply when Zara sauntered over, beautiful and stylish as ever in a pair of leather trousers and a black silk shirt that most likely cost as much as a month's rent on Cory's flat.

'Hi, Liberty, how are you?' she asked, flicking back her long blonde hair, which looked as if it had been freshly blow-dried in a salon.

Liberty forced herself to smile. 'I'm fine thanks, Zara. This is my friend Em.'

Zara glanced at her, in a way that said she didn't consider Em to be any competition whatsoever.

'On a girls' night out?'

'Yep, how about you?' Em asked, clearly not warming to Zara one little bit.

'Just out with a group of friends. We love this bar, it's got a good vibe. And, of course, now Cory works here, it's a great place to hang out.' She looked at Liberty. 'So has he told you about moving into my house? It makes perfect sense, doesn't it? I mean, I have so much space. And the light is fantastic for an artist as the house is north-facing.'

Thank God Cory had told her . . . Liberty could just imagine how happy it would have made Zara to be the first to break the news to her.

'Yes, he has. I guess it would be good for him to have somewhere cheaper to rent.' *If only it wasn't with you.*

Cory rejoined them at that moment. Liberty suddenly noticed how tired he looked. There were dark shadows under his eyes and his golden tan seemed to be fading; the late nights were taking their toll on him as well.

'So, I'm planning to have a party next Friday night, and of course you're all invited,' Zara continued.

Friday, the day when Liberty had to work a double shift, followed by a double shift on Saturday.

'Sure, I'll see if I can swap shifts with someone,' Cory replied.

'Cool. And I hope you'll be able to get a babysitter, Liberty?'

If anyone else had said that, Liberty would have thought they were being considerate, but she reckoned Zara was just trying to rub her nose in the fact that she wasn't as carefree and single as she'd once been. And as Zara was now.

'I work on Fridays, but maybe I'll be able to come after work.'

'Oh, I do hope so,' Zara replied, then thankfully she swished away to rejoin her friends.

'See, she's okay,' Cory commented, before he rushed off to serve another customer.

'Bloody hell,' Em muttered. 'She's a nightmare. Don't worry, Libs, he doesn't fancy her.'

'She fancies him though, doesn't she?' But Liberty didn't want to say any more about it. Em was leaving in two days' time, and this was their night.

Chapter 11

Em's departure left a gaping hole in Liberty's life. She missed her at work, after work, all the time. She had other friends, but no one she was as close to as Em. She felt terribly lonely, as if she had no one to confide in. Meanwhile, Cory had moved in with Zara. Liberty had imagined a student-style house, but in fact it was expensively decorated and furnished, with no one else living there apart from Zara and Cory. The other housemate was away travelling for a month.

As Liberty had feared, the move had a negative impact on their relationship. Whenever she went round there she was aware of Zara's presence. Even if she wasn't in, the smell of her expensive perfume seemed to linger in the air; her designer clothes would be strewn across the sofas, along with her copies of *Vogue* and *Elle*. Glasses and empty bottles of expensive wine would be left in the living room, all ready for the cleaner to come and tidy away. Liberty felt as if her old precious intimacy with Cory was being chipped away. It was made worse by the fact that he seemed oblivious to it; he was so caught up in work at the bar that he was taking on more and more hours.

By the time Friday came the last thing Liberty wanted to do was to go to Zara's party. She had already suggested that she and Cory skip it, that he come over to her house instead, as they had hardly seen each other that week, but Cory had insisted he had to go.

'Zara's been so good to me,' he said. 'She'll be upset if I don't show.'

Liberty was exhausted after the double shift. She had changed into her little black dress and put on some more make up when she finished work, but still felt drab compared to the other girls at the party when she walked in. They were all in beautiful designer clothes, their hair freshly washed and blow-dried, the jewels round their necks and on their fingers real rather than the paste ones which were all that she could afford. She found Cory in the living room, chatting to a group of girls that included Zara. For a moment Liberty watched him. He seemed completely at ease with these beautiful, rich, privileged people – hardly surprising, she supposed, as he had been one of them – but it made her feel left out, made her long for the two of them to be alone together, back in his flat, in bed, with the world shut out. Maybe that was the only place their relationship could work . . .

Cory caught sight of her and immediately made his way over. 'Hey, I was wondering when you were going to arrive. I've missed you, baby.' He kissed her and she wound her arms around his neck, aware that they were the centre of attention, and not caring. Somehow she wanted to stake her claim on Cory, especially in front of Zara.

'When did you get here?' she asked as he led her into the huge, glass-roofed kitchen to get some champagne. It would be champagne for Zara . . . the last

91

time Liberty and her mum had held a house party, they'd had a choice of red or white wine or lager.

'Oh, I bunked off work today so I could help Zara get the house ready. I thought it was the least I could do.'

She felt a stab of jealousy at the thought of Cory spending so much time with his housemate.

'Doesn't she have staff to do that?' Liberty knew she sounded sarcastic, but couldn't help it.

Cory chose not to pick up on it. 'They didn't come until six and there was a heap of stuff to do first.' He poured them each a glass of champagne, and she noticed that his hand was slightly unsteady.

'Are you pissed?' she asked, feeling a little resentful that she'd been stuck at work while he was already knocking back champagne.

He grinned and now she could see that his blue eyes seemed not to be quite focused. 'A little, I guess. But, hey, you know what they say? All work and no play makes Jack a dull boy.' He slid his arms round her and pulled her close to him. 'So why don't we go upstairs?'

The resentment was still there but the desire was stronger . . .

'Why not?' She drained her glass of champagne.

Upstairs Cory wedged a chair under the door handle to stop them being disturbed and then they were falling on to his bed, he was pulling off her dress and she unbuttoned his jeans. And while he lay back, she sucked and licked him, revelling in his groans of pleasure and feeling a flash of satisfaction that Zara was downstairs, wondering what they were doing. And then Cory pulled her on top of him and she was riding him, feeling the pleasure building inside her as he thrust into her and as his fingers expertly caressed her clit, sending whorls of pleasure through her body. Faster and faster she rode him, teetering on the edge of the most delicious orgasm.

And then someone knocked on the door. 'Cory, are you in there?' It was one of Zara's girlfriends. 'Zara needs to speak to you about something.'

They were both beyond talking but Liberty thought the rhythmic squeaking of the bed might have given a clue. Eventually the friend gave up.

'Was that very bad?' Cory grinned afterwards as they lay in each other's arms.

'No, it was very good,' Liberty teased, reaching out and touching his face. And exactly what she had needed. They stayed there for an hour, talking, catching up, and Liberty half hoped that they could remain up here until the party was over, so she could have him all to herself. But eventually Cory sat up. 'I guess we'd better go back down.'

Reluctantly Liberty pulled her clothes back on. She stifled a yawn, it was two a.m. and she was bone tired. She had to be at work by eleven the next morning and she knew she couldn't afford another shift where she acted below par. Marco had already given her a warning. Although she knew he was a kind-hearted man, she didn't want to push her luck.

Downstairs Zara and her gang of friends were playing a drunken game of Spin the Bottle. Some of the boys had already taken off their shirts, a couple of the girls were down to their underwear. Zara was still in her dress but seemed very drunk, her eyes glittering dangerously as she spotted Cory.

'There you are! Come on, you two, you have to join in. No chickening out!'

Cory looked at Liberty and shrugged. 'Shall we?'

No fucking way! Liberty wanted to reply, but she

imagined how that would go down, so reluctantly she followed him over to the circle. They found themselves sitting opposite Zara. The party girl grabbed the bottle. (Of champagne, naturally.)

'One more round of kissing then it's Truth or Dare,' she declared.

'Well, hurrah for that,' Liberty muttered, mimicking her voice, causing Cory to nudge her gently and say, '*Shush*.'

Zara spun the bottle and it came to a halt pointing at Hugo, one of her stuck-up male friends whom Liberty had never liked after she had overheard him mocking one of their other friends – a girl who was slightly overweight.

'You've got to kiss the two girls opposite you,' Zara decreed. The power was obviously going to her drunken head. 'For twenty seconds.'

Liberty curled her lip when she realised that she was sitting directly opposite him.

'Sorry, baby,' Cory said under his breath. 'I'll get you a glass of champagne to make up for it.'

'No problemo!' Hugo replied, and crawled over to the girl next to Liberty. He promptly gave her a full on snog while the circle around them clapped and counted down from twenty. Then he detached himself from the girl and lunged at Liberty. She tried to keep her mouth clamped firmly shut but he thrust his tongue straight in. And twenty seconds might not sound very long, but when it involved a man you didn't like, sticking his tongue down your throat, boy, it dragged.

'. . . seventeen, eighteen, nineteen, twenty!' yelled the partygoers. Hugo gave a cocky half smile to Liberty, as if to say, *Was that good for you?* Then he staggered back to his place. She wiped her mouth and took a long sip of champagne from the glass Cory handed her.

'Poor you,' he whispered. 'I've heard Hugo kisses like a vacuum cleaner.'

'That's an insult to vacuum cleaners,' she muttered, the post-sex glow rapidly leaving her. She wanted to get out of here – *now*. But Zara was already spinning the bottle and now it came to rest pointing straight at her. Great . . .

'It's Truth or Dare time now!' Zara cried gleefully, clapping her hands together. 'And because the truth is so dullsville, I think it should be a dare for you, Liberty.'

'So you've just decided to change the rules?' she asked.

'It's my party! It's just a question of the dare . . .' Zara put her finger on her perfectly chiselled chin and adopted a coy look.

God, she was annoying! If only Em was by Liberty's side to say something suitably cutting.

'Got it! I dare you to take a line of coke. I know you don't do drugs any more, so now's your chance.'

'That's a fucking treat!' Hugo drawled. 'Not a dare.'

Zara was staring straight at Liberty, challenging her, taunting her. How could she know that Liberty didn't take drugs? It could only have come from Cory. God! Why had he done that? Didn't he realise that Zara loathed her? She had told him that she had experimented with them a little when she was younger, before she'd had Brooke, but since then had vowed to stay off them. It wasn't exactly a hardship as she couldn't afford coke anyway, but a couple of years ago one of her friend's brothers had died of an overdose. It had devastated his family and Liberty knew she could never be casual about drugs again. She was a single mum; she couldn't afford to make any mistakes.

'So how about it?' Zara repeated. 'It's either that or a

95

forfeit, and the forfeit is to strip off and run round the circle three times.'

'Just say no to the drugs!' Hugo bayed.

'Fuck that, Zara!' Cory exclaimed. 'Why are you picking on Liberty? The reason she doesn't take drugs is because someone she knew died of an overdose. She's not going to take a line of coke in some dumb-ass juvenile game.'

He stood up and held out his hand. 'Come on, Liberty, we're going.'

They were almost at the door when Zara shouted, 'Oh, that's it! Run off to your girlfriend's council house. Your little experiment in slumming it. I can see through that. You're only with her for the novelty value. Fuck! You used to be interesting to be with. Now you're so fucking boring and under her thumb.'

Liberty felt her heart racing and a surge of anger rushing through her as she looked at Zara, seeing the girl's pretty face twisted with spite and jealousy.

'You're pathetic, Zara,' she said. 'We weren't all born with a silver spoon in our mouth, a trust fund and a rich daddy to bankroll us.'

The other guests were open-mouthed as they glee-fully listened to this exchange. Not one of them stood up for Cory. They were all spoiled rich kids, just like Zara.

'Come on, Liberty,' he repeated. 'We're out of here.'

In a way it was a relief that Zara had behaved like this – now her dislike was out in the open Liberty wouldn't have to pretend to get on with her any more.

'I'll find somewhere else to live as soon as I can,' Cory told her later as they lay in bed together. 'She's a psycho bitch and I'm not having you exposed to her. I'm sorry I ever told her about the drugs incident. I never realised she would use it against you.'

Liberty snuggled up to him. 'It's okay, I just wish you'd intervened before I had to kiss that wanker Hugo.'

'Yeah, sorry about that. How about I kiss you and make it better?'

'Yes, please,' she murmured, the incident with Zara already fading from her mind at the feel of Cory's lips on hers.

Chapter 12

But it proved easier said than done for Cory to find somewhere else to live that he could afford. Liberty wondered if he should move in with her, but it seemed too soon. Besides, it wasn't up to her, it was her mum's house. But then Zara apologised to him and whenever Liberty went round, his housemate was always out. So that was something. But work seemed to be getting Cory down. He obviously wasn't used to living to such a strict routine and on such a tight budget.

Worse still, he stopped talking about the future and his plans to go to art school. He never seemed to do any painting any more. To Liberty it seemed as if a light had gone off inside him. He had radiated such confidence and delight in life when they had first met. He'd been the golden boy with a glorious future stretching ahead of him. Now he seemed older, more weary, as if ground down by life, accepting that things were the way they were and would never change. And it looked like her life wouldn't either as there still had been no word from Zac.

Cory seemed to cheer up dramatically as Liberty's twenty-second birthday drew closer, saying that he had all kinds of plans. 'Promise me you won't spend too much money – you need it for college,' she told him, worried that he would blow all his savings in one extravagant gesture. It would be so like him to do that. 'Seriously, I'd be happy if we went out for a pizza. I don't need lots of money spent on me.'

He just grinned and tapped his nose. 'It's a secret. Wait and see.'

She might have guessed that Cory wouldn't listen to her. On the morning of her birthday an extravagant bouquet of pale pink roses and stargazer lilies was delivered to her. From Cory, naturally. And when she arrived back at the house from dropping Brooke off at nursery, a white Audi TT convertible was parked outside, with Cory at the wheel.

'Oh my God! Where did you get this from?' she exclaimed.

'I hired it. I'm taking you to London. We're going to be staying at the Ritz – so go upstairs and pack. We're leaving in ten minutes. It's all sorted out with Nina, don't worry. I'll have you back home at the same time tomorrow.'

Liberty had always fantasised about staying at that hotel. There was something about the elegant building on Piccadilly, with its name proudly displayed in lights, that had intrigued her ever since she was a little girl and had walked past it on a rare trip up to London. A few weeks ago Cory had asked where she most wanted to stay in London and she told him it was the Ritz – he must have been planning the surprise even then. She was torn between feeling charmed by the romantic gesture and panicking about the cost.

'But that's so expensive! Oh my God, Cory, you need that money!'

'I had some savings. Now hurry up – we have a five-star hotel room to make the most of.'

It was a magical day. Driving through London with the roof down, she felt like a movie star as people turned to look at the flashy sports car with the beautiful young couple inside it. At the hotel Cory had arranged for pink rose petals to be scattered over the double bed and for a bottle of champagne to be chilling. She wanted to say that it was too much . . . but he silenced her concerns by putting his arms round her and kissing her.

They stayed in their room, making love and drinking champagne, as the afternoon bled into the early evening and the streetlights went on outside their window.

'Thank you so much for this,' Liberty said, as she lay in his arms, stroking his shoulder. 'It's been perfect.'

'It's not over yet!' Cory exclaimed, sitting up. 'I've still got to give you your present.'

'No way! You didn't have to get me anything after all this!'

But Cory had leaped out of bed and was rifling through his overnight bag.

She couldn't believe it when he presented her with a duck egg blue Tiffany box. He must have spent every last penny of his savings. She opened the box to discover a sweet silver dragonfly necklace.

'I love it!' she exclaimed, lifting up her hair so he could fasten the chain round her neck.

'I wanted to get you a diamond, but they were a little out of my price range. One day, though. And I thought the dragonfly was a good symbol – to remind us to live in the moment, to seize the day, not sweat the small stuff. So come on, we have to go and eat and then we're going to see *Chicago*.'

'How did you know I really wanted to see that show?'

'I've done my research.'

They ate huge Margherita pizzas at a cheap Italian restaurant and drank a carafe of white wine that tasted rough after the champagne, but they didn't care. They were high on love and spending all this precious time with each other. It was as if they were in a bubble of happiness that lasted all night long, throughout the show, and walking back through late-night London, and into their hotel lobby, and feeling like VIPs as the uniformed doorman held the door open for them.

'I wish we could do this all the time,' Cory said regretfully as they checked out the following morning. He seemed subdued after yesterday, as if realising that it was time to go back to reality, one that he didn't want to face.

Liberty linked her arm through his. 'It wouldn't be so special if we could do it all the time. That was a perfect day, I'll always remember it.'

He didn't answer and she wondered if he was thinking that he used to be able to spend money freely and never worry about the consequences.

One evening after her birthday she met up with Cory before he started work. There was a chill in the air and it felt as if autumn was well on the way. As usual he asked her all about her day and how Brooke was settling into school. He had become very good at deflecting questions about himself.

'So did you manage to do any painting?' she asked.

He shook his head. 'Nope. I slept in and then I went on the PlayStation. I was too exhausted to do anything else.'

'Maybe you could cut down your hours, now your rent is so much less?'

Instantly he became defensive. 'I need to save all

I can if there's to be a chance in hell of me going to college here. I was thinking maybe of getting another job a couple of days a week, before I start at the bar.'

'Is there no way you could talk to your parents? See if they've changed their minds?'

'My mom never changes her mind once she's made it up – that's her specialty. *Never.* She'll be hoping I change mine.' He glanced at her. 'But I'm not going to, Liberty.'

These were fighting, confident words, but Cory seemed diminished. Was it her fault? Was she dragging him down? She couldn't bear the thought that she might be.

They reached the bar and kissed goodbye.

'So . . . I'll see you tomorrow,' Liberty said, sad at the prospect of yet another night without him.

'Yeah. I'll try and call you if I get chance.'

She knew it was unlikely that he'd be able to. He'd given up his mobile phone as he wanted to save every penny. She watched Cory go inside, his head bowed, shoulders hunched against the bitter wind coming off the sea.

Chapter 13

The phone was ringing when Liberty let herself into the house. It was Lizzie, her agent.

'Liberty! I hope you're sitting down because I have got some A-mazing news for you, sweetie!' Her voice seemed to have gone up an octave in her excitement.

'Oh?'

'I have just come off the phone to Zac Keller's assistant. And . . .' she paused for dramatic effect. Really Lizzie was wasted as an agent, she should have been an actress herself '. . . he wants to see you. Wants you to fly over to LA the day after tomorrow for a screen test for some major crime series he's producing. They wouldn't tell me anything more than that. But it's a leading role, I know that much. This is the moment we have been waiting for!'

It was amazing news, but immediately Liberty started panicking – she couldn't just drop everything and fly off. Who would look after Brooke? What about her job in the restaurant?

'I know it sounds mad, Lizzie, but I just don't know if I can go at such short notice. I'll need a bit of time to make arrangements.'

There was a sharp intake of breath from the other end of the phone. 'Liberty Evans, this is what is called a Big Break. They don't happen very often, believe me, especially not to twenty-two-year-old single mothers who are working in fast-food outlets.'

'It's a family-run Italian restaurant,' Liberty shot back.

'Whatever. So what do you want me to tell Zac Keller's assistant? He's most likely got a list of girls as long as your arm lined up.'

'Tell them I need more time.'

A heavy sigh from Lizzie. 'And that's your final answer?'

'It has to be.'

She'd got as far as pouring her mum and herself a glass of rosé when the phone rang again.

'I can't quite believe this,' it was Lizzie speaking, 'but Zac Keller is going to fly over tonight and will see you tomorrow evening in London. Tell me you're going to be available for that meeting?'

'Really? It seems incredible he would do that.'

'You said it, sweetheart. He must really want you. Remember I told you how impressed by you he was? I'm going to play hardball about the money, if he offers you the role. So, to confirm, you will need to be at Claridges tomorrow night at seven. They're faxing me the audition script over, and I'll get a bike to bring it to you. It's one of the lead roles. They gave me a little more background on the phone and you'll be auditioning to play a young female detective who survived a traumatic childhood experience and has developed unique powers of intuition that enable her to solve crimes no one else can.'

Liberty came off the phone in a complete daze. A leading director wanted to see her? Was flying all the way over from LA? It seemed too good to be true. There had to be some catch to it. Knowing her luck, he wanted her to star in a porn movie . . . But then surely he wouldn't go to so much trouble and expense? All she knew was that she was excited and nervous in equal measure at the prospect of seeing Zac Keller again.

At five p.m. the following afternoon Liberty was on the train to London. She had wanted to tell Cory, but hadn't seen him as he'd been working extra shifts and something had stopped her telling him the news over the phone. He had been so down lately that it didn't seem the right moment to reveal her amazing news. Her mum had told her she was being silly, and that she should, but Liberty wasn't so sure. It felt a bit too much as if it would put a revealing spotlight on Cory's own situation, and highlight how very far he was from realising his dream.

She had read through the script many times now, trying to get a feel for the character. And while she hadn't really had enough time, she supposed she was as prepared as she was ever going to be.

All the same she was a mass of nerves as she approached the impressive five-star hotel, and she heard her voice shaking as she asked the attractive brunette receptionist to let Zac Keller know Liberty Evans had arrived. Part of her couldn't help thinking that the receptionist would reply, 'Who?' and then the whole audition would be revealed as an elaborate prank. But no, the receptionist discreetly made the call then said, 'Mr Keller says to go straight up to his suite. He's in the Davies Penthouse. If you take the lift all the way to the top, turn to the right and you'll find it.'

Liberty felt as if her legs had turned to jelly as she followed these instructions. The mirrored walls of the lift showed her looking anxious, hardly the expression to blow the socks off a Hollywood director. 'I've got nothing to lose,' she told herself, wishing that her mum or Em were here to give her a pep talk. 'And either I'll be right for the part or I won't be. So what will be, will be.' She touched her dragonfly necklace for luck – she always wore it now.

Outside the penthouse suite she hesitated for a few seconds before knocking. Almost immediately the door was opened by a tall, athletic blonde woman, who smiled at her and said, 'Hi, I'm Tess, I work with Zac Keller, do come in.'

Liberty had never been anywhere as lavish as this suite. She could hardly take it all in: the French windows leading on to a terrace, giving a breathtaking view over London; the immense marble fireplace; the vases full of beautiful arrangements of fresh flowers; the ornate lamps. And there, sitting on one of the elegant armchairs and looking every inch at home, was Zac. He stood up and held out his hand to her, 'Liberty, it's so good to see you again.'

'Even if we did have to fly over,' Tess said dryly.

'It was worth it, though, Tess, wasn't it?' he replied, shaking Liberty's hand and holding it for a fraction longer than you usually would in greeting. 'She definitely has the right look.' He gestured to Liberty to sit down and she perched on the edge of the sofa.

'Now we just need to see if this one can actually act.' Tess again. She didn't seem nearly as impressed with Liberty as Zac was.

It was a little disconcerting, she found, having people discuss her as if she wasn't even in the room.

Zac grinned. 'You mustn't mind Tess. She's still furious with me for casting the wrong leading lady. So your agent mentioned that you had a daughter?'

'You didn't tell me that,' Tess muttered.

'It's not a big deal, Tess,' he replied. 'Are you and the father still together, Liberty?' he continued.

She shook her head, and feeling that she needed to get Tess on her side, she added, 'But really I don't think it should make any difference to whether I'm the right actor for the role or not. In fact,' she was gaining confidence now, 'I happen to think that having a child gives you a deeper insight into human emotions. And that can only be a good thing, can't it?' She tilted her chin and shot a defiant look at Tess.

'Well, I suppose we should get down to business,' Zac told her. 'I'd like you to read the first scene with Tess, who will take on all the other parts. And you're to keep your English accent.'

Initially Liberty made a complete hash of it. It had been so long since she'd had an audition and she felt she wasn't getting into the character at all – too aware all the time of sinking into the luxurious sofa and being in the presence of this powerful director.

'Heard enough?' Tess asked Zac, as yet again Liberty stumbled over one of her speeches. They must be regretting wasting their time on her.

Zac looked disappointed, but before he could reply Liberty said, 'Please let me try it again. I know that was rubbish. And I think it would help me if we stood up.'

'Sure. Do it again from the top,' Zac replied. But he sounded weary, as if he had nothing to lose.

But this time Liberty felt herself connect with the words and with the character. When she came to the end she looked over at Zac and Tess, and they seemed impressed. Well, Zac seemed positively excited and Tess actually cracked a smile.

'Liberty, would you mind stepping out to the other

room while Tess and I have a talk?' Zac asked. 'Help yourself to a drink from the bar.'

They seemed to be ages. Liberty felt too agitated to sit down and, after pouring herself a glass of water, paced up and down the room. Now she was here and had met Zac again and had the prospect of this amazing, life-changing role within her grasp, she suddenly realised how much she wanted it. With a fierce, burning ambition.

Tess popped her head round the door. 'Come on through, Liberty. We've made our decision.'

Zac smiled broadly at her as she walked back into the room. 'Well, usually we'd do all this through your agent, but there's no time. So, we'd like to offer you the role. We need to start filming next week. What do you say?'

For a moment she was too stunned to reply, and Zac took her silence for uncertainty. 'Obviously we would help you get settled into an apartment, arrange child care for your daughter, and make the move as trouble-free as possible for you.'

'I can't believe it!' Liberty finally exclaimed. 'Are you sure this isn't a joke? Things like this don't happen to me.'

'Believe it. You have just the quality we're looking for. You're perfect for the role.' He glanced at his colleague. 'Even Tess agrees and she is really tough to please.'

Tess smiled. 'It's certainly true that I had my doubts. But I'm ready to concede that Zac is right. You're just who we're looking for.'

'We should celebrate,' he went on. 'We'll order champagne and have dinner here. We all need to get to know each other better as we're going to be working together. Would that be okay with you, Liberty?'

'Sure,' she replied, as if room service in Claridges was an everyday occurrence, while inside she was brimming over with excitement.

Chapter 14

Nina was waiting up for her when she arrived home. Liberty had called her mum from Victoria station to let her know the brilliant news. As soon as Liberty walked into the living room, Nina got up and folded her into a hug. 'I'm so proud of you, Libs.'

Now she was back with her mum she felt like bursting into tears. It was overwhelming, and reality was starting to sink in. This would mean being away from Cory, from her mum, from her friends. Was she really strong enough to cope with all of that? Then she thought of the opportunity it would offer her and her daughter to carve out an exciting new life. There was no way she could turn that down.

'D'you think I should take it, Mum?' she asked, sitting by the open fire, which was dying down now.

'Definitely. No question. It's what you've always wanted to do. And I can come out for a couple of weeks to help you get settled.'

'That would be so good. But what about Cory?'

'What about him? Surely there's nothing to stop him moving back to the States and going to art school there. It's a win-win situation, isn't it? I'm

110

surprised you didn't stop off at the bar and tell him.'

'I phoned but they said he hadn't come in because he was ill. I'll go and see him in the morning.'

There was no answer when Liberty rang the doorbell the following day. It was after ten and she'd expected Cory to be there. She was just about to give up when the door was opened by a bleary-eyed Zara who was dressed only in a long white t-shirt and looked as if she'd just crawled out of bed.

It was the first time Liberty had seen her since the party and she forced herself to sound friendly. 'Hi, is Cory in?'

'Yeah, he's still in bed, I think.' Zara clutched her head. 'Ouch! I've got a major hangover. We had quite a session yesterday.'

'Oh? I thought he was ill?'

'No, he just couldn't face going into the bar. We both got a bit, well, rat-arsed. We had some friends over. I'm never going to be able to drink tequila again. It *really* doesn't go with champagne.' The hangover had made Zara's posh drawl even more pronounced.

Liberty was not impressed to hear about their drinking exploits. Whatever happened to Cory saving every penny for college? He'd only been working at the bar six weeks. She'd worked at the restaurant for the last three years and had never thrown a sickie.

She glanced into the living room as she walked along the hallway. It was a complete tip – talk about the morning after the night before. Empty bottles of champagne littered the mirrored coffee table, the ashtray was brimming with cigarette ends and the air stale with smoke. CDs were strewn all over the floor. It seemed as if they had got the late-night munchies too

111

as empty pizza boxes were piled up on the expensive Turkish rug. Nice.

Liberty ran up the stairs, taking them two at a time. Cory lay sprawled in bed, flat on his back. She sat on the edge of it and looked at him. Typically, he still looked good. There was an empty bottle of tequila on his bedside table. His clothes seemed to have been dropped where he had taken them off, including the t-shirt she had saved up to buy him. He stirred, rubbed his face then opened his eyes.

'Hi.' He struggled to sit, then gave up. 'Man, my head's killing me. I don't suppose you've got any painkillers, have you?'

She shook her head.

'Is there any chance you could go downstairs and get me some? I'm dying.' Cory groaned theatrically.

'Well, you certainly look like shit,' Liberty shot back. She had wanted to share her good news and his hangover had ruined the moment.

'Oh, baby, don't be mean. I feel so bad.'

'Are you going to go to work today?'

He shook his head and then winced. 'I don't think I'll be able to. I was supposed to be starting at midday, but there's no way I'll be up to it.'

She sighed. 'I'll get you some painkillers and a glass of water, and then maybe you'll be okay.' At this rate he'd get fired. Then again, would it matter now if he was coming to the States with her? She'd get his tablets and then surprise him with her good news.

Zara was downstairs in the kitchen, buttering a slice of toast and covering the sleek granite worktop with crumbs.

Now Liberty knew about her own acting role, she didn't give a flying fuck about seeing the other girl. She smiled to herself as she thought about the look on

Zara's face when she found out about it. That should wipe away her self-satisfied expression . . .

'I never usually eat bread,' Zara drawled. 'It's only when I'm hungover I have to carb load. I'll regret it, but it's essential. Do you want me to make some for Cory?'

'It's okay. I'm just taking him up a glass of water, and do you have any Ibuprofen?'

'Cupboard at the end.' Zara paused then continued, 'So has Cory told you about his idea of going to work in Thailand?'

What the fuck was she talking about? Not wanting to let on to Zara that she'd had no idea, Liberty muttered 'Yeah', which probably fooled no one.

'I think it's a brill idea. The cost of living is so much cheaper out there, so he can save and still have a great time. He's wasted in that bar. And maybe out in Thailand he'll feel like painting again. I keep nagging him to pick up a paintbrush, but he won't. I think he's depressed.' Zara looked at Liberty accusingly. '*Really* depressed.'

She didn't say 'And it's all your fault', but to Liberty her meaning was crystal clear. 'He'll be fine,' she replied, and grabbed the tablets. She ran back upstairs, spilling half the water in her rush.

By now Cory was sitting up properly. He smiled when she walked in. 'I've cleaned my teeth, so why don't you come into bed?'

She put the glass down on the bedside table and handed him the packet of pills, sitting down next to him.

'What's this about Thailand?'

'What? Oh, yeah, I was talking about an idea I had last night, about the three of us – you, me and Brooke – going off to Thailand for six months. There are

113

some beautiful places out there and I could easily get a bar job, or even work as an artist, painting portraits for tourists. We could rent a really cheap beach villa and go to sleep to the sound of the ocean. It would be awesome. What do you reckon?'

'Well, actually, I've got some news of my own. Some amazing news.' She couldn't stop the smile from breaking across her face.

'Oh, yeah? Go on, tell me.'

She quickly filled him in on what had happened, but instead of seeming happy for her, Cory seemed mightily pissed off.

She ended up by saying, 'And there's no reason why you can't come to LA with me. You could enrol in art school there. We could live together. I'm going to be earning really good money, I could help out with your fees.'

'No way am I going back to the States! I'm going to art school here, like I said I would.'

Liberty was shocked by his flat out refusal. 'What the fuck are you talking about?'

'If I go back, it will be like my mom has won. And that she knew all along that I wouldn't be able to make it on my own. And, no, I won't take money from you.'

'But I've *got* to take the role. It means I can give Brooke the life I want to give her. I won't have to be a waitress any more.' Liberty was struggling to imagine how they could manage a long-distance relationship.

Cory gave a bitter little smile. 'So I give up my dream for you, but you won't even consider giving up yours for me?'

'But you're just being stubborn! What does it matter what your mom thinks?' Again she felt that lack of understanding from him about what it was like to be a parent. He was behaving too much like a child.

'It matters. But look, if you got this role, you'll get other ones. Why don't we go to Thailand like I said. And then when we come back you can get another part.'

As if they grew on trees. He didn't get it. There was no way she could turn down this role.

'Oh, Cory, how can I? This is the break I've been waiting for, I can't just turn it down.'

He drew her to him. 'I know it's hard, but I can take care of you and Brooke, I know I can. And you're so talented, there's no way you won't get another role.' He kissed her. 'We're so good together. We can make this work.'

His blue eyes were fixed on her. She felt the familiar pull of attraction towards him, her body longed for his. And even though she knew she couldn't turn down Zac's offer, she found herself kissing Cory back and making love with him. It was tender and intense, as if they both wanted to put their argument behind them.

'Love you,' she said as she got ready to leave.

'Love you too,' he replied. 'And, Libs, we belong together. Nothing can keep us apart.'

Chapter 15

Walking back home, Liberty turned over her conversation with Cory in her mind. She loved him so much, and making love with him just now had been wonderful, but how could they ever make it work when they seemed to have such different dreams? She wanted to go back to the way they had been when they first started seeing each other at the beginning of the summer, and anything had seemed possible. Cory's stubborn refusal to go to the States had stunned her. It was so unreasonable, and his plan to go to Thailand was unrealistic. She just couldn't see any way they could stay together now.

Zac called as she was going to bed, and asked if she would consider flying out the following night.

'We've found you an ideal apartment in Santa Monica, and a nanny. I really want you to be settled and over the jet lag before filming starts. What do you think?'

For a moment she considered saying that she needed more time, but really what would that achieve?

'Perfect,' she replied. But even as she said it, she

116

knew it wasn't. Nothing could ever be perfect again if it meant that Cory wasn't in her life. She thought about calling him, but was worried that she wouldn't be able to say what she needed to say without crying. So she sat down and wrote him a letter, pouring out her feelings, begging him to come to LA so they could be together.

I know we can make it work so long as we're together. Please come to LA. I have to take this role, for the sake of Brooke and because I know that this is my big chance. I love you so much, Cory, more than I've ever loved anyone before. I can't be without you. You're everything to me. You always will be. Meeting you has been the most wonderful, incredible thing ever to happen to me.

Love you a million times,
L x

Liberty hesitated as she stood outside Zara's house the following morning. She could ring the bell and see Cory. Maybe he would be persuaded . . . No, it had to be the letter. She slipped it through the letterbox, then turned and ran down the steps. She paused when she reached the pavement, and looked back. She thought she saw a figure move behind the opaque glass panels of the front door, but couldn't be certain it wasn't a trick of the light.

'Phone me as soon as you get there,' Nina said, hugging Liberty tightly.

'You know I will.'

'And don't look so anxious. I'll be out in a week to help you. Everything's going to be fine.'

Liberty nodded, not trusting herself to speak. She had just checked in her luggage and she and Brooke were about to go through security. After that they would be on their own. She took one last look around her. In spite of everything, she had thought Cory might come. She'd told him the time of her flight. But it was clear that he wasn't going to. She held on to Brooke's hand and hugged Nina close one last time. Then, with her chin held high and her shoulders back, Liberty walked through to Departures.

Part 2

Chapter 16

August 2013

'Jesus Christ, couldn't you at least pretend that you're enjoying yourself?' Zac demanded. He and Liberty were at a TV industry party honouring his achievements as a director. To date he had directed series that had won over ten Emmys and five Golden Globes. He was very good at his job, Liberty gave him that. It was at being a husband he fell short. Or rather, *her* husband. Maybe some other woman would feel differently.

'I mean, you're good enough at faking it, aren't you? You do it enough in the bedroom,' Zac continued. He had grabbed hold of her arm and his grip was painfully tight.

She forced herself to stay calm and kept her voice even. 'I am enjoying myself. I'm very proud of your achievements.'

Fortunately at that moment Tess joined them and claimed Zac's attention, and Liberty was able to slip away on the pretext of getting another drink. The party was being held in some swish boutique hotel, just off Sunset Boulevard. The only colour in the ultra-minimalist white bar came from the huge canvases on the walls. She wandered over to one, a painting of a headless torso next to a bunch of bananas. What the fuck did that mean? She suppressed a smile as she thought of Em, whose favourite expression was 'top banana'. God, she missed her best friend so much. Sure, she had friends in LA, but no one she was as close to as she was to Em. She had seen her as much as she could over the years, but it hadn't been easy as Em and Zac didn't really get on. He thought she was an annoying hippy, and she thought he was an uptight control freak. Not exactly the basis for a beautiful friendship.

'What do you think? Would you like that in your living room?' Damon, a young English actor, had joined her. He played one of the detectives in Zac's latest series; Liberty played an attorney. She knew that Damon had a bit of a crush on her and was flattered as he was only twenty-three and, as Em would say, 'a hottie'.

'Nope. Not my taste at all. How about you?'

'To be honest, I prefer old film posters. You know, Hitchcock, that kind of thing. But I like that one.' He gestured at the painting of a woman sitting on the edge of a double bed in what looked like a hotel room. She had long red hair and was dressed in a green silk dress. Liberty instantly recognised the style – the vibrant colours, the way the picture seemed to suggest a story. It had to be by Cory. Sure enough, when she moved closer she saw his trademark signature in one corner. Oh, God, even after all this time, just the thought of him made her heart race and filled her with longing.

She knew that Cory had become a very successful artist who was in great demand for his portraits. A number of high-profile celebrities had sat for him. He had become the artist she'd always hoped he would be.

She barely had time to gather her thoughts before Zac joined them. He hated her talking to other men, always got jealous, even though there was never anything for him to be jealous about.

Sure enough his opening line was, 'So what are you guys so busy talking about?' And typically, without waiting for an answer, he followed it up with more questions. 'Swapping tales about life in the UK? Bet you're glad you're over here, Damon. Jesus, the weather in that place is shit. Who would ever want to live anywhere else but LA?'

He moved closer to Liberty, and put his arm round her waist possessively. My wife. Hands off. Damon actually took a step back. He was in awe of Zac, as were many of the actors.

'We were just talking about the pictures,' Liberty replied. She had never told Zac about Cory. Sure, he had known that she'd had a boyfriend in the UK, and that their relationship ended when she came to LA, but she had never told him Cory's name. She didn't want to hear him say it, didn't want him bombarding her with questions about what Cory was like. It was her past, not his to paw over and pick apart as he would one of his plotlines.

'I like that one,' Zac commented, pointing at the torso with the bunch of bananas. 'The other one is sentimental shit.'

And that, thought Liberty, said it all. She discreetly looked at her watch. At least another two hours to go, including the presentation ceremony. With any luck she could make sure that Zac was plied with enough celebratory alcohol for him not to want sex when they got home. She was fast running out of excuses.

Chapter 17

Brooke

Brooke sashayed along 3rd Street Promenade in Santa Monica enjoying the feeling of the warm sun on her skin and the admiring glances she attracted in her barely-there white shorts and off-the-shoulder t-shirt. She was a shopping ninja, a girl on Mission Find-the-perfect-dress-for-her-boyfriend's-eighteenth-birthday. She'd been into five designer stores already and had found nothing suitable, though she had managed to spend six hundred dollars on some other clothes that she needed. Well, maybe needed wasn't exactly the word, but wanted, especially when she had tried them on and saw how good they looked on her.

She tried not to think about the blazing row she'd had with her mom recently, over her credit-card bill. Her mom had insisted that she had to cut down her spending, that she had to learn the value of money, and blah, blah, blah, blah. Brooke had tuned out – she was good at doing that – and muttered something about promising to do better. She hadn't meant it. Like, why would she? Her mom and stepdad were loaded.

Money had never been an issue before. She didn't know why her mom was criticising her now. After all, it wasn't as if she set a good example – Liberty was always buying clothes and had an entire walk-in closet full of unworn garments. She probably had PMT or something. *Whatever*. Brooke was not going to let that row stop her from getting the dress that was going to blow her boyfriend away when he saw her in it.

She went to push open the door to her favourite designer boutique, only to have it opened for her by an attentive assistant, who immediately gave her the VIP treatment, showed her to a comfortable sofa, summoned some other minion to bring her iced tea and a fresh fruit platter and then rushed around gathering a selection of suitable dresses from the rails.

The garments were then held up for Brooke's inspection. 'No, that's not going to work . . . it's not me,' she said despairingly, after each dress was showed to her. 'I have to have one with the wow factor!' God! Why couldn't these people get it into their heads, mediocre was not going to cut it?

Finally, just as she was about to flounce out in despair, one caught her attention – a divine corset-style dress in black lace. 'OMG!' she declared, clapping her hands together. 'That's totally it!'

Once she had wriggled into the tightly fitted dress, she knew that her first reaction had been spot on. The dress clung to every curve and made her look much older than her seventeen years. It was artfully designed with nude panels underneath the lace, so it appeared that she was naked. She expected her mom would freak, but knowing Liberty she would be out at some event or other and wouldn't even see her daughter leave for the party.

Naturally she *had* to get some new heels to go with

the dress. The assistant immediately said that she had the perfect pair and proceeded to show Brooke a pair of Swarovski crystal-encrusted Louboutins. They were over three thousand dollars and she really shouldn't. Really, *really* shouldn't. But as soon as she'd slipped them on and considered her reflection in the mirror, and strutted around the shop in the five-inch beauties, she knew she had to have them. And, hey, they were designer; they were an investment piece. And her mom had at least twenty pairs. Surely she wouldn't begrudge her daughter one measly pair? Okay, actually she already had five pairs of Louboutins . . . but compared to some of her friends, that was *nothing*. Her best friend Kelly had fifteen pairs, and *her* mom didn't have a problem with that.

The rush of pleasure Brooke derived from her successful shop lasted until she pulled into the palm-tree-lined driveway of the house and wondered how she was going to smuggle the tell-tale designer bags upstairs without her mom seeing them. She decided to leave them in the car, and pretend that she'd been to the gym. But once she let herself into the ultra-modern house with its stunning views of the Pacific Ocean she was met by Rosa, their Mexican housekeeper, who told her that her parents were out at a party and wouldn't be back until late. On the one hand Brooke was relieved that she could smuggle her purchases in without being busted, but on the other, apart from the row, she hadn't seen her mum and stepdad all week. Every single night she had eaten supper on her own. She was supposed to be finishing a backlog of overdue papers, and so hadn't been allowed to go out in the evenings or have her boyfriend Christian over, or her best friend Kelly. And there was no getting around that order from her parents because even if they weren't there, there were the CCTV cameras recording who went in and who went out of the building. Her mom was quite capable of playing back the film as Brooke knew to her cost. Only last week she had slipped out to meet Kelly . . . and then had some explaining to do. Again.

'I've made you a crayfish salad, Brooke, and there's some of that strawberry frozen yoghurt that you like,' Rosa told her. Lovely Rosa, who had been with the family since Brooke was four years old, often babysitting for her when it had been the nanny's night off, or coming to watch her compete in school sporting events and school shows when her mom and stepdad were tied up with filming. She was the one who had picked up Brooke from school if ever she was unwell and sat with her until her mom came home. Brooke saw Rosa as her unofficial gran. She adored her.

'Will you stay and eat with me?' Brooke asked. Rosa would sometimes keep her company, and Brooke was pretty sure that she was doing it out of the goodness of her heart and not to get paid overtime.

Rosa frowned. 'I'm sorry, Brooke, I'm having dinner with my son's family tonight. It's my grandson's first birthday. You know I'd stay otherwise.'

Shit! Brooke felt terrible! She must have made Rosa late for the dinner. She had probably been waiting for Brooke to get home before she left.

'Sure, give him a birthday kiss from me. I'll make sure I get him a present tomorrow. And shall I get you a taxi?'

'No, no, I'll take the bus. It's no problem. You have a good evening, Brooke. Do your studies and your mom will be very proud of you, for sure. She left a note for you in the kitchen.'

Brooke managed a smile for Rosa, but she doubted her mom would ever be proud of her.

She waved Rosa goodbye, assuring her that she would be fine, and headed out to the garden to see Ozzy, her beloved, cute as a button Border Terrier. He went wild as soon as he saw Brooke, tail frantically wagging as he jumped up and thrust his nose into her hand. 'Did you miss me, boy?'

He looked at her with his expressive brown eyes as if to say, Yes! She let him into the kitchen – one of the few rooms he was allowed in. The pale grey units and white marble surfaces made the place seem even emptier. Her stepdad Zac was a complete neat freak and hated any clutter. Everything had to be put away the moment it was used, which had led to countless arguments between them. Her mom had stuck a pink Post-it note on the stainless-steel fridge, the one splash of colour in the otherwise neutral-toned room. Brooke peeled it off.

Hi, honey, hope you can get some work done tonight. Sorry about our fight the other day. Let's have a girls' night in soon. You choose the movie and the take away. Love you xxx

In spite of still being annoyed with her mom, Brooke smiled. It had been ages since they'd had one of their girls' nights in, where they would put on their PJs and order in pizza, Thai or Chinese, followed by their favourite salted caramel ice cream, and watch a movie in the cinema room. She missed having those cosy times. But Liberty was often away filming, and if she wasn't working she was out at various movie premieres and parties with Zac.

Brooke took the salad out of the fridge and perched on one of the stools at the island in the middle of the huge space – somehow it seemed a better option to eat there than at the glass-topped dining table that could seat twenty and always made her feel even more alone when she sat there.

Her phone rang and the smiling face of her best friend Kelly popped up on the screen. They had been close since second grade and hung out together practically every weekend. Brooke had also gone on many vacations with her friend's family. Kelly was African American, absolutely stunning to look at and also the sweetest, funniest person Brooke knew.

'Hey, girl, how you doing?' Kelly asked.

'I'm back at home now, on my own, having supper, on my own.' Brooke could hear voices and laughter in the background – it was bound to be Kelly's three younger sisters. She had always envied Kelly her large family, where there was always something going on. Brooke hated being an only child but apparently her stepdad hadn't wanted any children of his own, so it was just the three of them.

'Tragic! Are you sure you can't come over and we could study together? I could get my mom to text yours.'

It was tempting but Brooke knew that she had been pushing her luck lately and it was unlikely her mom would agree.

'I don't think she'll let me. It's cool, I do have a paper to write and I've already extended the deadline once.' It wasn't cool, though. She wished more than anything she could go round to her friend's, where Kelly's mom would make a big fuss of them, bring them up iced coffees and cookies, where everyone got on well and there were none of the strained silences that filled her house, whenever her stepdad and mom were in.

'So did you manage to find a dress?' Like the best friend that she was, Kelly knew how important this was to Brooke.

But not even describing her purchases to Kelly could really cheer her up, though she ended the call by promising to send her friend a picture of the dress and shoes.

Brooke checked through her messages. There was nothing from Christian, her boyfriend, but then he only ever sent a text in reply to ones she sent him. She didn't know whether this was his strategy to keep her on tenterhooks, or whether that was just the way he was. They'd only been seeing each other for three weeks.

Christian was easily the best-looking guy in her year. At six foot two, with sun-bleached blond hair that flopped adorably over his forehead, impressive biceps, and the cutest smile, he was the guy everyone wanted to go out with. On top of that he was a brilliant baseball player and the lead singer in a band – boys didn't come any more desirable than that. As soon as he'd joined the school after moving to Santa Monica two months ago, Brooke knew she had to have him. She had worked her hardest to attract his attention, planned out her strategy in minute detail, bought even more clothes to impress him, wearing a different outfit every single day, hung out at all the places he did, watched him play baseball even though she found all sport a big yawn. And of course went along to all his gigs and pushed her way to the front of the crowd so she got the best view of him on stage, even though he was in a thrash metal band and she hated that kind of music. She had always been a Motown, R&B and pop girl herself.

She'd focused on how good he looked clutching the microphone and showing off those muscles in a ripped black vest, rather than what he sounded like (strained yowling) and what he was singing about (death and the devil – kind of dreary). His group was called Hell Dogs, so she supposed the clue was in the title. If she could have got away with it she would have been listening to Lady Gaga on her iPod, but she couldn't risk being caught out. The people next to her, who were all jumping up and down wildly, punching the air, would probably have lynched her. Not even the sight of Christian's smooth, well-defined biceps was worth that fate.

Finally she got her chance at Kelly's birthday party where Brooke had homed in on him on the dance floor (like a heat-seeking missile, Kelly had told her afterwards), and, well, several Mojitos later, they were kissing by the pool. Christian had made it very clear that he wanted to go a helluva lot further than kissing . . . but Brooke wasn't going to give it up so easily. She reckoned after a month, anything sooner and there was too much of a chance she'd feel slutty, and possibly get dumped. And she had no intention of being dumped. She planned to sleep with him at his eighteenth birthday party – she figured that would be quite some present.

She selected his number, but it went straight to voicemail. She did her best to sound upbeat as she left a message, and appear happy and relaxed, not needy and insecure, though she couldn't help wondering where he was exactly at seven p.m. on a Thursday night, and why he didn't pick up his phone when he saw who it was calling him. She always took his calls, had her phone with her at all times, on the chance he might ring. She even took it into the bathroom with her.

She scraped her half-eaten salad into the bin, grabbed the bags out of the car, and carried Ozzy upstairs to her room. He wasn't supposed to go upstairs at all but Brooke always flouted that rule, causing even more arguments between her and her stepdad. Here at least, in her bedroom, she was able to express her personality and there was no sign of Zac's minimalist taste. An entire wall was devoted to photographs of Brooke and her friends over the years, and to her beloved animals, Ozzy and Fifi the cat, who had lived to the grand old age of fifteen; there was also a huge pop art canvas of a couple kissing, an enormous plasma-screen TV on one of the other walls, a four-poster bed painted silver with pale pink drapes. She'd had the bed since she was seven years old after begging Liberty to buy it for her. It had always made her feel like a princess when she was little. There was also a pink velvet sofa in the shape of a pair of lips, but best of all was the breathtaking view of the Pacific Ocean from her window.

Brooke sat down at her desk, switched on her laptop, and attempted to continue her psychology paper. She had wanted to drop out of school and go straight to drama college but Liberty wouldn't hear of it, had insisted that she had to have some qualifications behind her.

'But I want to be an actor, like you,' Brooke had pleaded with her. 'That's all I've ever wanted to do, you know that. Why do I need to take these stupid subjects? You dropped out of school and you did okay – more than okay.'

Usually if Brooke was persistent enough she got her own way with her mom. Not over this.

'Because in acting you never know what might happen. It's a brutal profession. You might not make it.'

'Big me up, why don't you, Mom?' she'd shot back sarcastically, hurt at her mother's apparent lack of confidence in her talent. 'And Zac is my stepdad, surely he'd give me a role?'

Liberty's face had softened when she saw how upset

Brooke was. 'Honey, you're hugely talented, far more talented than I ever was at your age, but sometimes talent isn't enough. And Zac agrees with me, you need to go to school. You'll be a better actress for it. Trust me on this.'

She looked away from the essay and out to sea, then checked her phone. Still nothing from Christian. This sucked. She picked up a remote control and selected Beyoncé on her music system. She could only work accompanied by music. Two painful hours later she finished the essay and flopped down on her bed. Ozzy crept out from under the desk where he had been lying curled up at her feet and hurled himself on to the bed next to her, turned round three times and then sat down with a contented sigh. She scratched his chin. Sometimes she envied him his simple life, even though she knew how completely mad it sounded to be envying a dog. No one ever gave him a hard time, or told him what to do.

After all that hard work, she felt like rewarding herself with a drink and was about to go downstairs and help herself to a measure of Zac's very fine vodka, for which she had recently developed a taste, when she heard the sound of the front door opening. Liberty and Zac were back. And they were mid-argument. Brooke's heart sank. She hated hearing them quarrel.

'Couldn't you at least have acted like you were enjoying yourself?' Zac shouted. 'Everyone commented on how miserable you looked. It was embarrassing.'

'Oh, I'm so sorry that I wasn't being the perfect Hollywood trophy wife tonight. Sorry for having any emotions of my own. Sorry for thinking that I might actually be allowed to think my own thoughts, instead of always being an extension of you!' Liberty responded. She had lived out in LA for fourteen years, but whenever she was angry her LA drawl slipped and her English accent took over.

Brooke sat up and hugged her knees, wishing she could block out the sound. It was as familiar to her now as the sound of the ocean she could hear from her bedroom, part of her day, part of her life, and not something she wanted to hear any more. There was a gentle knock at the door and her mom walked in.

'Hi, Brooke, are you okay?' Liberty looked as beautiful as ever. Her silky dark brown hair cascaded down her back; the floor-length black couture strapless dress showcased her enviable figure. An emerald choker caught the light and sparkled at her throat, accentuating her vivid green eyes, the only feature Brooke had inherited from her. Her make up was still perfect after the party.

'I'm fine. Stayed in, like you wanted, and didn't see anyone, like you wanted. Finished the essay like you wanted,' she muttered sulkily.

Liberty chose to ignore the tone – she was good at doing that. 'Brilliant. Well done, sweetheart, I knew you could do it if you put your mind to it.' She came over and lightly kissed Brooke on the top of her head, enveloping her in an exotic perfume. She managed a smile for her daughter, but Brooke could see the sadness in her eyes. She seemed strained and on edge, as if at any minute she might snap. Brooke suddenly felt sorry for her.

'So what were you and Zac arguing about this time?'

'Oh, it was nothing. I just didn't want to be at the party. I'd rather have been here with you, but he made a big deal of it, and then, as you heard, was pissed off with me for not putting on the big Hollywood fake smile.' Liberty's shoulders seemed to sag, as if she was worn out by the quarrel.

'So how about I make you a hot chocolate?' she continued. She had noticed Ozzy curled up next to Brooke, and raised her eyebrows but didn't say anything.

Brooke guessed she would have to forget the vodka now. 'Sure, thanks, I'll come downstairs.'

'I'll bring it up to you. Zac's in a pretty dark mood. He's best left alone until he's calmed down.'

'Okay.' It wasn't, though. Zac's dark moods could last for days. Brooke waited until her mom had left the room and then switched her music back on, anxious not to overhear any more of her parents' arguing. It was right at this moment that she could really do with hearing Christian's voice, to have him say something nice to her, to make her feel good. She dialled his number again. Voicemail. Again. She noticed the designer shopping bags by the side of her desk and quickly shoved them in her walk-in closet. She hadn't even sent the pictures to Kelly. Somehow she didn't feel like it. The excitement she had felt when she'd bought the clothes had fizzled out now.

Chapter 18

Brooke's school was a five-mile drive away. It used to be one of Rosa's jobs to give her a lift to and from it, but on her seventeenth birthday Zac bought Brooke a cherry red Mercedes convertible and from then on she drove herself and Kelly. She never ceased to get a thrill when she got behind the wheel and started the engine and hit the freeway, knowing how many people would be admiring and envying the blonde girl in the driver's seat. In fact for all the hours she had devoted to attracting Christian, and all her many tactics, the first thing he had said to her when they finally got together was, 'You're the girl with the bad ass car.' She could just have driven past his house a couple of times to get his attention . . . her ears could have been spared the sound of Hell Dogs.

She pulled in at the entrance to the school, a sprawling modern building set in attractive landscaped grounds, and parked in the student car park. She noticed that Christian's distinctive black-and-gold jeep was already there. It was a little too pimped up for her taste – not that she would ever tell him that. Good, so he was in school already and she could find out where he had been the night before, and what had been so important that he hadn't called her back.

Kelly saw her frown and guessed the reason why. 'He was probably playing baseball, don't stress about it.' She pulled out her lip-gloss and swiped some more on her already perfectly glossed lips.

'I guess.' But it hurt that he hadn't called. It would have taken Brooke's mind off her parents arguing. It would have made her feel that he cared about her, because sometimes she had her doubts.

As usual before class, the two girls went to the cafeteria to grab a skinny latte. They had just paid for their drinks and were making their way over to a table when Kelly nudged Brooke. 'There's Christian over there.'

Brooke followed the direction of her gaze and saw her boyfriend. The trouble was, he was not alone. Her boyfriend was talking to Taylor. Oh, please, anyone but her. She was blonde, rich, and the biggest bitch on campus. From the word go the two girls had loathed each other, and their relationship had taken a turn for the even worse when Brooke landed the leading role of Sandy in the school production of *Grease*, and Taylor, who was jealous as hell, had done her best to turn everyone against her.

She went around spreading rumours that Brooke had only got the role because of who her parents were, and because her stepdad made such generous donations to the school, and had even started a Facebook campaign against her. It had all got very nasty and Taylor came close to being suspended. Since then she'd restricted herself to looking daggers at Brooke, and Brooke did her very best to ignore her.

'Shit! What's *she* doing with him?' Brooke hissed at Kelly.

'Just go over and act natural,' her friend told her.

It was easier said than done as Brooke was dying to know what Taylor and Christian were talking about. Taylor was doing her best flirtatious routine: gazing into his eyes, leaning forward so she could show off her cleavage, twirling a lock of her blonde hair round one finger . . . Brooke knew exactly what she was up to, because those were just the kind of techniques she herself had used on Christian, very effectively. And she knew how susceptible he was to pretty girls . . .

'Hey,' she said, smiling warmly at him as she approached and completely blanking Taylor.

'Hey yourself,' Christian answered. He was sprawled back in his seat and made no effort to get up and kiss Brooke. Okay, she was used to this, he didn't do displays of affection when they were at school. But a little kiss on the cheek wouldn't have hurt. She wasn't just any girl; she was his girlfriend, for Christ's sake!

'Hi, Brooke,' Taylor said. 'How are you? Christian told me that you've had to study *all* week. Bummer.'

When did he tell her? Just now or had they met up last night? Brooke was itching to ask but didn't want to be thrown on the back foot in front of Taylor.

'Yeah, well, I had some papers to finish, but I've done them now.'

'That's lucky, 'cos I'm guessing you wouldn't have wanted to miss Christian's party. It sounds awesome.'

Shit! He had asked her.

'Yeah, I was just telling Taylor that we're going to have a marquee and my band's going to play. It's going to be *fucking* awesome!'

'Yeah, rock on Hell Dogs!' Taylor exclaimed excitedly. 'And Christian was telling me about one of his new songs – "Rip Out my Heart". It sounded so totally in the zone.'

Creep, Brooke thought, guessing that Taylor most

likely loathed thrash metal every bit as much as she herself did . . .

'So what are you wearing, Brooke?' Taylor asked, looking as if butter wouldn't melt in her mouth and that she and Brooke always had these girly chats together, which they'd had precisely never.

'It's an incredible outfit,' Kelly broke in. 'She looks amazing in it – like a runway model. But you want it to be a surprise for Christian, don't you, Brooke?'

'That's right.' She managed to flash him an adoring smile. And finally he put his arm round her and said, 'You always look incredible, Brooke.' She felt like high-fiving Kelly when she saw the look of jealousy flare up in Taylor's eyes. Clearly she'd decided she wasn't going to hang around and watch any more PDAs between Brooke and Christian. She abruptly stood up and muttered something about seeing one of her tutors, stalking off and wiggling her tiny denim-clad butt for all it was worth. *Tragic,* thought Brooke.

'Sorry I didn't call you back last night, babe. I was at baseball practice, and then we went to Bryan's and crashed. His parents are away and it turned into a bit of a late one,' Christian said, thankfully not staring at Taylor's ass.

Brooke wanted to say, Well, what stopped you after practice? But didn't want to come across as needy, so instead she shrugged and said, 'No problem. I was really busy.'

Christian smiled. 'You are my kind of girlfriend, Brooke. I can't stand girls being on my case. It does my head in when they want to know where I am all the time. When I've got something to say, I'll call you, but I don't have to check in every five minutes, like I'm on some kind of parole. I swear my ex would have electronically tagged me if she could.'

139

So it had paid off . . . but Brooke realised she had probably painted herself into a corner because now Christian would think she didn't have a problem with him not calling her back, and she *really* did have a problem with that. She glanced at Kelly, who smiled sympathetically.

'So come on, tell me about the party,' Brooke asked. And while he chatted away about the guest list and the DJ he'd chosen, and how his mom and dad were buying him a new jeep, Brooke allowed herself to relax slightly. She shouldn't get so tense. Christian was into her; he just had his own unique way of showing it.

'So a group of us are going over to Bryan's house after class, d'you want to come?'

Her heart sank. She would far rather have gone to the beach with him so they could spend some time on their own. But she was trying to be the perfect girlfriend, and so the perfect girlfriend replied, 'Yes. Love to.'

The rest of her day in school was actually pretty good. Mr Wilson, her psychology tutor, looked as if he was going to have a heart attack when she handed him her paper as she was notorious for getting work in late. Drama was as compelling as ever – they were working on *Romeo and Juliet* and she had to deliver Juliet's famous balcony speech. Her performance received much praise from Miss Rose, the drama teacher. She held Brooke back after class to say she had brought great sensitivity and depth to the part. Hearing that, Brooke broke into a smile like it was her birthday.

All in all she was in a brilliant mood as she drove up to Beverly Hills with the roof of her car down. Kelly Clarkson's 'Stronger' was blasting out of the stereo but she switched it off as soon as she reached the gates leading up to Bryan's dad's mansion, mindful that Christian always poked fun at her for liking such mainstream pop.

Bryan's dad was a movie producer and a multi-millionaire. He had recently remarried for the fourth time, to a model turned actress who Bryan didn't get on with at all. But his parents were supposed to be away, and when they were, that was when Bryan partied. Hard, by the look of his living room – he had his own wing in the house and seemed to have banned the cleaners from going in to tidy up. Brooke picked her way through empty cans of Bud and bottles of Bacardi, past take-out boxes of fried chicken and pizza, and took a seat on the leather sofa. It felt sticky against her bare legs and she didn't like to think about what might have been spilled on it.

She'd hoped Christian might sit next to her, but he sat on the floor by the large glass coffee table and immediately started laying out his gear to make a spliff. Okay, apart from his terrible taste in music, this was the one thing she didn't really like about Christian. He was a bit of a dope head. Brooke had tried dope in the past but didn't like it; it just gave her a pounding headache and the munchies. And her mom was really hardline when it came to drugs. A friend's brother had died of a drug overdose when Liberty was sixteen and it had had a profound effect on her. A year ago she had caught Brooke and Kelly smoking a joint, and had hit the roof.

Brooke's good mood began to fade. She felt insecure and self-conscious. She didn't know Bryan very well or his friends – there were two other guys here along with two girls she vaguely knew from school. They were all eyeing up the spliffs appreciatively and Brooke realised she might be in a minority when it came to disliking dope. Oh, well, she supposed one or two drags wouldn't matter. She didn't want to seem like an uptight killjoy, and hopefully her mom would be out by the time Brooke got home and she'd be able to shower and wash her hair. Liberty had a very acute sense of smell and always knew when Zac had been smoking, a habit which she hated. As weed had a far stronger smell, she would instantly be able to detect it. Really her mom was wasted on TV, she should have been working for the DEA sniffing out illegal drugs at airports.

Christian lit the joint and inhaled deeply. 'Man, that's good stuff,' he exclaimed, passing it on to Bryan. Brooke fidgeted on the sofa, wondering how much longer they would have to stay here and whether she could suggest that she and Christian slipped away to the beach. Bryan passed the spliff to her and she took a drag. Instantly her throat burned from the smoke, causing her to cough and her eyes to water. the girl with dyed black hair raised her eyebrows as if to say, What a baby.

The conversation was all about a gig they had recently been to and Brooke hadn't. And thank God for that, it sounded *so* not her kind of thing – Death Head something or other had been playing.

'What was the last gig you went to, Brooke?' the second girl asked. She had dip-dyed hair, brown at the roots, pink at the ends, which looked atrocious. She must have done it herself. Brooke couldn't help touching her own hair, to reassure herself that it was still there in all its glossy, blonde glory.

'Um, my stepdad got tickets for Rihanna,' she replied, hating herself for sounding apologetic because at least Rihanna could sing and put on a brilliant show, and Brooke had loved it. She would take her any time over some skanky group who looked as if they needed scrubbing down with disinfectant, and who were borderline tone deaf.

Bad dip-dye actually sniggered. Not wanting a confrontation, Brooke pretended she hadn't heard and got out her phone to check her messages. There was one from Kelly. *How's it going? Am at home by the pool if u want to come over later. Mom says stay for dinner if u want. xx*

That sounded so tempting . . . Brooke was about to reply when the door to the living room was flung open and Bryan's dad Wyatt and stepmom Lydia marched in.

'What the hell is going on in here?' Wyatt roared. 'I warned you about smoking weed in the house . . . or anywhere else!' He was red in the face with rage and Brooke guessed this was not the first time they'd had this row.

Lydia folded her arms and glared at everyone. She was twenty-five at the most, with platinum-blonde hair and a pretty heart-shaped face that was ruined by an unbelievably sulky expression – though that was possibly caused by the fillers in her pumped-up lips.

'And this place is, like, filthy!' she exclaimed, kicking at one of the fast-food boxes, and looking disgusted. 'The housekeeper just told us you wouldn't let the cleaners in. What is wrong with you, Bryan? I would never have dreamed of letting my room get in such a state when I was your age.' She glanced at Wyatt to back her up. 'You are spoiled and selfish and rude, and your dad and I think it's high time you were taught a lesson if you want to carry on living in this house.'

Brooke was actually starting to feel quite sorry for Bryan, being publicly humiliated in this way. It must be tough having a stepmom like that.

143

But Bryan wasn't going to take the attack lying down. 'It's none of your fucking business what I do in my rooms! I'll keep them how I want! Just because you control my dad, doesn't mean that you can control me! I've still got my balls, you gold-digging bitch! We all know *exactly* why you married my dad. And one day the scales are going to fall from his eyes, and you'll be out on your ass, just like all the other hos he's been with.'

Okay, he had just overstepped the line big time. Brooke looked over at Christian, who smirked and shook his head, like it was all a big joke.

Lydia's violet eyes bugged out of her head in fury as she jabbed Wyatt's arm. 'Are you going to let him speak to me like that? He is totally out of control!'

Wyatt stepped forward, clenching his fists, and for a moment Brooke was concerned he might throw a punch at Bryan, then he seemed to gather himself. 'You ever speak to Lydia like that again, and *you* will be the one out on your ass. This is *my* house, *my* rules, and it's high time you realised that. And just to make sure that there is no repetition of your little dope parties, I am now going to phone up each of your friends' parents and let them know exactly what you've all been up to.'

'What the fuck!' Bryan screeched. 'You can't do that!'

'You've had enough warnings. You need to know I'm serious.'

Wyatt threw a black garbage bag in Bryan's direction as he and Lydia left. 'And clear up this shit, it's a disgrace.'

For a moment the group looked at each other in stunned disbelief, then they all started complaining at once, talking over each other. This was going to freak out their parents and cause major grief for them . . .

and why the fuck didn't Bryan know that his folks were coming back?

Only Brooke and Christian stayed silent; Brooke because she was terrified of what Liberty's reaction was going to be, and Christian because he was nonchalantly gathering together all his smoking paraphernalia as if it had always been his plan to leave now. He glanced over at Brooke. 'Shall we split to the beach then?'

'Sure,' she replied, though she wondered if it might be better to go home and face her mom's wrath and get it over and done with. But then again, she hadn't spent any time alone with Christian for ages. She would go to the beach. Maybe her mom would have calmed down by the time she got home. She could say that it was only one tiny puff, and that Bryan's parents were over-reacting. And her mom was pleased that she had caught up with her schoolwork. Yeah, it would be okay, Brooke told herself. It was no biggie.

It was after ten p.m. when she let herself quietly into the house. She had ignored all six calls her mom had made to her and not read any of the texts she had sent. For a moment, as she tiptoed across the hallway, she hoped that her parents were out again. But just as she was about to go upstairs, her mom called out her name.

'Brooke, I'm in the living room, will you please come and see me now?' Liberty sounded as if she meant business – her voice was quiet and controlled, which was always a hundred times scarier than if she was ranting and shouting at her daughter.

Brooke turned round and reluctantly made her way into the living room. Her mom was sitting on the sofa in near darkness. There was only one lamp on in the room, but there was enough light for Brooke to see that Liberty had been crying. She stood in front of her and folded her arms, waiting for the onslaught.

'What did I do that was so wrong you would behave like this? I have always done everything for you, Brooke, tried to give you the best possible life. And then you go and do the one thing you know is completely unacceptable to me.'

Liberty's tone was weary, resigned. The martyred one, which made Brooke feel horribly guilty.

'I only had one pathetic drag of a joint! I don't even like dope, I swear. I don't know why you now assume I'm some kind of drug addict. Bryan's parents were pissed with him and wanted to get us all into trouble, but it really wasn't a big deal. It's not like we were smoking crack or anything!' Brooke felt it was totally unfair of her mom to over-react like this.

'It's not just about today. We had that talk the other week about your spending, but when I went up to your bedroom tonight I discovered a stash of designer bags and worked out you spent over five thousand dollars. Five thousand dollars, Brooke! How do you explain that?' Now Liberty was sounding less in control.

Okay, so that spending was a little excessive, but it had been necessary. 'Well, I promise I won't get anything else for a while. But I needed a new outfit for Christian's party at the weekend.' Brooke tried to claw back some moral high ground. 'And anyway, you shouldn't have been poking around in my room. It's private. I wouldn't dream of going poking around in yours.'

Liberty stared at her. 'Have you taken on board at all how serious this is? Your over-the-top spending, your spoiled brat attitude, the drugs! It has got to stop, once and for all. You are grounded, young lady, for the next month. There is absolutely no way that you're going to

146

Christian's party. He's clearly a very bad influence on you.'

No! She couldn't have heard her mom correctly. She couldn't miss Christian's party! 'You can't do that! He'll dump me if I don't go!'

'Well, he sounds like a keeper,' Liberty said dryly. 'And I *am* doing this, Brooke. You've had enough chances to improve and you've blown them all.'

For a moment she stood there, rooted to the spot in disbelief. Of all the arguments she had ever had with her mom, this was the worst. Brooke could see that there was absolutely nothing she could say that would change her mind. She sprinted out of the room and upstairs, not wanting to spend another second in the same room as Liberty, who was hell-bent on ruining her life.

Chapter 19

Liberty

Liberty heard her daughter slam her bedroom door shut, and put her head in her hands. She hated falling out with Brooke. Up until two years ago they had always been so close. She'd thought she had the perfect relationship with her daughter and felt that she could talk to her about anything. She'd almost felt a little smug when friends had told her about how obnoxious their teenage offspring were being. Brooke would never be like that, she would think to herself. And now here she was with a daughter who wouldn't talk to her, who had taken drugs, who was most likely sleeping with her idiot of a boyfriend. On top of that she seemed to have become unbearably spoiled. Zac gave her a huge monthly allowance and a credit card and seemed to have no problem with Brooke going out and blowing it all on designer clothes, and yet she was only seventeen. What kind of a person would she become if she carried on like this?

Wearily Liberty got up and wandered through the vast open-plan living room with its views of the infinity pool and ocean beyond. Only last month Zac had been interviewed by some magazine or other and they had photographed him in the house, where the journalist had raved about how beautiful and stylish it was. Liberty hated it. To her this place wasn't a home; it was a show house, purely there to display her husband's wealth and success. Everything in it was so perfectly designed. Press a button and the shutters came down, press another to dim the lights, press another to turn on the music centre or TV, press another to summon Rosa. Pity there wasn't a button you could press to make you happy.

Liberty reached the kitchen, pulled open the fridge and took out a bottle of white wine – from Zac's personal vineyard, where else? – and poured herself a large glass. She felt loneliness descend on her like a fog. She went outside and curled up on the sofa by the pool, looking out over the glittering lights of LA strung along the coast like jewels. She knew that she was envied by so many people who thought she had the perfect life, with the perfect husband, the perfect job, the perfect house, more money than she could ever possibly want. But none of those things mattered to her.

She didn't want to be with Zac any more. She'd been putting on a brave face for the last five years, and it hadn't been a happy marriage for a long time before that. The only thing she wanted to do was to be a good mother to Brooke and she didn't know if that was even possible out here in LA, with the lifestyle her daughter had grown used to. As for love . . . well, Liberty had had her chance of that a long time ago and she didn't think you got that kind of love twice.

After she'd moved to LA she had thrown herself into her new life. As he had promised, Zac had made her into a star. Over the course of two years he had pursued her romantically, until finally she relented. Liberty had persuaded herself that she loved him, but looking back she never had. She had been seduced by the glamour of being with someone as powerful and charismatic as Zac Keller, a man who could open doors in her career and give her the security she craved. But it could never be enough. She'd often thought of Cory, yearned for him, dreamed of him, and then out of the blue five years ago he had come back into her life.

Liberty had been to an art exhibition organised by one of her friends and there he was, completely by chance. She hadn't seen him for nine years, but the time apart fell away as they came face to face.

'You still have the most mesmerising green eyes,' he had told her. And he was as handsome as ever, but a man now, with broad shoulders and a muscular body. Same blue eyes, though, that seemed to see to the heart of her.

All night they had talked and talked, covering everything that had happened to them.

'Why did you leave and not say anything?' Cory asked her. 'Do you have any idea what that did to me?'

'But I did – I wrote you a letter where I explained everything, begging you to come out to LA with me.'

He frowned. 'I never got a letter.'

'Well, I definitely delivered it, by hand, so it can't have got lost in the post.'

'Zara must have kept it from me,' he said. 'She behaved really oddly after you'd gone.' He shook his head. 'You always said that you couldn't trust her, I should have believed you. But why didn't you call me once you were here? I didn't know where you were, thought you must want never to see me again, so I didn't dare ask your mum.'

'Oh, Cory, and I thought the fact you never answered my letter meant *you* never wanted to see me again! I thought you must have gone to Thailand so I just worked as hard as I could and tried to forget you. I never did, though. I've tried to pretend it's not true, but I've never stopped loving you.'

When they came out of the gallery, Ramon, Liberty's driver and security guard, was waiting for her. Brooke was staying with friends and Zac was away filming. She felt reckless, giddy with love and desire for Cory, so when Ramon asked her where she wanted to go, she told him to drive them to Cory's hotel.

When they woke up in the morning, still wrapped in each other's arms, they knew that they had to be together.

'Leave him,' Cory told her. 'I love you so much, Liberty, and I hate to think how unhappy you are with Zac. We have enough money. We could move down to San Francisco, I've got a house there, or we could go back to the UK. I've got a home there too.'

She couldn't think of one reason to stay with her husband. For the next two days she made her arrangements but told no one except her friend Tandi, Kelly's mom. The plan was that Liberty would fly down to San Francisco with Cory, get the house ready for her daughter and then fly back for Brooke.

But on the morning they were due to fly out together Cory didn't meet her at LAX as they had arranged. Liberty stood there surrounded by suitcases, feeling hope fade away as the time drew closer and closer to their flight being called. She phoned Cory and his phone went straight to voicemail. Their flight was called and then boarded. It took off; still Liberty waited. In films people didn't turn up because something terrible had happened. She phoned up all the local hospitals, the police. Nothing. Had she misread everything? Was this Cory's revenge on her for going to LA without him all those years ago?

She felt she had no other choice but to return to the Santa Monica house and unpack.

'So what did you do while I was away?' Zac asked her when he returned the following day.

'Nothing much. I hung out by the pool. Had lunch with friends. Shopped.' Had my heart broken all over again by my lover.

'You look tired, I hope you didn't overdo it with your friends.'

Was it her imagination or was there an edge to Zac's voice, the way he'd said 'friends'?

'No.'

'Good, because we start filming the new series next week and I need you to be at your very best.'

If she'd felt broken-hearted when she'd first come to LA, then Cory's betrayal had nearly destroyed Liberty. Work and Brooke were the only things that saved her from going under. She later found out from Em, who had moved back to Brighton, that Cory had bought a house on the Sussex Downs. Two years later she heard that he'd got married. So it must have been revenge after all. She couldn't believe that the warm, loving man she'd known could ever behave like that, but the evidence spoke for itself, and the faint hope she'd nursed that there was a good reason why he had abandoned her, died. She'd been so desperate and unhappy when she'd met Cory again that she'd taken everything he'd said at face value. After living with Zac in LA, she should have known that people rarely meant what they said.

She was still lost in thought when she heard footsteps.

Shit, it was Zac! She had been hoping he would be out all night, overseeing the edit.

'Hey, why are you sitting out here in the dark?'

It was typical that he wanted to know why – he never seemed to switch off from directing, wanting to know her every move and motivation at all times. It was one of the many things about him that drove her mad. At the beginning of their relationship she had found it endearing; now she found it controlling, possessive.

He bent down and kissed her. She smelled coffee and gum. He got through so many cups during the day, and the gum was because he couldn't smoke on set. He lit a cigarette now and inhaled deeply, even though he knew that Liberty hated him smoking near her. She had given up saying anything about it, though. There was no point. Zac always did exactly as he pleased. Funny that he wasn't Brooke's real father – she certainly took after him when it came to being selfish, and getting her own way.

Liberty shrugged, feeling a little light-headed after a glass of wine on an empty stomach. 'I just felt like some air. I had an argument with Brooke.'

'Again? I thought you guys were going to sort it out.'

It was always 'you guys' with him. He was a distant stepfather to Brooke, happy to hand out money but wanting little involvement in the nitty-gritty of actually raising a child.

'I got a phone call from Wyatt. He caught a whole group of them smoking dope, Brooke included.'

'Is that so bad?' Zac replied. 'Everyone has to experiment when they're young. It's only dope. Chill, it's not a big deal.'

It was as if he was deliberately trying to undermine Liberty. He knew how strongly she disapproved of drugs. This was his way of getting back at her because she was no longer the perfect wife to him. She was sure he must know that she didn't love him any more but it was a subject they never discussed. They just carried on growing further and further apart and pretending that it wasn't so, always pretending.

'Well, she's grounded for the next month. She has to learn a lesson from this. And I thought we'd agreed that you weren't going to give her any more money? But she's spent over five thousand dollars this week on an outfit for a party she's not even allowed to go to now!'

Zac blew out a plume of cigarette smoke. 'So I guess there's going to be a great atmosphere in this house.' He paused, then added under his breath, 'No change there then.'

She looked at him. Most women found him stunningly attractive. He was tall, powerfully built, with jet black hair and strong chiselled features. With his looks Zac could have been an actor, save for the fact that he couldn't act. He was over forty now and looked good for his age. He kept in shape with rigorous work-outs at the gym with his personal trainer, he watched what he ate, what he drank. Smoking was his only vice, and that was restricted to the house and his car as it was so difficult to find anywhere else to smoke in LA. He had it all, but nothing Liberty was interested in any more. She stood up and picked up her empty wineglass. 'I'm going to bed.'

'Let me guess,' he muttered. 'You've got a headache.'

'I'm tired, and upset because of what's going on with Brooke. So, yes, I've got a headache.'

Upstairs in her dressing room – always the place she retreated to if things were difficult between her and Zac – Liberty quickly got out her laptop and sent an email off to Em. *What we've been talking about. I think it's time. Expect us soon.* She clicked send then went to her sent mailbox and deleted the email, and just to be on the safe side set up a new password on her computer. She never knew for certain if Zac checked her emails as she had never caught him. But she strongly suspected he did. It would be just his kind of control-freak behaviour.

Chapter 20

Brooke

Brooke kicked off her crystal-studded Louboutins and then for good measure picked one up and flung it against the wall, not caring what happened to the insanely expensive shoe. She couldn't believe that her mom had actually gone ahead with her threat and grounded her. Fuck that, and fuck everything and everyone! Why did her mom have to be such an uptight pain in the ass? Majorly on her case just because she had been caught smoking weed. Her mom should have been grateful it hadn't been anything stronger – she should have seen what was going down in the bathroom at the last party Brooke went to, where there were lines of coke laid out by the black marble sink and someone was going around handing out tablets of MDMA as if they were Smarties.

She threw herself on the bed, and punched her pillow in frustration. She had got dressed up in her black lace dress and Louboutins and made it as far as the hallway before her mom caught her and sent her upstairs. Usually Brooke would have tried to brazen it

156

out but Liberty had seized her purse and taken out her wallet, cellphone and car keys. Brooke wasn't going to get very far without any money, and the Louboutins were hardly made for walking the seven miles to Christian's house.

There had been no alternative but to run upstairs to her room and slam the door shut, a habit that she knew drove her mom and stepdad crazy – which was no consolation at all. She reached for her laptop and logged on to Facebook.

I'm not going to be able to make it tonight, my bitch of a mom has grounded me, she quickly messaged Christian. *Wish I could be with you. Will see you tomorrow to give you your present. xxx* She pressed send and wondered if Christian would even get it. He would be caught up with saying hi to his guests, with generally being the life and soul of his eighteenth birthday party. She was supposed to be at his side. She could just imagine the look on that slut Taylor's face when she realised that Christian was on his own. And yes, she, Brooke, was his girlfriend and he claimed to be into her, but she didn't know if she could trust him, especially not on his birthday of all nights, surrounded by so many temptations, drink, drugs and Taylor, with her big tits and bad reputation . . .

Brooke clicked through her pictures on Facebook, settling on the ones of her with Christian. He was so good-looking, with that bad boy swagger she loved. She toyed with the idea of sending him a picture of her topless in the teeny-tiny black lace briefs she had bought 'specially from Victoria's Secret, then thought again. A year ago her then boyfriend had taken a picture of her topless that he had posted up online when they split. Liberty hadn't been too pleased about that either.

There was a knock at the door.

'Go away!' Brooke shouted. 'I don't want to talk to you!'

Typically Liberty ignored her and walked in. It crossed Brooke's mind that her mom looked terrible. She was too pale with dark shadows under her eyes, when usually she was an absolute knock out, sensationally beautiful, and lusted after by all the boys in Brooke's school – something that really pissed her off. No one wanted a mother who was hotter than them.

'What do you want?' she muttered sulkily, picking at her python-print manicure, which had taken the girl at the nail bar two hours to do. What did it matter what her nails looked like now?

'You know how I feel about drugs. You've always known, so I'm sorry if you think I'm being unfair but this is the second time you've been caught and you have to learn a lesson.'

Shit, she had hoped that her mom would have forgotten about that other time. She might have known that she wouldn't.

Brooke rolled her eyes, another habit which she knew drove Liberty crazy.

'Well, thanks to you, Christian is probably going to dump me! And I love him. You're ruining my life!' Actually she didn't love him, but it sounded more dramatic than 'And I really, really like him'.

In the past she had always been able to wrap her mom around her finger, but not now apparently. Liberty shrugged. 'I don't think he's good enough for you. He's a spoiled little rich boy with no idea about life. And by the way, you don't love him.'

Brooke sat up, outraged by her mom's casual attitude. 'You don't know anything!'

Liberty winced at her tone, 'Well, I know more than you think. I was a teenager once too and I only want you to . . .'

Brooke cut across her. 'Make a success of my life and not end up a single parent like you did. Yeah, yeah, yeah.' She had heard her mom say this so many freaking times, but the fact was that Liberty seemed to have made a great success of her life. She was a leading actress, she lived in a massive house and she had plenty of money. Brooke mentally skated over the fact that she knew her mom's marriage to Zac was less than happy, and that the rows between them had become even more bitter lately.

'I was going to order in some Thai food for us. I thought maybe we could watch a movie together? Your choice?' Her mom sounded so pathetically hopeful it set Brooke's teeth on edge. That was supposed to be her consolation prize for missing Christian's party?

'I'm not hungry and I'm not in the mood for a movie – unless it's about how much it sucks having you as a mother.'

She expected Liberty to blow up at her for that. Instead she said wearily,

'Okay, well, if you change your mind I'll be downstairs. And here, you can have your phone.'

Brooke snatched it from her without a word of thanks.

The moment her mom was out of the room she selected Christian's number. Typically it went straight to his voicemail. She almost cried with frustration as she threw it on the bed.

Taylor could hardly keep the smirk off her face on Monday morning when Brooke saw her in the cafeteria.

'Whatever she says to you, don't rise to it,' Kelly

muttered under her breath as Taylor made a bee-line for them, no doubt intent on rubbing it in that Brooke hadn't been at Christian's birthday.

Taylor stood in front of them both, twirling a strand of long blonde hair between her fingers. 'You missed such a great party at the weekend, Brooke. It was awesome. I don't think I got home until after five. It was easily one of the best I've ever been to.'

'Yeah, well, I had a fever and was too sick to go. I'm planning to celebrate with Christian at the weekend. Just the two of us. It'll be way more intimate than some big party. He told me he can't wait.' It was a blatant lie as Brooke had only received one text from Christian, saying that he was so hungover he couldn't see her yesterday. And he wasn't in school today either.

The smirk on Taylor's face turned into a smile. 'Seriously? That's the best you can come up with? 'Cos I heard from a reliable source that you couldn't come because your mommy had grounded you after the drug incident at Bryan's. That is so second-grade! My mom lets me do whatever I want. She says that now I'm eighteen, I'm an adult and free to make my own choices. I mean, imagine getting so wound up about a tiny bit of blow! I smoke it at home, all the time.' She actually giggled.

Kelly touched Brooke's arm lightly, as if warning her not to retaliate, but Brooke couldn't stop herself. 'That's because your mom's too busy screwing the gardener to realise what the fuck you're doing. Everyone knows.'

Taylor's face turned an unattractive puce, clashing with her tight pink polo-shirt, as she said angrily, 'Bitch! You think you know everything? Why don't you ask Christian what we got up to in his bedroom? He got a very special birthday gift from me.' She licked her lips suggestively. 'He said it was the best he'd ever had.'

Brooke felt sick. No wonder he hadn't wanted to see her yesterday.

'You've had enough practice, let's face it,' Kelly spoke up. 'Most of the soccer team have enjoyed your services, haven't they? And you might have sucked Christian's dick, but he won't respect you for it. He was probably so wasted he won't even remember it happening.'

That was Kelly, you could always rely on her for a killer putdown.

Taylor was temporarily speechless and, before she could come up with a reply, Kelly took Brooke's arm and practically dragged her out of the cafeteria.

'She's bound to be lying about Christian,' Kelly said reassuringly, once they were safely out of earshot and sitting on the grass, leaning against the trunk of an oak tree. 'She wants to get back at you because you're going out with him and she's jealous as hell.'

Brooke just looked at her friend. It was nice of Kelly to say it, but neither of them really believed it. Humiliation, anger and hurt were all vying inside her. 'It's all my mom's fault,' Brooke finally burst out. 'If she hadn't grounded me none of this would have happened! I should have been at the party.' Even as she said it she was aware of how ridiculous it sounded – she could hardly blame her mom for what Christian had got up to with Taylor.

Wisely, Kelly chose not to answer that. 'How about we go shopping after school?' she suggested instead. 'You don't have to be back until six, do you? I saw this divine dress in Bloomingdales. I need your opinion on it.'

Brooke shrugged. 'Sure.' She probably had a bit of

credit left on her cards and it wasn't as if she had any other plans. It had to be better than going home and seeing her mom and obsessing about Christian.

She checked her phone. Still nothing from him. Why didn't he call? Or text? Didn't he care about her at all?

'*If* Taylor was telling the truth, do you think it counts as Christian cheating?' Brooke couldn't believe she was really asking this. She had always been strong when it came to boys, and felt that she kept the upper hand. She didn't feel like that with Christian. But then, she had never been so into someone before.

'*If* Taylor was telling the truth,' Kelly said carefully, 'I think, yeah, it does count as cheating.'

'People do forgive their partners for cheating though, don't they? We can get over this, can't we? I mean, he was probably drunk and it was his birthday. Things aren't always black and white, are they? He probably regrets it.' God, she sounded so desperate; she just couldn't help it.

Kelly looked as if she couldn't believe her ears. 'Babe, who cares that it was his birthday? Does that entitle him to get blown by that slut? You've only been going out with him for three weeks. If he does this after such a short time, what does it say about his feelings for you? I know you really like him, but you can't let him treat you this badly. And you know you'd say exactly the same to me if I was in your position. He has to respect you, and you have to respect yourself! Come on, girl! This isn't like you at all.'

Brooke put her face in her hands. 'I know. Everything's such a mess.'

The afternoon dragged by painfully slowly. She couldn't concentrate in class, too taken up with thoughts of Christian and what she should do. She completely messed up her speeches in drama, even though she had been working hard on them, and could tell that her teacher was disappointed by her performance.

'Is everything okay, Brooke?' Miss Rose asked her afterwards. 'You seem very distracted.'

'I'm fine. I'm sorry . . . it's just a bad day for no particular reason.' Brooke couldn't tell her that it was too cruel to be playing Juliet and exclaiming about your great love, when in real life your boyfriend had cheated on you; Romeo would never have treated his Juliet like that.

As soon as she and Kelly hit the shops she felt slightly more hopeful. She would flex some plastic, buy a new outfit and then call by on Christian on the way back and find out what had happened. Maybe Taylor had lied. Brooke wouldn't put it past her. Yeah, that was possible. She couldn't believe that Christian could have cheated on her after just three weeks . . . No, there had to be another explanation.

She found the cutest little blue pleated skirt in Abercrombie & Fitch, which she liked so much that she bought the pink one and the white one too, along with a sexy white vest top. She changed into the skirt and vest there and then. Then they popped into Mac and Brooke bought a couple of new lipsticks, a blusher and a foundation – even though her mom was always saying that she had perfect skin and really didn't need to wear foundation. They stopped off at a nail bar and she had a manicure because she had wrecked her last one, and a pedicure because she always liked fingernails and toe nails to match. She emerged an hour later with perfect sweet sugar-pink nails.

Four hundred dollars later – oops, she hadn't intended to spend quite so much – she dropped Kelly home and headed over to Christian's house which was close to Santa Monica beach. She checked her watch. Shit, she only had an hour before she was due back. She had texted her mom to say that she might be late as she had a drama rehearsal. She felt bad about lying, but not that bad.

The Mexican housemaid who opened the door to her told her that Christian was in his bedroom. There was no sign that a party had ever taken place in the Italian villa-style mansion and it was as pristine as ever. She imagined that the Mexican housemaid and a team of other staff must have been working round the clock to get it back to this state. Brooke quickly ran up the wide mahogany staircase and along the landing to Christian's room. He was sitting at his desk, hunched over his laptop, when she walked in after knocking. Was it her imagination or did he look guilty as he closed the lid of his MacBook, preventing her from seeing the screen?

'Hey, I didn't know you were coming over.' He leaned back in his seat, legs sprawled wide, arms folded, and made no attempt to get up and greet her. His too-cool-for-school style had always been part of the attraction for her. Now she felt annoyed that he made zero effort. He looked rough, but still sexy in jeans and a baggy vest that showed off his biceps.

'I thought I'd surprise you,' Brooke replied, sitting on the edge of his bed and trying not to imagine him lying there while Taylor did what she did best apparently. 'I'm really sorry I couldn't be at your party.'

'Yep, you missed a good one. Bummer about your mom being so strict. She really needs to loosen up, I mean, you're nearly eighteen, for Christ's sake.'

She missed a good one? What about him saying that he had missed *her*?

'So did you have a good time?'

Again there was that evasive look in his eyes as he replied, 'I did, from what I can remember. *Way* too much alcohol and weed. Yesterday I didn't get up, except to puke.'

And they said romance was dead . . .

'So did you miss me?' She had to ask.

'Of course I did, babe. *Badly*. Wasn't the same without you.'

But he didn't meet her gaze.

'Did you really?' Oh, to hell with it, she had to ask. 'You weren't too busy hanging out with Taylor?'

'Taylor? Fuck, no. What makes you say that?' Now he got up and sat next to Brooke, draping his arm round her shoulder, giving her his brown-eyed intense look.

Brooke took a deep breath. She just had to know the answer to the next question, even if the truth hurt. 'So, she didn't blow you? Because that's what she said happened. Oh, and apparently you told her that she was the best you'd ever had.'

'No fucking way! Is that what she's been telling you? She's such a skanky slut! I wouldn't want her anywhere near me. That girl's bat-shit crazy to come up with that lie.'

Was he protesting too much? Brooke didn't know.

'Brooke honey, I swear I haven't cheated on you.' He gazed at her and she could feel her resistance weakening. It would be just like Taylor to make something up. She was such a devious bitch and Brooke knew how insanely jealous she was. Okay, maybe she should take Christian's word for it. She reached towards her bag and pulled out a black jewellery box.

'Happy birthday. I'm sorry it's two days late.' She had agonised over what to buy him and in the end had gone for a silver dog tag necklace with two tags. She had been planning to get her name engraved on one and his on the other, but she didn't know if she still wanted to. However, as soon as Christian opened the present he said, 'Wow, babe, that's awesome.' He slipped it over his head. 'I'll have to get your name engraved on one of these.'

Hah! She'd like to see Taylor's face when she heard about that . . .

Christian seemed to sense that he was being let off the hook and went in for a kiss, gently pulling Brooke back on the bed with him. Kissing was good, she reflected as she felt his lips on hers, his tongue sliding into her mouth, and she got caught up in kissing him back for a few minutes, then remembered that kissing was as far as it was going to go. Today, anyway. He hadn't done quite enough to win her over yet . . .

'Love the outfit,' he murmured, sliding his hands along her thighs and under the flimsy fabric of her skirt.

Instantly she squeezed her legs together. Christian stopped kissing her. 'I want you, Brooke. You're so sexy. I'm hot for you.'

Hmm, he didn't say that he loved her, or that she was beautiful. It was all a bit, well, unromantic. Hardly something that Romeo would have said to his Juliet. Brooke wanted to be wooed, to be made to feel that she was special.

But Christian had other ideas. He grabbed her hand and placed it on his now bulging crotch. 'How about giving me my other birthday present? I'm hard for you, baby.'

That did it! She pulled his hand away and sat up.

'*Seriously?* "I'm hard for you, baby!" You sound like the script from a porno movie!' she exclaimed, furious with how little effort he was putting in to winning her over, and once again not trusting him about Taylor.

'Well, Jesus Christ, we have been seeing each other nearly three weeks, I do have needs! I don't know why you're being so frigid. I know you had sex with Mason, he told me all about it, so it's not like you're a virgin or anything! In fact, he led me to believe that you were quite the expert. It was one of the things that attracted me to you.'

At that she leaped off the bed. This was the icing on the fucking cupcake! 'Where are you going?' Christian demanded. And when she didn't answer but headed for the door, he added, 'Oh, gotta get home to Mommy like a good little girl? Maybe I should get someone else to play with. Someone who isn't such a major tease.'

She shot him the middle finger as she ran out of the room, bitterly disappointed and hurt that she had ever been involved with him.

Chapter 21

Liberty

Liberty flipped open the jewellery box and looked at the glittering diamond necklace, her twelfth wedding anniversary present from Zac, which he'd given her this morning. He would expect her to wear it tonight for dinner. The dinner that was all about them pretending to be a happily married couple. Knowing Zac, he would have laid on the most expensive champagne, ordered a 'specially made cake from the restaurant with their names on it, circled by a love heart, which the waiter would bring out with a flourish. Zac would want to be the centre of attention with all the other diners gazing at them, admiring them, being jealous of them.

She picked up the necklace and held it to her throat. It was a beautiful piece that showed off her slender neck, but she couldn't wear it. The necklace was just another lie. 'I don't want to be married to you any more,' she whispered to her reflection in the mirror. The words that she had been rehearsing in her head over and over and over. Tonight, she was finally going to say them. She had to come out with her declaration in a public place. It wasn't that she thought that Zac would hurt her or anything like that, he never had before, but he had a vile temper.

On her way out she found Brooke sitting by the pool, hugging her knees, with ever-loyal Ozzy curled up at her feet. Her daughter was staring moodily at the view and barely glanced at Liberty as she approached.

'I've phoned Kelly's mom and she says you're welcome to stay over there tonight. I could give you a lift?'

'No, thanks. I'll drive myself.'

Again Liberty felt a pang at how distant her daughter was being with her. She had found Brooke sobbing in her bedroom earlier, but she'd refused to say what the matter was. Something to do with Christian, no doubt. Liberty had longed to put her arms round her daughter and comfort her. It had been so easy when she was a little girl, but now Brooke looked as if comfort from her mother was absolutely the last thing she wanted.

'Anyway, I thought I was supposed to be grounded,' Brooke muttered.

'Honey, I know you're still mad at me about missing Christian's party, but please, can't we put it behind us now? Go and see Kelly tonight, and maybe tomorrow you could ask Christian over for supper. I feel that I hardly know him.'

Brooke glared at her. 'FYI we had a massive row, all because you didn't let me go to his party. Happy now?'

'Of course I'm not! I'm sorry. Really I am. I don't want you to be upset.'

But Brooke had picked up her phone and was busy texting, her way of saying, Don't talk to me any more.

'Okay, I'll see you tomorrow, sweetheart.' Liberty blew her daughter a kiss, knowing that she wouldn't want a hug.

''Bye,' Brooke muttered. 'Oh, yeah, happy anniversary.'

The traffic was terrible and Liberty was running late as she pulled up outside the restaurant. Immediately a valet came over to open the door for her and park her car. Once inside the restaurant, Giorgio the owner made a fuss of welcoming her, taking her jacket and telling her how wonderful it was to see her again. She and Zac always received the star treatment here. It was Zac's favourite restaurant and he'd been coming for years. He liked to think that he was in an Italian Mob film, like *Goodfellas*. Liberty used to think it was sweet. Now, like so many other things about him, she found it intensely annoying.

As she was shown over to Zac's table she was aware of other diners looking at her – discreetly of course, no one outright stared in such an exclusive restaurant as this. To stare would have been an admission that maybe you weren't as famous as the person walking by. The attention was something she had never really grown used to, and it was not something that she relished. She loved acting and performing, that was everything to her. But she hated the constant scrutiny of the press, picking over her personal life and constantly analysing her appearance. Had she put on a few pounds, lost a few pounds? Had she had any work done? When she first moved to LA as an inexperienced twenty-two-year-old actress, she had naively read all the stories written about her, and had felt crushed by a negative piece or a bad photograph. And all the good stories never seemed to outweigh the damage done by the negative ones. By the time she turned twenty-five she had stopped reading them. And she absolutely refused to Google herself. She didn't read reviews any more either.

Zac was sitting at his favourite table. Typically he was working, frantically emailing from his iPad. He glanced up as the waiter pulled the chair out for Liberty and she sat down.

'I'll be with you in one minute, I promise.' He leaned over and kissed her lightly on the lips, then returned his attention to the screen.

The waiter poured her out a glass of champagne, and she took a long sip. So here she was, at her twelfth wedding anniversary, and all she could think about was how much she wanted to get out of this marriage. She could not imagine carrying on this relationship a second longer, papering over the cracks, pretending, always pretending.

Zac finally sent off his email and looked up at her.

'Sorry, there's a problem with one of the scripts. Ten writers and they still can't get it right.' He shook his head as if marvelling at their incompetence. 'Hey, why aren't you wearing the necklace? Don't you like it?'

'Of course, it's exquisite, I just wanted to wear this.' She touched the silver dragonfly necklace that she'd had for years. It had been a present from Cory. She hadn't worn it for ages, but somehow it had felt right to wear it tonight. It gave her a feeling of strength, reminded her that she was still the person she had been all those years ago.

Zac didn't look impressed by her choice. 'It's not exactly a statement piece, is it? It's a little bit dippy hippy bohemian. The diamond necklace would have looked better.'

Better to show off what a generous husband she had.

'So shall we order? I'm starving.' He held up his hand to summon the waiter. Zac always had exactly the same thing here – the Carpaccio and Risotto Nero.

171

Liberty had no appetite at all and ordered a Caesar salad. She was playing for time.

'Aren't you hungry?' he commented. Even after nearly fourteen years together he always noticed what she did or didn't eat.

'Not especially.'

'You could do with putting on a little more weight; you're beginning to look a little gaunt in the face. It can be ageing. Or you could go and see someone about getting some fillers. Greta –' he named another actress – 'has just had some done. She looks fantastic. Glowing. At least five, maybe even ten years younger.'

He didn't wait for Liberty's reply as he continued, 'So we're going to start filming in a month's time. I think it will be your best role yet – it's perfect for you. It should be, of course, I created it for you.'

Okay, she'd thought her declaration would come later, but it had to be now.

'Actually, Zac, I'm not sure if I want to do it.'

'What do you mean? What's not to like about it?'

'I should have been clearer. I don't want to do it. In fact, I'm not going to do it.'

She had his full attention now.

'You can't just drop this on me! You've had a bad couple of weeks with Brooke, it's affected you, I can see that now. You probably need a break . . .'

'It's more than that. I know this seems like the worst possible timing, but I don't want to be married to you any more. I think our marriage ended a long time ago. We both need to face up to that.' There. She had finally said it. The words were out there.

He looked at her as if she had sucker-punched him. 'What are you talking about? I know we haven't been getting on lately, but that's because of work . . . because of Brooke being so difficult. We'll take some time off

172

together. We could go to Hawaii – Brooke as well. You love it out there, baby, you know you do. And if that's not enough, we'll have some counselling. I'll do whatever you want. Whatever it takes.'

She shook her head. 'I'm sorry, Zac, I've been thinking about this for a very long time and I've made up my mind.'

He slammed his hand down on the table. 'You can't just call time on a twelve-year marriage because *you* want out! Don't I have any say in this at all?'

She shook her head.

'For God's sake, Liberty, you're the love of my life! You can't do this to me! Is there someone else?'

'No one else.'

The waiter came over, alerted by Zac's shouting, and asked if everything was all right.

'Actually we're leaving. My wife has something important to discuss with me.' Zac stood up and, reaching for his wallet, thrust a handful of notes at the waiter.

Liberty remained seated. 'I've got nothing else to say. I'm planning to stay with a friend tonight and I'll be at the house tomorrow morning to pack up my things. We can talk then about the practicalities. I'm not changing my mind, Zac.'

He stood rooted to the spot for a moment, as if in a daze, before Giorgio, realising something was wrong, came over and lightly touched him on the arm. 'Your car will be ready for you in just a moment, Mr Keller.'

Zac looked as if he had no intention of leaving, but Giorgio said, 'I think it's best, Mr Keller.' And finally Zac seemed to admit defeat and followed him out.

Liberty waited until he was safely out of the restaurant before making her own exit. She was shaking when she got behind the wheel of her car and it took a few minutes before she felt composed enough to turn on the ignition. She glanced back at the restaurant; somehow she had a feeling she wouldn't be going there again.

Zac was waiting for her at the house when she returned the following morning, as she'd known he would be. He looked pale and drawn as if he hadn't slept, but he kept his expression neutral when she walked into the living room. The only sign of tension was the ashtray overflowing with cigarette ends. Now wasn't the time to point out that she disapproved of smoking inside the house. From now on Liberty didn't care. It was his house.

'Have you changed your mind about what you said last night?' His voice was controlled.

'I haven't.' She paused, then added, 'I'm sorry. Really sorry. But I can't make myself feel something that I don't.'

'You won't be entitled to any big settlement, you do know that, don't you? You signed that pre-nup and it will hold. I spoke to my lawyer.'

Of course he had. Money meant a great deal to Zac. Money, power, it was all part of the same thing to him, as essential as oxygen.

'I don't want any of your money, Zac, or any share of the house, or the apartment in New York, or the vineyard, or the boat, or the art collection, or the company. I'll leave the marriage with what I came with and what I earned myself.'

Now he seemed rattled, angered by her apparent calm resolve. He had probably expected her to beg and plead, to say it had all been a mistake, that she hadn't meant it.

'And how exactly are you going to support yourself

and Brooke? I'm telling you now, you won't find work in LA. Your career here is finished. No one will hire you, I'll make sure of that. And I'll make sure Brooke doesn't get work either.'

She had expected this as well, had thought he would most likely turn vindictive, and knew that other people in the industry wouldn't employ her if they believed it would anger him. He was too powerful. He didn't understand that all his threats were only making her more determined to be free of him, once and for all. The door of the gilded cage was finally open.

'I understand. We won't be living in LA, so it won't matter.'

'You won't survive without me. Where are you going to go? What are you going to do?' He sounded increasingly desperate.

'I'll send you the address once I know it.' She had no intention of telling him until she and Brooke were long gone and out of his reach.

'Is there someone else? You owe me the truth after twelve years of marriage.'

She shook her head, desperate now to get away from him.

'I don't believe you! Did you think I never knew about Cory? He wrote to you, did you know that? Some sappy letter about how much he still loved you, in spite of everything.'

Liberty felt herself pale at the words. How had Zac known about Cory? When had he written to her? She longed to ask, but knew she would be playing straight into her husband's hands and then he would be pulling the strings, yet again. And she couldn't deal with this now. It would have to wait until she was away from here, then she would think about what he'd told her.

With a huge effort, she kept her voice level. 'Well, that's all in the past. Goodbye, Zac.'

Sensing he had lost his power over her, he shouted, 'I've made you into a star and this is how you repay me?'

She had nothing else to say. She was halfway across the room when Zac let out a roar and hurled the ashtray towards the wall where it shattered the huge silver-framed mirror. Liberty carried on walking. She didn't look back.

Chapter 22

Brooke

'Bastard! I don't believe it!' Brooke exclaimed, checking her Facebook page on her phone and seeing the picture Christian had posted of him and Taylor kissing – or rather eating each other's faces. Eww!

'Bastard!' It was all she was capable of saying right now.

'Well, at least she's sucking his face and not his . . .' Kelly stopped talking when she saw the look of anguish on her friend's face.

'Why didn't I dump him last night?' Brooke wailed. 'Now it's going to look like he dumped me! And I was so going to dump the fucker! Ahhh! What did I ever see in him?'

She shot out of bed where she and Kelly had been lounging in their PJs, taking advantage of the Saturday morning to have a lie in. Brooke was so agitated she couldn't stand still, but paced up and down the bedroom. She felt totally humiliated as she thought of Taylor and Christian laughing at her behind her back. The gruesome twosome.

'He's very good-looking,' Kelly replied. 'But, babes, it was only ever about him being hot, admit it? You weren't interested in him for his conversational skills and his emotional depth, were you? And you *hated* his music.'

As usual Kelly knew her so well and was absolutely right, not that Brooke was quite ready to admit it.

'We talked about stuff all the time,' she replied defensively, while trying to remember what exactly they had ever talked about, apart from how his baseball game was going and about the latest song he'd written. The lyrics of which always sucked . . . not that she ever told him that. God! She had been such an idiot! Totally infatuated by the pretty-boy loser.

'Yeah, right.' Kelly shot back. 'Forget about him. You are a hundred per cent better off without him.'

Brooke stopped pacing and sat back down on the bed. 'I know, I know.' She picked up her phone. 'So should I send him a message saying he's dumped, or what?' She was itching to type out something rude.

Kelly shrugged. 'No point having any contact with him.'

'How about I post something under the picture, like, "Hope you'll be very happy together, douche bags!"'

'Girl, you are totally going to occupy the moral high ground and say nothing at all. Anything else will just make them post up something nasty. Ignore them. That will be so much better. It says you don't care. You are the stronger person.'

Brooke put her head in her hands. 'But I'm a wreck. I need to eat a tub of Ben and Jerry's Peanut Butter Me Up, watch *The Notebook*, and cry.'

'You need to forget about Christian. So do you want to come to the beach today? I'll buy you a frozen yoghurt. You are not going to eat Ben and Jerry's and calorie load because of that dickbrain. And I can lend you a bikini, to save you going home?'

It was a tempting offer as she had no plans, but then again Kelly was bound to be meeting her boyfriend Ray, and Brooke didn't know if she was ready to be around a happy couple.

'I think I'm going to head home. I should check on Ozzy. And my mom's left loads of messages, saying she needs to speak to me urgently.'

'Well, if you change your mind, just text me. And promise me you're not going to waste any more time thinking about Christian? He *really* isn't worth it.'

'Who?' Brooke joked back, though she knew she was still bound to go over and over what had happened.

'Atta girl!'

A scene of complete chaos greeted her when Brooke let herself into the house. Half-filled suitcases, plastic bags overflowing with clothes, framed photographs of her and her mom stacked up against the wall . . . and in the middle of it all, Rosa, looking uncharacteristically flustered.

'What's going on?' Brooke asked her in bewilderment.

'You'd better ask your mom,' Rosa replied. 'She's upstairs.' She sniffed and rubbed her eyes. She'd obviously been crying.

'Are you okay, Rosa?'

The housekeeper shook her head. 'I don't know, Brooke.'

She raced upstairs and found Liberty in her bedroom, surrounded by yet more piles of clothes. Her mom was dressed in sweat pants and a vest, her hair was tied back in a ponytail, and she looked as if she had been busy packing for some time.

'Can you please tell me what's going on?' Brooke demanded.

Liberty dropped the pile of clothes she was holding on to the bed and walked over to her. 'I've left Zac. Our marriage is over.' She reached out and rubbed Brooke's shoulder. 'I know it might come as a shock and you're bound to be upset, but it's for the best, I promise.'

'What!' The news completely derailed her. She knew her parents hadn't been getting on for a while (okay, years if she was honest), but she'd never thought they would break up. *Never.*

'But . . . it's so sudden. Are you sure? Isn't this just, like, a blip?'

'I've never been more certain of anything. And, no, it's not a blip. We're getting divorced.'

'But this is our home, where are we going to live?' Brooke could feel tears welling up in her eyes.

'I promise I'm going to sort everything out, honey. We're going to stay with Kelly's family for a few days. You'll like that, won't you?'

Her mom seemed incredibly calm. In fact, Brooke would go so far as to say Liberty had a new sense of purpose and energy about her. She seemed confident and determined.

'Was it your decision, or was it Zac's as well?' She knew that for all his faults her stepdad really loved her mom.

Liberty bit her lip. 'It was just mine.' She hesitated. 'He's very angry with me at the moment, which is why I want to get packed up as quickly as possible. We need to be gone before he gets back.'

'Will I see him?' Brooke might not have been that close to Zac, but he had been a part of her life for the last fourteen years. The way her mom was talking, it sounded as if they were never going to see him again.

Now Liberty looked uncertain. 'Yes, sweetheart, just

not straight away. Give it a little time. It's all a bit raw right now. So if you could make a start on packing, that would be great. You'll need to pack a suitcase of the clothes you know you can't do without, to last you a couple of weeks. Rosa will pack the rest of your things once we've gone and send them on to us.'

'And what about her? Will she be coming with us?'

'I'm afraid not, honey. She'll stay here in LA, she wouldn't want to leave her family. But I'll make sure I give her brilliant references and a good pay off. Unfortunately Zac doesn't want her to carry on working for him. He's firing everyone and replacing them with new staff.'

'What!' Rosa was part of Brooke's life. How could she not see her every day? Liberty went to say something else but Brooke bolted out of the room and slammed the door. Just when she thought things couldn't possibly get any worse, she discovered a new level of complete crap!

'D'you want to go to the beach?' Kelly asked. The two girls were lying by the pool, attempting to do some homework after class. Brooke and Liberty had been staying with Kelly and her family for the last week, while Liberty tried to sort out somewhere else for them to live. Brooke adored Kelly and her mom, dad, and three younger sisters, but their perfect happy family where everyone got along was too much of a reminder of the way her own small imperfect family had been ripped apart and set adrift.

'No, thanks, I'm cool here.' The truth was Brooke couldn't face running into anyone they knew. School had been bad enough, where she was aware of other students looking at her when she passed them. News travelled fast and the ending of a high-profile marriage

181

like her parents' was a major source of interest as people speculated about how nasty the divorce was going to get.

Brooke felt as if her world had been turned upside down and inside out. Nothing she'd thought about anything seemed to hold true any more. Last night Liberty had told her that she hadn't been happy with Zac for the last eight years; that she didn't even know if she wanted to live in LA any more. Not live in LA! The thought was unimaginable to Brooke. She was sure that her mom couldn't mean that; after all, LA was where she worked.

There was nowhere else Brooke wanted to live unless it was New York. But then she imagined dividing her time between New York and LA when she was a successful actor. She would have an apartment in New York for all the times she felt like going under the radar and didn't want the attention she was bound to attract in LA. But even then, she predicted, she would always prefer LA. It was her spiritual home.

She picked up her copy of *Romeo and Juliet* and half-heartedly tried to concentrate on the text. She failed to take in a word. But then, who wanted to read about a great love story when their own love life was such shit? She had done her very best to ignore Christian in school, but wherever she went she seemed to bump into him and Taylor, with their arms wrapped round each other, a pair of loved-up fuck wads. It made her want to puke. She was furious with him, but angrier with herself for the hours and hours she had wasted on him.

She abandoned her book and got up and dived into the pool. Swimming usually helped to clear her head, but with every length she found something else to worry about. Would Zac still help her with her acting career? He had always promised to, but since Liberty had walked out on him Brooke hadn't heard a word from her stepdad. Everyone knew how crucial contacts were in the film industry. It simply wasn't enough to have talent. And where were she and her mom going to live? Brooke loved Beverly Hills and Santa Monica, and didn't want to live anywhere else. She hauled herself out of the pool and saw that her mom had come out of the house. She seemed very pleased about something.

'Hey, I've got some great news!' she exclaimed as she handed Brooke a towel. 'I think I might have found us somewhere to live. And you'll love it, it's right by the sea.'

Oh, thank God! They weren't leaving LA after all. Nothing would have to change that much. She'd get to see Zac at weekends, which were pretty much the only times she got to see him anyway. He would still be able to help her.

'Awesome!' she exclaimed, caught up in her mom's excitement. 'So can we go and see it this afternoon? I'm through with studying for now.'

'It's a little bit too far away for that.' For some reason Liberty seemed amused by the question.

'So where exactly is it?'

'Brighton.'

Brooke frowned; her mom couldn't possibly mean Brighton in the UK, where she was born. It must be a part of LA that Brooke hadn't heard of. 'Is that beyond Malibu?'

Liberty laughed. 'Just a little bit. Brighton, England, sweetheart! We're going home! I know it's going to be a big change for you, but there are so many positives. And we'll be close to Nina . . .'

For a moment Brooke couldn't quite take in what

her mom had said. She stood there with the water dripping off her body before she exploded with rage. '*What* are you talking about? LA is my home. I don't want to live in the UK. Why the fuck would I?'

'I know it's a lot to take in right now, but it's the best thing for both of us, I promise.'

'No, it's not! You're only thinking about yourself. You're a selfish bitch! I'm not going. I'm staying here with Zac. You want to go to the UK, fine, you go there, we can Skype. We'll probably have a more meaningful relationship that way.'

'Sweetheart, I'm sorry. I really didn't mean to upset you. But I don't think it would work out living with Zac.'

Brooke glared at her, desperately trying to hold back the tears that were threatening to spill out. 'I don't want to hear any more! I'm not going, so get over it. You can't make me do something I don't want to do. I have rights as well!'

And before Liberty could come out with anything else, Brooke sprinted inside where she hastily put on some shorts, a t-shirt and the first pair of shoes she could, which happened to be orange neon trainers, and raced out to her car. She would go and see Zac, say that she wanted to live with him. He would understand. She would promise to be more considerate round the house, completely abide by his rules, and not even sneak Ozzy upstairs. Everything would be okay.

Zac's production company occupied a swish office complex in Beverly Hills. Usually Brooke would have made an effort to be ultra-groomed when she made a visit – always mindful of being spotted by producers and directors. Now she was going to have to settle for dark glasses to cover her puffy eyes and hope that no one noticed her. She had reckoned without Zac's snotty PA, a stunning redhead called Alyssa who insisted that Zac couldn't possibly see her now and that he didn't have a window until tomorrow afternoon at the earliest.

'Please can you let him know that I'm here? I can't go until I've seen him. It's really urgent.' The tears were threatening to fall again.

Alyssa sighed and signalled that Brooke should take a seat, before sauntering into Zac's office. Brooke perched self-consciously on the edge of one of the taupe leather sofas. The air con was turned on so high that she was freezing in her vest and shorts, and her hair was still wet from the swim. She must look like shit. She hadn't even put any make up on. Alyssa emerged from the office. 'You can have two minutes.'

Patronising cow! She was just saying that, Brooke tried to tell herself, of course he would give her more time. But as soon as she walked into his spacious office she felt her courage desert her. Zac remained sitting behind his glossy white lacquer desk and looked at her without a hint of warmth in his expression. Okay, he was pissed off with her mom, she got it, but he must know that it had nothing to do with her.

'You wanted to see me, Brooke?'

He sounded so formal, as if he hardly knew her. She stood in the middle of the room, hardly knowing what to say. He gestured to her to sit down and she took a seat opposite him, feeling as if she was there for an interview.

'Um . . . I'm really sorry about you and Mom. It's not what I would have wanted. And, for what it's worth, I think she's making a big mistake.'

He shrugged. 'It's not what I want either, but Liberty is determined, she's made that crystal clear. The divorce is going ahead.' His tone was cold, stripped of any emotion. It didn't give Brooke much hope, but she ploughed on.

'Mom's talking about going back to the UK, but I really don't want to go with her, Zac – LA is my home, I belong here.' She paused, waiting for him to step in and say that of course it was, and that she could live with him. Nothing was forthcoming.

'I wondered if I could carry on living with you? I promise I won't be any trouble. I know I've been a bit slack lately with my schoolwork, but I'll make more effort. And you'll hardly know I'm there. I won't make a mess, I'll make sure Ozzy doesn't come upstairs any more . . .' She had clasped her hands together as if praying, feeling that her whole future hung on his reply.

When it came, it was like a body blow. 'I'm afraid that's simply not possible, Brooke. I'm not your father.'

'I know, but we've always got on, haven't we?' She was struggling to come up with some examples of happy times they had shared. There must have been some, though none sprang to mind.

'I couldn't live with you, Brooke. Every minute of every day would be a reminder of your mother and what she'd done to me. I need to make a clean break from both of you. I don't wish you ill, truly I don't. I just never want to see you again.'

'What? You can't mean that, Zac?' Her head was spinning. This was the worst news ever. Her dreams of being an actor, the life she'd had all mapped out, had been demolished in front of her.

Zac pressed a button on his desk. 'Alyssa, can you show Brooke out?' He looked at her. 'And just one more thing before you go . . . can you give me your credit cards? I'm not going to be subsidising your lifestyle any longer. Goodbye, Brooke.'

It was late afternoon by the time Brooke arrived at the beach. After seeing Zac she had driven around Beverly Hills in a complete daze, unable to think straight. She had nowhere to go. She had just enough money to buy herself a coffee and took it on to the beach where she sat watching the sunset, feeling more lonely and lost than she ever had before in her life. She couldn't believe that Zac had rejected her. God! First her real father wanted nothing to do with her, and then her stepdad. It was too much.

She stayed on the beach for several hours, gazing out at the ocean, lost in her thoughts. Everyone else around her was so happy and carefree. She watched a teenage couple walking by the sea, the boy with his arm draped round the girl, entirely caught up in each other. A few days ago that would have been her and Christian. And where was he now? Most likely with Taylor. Somehow in the middle of everything else that had happened it seemed like the very least of her problems. She had no more emotions to waste on Christian. Her phone beeped with a message from Kelly.

Where r u babe? We're all worried about u. Please let us know u are okay. xx.

It was tempting not to reply, to let them all carry on worrying, but while Brooke felt Liberty totally deserved that, she didn't want to upset Kelly and her family.

Back soon x, she replied, and stayed a few minutes more to watch the flaming orange sun sink into the ocean on her beloved beach.

Chapter 23

Liberty

Home, she was home at last, and it felt absolutely fantastic. When Liberty had arrived at Heathrow, she'd had a mad urge to kneel down and kiss the ground, she was so relieved to be away from Zac, except Brooke would have killed her for embarrassing her. Brooke already wanted to kill her mother for making her move as it was. God, Liberty hoped she would come round to it soon; it was like sharing the house with a ball of pure fury. A ball of pure fury who swore and slammed doors a lot.

But tonight was all about celebrating Liberty's return. She was out at Hotel du Vin – the kind of place she could never afford to go when she and Em used to hit the town all those years ago – with Em, Angel Summer, and her flamboyantly over the top camp hairdresser/best friend Jez. Em's husband, Noah, had been redesigning Angel's garden and the two women had become friendly again, after losing touch on leaving school. Angel was as beautiful as ever if not more so, as her cheekbones seemed to have become even more defined with age, and motherhood had given a new strength and confidence to her features. She was so friendly and unaffected, even after years of being one half of the UK's most famous celebrity couple. Liberty had seen her a few times when Angel had been living in LA before, and she'd always made a refreshing change from some of the other celebrities Liberty knew, who thought everything about themselves was automatically more significant and interesting than it was for anyone else on the planet. But Zac hadn't liked her, and it had been difficult for Liberty to see her. Once Angel had gone back to England, they had lost touch again.

'So was being with Zac a bit like that film *Sleeping with the Enemy*? You know, all the tins lined up in alphabetical order and the towels arranged just so,' Jez asked, after she'd mentioned in passing how controlling her soon-to-be ex-husband was and how that had been one of the reasons she left him.

Angel punched him on the arm. 'Jez! Inappropriate!' She turned to Liberty. 'I'm so sorry about him. He can't help himself. And he's a diamond really. One of my oldest friends. I've known him since I started modelling.'

'Yeah, a hundred years ago,' he quipped.

'Honestly – that's loyalty for you.' But Angel smiled fondly at Jez, and Liberty guessed that their relationship was built on banter.

'I'm sorry, Liberty, she's right, I can't stop myself,' Jez added.

She laughed. 'I'm not offended.' She could laugh about Zac, now there was the Atlantic between them and the divorce was going through. 'And he wasn't quite as bad as the guy in the film. Let's just say, I'm so very glad not to be married to him any more.'

'And we're glad you're not!' Em declared with

feeling. 'Let's have a toast. To your brilliant new life, away from that cold-hearted fucker.'

'Em!' Liberty exclaimed, worried that people at other tables would be offended, but everyone else round about them was laughing.

'I'm just telling it like it is,' Em defended herself.

'So what are your plans now you're back?' Angel asked Liberty.

'I'm going to get a new agent – I've got some meetings set up over the next few weeks. I want to get Brooke settled and I want to enjoy myself. God, I want to enjoy myself! I want to slob about in my trackies and watch crap TV and not have someone criticise me for it. I want to go running by the sea, I want to eat my favourite caramel ice cream at Morocco's, and have fish and chips. I want to—'

'Have a shag with a totally hot stranger?' Jez interrupted.

See Cory again. The thought had been constantly in her head since Zac had told her about the letter. Half of Liberty really wanted to see him, to find out what he had written to her and whether he still had feelings for her, the other was too scared of him rejecting her.

'Yeah, maybe,' she bantered back, not wanting to let on what she was thinking. 'Are there any in Brighton?'

'Well, there might be a few at the party I'm having at the beginning of October,' Angel put in.

'Yeah, some loaded footballers,' Jez added. 'Admittedly none of them will be in Cal's league looks-wise.' Cal was Angel's drop-dead-gorgeous husband. 'But you could always lie back and think of their weekly pay packets. Money and power can go some way towards making up for shagging a guy with a face like a bulldog sucking a wasp. Or so I've heard. Never done it myself.'

An eye roll from Angel. 'Anyway . . . the point is, you're both invited. If you can put up with a night of Jez. He'll have his husband Rufus with him, who can usually keep him in check.'

Of course that prompted Jez to whip out his phone and show Liberty and Em pictures of Rufus, who looked like the strong, silent type. Just as well really as Jez could talk for England. They should make it an Olympic sport – he'd get gold every single time.

It ended up being one of the best nights Liberty had had in years. Admittedly she drank too much champagne and knew she would have a wicked hangover next day, but it was worth it.

'Shall we get some fish and chips?' Angel asked as they stumbled out of Hotel du Vin, slightly the worse for wear.

'Can't we go back in there and have some proper cuisine?' Jez protested, wrinkling his nose.

'Nah, I'm in the mood for fish and chips,' Angel replied. Liberty and Em were up for it too and they went into the cheap and cheerful restaurant on the corner.

'I can't believe you've brought me here. I don't do this kind of place,' Jez declared as they sat round the plastic-topped table. There were bright fluorescent lights overhead, and a strong smell of frying. The contrast with Hotel du Vin could not have been greater.

'Oh, shut up, I bet you eat everything,' Angel told him. And sure enough Jez polished off all his cod and chips and half of Em's.

'So that's one thing you can tick off your to do list,' he told Liberty as they said goodbye afterwards. 'Now for the hot shag.'

'And on that bombshell . . .' Liberty joked as she and Em got into the taxi.

Chapter 24

Brooke

As far as Brooke was concerned her life was shit, and it was going to remain shit until she could save up enough money and go back to LA. Yes, her mom had rented them a house by the sea, and if Brooke was honest it was a beautiful house and even had its own strip of beach and a swimming pool. It was on a private road, the last in a select row of bright white houses, all built in the same unusual style with castle battlements and turrets, all over a hundred years old. Apparently it was known locally as Millionaire's Row. But the house didn't come anywhere close to her old one in LA. Nor did the shingle beach and grey-blue English Channel compare well to the wide sandy expanse, fringed with palm trees and the glittering sapphire-blue Pacific Ocean, of her Santa Monica beach. Everything here seemed smaller, duller and more insignificant than in LA.

She spent her first week in Brighton hardly leaving her room, dressed in sweat pants and a hoodie, messaging Kelly and watching DVDs. She refused to eat supper with her mom and carried her meals upstairs to eat on her own. Brooke had emerged only to see her gran, Nina, who had been a frequent visitor, and to take Ozzy for walks. He, at least, seemed to have adapted to his new surroundings very happily, especially since he was allowed to sleep in Brooke's room. But she barely spoke to her mom. And every time she caught sight of Liberty looking happy, Brooke wanted to scream. She couldn't forgive her for forcing them to make this move. The day they had left LA had been without doubt the worst one of Brooke's life. Rosa and Kelly had come to LAX to say goodbye and she had clung to them both, sobbing her heart out. Her mom literally had to prise her away.

But after five days of being a virtual recluse she was just about ready to go stir crazy. She had to do something! She changed into jeans and a t-shirt, put on her favourite pair of crystal-studded white Converse, and for the first time all week applied some make up.

Downstairs she found Liberty in the kitchen checking emails on her laptop. Her mom stopped what she was doing when Brooke walked in.

'Hey, you look nice. Do you want to go into town with me and I can show you around? It's got some great shops – all the ones you love, like MAC, Superdry, Hollister – and lots of quirky, vintage boutiques as well.'

Brooke gave her mom her best withering WTF look. Like she would want to spend any time with her. The antichrist, the mom from hell, the woman who had ruined her life!

'No, thanks, I'm going to see Nina.'

Her mom's mom had always outright refused to be called Granny. Being able to see her was the only good thing about being here. Brooke adored Nina and had always loved her visits over to LA. The big house had felt even emptier after she'd left.

'Oh, well, I could always meet you afterwards,' Liberty said hopefully.

Why didn't she just give up and accept that she had ruined any chance of a good mother/daughter relationship between them? It wasn't going to happen. *Ever.*

'I haven't got a credit card any more, if you remember. Zac got his PA to cut it up in front of me. Can you imagine how humiliated I felt?'

That wiped the smile off her mom's face. 'I know. I was going to buy you some clothes, as a treat.'

Brooke shrugged. 'Maybe.' She meant, No fucking way. Her mom couldn't buy her approval. The way Brooke felt right now, all the money and all the designer clothes in the world couldn't buy her approval.

Liberty had sold Brooke's cherished cherry red convertible just before they left LA. She claimed to have put the money into a savings account for Brooke for when she was older, and said that she wouldn't need a car in the UK. She had bought herself one, though – a flash stick-shift BMW which Brooke had no idea how to drive, having always driven automatics. So here she had a choice between walking or riding a bike. God, if her friends could see her now, she reflected as she pushed the second-hand mountain bike out of the gate and on to the private road. She hadn't had her hair done for over three weeks when usually she had it done every week, nor had she had a manicure. She must look such a wreck. She put on her black Ray-Ban Wayfarers – she had a pair in every colour – and began pedalling. She was too gloomy to take in the glorious view of the sea, the beach and the brightly painted beach huts. And the sun was actually shining. Brooke didn't care. It might as well be raining.

She arrived at her gran's still feeling as if the world

was against her. Not even the sight of Nina's bright pink-painted house with its window boxes full of even pinker geraniums could cheer her up. It stood out in the red brick Edwardian terrace and absolutely summed up her gran's extrovert character.

'Is it still that bad?' Nina asked when she opened the door and registered her granddaughter's miserable expression. Brooke had poured her heart out to her yesterday about how much she was missing LA and her friends and Rosa, who had been a part of her life for so many years.

'Worse. So much worse,' Brooke muttered, pushing her bike inside and leaning it against a wall in the hallway. She followed Nina into the sunny kitchen.

'What do you want to drink? I don't have any of your decaff skinny Mocha-frigging-ccinos or 'erbal tea or whatever it is you drink in the States. It's a choice between builder's tea or instant coffee. Or there might be some Diet Coke.'

'Have you got any mineral water?'

Nina gestured at the sink. 'There's an unlimited supply of tap water.'

Gross! Brooke wasn't drinking that; everyone knew it was polluted. Full of fuck knows what! Did her gran have a death wish or something?

'I'll have Diet Coke, please.'

They settled on deckchairs outside in the tiny south-facing garden. Nina was in her late-fifties and looked great for her age. She dyed her hair a vivid auburn, liked wearing tunics and leggings – the brighter the better – and lashings of black eyeliner. She was always tanned from spending so much time outside, cycling or walking by the sea or working in her garden. She'd had a tattoo of a mermaid put on her shoulder when she turned fifty as she had always wanted one, and was considering getting another on her back. It was fair to say that she was a bit of a hippy and a free spirit. She had just ended a six-month relationship because she found the guy too boring.

'I mean, I like gardening programmes, but I don't want to stay in *every* single night and watch them!' she had told Brooke. 'He never wanted to go anywhere and this was after only six months – we should have still been in the honeymoon phase, not vegetating in front of the TV. I want to go out and have fun. The deal breaker was when he didn't want to come to Glastonbury with me.'

She was the coolest gran Brooke knew.

'So when do you start college?' Nina asked her.

Brooke grimaced. 'Next week. I don't see the point. I want to audition for drama school – at least that would be one good thing about living here. But, typically, Mom won't let me yet. She still says I need to get some qualifications first. Big yawn and a total waste of time.'

'She's right on that score. There are plenty of out-of-work actors. You need something to fall back on.'

'Oh, and that's not all. She's got me a job working at some crappiola Italian restaurant on Saturday nights, the same one she used to work in. She says that I need to learn the value of money, that I've become too spoiled. I've got to go there tomorrow to have some induction training. Like, how hard is it to wait tables?'

This had caused a massive row between Brooke and Liberty, who had revealed that her daughter would no longer have her own personal credit card. From now on she would get a monthly allowance of £150 and that was it. Back in LA that didn't even cover the cost of having Brooke's hair done!

Nina raised her eyebrows. 'That's something else I agree with Liberty on. You were becoming a little bit of an LA princess, expecting to have whatever you wanted, whenever you wanted it. It's not attractive, sweet pea. You have to work for things. You'll appreciate them more if you do. And it would be good for you to mix with some real people – not all those LA types who only care about money and looks and being seen in the right places.'

'Aren't you going to say it will make me a better person?' Brooke said sarcastically. She could really do without the character assassination right now, especially from her gran who was supposed to be on her side.

'Yes, I think it probably will,' Nina said cheerfully, not rising to the bait.

'Well, it sucks being here. I love LA . . . it's my home. And then there's the whole deal of my real dad living in the UK and not even wanting to know me. Plus I haven't got any friends. Being here is doing my head in. I literally have nothing to look forward to. Nothing at all.' Brooke could feel her eyes fill with tears of self-pity. Again. That's all she seemed to have done since arriving here, got angry then cried. Pathetic.

'You'll make some friends. And your dad is a loser, don't waste any time on him,' Nina said gently. 'You and your mum can have a great life here and I'm thrilled to have you back, even though you haven't stopped moaning! I missed you so much when you left. Those annual visits never made up for not having you living around the corner.'

'You're the only good thing about being here, Nina,' Brooke muttered, trying to hold back the tears.

Nina reached out for her hand and squeezed it.

'And your mum had to get away from Zac. He was completely controlling her life. Wanted her to sign up for another series, when she didn't want to. He was even pressurising her to have surgery, for God's sake

– as if she needed it! He wanted to turn her into a clone of every other actress out there. Liberty only stayed with him for so long because she wanted to give you a good start in life. She's always put you first in all the decisions she's ever taken. You've no idea of the sacrifices she's made for you.'

Nina certainly knew how to guilt trip her . . . Brooke was starting to feel bad about the barrage of negative comments she had been directing at her mom.

'Anyway, I'm sure that you'll soon feel settled here and then you'll wonder what you ever saw in LA,' Nina continued.

Her gran was sweet, but deluded.

Back home, Liberty was in a great mood as her best friend Em had come over. Even though Brooke still felt as if the world was against her, she really liked Em, who was full of energy and always optimistic. She had returned to Brighton three years ago after living in Australia for over ten years, and that experience seemed to have added to the 'can do' vibe she always gave off. The two women were on the verandah, which looked out across the sea, watching the sunset. They had cracked open a bottle of champagne and already seemed a little drunk. Maybe it wasn't the first bottle of champagne . . . Hmm, and her mom had given Brooke a hard time about smoking a spliff. The word 'hypocrite' sprang to mind. But because Em was there, she wouldn't say anything . . . just yet.

'Brooke! How fantastic to see you. My God, you look so grown-up!' Em declared, getting up and giving her a big hug.

'Well, you haven't seen me for over two years, so yeah, I'm sure I have changed.'

'You look beautiful, doesn't she, Libs?'

'She does.' Liberty smiled at her daughter.

'I can't believe that you had a daughter who is naturally blonde when you have such dark hair.'

'Well, my dad had blond hair, if you remember,' Brooke muttered. 'Not that I do as I've only ever seen him about three times.'

'His loss,' Liberty said quietly.

'But Brooke has your wonderful green eyes. The boys at college won't know what's hit them when she arrives,' Em declared. 'They'll be like bees round a honeypot.'

'Well, they can look but not touch, I'm totally off boys.' Brooke sat down on one of the chairs and tucked her long legs up under her. She felt more relaxed with Em there, less inclined to be the spiky and sarcastic teenager, who stormed up to her room and slammed the door shut on her mom.

'Oh? That's news to me,' Liberty replied. 'I thought you were still in touch with Christian and that's why you were so mad at me for moving. I was going to suggest you ask him over.'

Her mom really was trying to make things up to her if she was prepared to do that . . . Brooke had been far too angry to confide in her in LA about the break up.

'No, I dumped him. Well, actually, he dumped me before I got chance to dump him. He was cheating on me with Taylor.'

She wasn't prepared to go into the full sordid details. Even so, she still hadn't been able to resist checking up on him on Facebook, and it looked like he and Taylor were still going strong. He'd posted up pictures of her posing on the bonnet of his new jeep in a leopard-print bikini. The temptation to post a message that she looked like a ho had been almost overwhelming, but somehow Brooke had resisted.

'Bastard!' Em declared. 'How dare he do that to you? What a scumbag tosser!'

'Yep, he's all of those. I don't know what I ever saw in him.'

'I bet he was a good-looking bad boy,' Em continued. 'We've all been there, haven't we?'

When Liberty didn't say anything, Em tactfully changed the subject and then Brooke asked to see pictures of her children. Em had three: a six-year-old daughter, four-year-old son and eight-month-old baby girl. 'God knows, I love them more than anything else in the world, but it's good to have some time out,' she said, draining her glass and filling it up with more champagne. 'Noah had better have got them off to sleep when I get back – honestly, they can twist him round their little fingers! I dread to think what will happen when they're teenagers.'

'They're lucky to have each other,' Brooke said wistfully, clicking through the images on Em's mobile. She had always, *always* wanted a brother or sister. As an only child, she'd had her mom's undivided attention when she was there, but it could be intensely lonely at times, especially when Liberty was away working. When she was little Brooke had even invented an imaginary sister called Lucy, to keep her company. She would get Rosa to set out an extra plate for her at dinner, and whenever they did any baking she would always make a special cake for Lucy. When her mom had found out she had seemed really upset.

'Zac never wanted to have children of his own,' Liberty said. 'But who knows? Maybe I'll meet someone else and have a baby.'

It was Brooke's turn to be surprised by her mom, and when Liberty saw the look on her daughter's face she said defensively, 'I'm not that old!'

'It's not that. I didn't even know you wanted to have another baby?'

'I always did. Just not with Zac.'

Em raised her glass. 'Well, there's life in the old girl yet, I'm sure. D'you want a glass of champagne, Brooke? I think we should have a toast to new beginnings. It's so brilliant to have you both back in Brighton.'

Liberty poured her daughter a small glass, and handed it to her.

'Cheers,' they all said in unison, clinking glasses.

As they seemed to have got on so much better tonight, after Em left Brooke decided to take a chance and ask her mom if she *really* had to work at the Italian restaurant. Liberty's reply was not at all what Brooke had wanted to hear.

'Yes, honestly, honey, I think it would be good for you to earn some money while you're at college. And I promise it won't be as bad as you think. You'll probably meet lots of people your own age – it'll be fun.'

'You've got a seriously weird idea of fun!' Brooke retorted. 'You told me you hated waiting tables, so why are you making me do it? You're being so mean! Isn't it enough that you drag me away from the place I love? Do you have to make me suffer doing some menial job as well? How much more of this do you think I can take? It's mental cruelty!'

When Liberty didn't reply, Brooke stormed upstairs and slammed the door on her mom. She stayed up in her room until ten when hunger drove her back downstairs. She made herself a peanut butter sandwich, which she knew wasn't healthy but by then she was too hungry to care. She was still hungry after that so ended up scoffing two of the fairy cakes Em had brought round and only just stopped herself from tucking into a third. Fuck! Now on top of everything else she was going to end up fat! And it would be all her mom's fault.

Her mood was no better the following day, getting ready for her induction at the restaurant. An Italian restaurant of all places, and she didn't even eat pasta! Once in a blue moon she might allow herself pizza, but that was it. She tried to avoid all carbs. Ugh! She so didn't want this job, she griped to herself as she rummaged through her suitcases – she still hadn't bothered to unpack – trying to decide what to wear. Maybe if she wore a completely outrageous outfit the manager would refuse to hire her . . . Then again, her mom would probably only find her something even worse to do and get her a job at some fast-food hellhole, which didn't bear thinking about.

In the end Brooke went for a pair of tiny denim shorts and a white shirt that she tied around her waist, showing off her flat brown stomach, and the white Converse that emphasised her bronzed legs. Though as the sun had barely showed itself since she had moved over here, she'd better book herself in for a spray tan soon. She had never been pale in her life, and as far as Brooke was concerned that was not an option for her. She was all about the sun-kissed, blonde beach-babe look.

Paradiso was in a prime location, near Brighton Pavilion. Okay, even Brooke had to admit that was an impressive building – all those insane turrets and pillars and minarets or whatever Nina had said they were called – but no doubt the location would mean the restaurant was constantly busy. Sure enough, when she pushed open the door and stepped inside the place was buzzing, and it was only Tuesday lunchtime.

202

'Hi there, can I get you a table for one?' A young waiter instantly approached her.

Brooke chewed hard on her gum and looked bored. Like she would ever want to eat in a dump like this! With its red-checked tablecloths, pictures of the Leaning freaking Tower of Pisa, gondolas, the Trevi fountain and the Italian flag hanging on the wall, and some cheesy tune playing, it was so tacky and cliché-ed. The owner ought to be sued under the Trade Descriptions Act for calling it Paradiso. She had never been anywhere less like paradise in her life. It should have been called *Inferno* . . .

Back in LA she ate at places where the food and décor were achingly stylish, where you went to be seen and had to be in with the right crowd even to get a reservation. By the look of the casually dressed clientele that was not true of Paradiso. They were here on a mission to stuff their boring faces with pasta and waddle off, loaded up with carbs. It was too tragic. And even more tragic was the fact she was going to be waiting on them.

'Oh, I'm not eating. I'm here to see . . .' Shit! She'd forgotten the manager's name, what a great start. At this rate it would be McDonald's here we come. Nooooooo! Anything but that. She would rather die than utter the words, 'Do you want fries with that?' At least this was an Italian restaurant, and she could kid herself that she was researching for future roles when she would be in some stylish Mafia-type movie. Immersing herself in that whole method acting thing.

'Um . . . Mario or something.'

Waiter Guy grinned at her. He was certainly very cute, with chocolate-brown eyes, dark brown hair cut in a cute spiky style, and a sexy mouth. Too good-looking really to be a waiter, but he *was* a waiter, and waiters didn't feature in Brooke's life unless they were waiting on her . . .

'You mean Marco. It's probably a good idea to get the manager's name right if you're here for a job interview. And to give you the heads up, he hates gum, really, it drives him crazy. I'll go and tell him you're here. What's your name?'

She liked his British accent; it too was cute. But again, he was only a waiter, so it didn't matter what he sounded like.

'Brooke.'

'Okay, I'll be back in a minute.'

'Thanks,' she muttered when he seemed to be waiting for her reply. Gee, did he expect the Nobel Prize just for doing his job and fetching the manager?

She sat down at one of the tables and got out her phone. She was halfway through sending Kelly a message, or rather a rant about where she was, when a short Italian-looking man wearing a crisp white shirt, smart black trousers and shiny black loafers, appeared. Brooke detested loafers – as far as she was concerned they were the very pinnacle of un-cool. And the fact that his were shiny made them even worse. Plus the smart black trousers looked as if they were fresh from a trouser press. Reluctantly she put down her phone and stood up. Better look as if she was making some kind of effort, even when she was wondering what the fuck she was doing here.

'You must be Brooke.'

Wow, they bred them intelligent here. She moved the gum to the side of her mouth and hoped Shiny Shoes hadn't noticed.

'Yep, good to meet you . . .' Shit, she'd forgotten his name already! Fortunately Waiter Guy was standing behind the manager and mouthed 'Marco'.

'Good to meet you, Marco.' Brooke tried to sound as if she actually meant that.

'So have you done any waitressing before?'

Brooke hadn't done a stroke of paid work in her life.

'Nope, but I've eaten out a lot, and I figure how hard can it be? I can do all that "Hi, my name is Brooke and I'll be your waitress today. What can I get for you?"'

She grinned at them both, rather pleased with the cheerful tone she had managed to put on, even if it did sound fake.

However, neither Marco nor Waiter Guy seemed at all impressed.

'Well, being a waitress is probably a lot harder than you think,' Marco replied. 'I'm surprised your mother didn't talk to you about it. How is Liberty, by the way? Tell her I said hello.' He kind of went all dewy-eyed then and Brooke guessed he had the hots for her mom. Gross.

'She's good, thanks,' Brooke replied, resisting the temptation to roll her eyes.

Marco glanced at her shorts, and frowned. 'And I expect all my waiting staff to wear smart black trousers – not jeans – and a white shirt. This is a respectable family restaurant. Long hair must be tied back and any make up must be discreet. And absolutely no chewing gum.'

Damn, she'd thought he hadn't noticed.

'I start all my waiters on a one-month probation. So welcome to Paradiso, Brooke.'

Marco reached out his hand and reluctantly Brooke shook it. This did not seem like anything to celebrate. She felt as if she was making a pact with a devil in shiny black loafers . . .

'I must get on now. Flynn here is going to show you around. I'll see you on Saturday, Brooke – an hour

205

before your shift starts, to go through the basics. And please do remember to say hello from me to your mum.' With that he walked briskly away to talk to one of the diners.

Brooke pulled a face at Flynn. 'I got off to a fantastic start, didn't I?'

He nodded. 'You said it. Come on then, I'll give you the grand tour. Just try not to give the chefs a heart attack with those shorts.'

Waiter Guy was commenting on her outfit? 'What's wrong with them?'

'I don't have a problem with them at all, but in fairness to Marco, you're not hanging out on the beach and not everyone wants an eyeful of your bum with their pizza.' He glanced at her behind. 'However peachy it is.'

Was he flirting with her? He could jog on.com! No one who worked as a waiter could possibly be Brooke's type. She didn't stop to consider that she was about to start work as a waitress.

'Okay. Whatever.'

Another grin. 'You're American, right? Where are you from?'

He'd spotted the accent, what a genius!

She sighed theatrically. 'I'm from LA, living here now.' She paused. 'But LA's my real home, this is just a temporary move.'

'No need to sound so down about it. Brighton's a really cool place, and from all I've heard LA is full of fakes. Fake people with fake bodies. Isn't it, like, the plastic surgery capital of the world?' Flynn stretched back the skin from the side of his face. 'All those people with cat faces after they've OD'd on surgery. Man, I feel sorry for them. Their lives must be so shallow and dull.'

He might look cute, but he was annoying and he

knew *nothing* about things that mattered to Brooke.
'Ever been?' she asked.

'Nope – never want to go either.'

'Well, probably best not to judge somewhere until you've actually visited.' It cost her some effort to sound polite when really she wanted to flip him the finger for daring to criticise her home.

Flynn seemed to want to say something else, but the look on Brooke's face stopped him. Instead he took her round the restaurant and kitchen. She smiled and said 'hi' to all the other waiters, chefs and kitchen staff he introduced her to, but felt more and more miserable at the prospect of working here. This was so not how she wanted to spend her Saturdays. She'd thought things couldn't get any worse when she'd left LA, but it seemed they could.

'So are you going to college here?' Flynn asked, once they'd gone through the menu together and he'd checked that she knew what everything was. Like, doh, she could actually read! The dishes here were hardly the height of culinary sophistication. Basically some kind of pasta with some kind of sauce, or a pizza with some kind of topping. She was used to eating out at top LA restaurant Koi with its mouth-watering Asian fusion cuisine, and ordering her favourite dishes of soft-shell crab and ponzu sauce or miso-bronzed black cod. She almost wanted to cry, thinking of it. When would she be back there again?

'Yeah, it's called Chester College or something. I'm taking drama and English literature.'

'Hey, that's where I'm going, and I'm doing drama as well. And so's Mila, the other waitress you met.'

Mila the fat girl? Who looked as if she spent all her spare time scoffing garlic bread, the kind that came with melted mozzarella on top, as if bread wasn't

207

calorific enough on its own? Was Brooke supposed to crack a smile over that? She would be hanging out with a cute waiter guy and a fat waitress. Wowzah! How the other students would envy her . . . And okay, she could admit that Flynn was good-looking, but definitely not her type. No, absolutely not. How could she ever have any respect for anyone who didn't like LA?

'Great,' she managed to say. 'Well, thanks so much for the tour. It was a real eye-opener. Who knew that restaurant kitchens were so exciting? You know when those guys were tossing the pizza dough in the air? It was like a move from Cirque du Soleil. And their skill with the knives when they were chopping up onions – awesome! But my personal favourite was the bin area. It was exactly what I would imagine a bin area to look like – not that I've ever wasted any time imagining it.' She couldn't help sounding sarcastic.

'Do you actually want this job?' Flynn asked. 'Because it doesn't exactly sound like you do.'

How could she begin to answer that? With another helping of sarcasm.

'It was always one of my main ambitions in life to wait tables. You know, from a really young age. Most little girls dream of being a princess and wearing a beautiful dress. I dreamed of being a waitress and wearing a pair of cheap black trousers and, well, waiting on people.'

Flynn shook his head. 'Believe me, you won't be doing it here for long with that attitude.'

God, he sounded so serious. Lighten up!

'Are you related to the owner or something?'

'No, but I like Marco, and we all work as a team here.'

It was tempting to make another sarcastic comment, *Team Loser* sprang to mind, but even Brooke realised it was time to stop. 'Sure, I'm sorry. It's been a bit of a culture shock coming here. And that's an under-statement. So I guess I'll see you Saturday.'

'Actually you'll see me tomorrow, there's an induction morning at college.'

She felt like banging her head against a wall. Her life just got better and better.

Chapter 25

Liberty had a meeting with her new agent in London and left the house early the following day or she might have had something to say about Brooke's choice of outfit for her first day at college: skintight black wet-look leggings, spike-heeled ankle boots, leopard-print vest and her black leather biker jacket, worn with fake eyelashes, a ton of black eyeliner and pink-glossed lips. With any luck Waiter Boy Flynn wouldn't recognise her and Brooke could make some cooler friends. People who would be sympathetic to her for having to live in a dump like this, and who shared her love of all things LA. There must be someone like that? Please God, let there be someone like that . . .

She didn't have enough money for a taxi and nor did she think she could cycle in her heels so she took the bus. The driver very nearly didn't let her on as she only had a £20 note and he claimed not to have any change. Her LA self would have said, Keep the freaking change! Then again, her LA self wouldn't have been on a freaking bus in the freaking first place! This was only the third time she had ever been on public transport. In LA she either drove herself or took a taxi. And she actually needed the change from that £20 note; she didn't have any other money.

The college was an imposing red-brick building, much larger than Brooke had realised. And what she also quickly realised was that while her boots were fabulous for posing in at parties, which she was whisked to in a limo, they were much less fabulous for actually walking any distance in. As she tottered precariously along corridor after corridor, trying to find the class where she was supposed to be meeting her drama tutor and fellow students, she looked enviously at the groups of girls who passed her, in their skinny jeans and Converse.

She stopped for a minute to rest, and pretended to be checking her phone. By now her feet were killing her. Every step was sheer torture – her toes felt as if they were being squeezed in a vice, and she could feel blisters popping up on her heels. She would need a major pedicure after this.

Someone said her name and she looked up to see Waiter Boy Flynn with Mila. Damn, the last two people she had wanted to run into.

'Wow, those boots are wicked, are they Louboutins?' Mila gushed. She had been like this at the restaurant, full of questions for Brooke and ceaseless compliments.

Brooke raised her foot and showed off the iconic red sole. 'Sure are. I'd never wear fakes.'

'Lucky that you can afford them,' Mila said ruefully, looking down at her own battered grey suede ankle boots that looked as if they'd seen better days.

God, the girl had no taste! She was wearing a shapeless black sweatshirt and a pair of grey leggings that did nothing for her figure. 'Curvy' would have been the polite way of describing it; 'fat' a more accurate description. In her place Brooke wouldn't have left the house without wearing a full Spanx body stocking, sucking everything in. Then again she would never have allowed herself to get that fat in the first place. Some people had no self-respect. Mila had a pretty enough face, Brooke supposed, but let herself down with her bleached blonde hair, cut in some kind of jagged bob with shocking trailer park roots. No one could get away with such bad hair, never mind someone with Mila's body issues.

'Can you actually walk in those boots, though?' Flynn asked. Trust him to ask a question like that.

'They're really comfortable,' Brooke lied as they continued along the corridor, Flynn closely observing her painfully slow progress.

'Yep, they look it. You should watch it, wearing shoes like that. My aunt ended up with bunions because she wore such high heels when she was a teenager. She had the ugliest feet . . . like something out of a horror film. All the kids would scream and run away if she ever took her shoes off. Revenge of the Killer Bunions. Then she had to have them removed – the bunions, that is, not her feet – and now she has to wear flat shoes for ever.'

That was so not going to happen to Brooke. 'I don't wear shoes like this all the time, and I have not got ugly feet,' she said through gritted teeth. Why was he saying all these mean things to her?

'No, I'm sure everything about you is perfect in every possible way,' Flynn replied, not particularly nicely Brooke felt.

'I'm sure it is,' Mila put in kindly. 'You're soooo pretty.'

If only Brooke could return the compliment. 'Thanks,' she muttered.

'So do you want to be an actor? You've definitely got the looks for it,' Mila continued enthusiastically. 'I bet the camera loves you. I could only ever get character roles – I'm not leading lady material, I'd always have to be the fat funny one.'

There wasn't really an answer to that last comment as Mila was spot on . . . so Brooke ignored it. Mila might not be her kind of person but she didn't want to hurt her feelings.

'Yep, being an actor is all I've ever wanted to do. If I had my way I'd skip college and go straight to drama school. But my mom's hung up on the whole college thing. I don't know why, she never went and she's a really successful actor.'

'Is she?' Mila said excitedly. 'What's her name? I'll have to Google her.' She whipped out her phone in anticipation. Did she have, like, no idea how to play it cool? She could at least have waited until she got home. That's what Brooke would have done.

'She's called Liberty Evans.'

'Maybe do it after the meeting?' Flynn suggested, as if embarrassed for his friend. But Mila had already accessed images of Liberty and exclaimed, 'Oh my God! She's absolutely beautiful!' She held up her phone for Flynn to see.

He whistled in appreciation, and Brooke was torn between feeling proud that her mom was such a beauty and jealous at the response her picture had provoked. Mila thought Brooke was pretty, while her mom was beautiful. She would have preferred it to be the other way round . . . Brooke sulked all the rest of the way, giving Mila monosyllabic answers in reply to her many questions about what Liberty had been in and what she was doing now.

Their drama teacher, Ms Wilson, seemed nice enough, though Brooke found the whole introduce-yourself-to-the-class an exercise in cringe. And far from seeing anyone who looked like a kindred spirit, everyone there was as casually dressed as Mila and Flynn. Minimal if any make up, no designer labels she revered. Everyone looked so scruffy in their unimaginative uniform of jeans and trainers. And did these people not have orthodontists? She had never seen so many crooked or less than perfect teeth in one room in all her life! She had always thought it was a stereotype that Brits had bad teeth. Apparently not. Brooke had spent years wearing a brace to straighten hers, still slept in a retainer at night to ensure they stayed perfectly straight, and regularly had them bleached. Everyone she knew in LA had done the same. Maybe there was a mass shortage of dentists in the UK. There had to be some reason for the snaggled, greyish horrors she saw before her. Or maybe they all thought it would help them get parts in some period drama where bad teeth were the norm . . .

She was just daydreaming that she was back home in LA when the door opened and in walked an absolutely drop-dead gorgeous guy. Hallelujah! That's what she was talking about! Brooke watched him saunter across the room, apologising for being late with an easy charm. Perfect features, check; immaculately styled brown hair, check; sexy, bad boy grin, check. Gorgeous body, shown to maximum advantage in a tight white t-shirt, black skinny jeans and silver-studded black belt round his slim waist. Check! She could tell the clothes were designer, check! Brooke immediately sat up straighter, stuck out her chest and shook back her long blonde hair, willing him to notice her. For good measure, she rifled through her bag and quickly spritzed on some more perfume. Maybe college was going to be bearable after all.

She noticed Flynn looking across at her, as if he

knew exactly what she was up to, and felt slightly self-conscious. But when Good-looking came and sat next to her (yay!), she immediately flashed him her most winning smile and said confidently, 'Hi, I'm Brooke.'

'Hi, I'm Harry. Love the jacket, is it Balmain?'

He knew the designer! He really wasn't like the others in their grungy baggy jeans and hoodies. And he had good teeth! In fact, he had perfect, white, shining teeth! He had American teeth! Brooke's smile got wider. She was itching to carry on talking, or rather flirting, but Ms Wilson was in full flow so Brooke dragged her eyes away from Harry. He even smelled gorgeous, of a lovely citrus aftershave. Could be a Dior or Gucci, she mused. Definitely not Hugo Boss, which was what that bastard Christian had worn. No, no, back to happy thoughts. Harry – that was a nice name, the same as that hot royal prince she had always fancied, even more so when he got caught out playing strip billiards in Vegas and she and Kelly had Googled all the pictures.

She didn't get another chance to talk to him until the session finished and they were all spilling out of the room.

'So where are you from?' Harry asked.

'LA . . . Santa Monica.'

'Oh my God! I so want to go there! And all those iconic places – Chateau Marmont, the Hollywood sign, Rodeo Drive! And Santa Monica is supposed to have such a cool, stylish vibe. I've always wanted to go to Venice Beach.' He seemed genuinely thrilled; there was no trace of Flynn's judgmental bullshit.

She beamed at him. A kindred spirit at last!

'So why are you over here? If I lived in Santa Monica, I swear I'd never leave. Well, maybe to go to my apartment in New York or my estate on Martha's

Vineyard. Oh, and I suppose I might have a house in the Hamptons for holidays. And then I'd have to go skiing at Aspen, I suppose. But I'd always go back to LA. It would be, like, my lodestar.'

Yay! These were some of Brooke's most favourite places as well!

'My mom's English and she was brought up in Brighton. She split up with my stepdad a few weeks ago and wanted to move back home. A fresh start, I guess.'

Harry pulled a sympathetic face, as if he totally got how tough that was for her.

'Never mind, sweetie, I'll show you all the cool places here. And we're not far from London, which I always think can hold its own against New York. It really won't be as bad as you think.'

He was adorable!

'D'you have any brothers or sisters, Brooke?' Mila piped up then.

'Nope, I'm an only child.'

'That's a pity,' Mila said cheekily. 'I bet any brother of yours would be stunning.'

Like any brother of Brooke's would be interested in someone who thought grey sweatpants were a fashion statement! And who needed to drop at least four dress sizes, get her hair done, and buy an entire new wardrobe of clothes! Though in fairness Mila did have quite good teeth, by comparison to everyone else.

'We're going to have some lunch – there's a great café nearby,' she continued.

'Oh, I don't usually have lunch,' Brooke replied. 'I have to really watch what I eat, if I'm going to make it as an actor.'

Instantly Mila went bright red, and Brooke was aware of Flynn giving her the stink eye. She hadn't meant to upset Mila. She couldn't help it if the girl had zero self-control. And if you wanted to act, it was important to realise that it was a brutal world where looks were everything . . .

'It's really unhealthy to skip meals,' Flynn muttered. And Brooke was tempted to say, *So what? So long as it keeps me slim!* But thought better of it. And she didn't want to bicker in front of Harry. It hardly said sexy, hot new girl. It was just that there was something about Flynn that made her want to provoke him. And he clearly felt the same way.

'Oh, come with us, Brooke,' Harry put in. 'You can always have a Diet Coke.'

'Yeah, that's really nutritious. Maybe she could chew on the ice cubes and suck a slice of lemon, or would that be too many calories?' That from Flynn, who continued, 'Maybe just tap water then, though I'm betting you don't drink anything but mineral water. You probably bathe in Evian, don't you?'

Brooke wanted to retaliate that she had only ever washed her face in Evian one time at summer camp when there was a problem with the water supply. And as for not drinking tap water, that was just a sensible precaution. But she didn't want to spark a row with Flynn and hadn't realised that the gorgeous Harry was friends with these two – she'd better rethink her strategy.

'Sure, lunch would be great. Why not? I haven't got any other plans.' She hadn't intended the comment to sound so dismissive, but Flynn burst out laughing. 'Are you always this rude? You'd better tone it down when you start working at Marco's or you'll end up with no tips.'

Crap! She hadn't wanted Harry to know that she was going to be waiting tables; it hardly went with the achingly cool image she was hoping to project.

But Harry didn't seem at all bothered. 'When I come and eat there I'll give you a big fat tip, sweetie,' he told her. 'Anyway I bet you'll get loads of tips – the pretty ones always do. Learn from Flynn. He has a special smile for the older ladies and gay gentlemen, to ensure they tip him well. It works like a dream every time. Don't be taken in by him pretending to be all holier than thou. He's an absolute tart and knows perfectly well how to use his good looks.'

Flynn rolled his eyes at that, but Brooke appreciated the way Harry had showed him up as well as the compliment to herself. It was just about the first one she'd received since arriving here. England, the place of bad teeth and rarely given compliments . . . No one had even told her to have a nice day when she bought coffee. No wonder everyone was so miserable here.

What they didn't mention was that the café was a fifteen-minute walk away on the seafront, and by the time they arrived there Brooke was hobbling. *So* not a good look.

'Are you okay, Brooke?' Flynn asked. 'You're walking strangely. Is it your bunions playing up?'

'For the last time – I haven't got bunions!' she shot back through gritted teeth. But frankly she was ready to chuck her designer boots in the bin; her feet were in agony.

However, she was pleasantly surprised by the café with its choice of smoothies, juices and delicious-looking salads, which almost looked as good as the ones in her favourite café in Santa Monica . . . almost. And the sun was actually shining. And there were even some people rollerblading by, and others running. It wasn't quite Venice Beach – there was no expanse of golden sand for a start, just banks of brown and

218

orange shingle – but it wasn't so bad either. And maybe it wouldn't hurt if she had a salad. She'd skipped breakfast and was starving.

The boys, lucky things, could eat whatever they wanted and ordered burgers and fries that looked and smelled so tempting. Ketchup and fries were one of Brooke's guilty pleasures, that she allowed herself once a month, but she wasn't going to tell them that. Mila ordered a salad like Brooke. She would probably sneak off to Krispy Kreme Doughnuts later, Brooke thought bitchily. And then felt guilty as Mila had been kind to her, which was more than could be said for Flynn.

She surreptitiously unzipped her boots and slipped them off. Her feet were actually throbbing. She would have to walk back home barefoot at this rate. Mila, Harry and Flynn clearly knew each other very well; they had been to secondary school together, which Brooke assumed was like high school. They bantered easily with each other, Flynn taking the piss out of Harry who admitted that his new Prada sunglasses cost over £150.

'But what's the point of buying cheap stuff?' Brooke spoke up. 'It never lasts. It's much better to make an investment purchase. And it's better for the environment too because more expensive things don't get thrown away.' She smiled, rather proud of herself for that last comment. *See*, she wanted to say to Flynn, *I'm not the airhead you think I am. I think about things. I have opinions.*

It didn't go down well with him. 'Not everyone can afford to make "investment purchases". You're clearly only working at the restaurant to get a bit of extra pocket money – no doubt to buy some more uncomfortable designer shoes – but some people have to live off those wages, run a home, bring up a family. Do you even have any idea what the minimum wage is?'

'Not enough, I know,' Brooke muttered. She *hated* being criticised and couldn't think of a smart comeback.

'She doesn't need a lecture, Flynn, it's her first day, don't be mean to the new girl,' Harry spoke up for her. 'Play nice.'

'Okay. Right. Sorry,' Flynn managed, not sounding especially sincere in his apology.

Brooke pushed her salad round on her plate. He obviously didn't like her and she felt awkward around him. She was used to people *adoring* her. Flynn's less-than-adoring attitude was completely unsettling and made her feel even more homesick.

'So where are you living?' Mila asked her.

'Oh, just along the seafront, you know, beyond the lagoon.' She gestured vaguely in that direction.

'Oh my God! You live in that row of houses with their own private beach! I have always, *always* wanted to see what they look like inside! They are so glam. Have you met any celebrities yet? Zoe Ball and Fat Boy Slim live along there, you know,' Harry exclaimed excitedly.

He and Flynn were like a positive and negative charge. She knew which one she preferred.

Brooke rewarded him with a beaming smile. 'Well, you'll have to come over and check it out.' Shit, she didn't want them all to come, but it would look bad if she didn't extend the invitation. 'You all will. I'll fix something up. The place is in a bit of a mess at the moment because we haven't unpacked.' She thought of her bedroom with clothes strewn all over it, the half-empty coffee cups she had abandoned, the cans of Diet Coke spilling out of the bin. Her way of saying to her mom that she hated living there. No, she didn't want them to see that – it would just confirm Flynn's opinion that she was some rich brat.

'Don't you have staff to tidy up?' he asked. She guessed it was a question designed to show up how spoiled she was, but frankly she didn't care what he thought, so answered flippantly, 'Not any more. We used to in LA. I mean, OMG, only this morning I actually had to squeeze toothpaste on my own toothbrush myself! And then, would you believe, I had to run my own bath, and make my own bed? It was exhausting *and* I nearly broke a nail doing it. I'm going to have to speak to my mom about the slave-labour conditions she's keeping me in . . . I mean, there are laws about that, aren't there?'

Flynn rolled his eyes, while Harry asked if she'd had a chef in LA. 'I think having a chef must be the sign you've really made it. And when I've reached that stage, I either want a chef or to have all my food delivered.'

Brooke had to admit that they'd had a housekeeper who cooked, a gardener and a chauffeur, and a stylist for when they needed outfits for one of Zac's film industry parties, and a personal trainer . . . She had intended to sound flippant but mentioning Rosa almost made her eyes fill with tears – Brooke missed her so much. She had tried to keep in touch, sending Rosa texts and pictures, but she wasn't the best correspondent and her replies were always frustratingly brief. Brooke guessed she was busy with work and her own family. She picked up her phone and found a picture of Rosa and herself, holding it up for the others to see.

'This is Rosa, she was our housekeeper and my unofficial nanny. I've known her all my life.'

'She looks nice,' Flynn commented, giving her a sympathetic look. 'You must really miss her.'

Shit! Brooke actually had a lump in her throat as she nodded then looked away, not wanting him to see how upset she was.

'Poor you, leaving all that behind. But I'm sure you'll have it all again,' Harry told her.

'No one could ever replace Rosa,' she said quietly.

Mila and Flynn had to leave after lunch as they had an extra shift at the restaurant so Brooke was left alone with Harry, something she was very happy about. He was dreamily good-looking, with such perfect skin, golden-brown as if he had been hanging out on Venice Beach, and lovely long eyelashes. She *had* to find out if he had a girlfriend. She really hoped not, though maybe even if he did, he might realise that she, Brooke, was a much better option . . . She didn't like girls who went after other girls' boyfriends – that slut Taylor, for example – but this was something of an emergency. She was currently in Dullsville and badly needed to get out. Fingers crossed, Harry was going to be her exit pass.

However, the topic didn't come up. Instead he wanted to know everything about her life in LA, and Brooke found herself talking to him about her favourite stores and restaurants, what her house had been like, her friend Kelly, her acting ambitions. It was lovely at first chatting about those things, but eventually it added to her feelings of homesickness. And while Harry had been very attentive, and interested in every single thing she had to say, hanging on her words in fact, she wasn't sure she could detect any chemistry between them. She couldn't, hand on heart, say that he had flirted with her. Sure, he called her sweetie and darling and princess and angel, but she had heard him call Mila those things too. Maybe he was a slow burn . . . But then he asked Brooke what she was doing on Sunday night.

'There's a new Julia Roberts film out . . . I just love her, don't you? And we could get some dinner somewhere afterwards. There's a divine sushi restaurant I know. Okay, it won't be up to LA standards, but sushi is so good for you, isn't it? So healthy. I never feel bloated after I've had it.'

He was obviously asking her out on a date! Brooke gave him her most dazzling megawatt smile, one that Julia Roberts herself would have been proud of.

'I would love to! Thank you!'

And as if to seal the deal he kissed her on both cheeks when they said goodbye. 'You smell delicious!' he exclaimed. 'What's that perfume?'

'It's a Tom Ford private blend. Santal Blush.'

'You're a goddess, Brooke! I'm so glad you've moved here. You can transform our humdrum lives. We need your LA glamour sprinkled over us like fairy dust. You're like a dream come true!'

The image seemed a little over the top . . . All the same, she couldn't wait to see Harry again. At last some excitement and flirtation to brighten up her tedious dead-end life.

Brooke was still smiling when she arrived home, and spent the rest of the afternoon unpacking her clothes and tidying her room without Liberty having to nag her for once. And when her mom returned from London they actually had a conversation where they spoke politely to each other, Brooke didn't resort to shouting and swearing and Liberty didn't look upset. No, instead they ate supper together, and Brooke didn't feel like throwing her plate of grilled salmon and steamed vegetables on the floor and storming upstairs in a huff. It made a pleasant change. Being so angry all the time was exhausting and boring.

'I'm so glad you seem a little happier, honey. I know this move is a big deal for you,' Liberty said, when they settled down in the living room together to watch an episode of *Dexter*.

'I wouldn't go so far as saying happier . . .' Brooke muttered. 'But I'm trying to make the best of it. Anyway, it won't be for ever. Once I've been to college and drama school, I'll go straight back to LA. It's where I need to be to fulfil my potential, I just know it. You understand how important contacts are, and hopefully by then Zac won't be so angry with you and will consider hiring me.'

The expression on Liberty's face said that she didn't share her daughter's optimistic view, but she tactfully changed the subject.

'And we should start thinking about your eighteenth birthday party. I want you to have something special. Eighteen is a real milestone birthday.'

It was only six weeks away and Brooke supposed her mom was right. She couldn't get too excited about it, though, not now she lived here. In LA there had been talk of Zac hiring a room at the legendary Chateau Marmont . . . Oh my God! She would have absolutely loved that! It would have been the most talked about party *ever*. But she was willing to bet Brighton didn't offer the equivalent, and her mom wouldn't have Zac's budget.

'Would you like to have it here at the house or I could hire a club? Or maybe we could have a themed marquee in the grounds of a hotel somewhere?' Liberty looked so pleased at the prospect of organising something for her. Only a day ago Brooke would instantly have wanted to rain on her parade, but now she had Harry to cheer her up. And a party would be an ideal way of letting Brighton know that she had arrived . . . and a great way to impress her new classmates, especially Harry.

'I think here would be good – everyone's really interested in seeing the house. Maybe I could have a fancy dress party? The twenties theme is hot right now, isn't it?' Already she was imagining herself in a beautiful, gold sequined dress and headdress, stunning all her guests as she sauntered down the impressive staircase after pausing for maximum effect. And Harry would look incredible in a tuxedo . . . They would easily be the most glamorous couple in the room. Everyone would be looking at them as they danced together . . .

'Whatever you want, honey, you know I only want you to be happy.'

Brooke was tempted to reply that if her mom *really* wanted that, then they would never have left LA, but she didn't want to spoil the moment.

Chapter 26

As the week went on Brooke was actually thinking that things were beginning to look up for her. She was enjoying college and loving her drama course. She had made some friends, she had an actual date and she was getting on better with Liberty. That was until Saturday when she had to go to work. As she had predicted the restaurant was packed with a constant stream of diners. She began her shift at five o'clock and worked practically non-stop until her break at nine. By then she was exhausted, and still had two more hours to go. Customers were so demanding! So rude! She'd had to bite her tongue so many times when they didn't even bother to say thank you after she put their food down in front of them. And even in her conservative white shirt and black trousers she had still noticed a few of the men leering at her. Men with wives and children, who definitely should have known better. She suddenly saw exactly why Marco hadn't wanted her to wear shorts.

She leaned against the wall outside the restaurant and sipped her Dict Coke. Big Bruno the chef (she didn't know why he was called that as he was beanpole skinny, maybe it was the Brits with their ironic sense of humour) had offered her a bowl of spaghetti bolognese and some garlic bread, which Brooke had politely turned down. She was regretting that decision now, as she was starving and must have burned up, like, hundreds of calories racing round the restaurant. It was more tiring than going on the StairMaster at the gym or doing a kick boxing class. Her arms ached from lugging the heavy plates around, and her legs ached from rushing from table to table, her feet hurt from standing up all the time, and she was even wearing flat shoes!

'How's it going?' Flynn asked, joining her outside for his break.

'Honestly? I had no idea how exhausting it was,' Brooke confessed. He had been kind to her during the night, helped her out with a couple of tables when she couldn't carry everything. Maybe he wasn't so bad after all.

'Bet you're glad you're not wearing your pointy boots?'

She rolled her eyes. 'Yeah.' She didn't know if she would ever be able to wear her pointy boots again, which was a shame because she knew that Harry liked them and she wanted to wear something impressive for their date. Maybe her crystal-encrusted Louboutins? Or was that a bit much for Brighton on a Sunday night? She had no idea. She wished she had a girlfriend like Kelly over here to advise her, but Mila didn't exactly look as if she knew anything about fashion.

'So what other plans have you got for the weekend?' Flynn asked.

'Chilling out tomorrow in the day and then I'm meeting Harry. We're seeing a movie together.' Brooke lowered her eyes, not wanting to let on how thrilled she was. 'So, I was wondering . . . does he have a girlfriend?' It seemed incredible that someone as eligible as Harry could be single. She crossed her fingers behind her back.

Flynn shook his head. 'Nope.' He paused. 'Why, have you got your eye on him?'

'No, I just wondered.' She knew she was blushing – she was such a bad liar. Liberty always knew when she wasn't telling the truth. Brooke just couldn't seem to use her acting ability when it came to her own life; apparently it was something she had in common with her mom.

'I suppose he would be your type,' Flynn mused. 'All those designer clothes, the spray tan, the bleached teeth, the obsession with his looks. Man, he's vain! He can't pass a mirror or a window without checking out his appearance.' He didn't actually say 'shallow' but Brooke was pretty sure it was included in the list.

'I thought you were meant to be his friend?'

'I am, but he is really vain. We went camping one year at secondary school and he spent ages doing his hair. Every single morning he'd get up extra early so he could style it, which was pointless because we would then spend the entire day canoeing, or wading through streams, or doing obstacle courses in mud. I swear if he was drowning, his first thought would be about the state of his hair. Justin Bieber has nothing on him.'

Hmm, that didn't exactly sound sexy, or especially manly, but Brooke could sympathise. She too spent ages doing her hair every morning. And a bad hair day could seriously interfere with her mood.

'There's nothing wrong in wanting to look good,' she muttered, once again feeling that Flynn was criticising her.

'Sure, but it doesn't have to take over your entire life.'

228

Mila wandered out at that point, which was a relief as Brooke didn't want any more judgmental comments from Flynn, thank you very much. As soon as Mila saw her she smiled warmly. 'First shift is always full on, isn't it? You'll soon get used to it. You looked like you were doing really well.'

'I don't mind the hard work but it's the way hardly anyone says thank you. I mean, *hello*, I'm a person too, I do have feelings.'

'I know, it used to drive me mad. Now I don't even notice – in fact, it's almost a shock if someone is polite back to me.'

'Maybe you should look at how you welcome people, Brooke,' Flynn commented. 'I saw that you looked a bit moody. If you smile, you get a better response.'

There he went again!

'I'm perfectly polite! I'm working in a low-key Italian, not fucking Nobu!'

'It shouldn't matter where you are, you should treat everyone the same.' Flynn again.

Ahhhhh! Enough! She clapped her hands over her ears. 'Oh my God, Flynn, you sound like my mom. Change the fucking record, can't you? I get enough abuse at home.'

She waited for him to come back with yet another put down. Instead he spoke to Mila. 'Brooke's going on a date with Harry tomorrow night.'

'Really?' She seemed surprised. 'A date date?'

'Yeah. Brooke wanted to know if Harry had a girlfriend, but I told her he doesn't. Does he?'

'I don't want to piss anyone off,' Brooke added. She glared at Flynn. 'I'll save that for work.' Every time she thought they might actually be getting on, he went and blew it with some dig at her. Honestly, he was infuriating.

'No, Harry definitely hasn't got a girlfriend,' Mila replied, looking slightly awkward. 'But—'

Flynn interrupted her, 'I'm sure he and Brooke will have a great time. They have so much in common. They can talk LA all night for a start. You'll be in your element, Brooke.'

Mila still looked awkward, but Brooke put that down to Flynn being a general pain in the ass. And then her pathetically short break was over and she was back in the restaurant, once more at everyone else's beck and call.

'Enjoy your date with Harry,' Flynn told her at the end of the night as she was wearily getting into a taxi – her mom was paying otherwise she would have been eating into her wages and might as well not have bothered to work her butt off for the last six and a half hours.

Did his comment sound ironic or was it Brooke's imagination? It was impossible for her to tell from Flynn's English accent. The people around her might be speaking English, but sometimes it didn't seem like the same language to her.

'Thanks. I will,' she replied.

Brooke spent most of Sunday afternoon getting ready, giving herself a face mask, a hair treatment, painting her finger and toe nails – usually she'd have had a trip to the beauty salon to get it all done, but that was in her other life. She sucked at painting her own nails. She got most of the red varnish on her toes – *so* not a good look. It took her a good two hours to decide what to wear, as she tried on outfit after outfit and then rejected it. In the end she went for her Roberto Cavalli mini dress, with its striking exotic flower print, worn with a shocking blue biker jacket. And she couldn't resist wearing her Louboutins – fortunately they had been unscathed by their collision with her bedroom wall . . . that was quality for you . . . they really were an investment piece.

'Don't you think you're a bit too glammed up for a night at the cinema?' Liberty commented as Brooke sashayed into the living room like a model on a runway. 'The Odeon isn't exactly like Grauman's Chinese Theater with the handprints of the stars outside it. There's more likely to be a pool of sick and a pile of cigarette ends.'

Brooke rolled her eyes. 'Thanks a lot, Mom!' She was about to go upstairs and change into her jeans when the phone rang – her taxi was there already, and she was running late. She didn't want Harry to think that she wasn't interested, when she was *very* interested.

However, when the taxi pulled up outside the Odeon, a staggeringly ugly seventies-style building with a series of what looked like dirty glass pyramids dumped on the top of it, she realised that her mom had been right. She was totally wearing the wrong outfit. She picked her way carefully along the pavement, skirting one splatter of vomit and a sinister-looking stain, which was possibly, dried blood. Yuck! She wouldn't put her hands on this pavement if you paid her! You'd need to have a tetanus and Hep B jab immediately afterwards.

Harry was waiting for her in the foyer, the very unglamorous foyer, where her shoes crunched on the spilled popcorn that littered the floor. Thankfully he had made an effort, wearing a pair of white jeans and a black shirt, and he looked even more tanned. Maybe he'd had a fake tan in her honour? Flynn would have thought that incredibly vain, but it was okay with Brooke. More than okay in fact, it showed that he wanted to impress.

'Brooke! You look gorgeous! So stylish! So Hollywood!' He reached out and held both her hands while he considered the dress. 'So overdressed for here! I feel like you need a red carpet. And there definitely isn't one here, sweetie.'

They both burst out laughing.

'So do you want anything to eat? A box of popcorn? A delicious hot dog with some mustard and onion relish? Nachos? Some pick-and-mix? So many delicacies to choose from, I hardly know where to begin!' He grinned at her.

'*Please!* Do you know how many calories are in those things?'

'I was joking. I've got something better.' He patted his jacket pocket and whispered, 'A hipflask of vodka and Diet Coke. Zero calories in that, sweetie.'

'Yummy, that is my kind of drink.'

'So how was your first shift?'

She shrugged. 'Just about bearable, I guess. I'm hoping if I do it without complaining for the next couple of weeks, my mom will say I can give it up. She's trying to make the point that I was spoiled in LA.'

'Poor you, I can't imagine you in such a place. It's all wrong, you're wasted on those diners, like pearls before swine. Still, at least you're with Mila and Flynn, and they're great.'

He seemed so enthusiastic that it wasn't the moment for her to say that she wasn't at all sure she liked Flynn.

Upstairs they settled down in their seats, after Harry had taken a few minutes to decide where he wanted to be. 'I have to have the absolute perfect view of Julia,' he told Brooke, who frankly didn't care where they sat.

Throughout the trailers she was hoping that Harry would make some kind of move, give a sign that he was interested in her, but while he handed her the hipflask and kept up a stream of witty comments about the upcoming films, there was nothing she could interpret as flirtation. She inched her legs closer to his, but when his thigh accidentally touched hers, he immediately apologised and moved it away. It was very frustrating! She didn't understand why he was being so reserved. He didn't seem like the shy type, and he had said all those lovely things about her.

A trailer came on for the new Colin Farrell film and now Harry clutched her arm. 'Oh my God! I so would, wouldn't you? I totally fucking love him! I know he's probably too old for me, but it's those eyes. Well, actually those biceps as well . . . and those abs . . . and, oh, everything!'

Him. He had definitely said him. It was all becoming clear to Brooke now. Harry's immaculate appearance, his knowledge of designer clothes . . . the fact that Flynn and Mila had given her such strange looks when she had told them that she was going out on a date with Harry. Fuck! They must both be pissing themselves laughing! How could she have got it so spectacularly wrong? She'd always thought she had good gaydar . . . apparently not. What a loser! She thought of the afternoon she had wasted, getting ready for her big date. Her big date with a gay man.

'I always think that Flynn looks a bit like him, it's those melting brown eyes . . . eyes you could lose yourself in,' Harry continued, oblivious to Brooke's inner turmoil. 'Flynn is so fit, isn't he? But straight. Oh, God! Why did he have to be straight? It's my tragedy. When we went camping with the school, we shared a tent. I was hoping for a *Brokeback Mountain* moment. I mean, I know he's straight, but there's always hope. But, no. He nipped out, leaving me all on my own, and copped off with Lacey Johnson. The lucky slag! She had a grin on her face the entire week. So did he.'

And there was the confirmation. For a moment Brooke considered flouncing out of the cinema. She felt ridiculous in her flirty dress and killer heels. But that would make the whole situation even more embarrassing.

'D'you really think he's fit? He's so arrogant and always acts like he's looking down at me.'

'I know. I love it! It's so sexy when he comes over all self-righteous, the way he does with you if you say anything he judges to be shallow.'

'Oh, that's everything I say then,' Brooke muttered.

'Don't look so serious! I reckon it's a defence mechanism and he secretly fancies the pants off you. He'll be in torment, knowing that he shouldn't really like someone like you but unable to resist the feeling. I can read that boy like a book, I've known him so long.'

'I really have no idea. Now vodka me up.' Brooke held out her hand for the hipflask. God knows, she needed a drink after that bombshell. Or five.

By the time the film was over – a feel-good rom-com that did actually make her feel better – Brooke was slightly tipsy, which thankfully numbed some of the embarrassment. Harry was so adorable, and such good company. She couldn't believe she hadn't realised he was gay. She supposed it was because she had so wanted to find an ally. Well, he could be her gay BF. If she was honest, she was still feeling bruised from her short and un-sweet romance with Christian. She needed a friend far more than a boyfriend. And so as they made their way to the sushi restaurant, she decided to come clean.

Harry laughed so much when she told him she had thought tonight was a date that they had to stop. He clutched her shoulders and bent double, trying to get his breath back.

'Darling, I can't believe you didn't realise! I'm camper than Christmas! But it's so sweet, and really, I'm flattered. You're a gorgeous beautiful girl, who deserves a gorgeous beautiful boy. But a straight one.'

'I'm such a fool.'

'You probably had jet lag. You were feeling homesick for LA.' He leaned in and kissed her on the cheek. 'But don't worry, your secret's safe with me.'

She believed him, but she hated to think of Flynn and Mila laughing at her mistake. Airhead LA girl falls for gay guy . . . She was certain that Flynn would absolutely love that. He would think it served her right for being so superficial.

Harry linked his arm through hers and they carried on walking. Now this was a novelty. In LA they would have driven to their next destination. No one walked. But this was kind of sweet, walking arm in arm by the sea and looking at the lights of Brighton Pier, flashing on and off. Okay, it wasn't as impressive as Santa Monica Pier, being considerably smaller, but it had a certain charm. And the Brighton wheel, slowly revolving and lit up in blue, looked pretty.

'Actually, could we play a little trick on Flynn about tonight?' she asked. 'I hate to think of him laughing at me. He's so superior.'

'What? Make out that you've converted me to all things straight?'

She nodded, not sure what Harry's reaction would be. But he rose to the challenge.

'That would be such a laugh! You're right, he does always act too cool for school. We could snog in front of him. Do you have that word in the States? FYI it means kiss. It will blow his mind. I've never actually kissed a girl, but I'll make an exception for you, sweet cheeks.'

'You never know, you might be like Katy Perry – kiss a girl and like it. I probably don't taste like cherry chapstick, but I did clean my teeth.' And flossed and gargled with mouthwash, hoping at the start of the night that she might end up kissing Harry, but not exactly like this.

He shook his head. 'Nah, that's not going to happen, but it'll be fun pretending.'

Chapter 27

Liberty

Liberty walked by the sea, looking out at the beach and the old ruined West Pier still hanging on in there, with the Palace Pier beyond it. Since moving back to Brighton, she couldn't get enough of this view. She had loved Santa Monica but in the end it had become tainted by the unhappiness of her marriage. But there were memories here as well, so many of them, crowding into her head. Of being with Cory on the beach, at his flat, in bed . . . Memories that haunted and tormented her with their bitter sweetness.

The thought of Cory living so close was tantalising. It seemed crazy after all these years and all that had happened, but she couldn't get him out of her head. Zac's comment about the letter from him had intensified that feeling.

Em was already installed at a table in the bar when Liberty arrived, and halfway through a large glass of white wine.

'I couldn't wait any longer,' she said, giving Liberty a hug. 'This has been the longest Sunday in the

237

history of the world! The kids have been so full on all day. Literally as soon as Noah walked in the door after football, I was out of there!'

Liberty smiled sympathetically, but really she envied Em her busy, full on family. She had always wanted to be part of one. Her marriage had never felt like that. Right from the start everything had to be controlled and ordered. Zac didn't like surprises, or noise, or mess, or anything that might upset his well-ordered life.

Em poured her a generous glass of wine. 'So, cheers, you've got some catching up to do.'

'Cheers.' Liberty clinked her glass against Em's. Being able to see her again was one of the very best things about coming back to Brighton. She had missed her so much when she was in Australia. Skype, Facebook and email came a poor second to knowing that her best friend was ten minutes away and they could meet up whenever they wanted.

'So how's Brooke? Not still dressing up to go to college as if she's about to strut her stuff on a catwalk?' Em had thought it was hilarious when Liberty told her about Brooke wearing her designer clothes on the first day.

Liberty smiled. 'No, thank God! And I didn't even have to say anything. She sussed out the dress code for herself. So now she wears jeans and Converse, like every other student – though typically her Converse are studded with crystals. She's gone out to the cinema with a boy tonight, so I hope she's getting on okay. She did get a little too dressed up for the Odeon.' Liberty doubted there were many other girls there in three-thousand-dollar Louboutins.

'Oh, bless her! She'll get used to the lifestyle here soon.'

'Yeah, and she seems so much happier now she's

238

made some friends and has her party to plan.' Liberty paused. 'I hope she doesn't blame me too much for taking her away from LA, but you have no idea what it was doing to her, Em. I felt I was losing my girl. She had become so spoiled and materialistic, only caring about shopping and looking good. And I felt guilty all the time because I knew I wasn't there enough for her. Now it feels like she's back with me again. We're actually having proper conversations.'

'She's a lovely girl and she'll be fine. And speaking of parties, did you get your invitation to Angel's? I literally cannot wait! At last, some excitement in my life. I can see it now: vintage champagne . . . say Cristal, delicious canapés, and Cal Bailey up close. Seriously he's the one man I would ever consider being unfaithful with, apart from Alexander Skarsgård. Obviously. Oh, and Ryan Gosling. And, I guess, Bradley Cooper.'

When she saw Liberty looking doubtful, Em explained, 'In my fantasy world, of course. Noah's fantasy fuck was Megan Fox, until she had a son called Noah, which kind of killed it. So now it's Clare Danes.'

'Ah, that's so sweet – you look a bit like her.' Em had always been the love of Noah's life, and Liberty could just imagine him choosing someone who resembled her.

'So who's yours?'

She shrugged. 'I really don't have one.' It was Cory, there was no one else she had ever fantasised about.

'Oh, come on! You must have. Everyone does. All those sexy actors you hung out with in LA. That sexy co-star of yours for a start . . . Jeff whatever his name was. He was hot to trot! Cute bum – I don't know how you resisted squeezing it every time you saw him. It is *so* squeezable!' Em actually mimed performing the action; she really did need to get out more.

'Actually he was gay and had no sense of humour. He would have seen any bum squeezing as a form of sexual harassment, and sued me. The sex scene we did together had to be the most awkward one I ever had to do.'

'Well, who then?'

When Liberty still insisted that she didn't think about anyone in particular, Em suddenly went quiet and then said, 'Oh my God – it's Cory, isn't it?'

'I'm so predictable, I know. Do you think one day I might be over him?'

She'd meant to say it lightly, but Em seemed to take it seriously. 'He's got an exhibition on in Brighton. I passed the gallery the other day. I was wondering whether to tell you or not. I didn't see him though.'

Instantly Liberty felt as if her heart was racing that little bit faster. So much for thinking she could keep it together if she ever saw Cory.

'Maybe you should try and meet up with him. It might be good for both of you. You never did get any – I hate that word – closure.'

It was what Liberty both longed for and yet feared. While they didn't see each other, she could pretend that there was still a chance that Cory might want her; that the rejection hadn't happened. She would rather keep the fantasy.

She shook her head. 'I doubt he'll want to see me again. If he really wanted to, he would have found me. I just hope that if we did see each other, we could be friends.' She sounded so grown up and sensible . . . Sounded it, didn't feel it.

'God, Libs, I don't know how you can say that! I know what he meant to you. I know he was the love of your life.'

Liberty twisted her mouth into a smile. 'Yeah,

well, I've had a lot of practice at dealing with it. And if someone left you waiting at the airport when you thought you were supposed to be starting a new life together . . . well, it's not something you really get over, or forget.' No, definitely not. Standing there in Departures, surrounded by her suitcases, looking hopefully towards the door and then realising as the minutes passed that Cory wasn't coming. Then calling him, only to hear his voicemail. And yet maybe the letter from him had explained why.

Em reached out and rubbed Liberty's shoulder. 'I know, but I just can't make that image fit the Cory I remember. I still think something must have happened.'

'Nothing happened, Em, just that he changed his mind.' She wasn't ready to tell her friend about the letter yet. She needed to work out what she wanted to do first.

'Oh, look, there's Nina.' Em waved at Liberty's mum as she walked into the bar.

Nina had said she would pop in for a quick one, on her way to meet up with a group of her friends who were planning to walk the Inca Trail next year. Liberty loved the fact that her mum was still so intrepid, and always seizing hold of life. She wouldn't approve of obsessing over someone, the way Liberty did.

While Em went off to the bar to get her a glass of red wine, Nina took out a large envelope and handed it to Liberty.

'What's this?' she asked.

'I was having a clear out and I found all these photographs. There are lots of Brooke and . . .' she hesitated '. . . Cory.'

There seemed to be no getting away from him tonight. Liberty reached inside and pulled out a pile of pictures. And as if to hammer home the point, the first she saw was one of her and Cory. They were standing on the beach together, arms round each other. Liberty vividly remembered being there with him – the feel of the sun on her face, the sea sparkling in the August sunshine, and thinking that she wanted to be with him always.

'Oh,' was all she could say. She shoved the pictures back in the envelope.

'Someone's in denial then,' Nina said dryly. 'You have got to see him, Libs. Find out once and for all where you stand. Otherwise you'll be stuck. Never moving on. You know I'm right, and you would say the same if it was Em in your position.'

Liberty put her head in her hands. 'I know I've got to do something, Mum, it's just that I don't know if I'm strong enough.'

'Listen, you were married to a very controlling man, it's bound to have left its mark on you. But you are a strong woman. You've left Zac behind now. You can do this. Don't live a life of regrets and what ifs.'

Liberty managed a smile. 'Are you going to print that on a t-shirt?'

'I might do.' Nina reached out and hugged her daughter. 'I know I'm sounding tough, but I only want the best for you.'

And just as Liberty was thinking that was it, Nina said, 'You know I'm right, Libs. Not knowing where you stand or why he didn't show up means you'll never be able to move on. And if you can't move on, you'll never be happy.'

Chapter 28

Brooke

'Are you still up for the kiss?' Brooke asked Harry the following morning. They had got to college deliberately early so that they could be in position outside the drama studio well before Flynn and Mila arrived.

'Darling! I am an actor, of course I'm ready! Ready to throw myself into any role. I can be as hetero as the next man. I'm channelling Tom Hardy and Jason Statham – can't you tell?' Harry clenched his jaw and squared his shoulders, then ruined the effect by checking that his hair was still sweeping across his forehead.

She had to smile. Now she knew Harry was gay, he seemed camper than ever and she could swear that he'd had his eyelashes tinted black and was wearing lip-gloss. Not exactly a look that she'd seen on Jason Statham . . .

'Okay, full concentration now!' Brooke whispered. 'I can see them coming along the corridor.' This was payback time for Flynn and Mila. She was going to mess with their minds. It would serve them, specifically Flynn, right.

'I'm going in!' Harry exclaimed, moving closer and locking lips with her.

Brooke deployed all her acting ability and was pretty sure that Harry was doing the same as she thrust her tongue into his mouth and ran her fingers through his perfectly styled hair. She couldn't resist sneaking a peek at Flynn and Mila as they walked by. They looked gratifyingly gob-smacked. Job done!

'Hmm, very nice, and completely unarousing,' Harry commented as they disengaged. 'Though, I beg you, never mess with the hair again.' He put his hand up to check it was still okay. 'Did they see?'

'Yep! I wish I could have taken a picture of their faces hashtag whatthefuck!' She high-fived him and they went into the studio hand in hand.

Brooke was delighted when Flynn and Mila could hardly keep their eyes off them throughout the workshop, watching their every move. Brooke made sure that she gazed at Harry whenever she could and he did the same to her, both acting the part of starry-eyed lovers. It was a challenge not to laugh, but they pulled it off.

After class the four of them headed to the college café for a coffee. Harry and Brooke had their arms round each other as if they couldn't bear to be parted. When they found a table, Brooke actually sat on his lap, ignoring his whispered protest that he didn't think his thighs could hold out. Cheek! It wasn't as if she was carrying Mila's weight.

'So are you two seeing each other? Like, going out together?' Mila finally asked, when they were halfway through their coffees. Naturally Flynn was too cool to ask outright.

'Oh, yeah, absolutely. Brooke is my soulmate and girlfriend, my lover and my best friend,' Harry replied, typically overdoing it. 'There's so much chemistry between us. I mean, you can feel it as well, can't you? It's, like, electric. I never thought that I'd get that with a girl. My dad is going to be *beyond* thrilled when he meets her. I think my mum will start planning the wedding.'

'So you do know Harry's gay?' Flynn asked Brooke.

'Like, der! How could I not? But like he says, you can't ignore chemistry like ours. And who needs these boundaries . . . gay, straight? I think sexuality is more fluid than that.' She bit her lip to stop herself from grinning and held out her hand for Harry to kiss. A gesture which was only slightly ruined when he groaned and said, 'You'll have to get off me now, sweetie, I've got terrible cramp.'

Brooke could have sworn that they had convinced Mila and almost convinced Flynn with their performance, but then Harry spectacularly blew it by blatantly ogling a workman who was outside the café, repairing one of the windows.

'Hang on a minute, are you two taking the piss?' Flynn demanded. 'You're not going out together at all, are you?'

The game was up. Brooke and Harry looked at each other regretfully, 'If I could ever consider going out with a girl, then it would be Brooke. She is gorgeous, and she has lovely lips and the sweetest breath, and her tongue can really work it! I'm sure the gentlemen must love her technique. It's first-rate. Top notch. The business.'

Okay, that was probably too much information there . . .

'But I'm simply not wired that way.' And with that, Harry blew them all a kiss and rushed outside to get a closer look at the workman. He was convinced that the guy had been giving him the eye, even though Mila had told him that he was obviously looking at Brooke.

'I can't believe you did that!' Flynn exclaimed. 'What a pair of wind-up merchants!'

'You totally deserved it. When I asked you if Harry had a girlfriend, you said no!' She shot an accusing glance at Mila. 'And you as well. I expected more from you, sister. Ever heard of female solidarity?'

'Sorry, Brooke,' Mila replied, 'Flynn made me.'

'Yeah, I bet he did.'

'Come on, it was too funny to resist,' he said. 'And we weren't exactly lying, as he really doesn't have a girlfriend. But it looks like you had a great time together. And you're some actress – you actually had me fooled in the corridor with that performance.'

'I'm kinda pissed off that I couldn't convert him. I used tongues and everything . . . and he didn't get so much as a hard on. What a spoilsport!'

Mila burst out laughing. 'Well, why don't you go and try your luck on the hot workman? You'll probably have more success.'

Brooke pretended to consider the young guy in the baggy black trackies, which in fact she hated as they reminded her too much of what Christian wore, and the chunky Timberland boots. Then she caught Flynn looking at her, and grinned.

'Seriously? He's not in my league. His clothes aren't designer, and where could *he* afford to take me for dinner? Burger King? KFC? Subway? I mean, *perlease*.'

Flynn raised his eyebrows.

'She's taking the piss, can't you see, Flynn?' Mila put in.

'Yep, I'm not such a ditzy airhead. You'll have to revise your opinion of me. Except I bet you've made your mind up and won't change it. Whereas I, at least, have shown that I am open to new experiences – even though I am so far out of my comfort zone here, and anyone, except you apparently, would be sympathetic to that,' Brooke replied.

And before Flynn could say anything more, she picked up her bag, swung it over her shoulder, and she and Mila headed back to class together.

But there were no hard feelings between them when after class she invited Mila, Harry and Flynn over. Her new friends were stunned by the house, its location, the sea views, and the luxurious rooms with their expensive furniture. Harry and Mila exclaimed over every single room that she showed them and squealed with excitement when they saw the swimming pool. Flynn was quiet, but Brooke expected that was because he thought she was such a spoiled rich kid brat.

'OMG!' Mila declared, sinking down on the soft-as-butter brown leather sofa after the tour. 'I'll never be able to invite you over. My house is, like, tiny. And we've only got one bathroom!'

Brooke's house had four . . . or was it five?

'Don't be silly, I'd love to come over.' She smiled, though she did think it a little unusual that Mila only had one bathroom. Flynn stood by the huge French windows, staring out to sea and looking moody. Brooke didn't know why he had bothered to come if he was going to be like this. What – was she supposed to go around apologising for her mom being successful and able to afford a nice house? She didn't get him at all.

'Hiya.' Liberty walked into the room, fresh from a shopping trip in town judging by the number of designer carrier bags she was holding. Typical that while she had a go at Brooke for spending so much money on clothes, she was perfectly happy to go and blow a fortune herself.

Brooke introduced her friends, all of whom seemed to be in awe of Liberty's beauty. Even Flynn seemed to cheer up in her company, and he asked her all about her acting work and seemed genuinely interested – no sign of the cynical, judgmental side Brooke was used to seeing in him whenever he talked to her.

'So do you guys want to stay for supper?' Liberty asked. 'I was going to make a chilli and there's always plenty to go round.'

Hah! Her mom rarely cooked. They had lived off salads and grilled fish since they'd moved here. This was all part of her acting the role of perfect mom. Back in LA Rosa did all the cooking. Liberty had never had to lift a perfectly manicured finger.

'Sure, that would be great,' Mila replied, looking at Flynn and Harry who nodded in agreement. In fact, Harry looked as if he never wanted to leave.

'Okay, I'll get started, and Brooke can hand out some beers. You're all nearly eighteen, aren't you?'

Liberty smiled and Brooke scowled as she noticed the warm smile Flynn gave her mom in return.

'I can help you, if you like,' he said.

Lickarse! Her new favourite word from Harry! Flynn probably fancied her mom! It was too much for Brooke. She muttered something about checking her emails and stomped upstairs, closely followed by Ozzy – her good mood after teasing Flynn about Harry had completely evaporated.

Upstairs Brooke threw herself on her bed. She knew she was being childish but couldn't help it. Nothing seemed to be going her way, and she felt as if it never would ever again. There was a quiet knock on the door.

'Come in unless you're my mom. In which case, Mom, leave me alone!'

Mila opened the door and came in. 'Hi, are you okay?'

Brooke sat up and pushed back her hair. 'Yeah, I just wanted to see if my friend Kelly had sent me a message.'

Mila perched on the end of the bed. 'You must really miss her.'

Brooke nodded. 'Yeah, we've been best friends for, like, ever. Every time something funny or bad happens, my first reaction is always that I can't wait to tell her, and then I realise she's not here. And I've got no one else to tell.'

Fuck! She was going to cry! She couldn't do that, not in front of Mila. She was supposed to be cool and stylish, not some stupid crybaby. Ozzy jumped on the bed and put his head on her knee. At least someone liked her.

'I'm your friend, and so are Harry and Flynn.'

Brooke pulled a face. 'You and Harry, but I don't know about Flynn. I don't think I'm his type of person at all – he's made that pretty obvious. Anyway it looked like he was more interested in flirting with my mom. How gross is that! I should be used to it by now, it always happens.'

Mila laughed. 'Your mum is very beautiful, but I think Flynn's just being polite, helping her cook. Why don't you come back downstairs and have a beer? Harry's being hilarious.'

It probably was a better option than staying up in her bedroom, so Brooke returned downstairs and hung out in the huge kitchen-diner, chatting with Mila and Harry while her mom and Flynn got on with cooking. She had to concede that there was no sign that Flynn actually fancied her mom – so, great, now she was imagining things. It was official: she was going nuts.

'Come on, Brooke, you can make the salad dressing.' Flynn came over to her, holding a bottle of olive oil.

'I don't know how to make dressing, I never have it,' she protested.

'Well, we all want one, so I'll show you how.'

'How come you're so good at cooking?' she asked, reluctantly getting up and waiting to be given her orders.

'My mum's a nurse and often works shifts, so I took over cooking in our house. My dad's the worst cook in the world – if it was down to him we'd be eating burgers and chips every single night. I don't mind it. It's a good unwind.'

Ugh! He was such a goody-goody! The boys she liked in LA wouldn't have been seen dead cooking; they would have been out with their friends, hanging out on the beach or going to gigs.

'And it earned me massive brownie points with my mum, so I could stay out late.' Flynn grinned. 'What? Did you think I was some kind of domestic god who would rather stay in than go out on the lash?'

'He's so not,' Harry put in. 'His room is a total tip. Honestly, I don't know how he finds anything in it. Such bad feng shui.'

'A bit like Brooke's until she tidied it,' Liberty said. Then added, 'Sorry, honey, that was bad of me. I'm going to call Em while you guys finish off in here.'

Harry waited until she was out of earshot before exclaiming, 'Your mum is even better-looking in real life than she is in photographs! She's got such amazing skin. Flawless. She probably doesn't even need to be airbrushed, does she?'

That was exactly what Brooke didn't need to hear. Her self-esteem was currently at rock bottom. Harry caught sight of her glum expression, and seemed to realise his mistake. 'Oh, sweetie, don't come over all jealous, you are beautiful too. And you're younger, so you win!'

'God, Harry, it's not supposed to be a competition between me and my mom!'

'At least your mum's around,' Mila put in. 'I never even see my parents. They're always working. And the only time I ever do see my mum, I can tell she's really disappointed that I'm so fat. I mean, I know I am really fat. I just don't need her criticism on top of everyone else's. It's not as if I look like this just to spite her.'

Brooke had been so caught up in her own problems that she hadn't given any thought to Mila's emotions – writing her off as the happy-go-lucky girl, who was perfectly happy being, well, there was no other word for it, fat . . . She thought of Mila making the effort to be friendly to her, sticking up for her when Flynn was having a go, even though Brooke hadn't given her one scrap of appreciation in return.

She suddenly had an idea. 'I'm thinking of joining a gym. Why don't you join with me? It would be so great to have someone to go with.'

Mila was usually so easygoing, her reaction took Brooke by surprise.

'No fucking way! I hate those places. Full of skinny bitches looking down at me as I flobber and flab around. And the last time I went to one and had an assessment with this trainer, I could see that he was wishing he'd got the fit girl that his friend had. He spent the entire time perving after her. I swear I could have dropped down dead on the treadmill and he wouldn't even have noticed.'

Brooke was outraged on her behalf. 'You should have complained! God, what a jerk!' She would never, *ever* put up with that kind of treatment.

Mila shrugged. 'I doubt I would have got anywhere. Haven't you noticed how fat people get treated differently, as if we don't have feelings or we're invisible? Which is ironic when there's so much of us to see . . .'

Brooke couldn't answer honestly as she knew she was guilty of thinking exactly that. 'Well, I'm serious about joining the gym, and I'll make sure no one treats you badly.'

'I don't know. I'm not promising anything.'

'Please think about it? For me? Pretty please?'

'Okay,' Mila replied, and Brooke felt a small sense of achievement that usually she only got when it was all about her . . . Shit! Was this her transformation into the better person that her mom was hoping for? Next off she'd be slobbing around in sweat pants and not caring what she looked like. No, that was *never* going to happen. Sweat pants were strictly for the house on days where she wasn't going to see anybody.

Later, after dinner, as she cleared the table with Flynn, he commented on her gesture. 'Did you really mean that about going to the gym with Mila?'

'Of course, I wouldn't have offered otherwise. Why? What's wrong with that?'

She stopped what she was doing and looked at him, arms folded, all set to defend herself against whatever criticism he was going to level at her. Maybe he had a problem with gyms – Brooke wouldn't put it past him.

But Flynn just smiled. 'Great. I'm sure she'll really appreciate it. She had a rough time at our secondary school, being bullied by a gang of girls. It's really good to see her making friends with you.'

'See,' she challenged him, 'I'm not so spoiled as you think. I'm not such a terrible airhead person, who only lives to shop and spend money and never lifts a finger to help anyone.'

'No? Then I guess you won't mind finishing the clearing up, I've got to go.'

'Oh, right, hot date with someone?'

She'd meant it as a joke, but what was this? Cool, self-assured Flynn actually looked awkward and didn't meet her eye.

'Sort of. With my ex. So I'll see you in college tomorrow. Say thanks to your mum for me.'

Brooke was surprised to find that later on, when she was lying in bed and listening to Emeli Sandé singing 'Clown', she wondered how Flynn's meeting with his ex had gone. Were they going to stay just friends? Or were they going to get back together? And, more to the point, why did Brooke even care? Except . . . *except* . . . he was very good-looking, and she sort of minded what he thought about her. It was only because there was absolutely no one else on the horizon, she told herself.

Flynn definitely wasn't her type. He couldn't be. He didn't like LA, her spiritual home.

Chapter 29

Liberty

Liberty walked slowly through the Pavilion gardens. She had decided to listen to her mum and Em and was going to see Cory's exhibition. She thought it was unlikely that he would be there, but it felt like a first step in getting back in touch with him. It felt like she was taking control at long last.

They'd been having something of an Indian summer lately, with days of sunshine and bold blue skies. Students, office workers, mothers and toddlers, were sitting out on the grass having picnics. It was an idyllic scene, if you could ignore the seagulls ever on the look-out for food. She smiled as she saw a young woman frantically waving her arms at a gull who had just tried to raid her son's packet of crisps, and then froze as she saw that the blond man sitting beside them looked like Cory. Oh, my God, it really was him, and he looked just as good as he had five years ago. Getting older suited him; he was astonishingly handsome, and looked tanned, healthy and happy. So tanned and healthy-looking and so happy. And was that young woman with him his wife? She seemed incredibly young, barely in her twenties, and very pretty in shorts and a t-shirt. Her long honey-blonde hair was pulled back in a messy ponytail and it didn't seem like she was wearing any make up. The little boy between them, who was probably around three, looked like a mini Cory, with thick blond hair and a cheeky expression. This should be Liberty's moment to go over and see him. But she just couldn't barge in on a family scene like that; it felt all wrong.

She carried on walking, her head down, intent on getting away before she was seen. But she found herself stopping at the café that overlooked the gardens, drawn to watch Cory a little longer, even if it was painful to see him with his wife. For the next half-hour she sat at a table, ostensibly reading her magazine and sipping a latte but all her attention fixed on Cory. He played football with his son and chatted to his wife. Later, another couple with a baby joined them and they seemed to be good friends. He clearly led a happy life. She wondered if he even thought of her any more.

Liberty got up and headed out of the gardens. She'd seen enough. As she reached the end of the path she hesitated – left was her way home, right was in the direction of Kensington Gardens where Cory's exhibition was on. She could just walk past the gallery and have a look. It seemed as if he was going to be in the gardens a while longer.

A painting of a black female singer dominated the gallery window. Bold, contemporary and powerful, it captured the intensity of the woman's expression and the energy of her performance. It reminded Liberty of the painting she had seen when she'd first met Cory, but she could tell that this one was executed with far greater skill. What a talent he possessed. He had clearly fulfilled his potential as an artist.

There didn't seem to be anyone else in the gallery, except for the young woman working at her laptop. Liberty could just have a quick look inside. The paintings made her feel close to Cory, and even if that was an illusion, it was one she needed to have. For a moment when she walked through the door she just stood there, taking in everything: the vivid colours, the scenes from urban life, the portraits.

The young woman looked up from her laptop.

'Hi there. Is there anything I can help you with?' She had dyed bright red hair, a nose ring, and an intricate tattoo of a pink lily on her shoulder. Typical Brighton look which Liberty had missed over in LA, where so many of the actors she knew looked exactly the same.

'Oh, no, thanks. I just wanted to have a look.'

'Go right ahead, you can see that quite a few paintings have been sold already. Cory Richardson is a very popular artist.'

Liberty walked round the room, considering each painting in turn. She finished up standing in front of a painting of a couple sitting outside a bar, which looked as if it might be in Brighton. A small part of her had wondered if there might be any pictures of her. But there were none. Had Cory even kept the ones he had done of her? She was deep in thought when the gallery door swung open. She glanced over. It was Cory. He strode in, smiling broadly at the woman behind the desk, and then seemed to do a double take as he realised it was Liberty standing in the gallery.

Countless times she had rehearsed this meeting in her head. In her fantasy version they would gaze at each other and she would know that he loved her still. The years that they had spent apart would fall away and she would be that same twenty-one-year-old girl who had fallen in love with that nineteen-year-old boy. But now she was confronted with the stark reality. For an instant she saw hurt flare up in his eyes, then he seemed to shut down and she was locked out. Those blue eyes that had once looked at her with such passion were ice cold.

'What the hell are you doing here?'

'I'm sorry. I was in the area, and I saw your painting in the window, and I—'

He cut across her explanation. 'What? You want to buy one of my pictures? Because I can't imagine why else you'd be in here. It can't have been to see me. Or did you come to gloat? To see if I was the same stupid fool I was five years ago?'

It was like a wave of anger coming at her.

The young woman behind the desk coughed quietly. 'Cory, shall I go and get some coffee? Give you two some space.'

'There's no need. Mrs Keller, or Ms Evans, or whatever the fuck she's called, is leaving.'

Liberty couldn't leave like this, though, she had to tell him about the letter. 'Cory, I need to talk to you about what happened then—'

Again he stopped her. 'Don't bother. You think I'd believe anything you ever told me again? You really must think I'm dumb. Or now your husband's dumped you, are you looking for your next dupe? Well, let me tell you, it won't be me.'

And to underline the point he flung open the door, leaving Liberty with no choice but to leave.

Outside she walked away swiftly, almost breaking into a run, trying to hold it together, trying so hard not to cry. But as soon as she'd turned the corner, she reached for her mobile. Her friend answered almost immediately.

'Em, can I come over? I need to see you.'

Chapter 30

Brooke

The following day when Brooke arrived at college, Flynn was standing by the entrance with a beautiful auburn-haired girl. They seemed to be locked in an intense conversation, with eyes only for each other. They didn't see her so she knew that what happened next was not an act, or Flynn getting his own back for the stunt she and Harry had pulled. The beautiful girl put her arms round his neck and kissed him. And he kissed her back. So the ex was not so ex after all . . . Just perfect. She got to fake passion with Harry, while Flynn got the real thing. Brooke was slinking past them when they stopped their snogfest (another new word courtesy of Harry) and Flynn noticed her.

'Hey, Brooke.'

'Hi,' she replied, aware of the girlfriend sizing her up. God, she really was something, with big blue eyes and gorgeous skin – okay, *way* too pale for Brooke's own taste, but she could see it was perfect, plus she had a gorgeous mouth and her hair was stunning. And natural by the look of it.

'This is Eve,' Flynn continued.

'Hello, Brooke. Even if Flynn hadn't told me, I would have guessed you come from LA, you have that look about you.'

She had a cut-glass English accent that Brooke reckoned her mom would describe as 'posh', and Nina would describe as sounding as if she was 'up herself'. Eve didn't exactly sound as if she thought '*that look*' was a good one. Well, screw her.

'Yeah, well, I always want *that look*, because LA's my home, it's where I belong.' She made a point of looking at her arms. 'In fact, I'm going to have to start faking the tan – I'm nearly as pale as you. I mean, no offence, but you are so white you look as if you've got a part in the *Twilight* movies.' She meant it as a joke but Eve didn't look too pleased.

'Just be careful you don't overdo it. It's a thin line between being brown and being a kind of toxic orange. No offence.'

There was now a definite edge to Eve's voice. Brooke wondered why she was getting so uptight – she was the one with the boyfriend, and the life in Brighton! She, Brooke, was the newcomer who was suffering.

She shrugged. 'The browner the better as far as I'm concerned. Bring it on.' She looked at Flynn. 'Oh, my mom says thanks for helping to cook last night. I think she was stunned that any guy would ever offer to help. My stepdad never did anything round the house.'

She noticed Eve narrow her exquisite eyes. No doubt she was put out that she hadn't been there too, to lord it over them with her flawless skin, shiny hair and pale face.

Flynn looked slightly awkward as he turned to Eve and said, 'A couple of us went to Brooke's last night for dinner. It was kind of a spur-of-the-moment thing.'

Oh, what? He had to justify himself to her! 'Yeah, don't worry, Eve, it was just dinner, we had the orgy after he'd left.' And then, because she'd really had enough of Eve, Brooke muttered something about needing to get to class early and left the beautiful couple to each other. But something about the encounter put her in a bad mood for the rest of the morning.

At lunch Flynn disappeared off somewhere – more snogging with Eve, no doubt – and Brooke went to the beach with Harry and Mila. It was a warm English afternoon, but only like a spring day by Brooke's standards, even though Mila complained that she was boiling. Brooke glanced at her black leggings and baggy black t-shirt.

'No wonder you're hot in all that black,' she commented.

'Black is supposed to be slimming. You can see how well that's working for me,' Mila said sarcastically.

'Well, come to the gym! I'm planning to go after class and sign up.'

Mila was usually so upbeat, but definitely not about this. She sounded completely dejected as she said, 'I just don't know if I can put myself through all that again. It's too depressing. I may as well accept that I'll look like this for ever.'

Brooke decided to go for a different tactic, already knowing how kind-hearted Mila was. 'Couldn't you come for my sake? To keep me company? I really hate doing things like that on my own. I'll feel so lonely and self-conscious. *Please*, it would mean so much to have a friend go with me. Kelly always used to come with me in LA.'

She was laying it on thick and it seemed to be

working as Mila sighed and said, 'Okay. But if anyone is rude to me, I'm out of there.'

'If anyone is rude to you, they'll have me to answer to!' Brooke exclaimed. 'And believe me, I can kick ass.'

From behind Mila's back, Harry gave Brooke the thumbs up. At least there was something she was doing right.

Mila checked her phone. 'I thought Flynn might be here by now. He said he'd try and meet us.' She sighed. 'Unless Eve's got other plans for him.'

'So what's she like?' Brooke asked as casually as she could. She had been itching to ask all morning, but didn't want to seem as if she was actually interested in the answer.

Harry rolled his eyes. 'High-fucking-maintenance! One minute she wants to have a relationship with Flynn and she's all over him, then she's pushing him away because she claims she wants her own space. And he's gutted, and a mess, and the second it looks as if he might be getting his life back together, she calls him and the whole cycle starts over. I can't fucking stand her. She's a selfish, heartless, manipulative bitch.'

'Wow! Don't sit on the fence, Harry,' Brooke joked, but really she was intrigued to hear about any girl who had that much control over Flynn. He'd always seemed to act so in control himself, as if he would always be the one with the upper hand in any relationship.

'He's right.' Mila spoke now. 'She'll seem like your best friend, but it's all about her. She was only ever friends with me because she wanted to get to Flynn. I could never say that to him, though. Even when she's treated him like shit, he can never see it. He's completely taken in by her.'

'I don't even think the sex is that good,' Harry put in bitchily. 'She has the look of someone who wouldn't really enjoy it, but would be doing it just to prove how much power they had over you.'

Brooke was taken aback to hear how much Mila and Harry seemed to dislike Eve. And okay, maybe this was bad, but she couldn't help feeling pleased. She hadn't warmed to Eve at all.

'I can't imagine Flynn being like that,' Brooke mused. 'Maybe he really loves her.'

'It's obsession. Infatuation. It won't last, and she'll break his heart. Again,' Harry muttered. Then he seemed to snap out of it. 'Sorry, Brooke, we're all a tiny bit in love with Flynn ourselves and that girl just puts me in a foul mood. I hate what she does to him.'

All a tiny bit in love with him? Well, Harry could speak for himself and possibly Mila . . .

'Let's talk about something else.' Harry grinned. 'Something glamorous, something gorgeous!'

Brooke looked blank.

'Something you're going to be having really soon,' he prompted.

She finally twigged. 'Oh, yeah, my party! I don't know that many people yet, but I was thinking of having a fancy dress theme. What do you reckon? Would that be cool or what's the word you use . . . naff?'

Instantly Harry looked radiant and Mila looked glum.

'Ooh, I can come as Richard Gere in *An Officer and A Gentleman,* in a white uniform to show off my tan!' he declared.

How could she *ever* have thought Harry was straight?

'And I can be Tweedledum,' Mila muttered. 'Again. Or Beth Ditto. Again.'

'Don't be silly,' Brooke told her. 'You'd look fabulous in a fifties-style fitted dress. You know, curves are really in at the moment.'

When Mila still didn't look convinced, Brooke carried on, 'And you're going to come to the gym with me, so that will make you feel better. Plus I'll help you find the perfect dress, and on the day I'll get someone to do our make up and hair.'

Fingers crossed. It would be quite a task, but Brooke had great faith in the power of Spanx and cosmetics.

'You're like the Party Fairy!' Harry declared. 'I love you!'

And even though she knew he was only saying it because actually what he loved was the prospect of getting dressed up for her party, she still smiled.

'Oh, look, there's Flynn,' Mila commented, waving her hand to attract his attention.

'And Eve,' Harry muttered. 'Shit. I was hoping that he wasn't going to get back with her. Bummer.'

Brooke watched the couple make their way over to them, hand in hand and looking sickeningly loved up. Why didn't they just go and snog somewhere in private? She was now going to be subjected to their PDAs and she so didn't want that. It was a reminder of everything that she didn't have, and she found it unsettling watching Flynn kiss someone. It stirred something in her that she didn't want to analyse. No, it was nothing she was going to worry about, it was just because her own love life was so non-existent, a desert. A desert with no oasis in sight. It was absolutely not because she fancied him . . .

However, it seemed that Eve was making more of an effort to be nice to Brooke this time – either Flynn had said something to her or she had realised what a bitch she had sounded. Now she made a point of sitting down next to Brooke and saying how lucky she was to live where she did, and that Flynn had told her how amazing the house was.

Brooke supposed there was no way she could avoid mentioning the party. 'You'll get the chance to see it as I'm going to have my eighteenth there and you're all invited.'

'It's fancy dress,' Harry exclaimed, clapping his hands together in glee.

'Isn't every day fancy dress for you?' Flynn commented.

'Harsh,' Harry shot back. 'Just because I don't like hiding my light under a bushel, or rather a pair of baggy shorts.'

Flynn shrugged. 'They're just clothes, man,' he exhaled. 'It's so hot.' And then he peeled off his t-shirt.

Suddenly Brooke saw exactly why Harry was so taken with him. Flynn had the most gorgeous body. Muscular, but not in a pumped up, I-love-myself-and-spend-all-my-time-at-the-gym way – like Christian. And while he might have teased Brooke for her LA look, he would have fitted right in as well, once he had an even golden-brown tan. She forced herself to drag her eyes away from the sight of the band of his black Calvin Klein boxers peeping out of the top of his shorts, and his rock-hard abs. She suddenly felt hot all over . . .

'D'you want me to put some sun cream on your back?' Eve asked, playing the part of the perfect if rather annoying girlfriend.

'No, it's not that hot, I'll be fine.' He didn't seem to like being fussed over. He looked at Brooke. God, she really hoped he hadn't noticed her checking him out . . . that would be too shameful.

'So what are you going to wear, Brooke, or is it a secret?'

'Probably a twenties-style dress, I love that look.'

When he seemed surprised, she grinned. 'What, did

265

you think I'd be going as someone out of *Baywatch* or some other LA cliché?'

He frowned. 'Not at all.'

'I think you should go in an LAPD uniform and go around threatening to arrest people and cuff them. Kinky. I like it!' Harry, of course. 'Ooh, and then you could strip it off and parade around in a basque and stockings.'

'Let me think about that,' Brooke joked. 'Oh, yeah, I have. No fucking way! My mom and gran are probably going to be there!'

'Well, you might have to stay out of the sun before your party – I don't think girls in the twenties had such deep tans,' Eve put in.

'Well, honey, I'd rather look good than historically accurate,' Brooke drawled. There was something about Eve's posh voice that brought out the LA girl in her, and she exaggerated her American accent.

'Absolutely!' Harry agreed. 'So what do you think you'll come as, Flynn?'

'Oh, Flynn and I will need to discuss it, so we can co-ordinate our outfits,' Eve spoke up for him.

'How very Posh and Becks circa 1999.' Harry smirked. 'Flynn would look so good in leather. And of course you would too, Eve.'

Neither Flynn nor Eve looked too pleased with that comment, though Brooke guessed that Flynn was more pissed off with Eve for talking for him. It was plain to see who wore the leather trousers in that couple.

Planning the party took up a lot of Brooke's time that week – she spent several evenings after college discussing arrangements with her mom, giving her an idea of what she wanted in terms of food and music, though Liberty also promised some surprises. She researched her party dress as well. She saw a drawing of a beautiful gold beaded flapper dress that she thought would be perfect. Her mom was going to get it made for her by a dressmaker she knew in London.

The list of guests wasn't quite as pitifully short as Brooke had feared – she was going to ask all the people in her drama and English classes, some thirty in total, plus some partners, and several of her mom's friends, including Em and Nina. So it would be getting close to fifty guests, which seemed reasonable. She tried not to think about the party she might have had in LA, with over a hundred guests at Chateau Marmont. It was best not to.

And true to her word she signed up to her local gym with Mila, and the pair of them went several times. Brooke had joined with Mila solely because she wanted to help her, but in fact it made exercise so much more fun. They worked out in the gym together and then swam and hung out in the Jacuzzi. Mila was incredibly self-conscious about her body and insisted on swimming in a pair of black shorts over her black swimming costume – enough of the black already!

Brooke started to see Mila as a real friend and to feel relaxed in her company. They chatted about their college work, favourite films and TV dramas: Mila was into all the vampire series while Brooke preferred dramas like *Homeland*. They spoke about their families, and spent quite a lot of time discussing Flynn and Eve. Brooke wanted to know the full story of their relationship, and Mila was happy to oblige. Apparently they had got together two years ago. Flynn had been going out with someone at the time, but Eve had managed to break that up.

'I just wish he wasn't going out with her again. We never see as much of him when he is, and when we do she's nearly always there, looking down her perfect little nose at me and Harry. I bet she didn't like your arrival on the scene.'

'What difference would that make to her? It's not as if Flynn likes me especially.'

'Eve's used to being the Queen Bee and lording it over everyone. But you're easily as good-looking as her, if not more so. She won't like that. And your mom is really successful, and you live in a big house. That kind of thing would bother her. I reckon underneath the confident act she puts on, she's pretty insecure.'

'Yeah, but I bet she doesn't have to work at an Italian restaurant,' Brooke replied. Her second shift was the following day and she wasn't looking forward to it at all.

'Cheer up, me and Flynn will be there. Just think of what you can get with your wages – I'm putting mine towards buying a dress for your party.'

And now Brooke felt terrible because the money she earned obviously made a real difference to Mila, whereas Brooke just used hers to top up her allowance.

The restaurant was even busier than it had been the previous week, and what made it even worse was that there were several large groups of diners, including a hen party, who had clearly been spending most of the day drinking and were now hitting the pasta in an attempt to soak up some of the alcohol before going on clubbing. It was Brooke's luck to end up with the hens, who were loud, aggressive and rude.

'Can't you go and serve them?' she begged Flynn when she passed him.

'They'd probably sexually harass me,' he replied, looking over at the table where the girls were checking out pictures on someone's phone and cackling loudly. They made a coven of witches seem shy and retiring

. . . He smiled at Brooke. 'You'll be fine, just use your LA charm.'

'I don't know why Marco let them in, all the other diners look really pissed off.'

Then there was no further time to talk as she had to race to the pass to collect the hens' main courses. It was a nightmare trying to match up the diners with their meals; no one paid her any attention. She ended up with three ravioli, which the hens claimed they hadn't ordered when she knew perfectly well that they had.

'I would never order that,' the bride-to-be snapped at her. Brooke knew she was the bride-to-be because that's what she had printed on her tight white t-shirt. And the bright pink tiara, now slightly askew, was a bit of a giveaway as well. What a lucky man the groom was . . . Mind you, God knew what he was up to.

'Well, you guys did actually.' Brooke was doing her very best to be polite.

'Well, you guys did actually,' the lairy bride-to-be mimicked her. 'Who do you think you are, Waitress Girl? I didn't, so take this shit away and get me the risotto I actually ordered.'

No one had *ever* been that rude to Brooke before. For a second she stood rooted to the spot, before gathering up the rejected dishes. Fuck! She yelped in pain as she burned her hand on one of the plates and very nearly dropped it, which would have capped the night off perfectly.

'What's going on with that table?' Marco demanded, catching her offloading the unwanted meals at the pass. 'We need to get them served and out of here as soon as possible, they are not good for business.'

'They're saying they didn't order the ravioli, but they did. I've got to get them the seafood risotto instead. They're probably too drunk to remember.'

He looked furious. 'What a waste! I'll take over from you. Have your break now. I hired you in good faith, as a favour to your mother, but you are letting her and me down with your attitude, Brooke.'

'It's not *my* attitude! Those women are being so obnoxious! No one should have to put up with that.'

'Enough! I have to go and sort out your mess otherwise those women will be writing some terrible review on Trip Advisor. And up till now I have never had a one-star review!'

Brooke slunk out to the back yard. Her hand throbbed painfully from where she had burned it, but she couldn't face seeing anyone in the kitchen where she knew the first-aid kit was. She sat down on one of the broken chairs from the restaurant, which wobbled precariously, trying her hardest not to cry.

'Cheer up, I got you a Diet Coke,' Flynn said, taking a chair next to her and handing her the can. 'You shouldn't let it get to you. We all have shifts like this.'

'Thanks,' she muttered. It would take more than a fizzy drink to raise her spirits, but she appreciated the gesture.

Flynn noticed the burn as she took the can. 'Hey, what have you done?'

'It's nothing.'

He reached out and gently turned her hand over, revealing the red mark. 'Ouch, that must hurt! Come on, we'll run it under cold water.'

Maybe it was because Flynn was being nice to her, or because she was exhausted, but suddenly Brooke's eyes were welling up with tears. She was going to win Loser of the Year at this rate . . . no contest.

'What's the matter?'

'Nothing. Everything. Being stuck here at this restaurant just about sums up my crappy life. I get abuse hurled at me by a group of drunk women, I'm miles from where I want to be and who I want to be with. I'm trying to do what my mom wants by working here and going to college, but nothing I do ever goes right. Everything is shit. And I feel so lost. I don't think I can take it any more.'

She waited for Flynn to tell her to stop being such a baby and to pull herself together. But instead he said quietly, 'Is it really that bad?' And putting his arms round her, he hugged her close. 'You'll be okay, Brooke. You're tough, you can get through this.'

For a few seconds she felt comforted by the gesture, and rested her head on his shoulder. But then that feeling turned to something else as she registered how good Flynn's body felt against hers. Far too good. Solid . . . strong . . . sexy. She was so close she could feel his heart beating, could smell his delicious musky aftershave. She had an overwhelming urge to kiss his neck, to slip her hands under his shirt and feel his warm skin. She felt tendrils of desire unfurl within her . . . No! She absolutely could not go there. What was she thinking! She awkwardly pulled away.

'Thanks,' she mumbled, certain that her face was flushing red.

'All part of the service,' Flynn replied, seeming completely together. Clearly she had not had the same effect on him.

She stood up, ready to go back inside and get on with her night from hell.

'Hey, you've got a few more minutes yet,' Flynn told her.

'No, I'm fine, Marco's already pissed off with me. I might as well try and get back into his good books.'

Inside, there was quite a scene. Marco and Big Bruno, plus Vince who did the washing up, were escorting the hens out of the restaurant. The women were not going quietly. 'You fucking wankers!' seemed to be a common refrain. Classy bunch of ladies that lot.

'What happened?' she asked Mila.

'The bride-to-be groped Marco's bum, not once, not twice, but three times. And the third time he lost it. He told them he would rather serve a table of farm animals than them.'

'And you are banned from ever coming back here!' Marco shouted as he slammed the door on the last of the drunken women. Then he addressed the other diners, all of whom had been riveted by the drama of what had happened. 'There will be a free glass of wine for all of you, and a free dessert. I sincerely apologise for that scene.'

At that the tables broke into a round of applause. Catching sight of Brooke, Marco walked over to her. 'And I am sorry for having a go at you. I should have listened when you told me about them. I didn't mean what I said. You're a very good waitress and a real asset to my restaurant. Come, we'll all have a glass of wine to make up. I need one after dealing with those –' he shuddered '– I can't call them women, they were beasts and barbarians!'

Instantly Brooke's mood lightened, and the rest of the night passed without incident. In fact, although she would never admit this to her mom, it was kind of fun. There was a party atmosphere in the restaurant. The diners were all in excellent moods after their freebies. And she felt that she was getting to know the rest of the waiters, chefs and sous-chefs, who by and large were all really nice and seemed to like her. For the first time ever she felt part of a team and didn't wish that she was the one being waited on.

'D'you fancy having a beer at my house?' Flynn

asked her, as she was getting her jacket at the end of the shift.

Brooke thought of their hug. Was it such a good idea to go with him? Then again, it was probably all in her imagination. It would be good to clear the air.

'Sure.' She grinned. 'Do we get a taxi there? You know what us LA natives are like, we never walk if we can help it.'

Flynn rolled his eyes. 'You're going to have to walk on your pretty little feet. But it's not far.'

She expected that he'd ask Mila as well, but he didn't and Brooke realised that she was glad that it was going to be just the two of them.

It might not have been that far, but Flynn's route home included what seemed like the steepest hill Brooke had ever climbed in her life.

'I can't go on!' she protested, coming to a halt halfway up. 'I've been on my feet all day. Have mercy!'

Flynn carried on walking and called out, 'Okay then. More beer for me. Just think of it, though, ice cold and waiting for you.'

'I'd prefer some harder liquor – Harry let me drink vodka when I went out with him.' Oops, she hadn't meant it to sound as if she thought that this was a date! Fortunately Flynn didn't answer and so she caught up with him and pretended she hadn't come out with her last comment.

Flynn's house reminded her of Nina's. It was in a Victorian terrace, painted sky blue, and inside was a riot of colour, with pictures on every wall alongside photos of Flynn and his two younger sisters. It was small, but very cosy. When Brooke saw the shoe rack with everyone's shoes lined up, she had that pang she sometimes felt when she used to go round to Kelly's, about missing out on what it was to be part of a big family. Not that Kelly had a shoe rack, more like a shoe room . . . and soon she'd need a shoe wing.

Brooke paused at a picture of Flynn, aged around five, riding a bike and looking incredibly pleased with himself. 'Ah, you were so cute!' She shot him a cheeky glance. 'Where did it all go wrong?'

'Do you want that beer or not?'

'After tonight? I definitely want.'

She followed him into the kitchen at the end of the hallway.

'Where's the rest of your family?' she asked, leaning against the work counter.

Even in the kitchen there were pictures and photographs on every available space. The large stainless-steel fridge was covered in magnets, underneath which were reminders of appointments, more drawings and postcards.

'They're away camping for the weekend,' he replied, opening the fridge and getting out two bottles of Beck's.

Oh, so she was alone with him? Suddenly Brooke had a very vivid flashback to their hug. She experienced a fresh upsurge of butterflies . . .

'It's so rare that I have the house to myself. You don't know how lucky you are to have all that space in yours. I keep having to chuck my sister Rosie out of my room, she's always trying to use my computer. I'm going to have to get a lock.'

He handed her the beer and they went into the living room. He shifted a large tabby cat out of the way and sat in a battered leather armchair; she took the sofa. See, it had been her imagination after all; he couldn't actually be sitting any further away from her if he tried. This was a friendly drink together, nothing more.

'Actually I envy you, having a big family. It sometimes

feels kind of lonely with just Mom and me. In a funny way, I guess it's better now we're here. Back in LA we hardly ever saw each other – she was always working or I would be out. We ate at different times. There was even one week when we had to text each other to arrange a time in our schedules to meet, and that was mainly for her to give me a hard time about my grades.'

Flynn shook his head. 'That's the other extreme, I guess – I'll try and remember that when Rosie is next winding me up. So how are you feeling about living here now? Does it still feel so alien?'

'Well, there's the lack of sun and sand, the fact that you don't have a Nobu here, and Omigod, I haven't had a manicure in three weeks! And do you know where you can buy 7 For All Mankind jeans in Brighton? I totally have to have a new pair or I'm going to freak.'

'I know you're joking. You pretend to be this shallow girl who only cares about how she looks, but I've seen through all that.'

'No way! I work so hard at it!'

'Yep, exhibit one is you being friends with Mila and being kind to her, exhibit two is the fact that you are working in a restaurant, and exhibit three you're a really good actor and would have to be drawing on something other than being a shallow airhead to convince an audience of your feelings.'

Flynn thought she was a good actress? Wow, that was quite a compliment coming from him, Mr Integrity.

'Okay, you got me, I'm real profound,' she teased. 'I could give you lessons, if you like. My fees are very reasonable, though I am saving for a new pair of Louboutins.'

'Don't take the piss.'

They were both silent for a moment while they sipped

their beers. His next question took her completely by surprise. 'So did you leave a boyfriend back in LA?'

Did it sound as if he cared about the answer? Did she want him to care? Probably more than she wanted to admit to herself . . .

'No. Just before we left, I dumped him.' Brooke paused. 'Okay, he dumped me first, but I was about to dump him. He cheated on me with this skanky girl.' She grimaced. 'It was so humiliating.'

'That's tough. And he must have been an idiot to cheat on you.'

'I was the idiot for ever getting involved with him in the first place. I don't even know what I saw in him.'

She really meant that. She couldn't imagine being with Christian now. Sure he was good-looking, but there had to be more than that to a person. What did they ever talk about? She couldn't even remember. She thought of having to go to his dreadful concerts and wanted to laugh. She had been crazy.

'So, have you met anyone over here who you like?'

Oh, God! She had an overwhelming desire to blurt out 'You'! What the fuck was wrong with her? She quickly turned her confusion into a joke. 'Plenty, but they all seem to be gay. But that didn't stop me with Harry, did it?'

'So is Harry really the type you go for?'

Why all these questions? Did he care what her 'type' was?

Before she had a chance to answer, they were interrupted by a knock at the door. A lucky escape, she couldn't help thinking. But she didn't have that feeling for long as Flynn opened the door to Eve. Brooke hadn't expected her to turn up and suddenly felt incredibly deflated. Although Flynn had been asking some difficult questions, she was loving spending time alone with him.

She could hear Eve laying into him, out in the hallway.

'I've been calling you for the past hour, why wasn't your phone switched on?'

'I thought you were going out tonight with your friends.'

'I did, but then I really needed to see you.' Eve sounded on the verge of tears. That was a bit odd. Surely it was no big deal that Flynn didn't have his phone on?

Brooke glanced up as Eve walked into the living room. Flynn's girlfriend looked stunned to find her sitting there, but quickly composed herself.

'Oh, hi, I didn't realise you were here.' Not said in an especially friendly way . . .

'I'm just having a quick beer on my way home. It was quite some shift we had. We needed to unwind after serving the great British public. I was nearly assaulted by a group of hens or whatever you call them.'

'Not exactly in your direction, is it? You're the other end of town,' Eve said icily.

If looks could kill, Brooke would be stone dead, that was for sure. She was conscious of her waitress uniform. Her white shirt had pasta sauce spilled on it and she probably smelled of garlic bread. Eve, on the other hand, looked incredible in a pair of black skinny jeans and a black sequin top, with perfect understated make up that made her blue eyes look even more intense. But she seemed very on edge. Brooke hadn't seen her like this before, usually she was supremely confident.

'D'you want a beer, Eve?' Flynn asked.

She tutted. 'You know I never drink beer, it really bloats my stomach.'

At that Brooke had a terrible desire to giggle. Harry had been right. Eve was so annoying and so

277

high-maintenance. She put her hand over her mouth to stifle any outburst but she was too late. A sound escaped her, something between a snort and a giggle. Whoah, she was discovering new levels of sophistication . . .

Eve glared at her.

'Sorry, it was the beer, it gives me terrible gas. Shit, d'you say that over here? It's like when I hear people say they're dying for a fag, I keep doing a double take . . .' She was burbling away, conscious of the Arctic freeze coming her way from Eve. 'Anyway, I'd better go.' Brooke stood up and grabbed her bag. 'D'you have a number for a taxi?'

Flynn didn't even suggest that she stay for another beer . . . and Brooke guessed he was going to get it in the neck from Eve after she left. There was an awkward five minutes while she waited for the taxi to arrive. Eve didn't say a word and Flynn seemed on edge. And when she left there was none of the banter that they'd shared earlier in the night. Just a quick goodbye and absolutely no hug. It shouldn't matter, she told herself as the taxi pulled away. But it did.

Chapter 31

Liberty

After her confrontation with Cory, going to Angel and Cal's party was the very last thing Liberty wanted to do. She wanted to stay at home and brood and try somehow to get over the man who didn't want her at all. But Em wasn't going to allow her to do that. Em, who had sat patiently with her as she sobbed her eyes out after seeing Cory, had decided enough was enough. So she'd turned up at Liberty's front door.

'We're going shopping for something to wear for the party. And I'm not leaving until you come. I'll move in with Noah and the kids if necessary. Or you can go and get dressed. You have ten minutes. Oh, and I'll make you some tea and toast, you look terrible.'

Em was like an unstoppable force and Liberty knew better than to try and convince her that she was fine and that she wasn't going to the party. An hour later they were sitting on the silver velvet sofa in their friend Denys's boutique, sipping white wine spritzers while Denys selected various dresses for them to consider.

Denys was a gorgeous, curvy blonde, who modelled

herself on Marilyn Monroe and always wore red Chanel lipstick and sweeping fake eyelashes. It was a look she'd been working since the age of fifteen. Liberty imagined she would probably always look like that. She always told everyone that they looked 'wonderful, darling', no doubt to encourage them to buy her designer clothes. She was also a terrible gossip, who Liberty would never trust to keep a secret, but at heart she meant well.

'You must wear something to show off that fabulous figure of yours, Liberty,' Denys declared. 'Like this, for instance.' She held up a strapless pink flared hem Hervé Léger bandage dress.

'That's way too short!' Liberty protested, out of the habit of wearing such figure-flaunting numbers.

'With those legs and that body? Are you crazy?' Denys replied. 'Go on, give it a try.'

Reluctantly Liberty got up from the sofa and went into the fitting room. She slipped out of her grey skinny jeans and black jumper and into the dress. It was an amazing fit and hugged her figure perfectly.

Denys knocked at the door. 'I've got some heels for you, darling.'

Liberty opened the fitting-room door and Denys let out a whistle of appreciation. 'That looks stunning! I'm not even going to attempt to find you anything else. That's the one. You'll have men queuing up to talk to you at that party. Incidentally,' she lowered her voice, 'I was so sorry to hear about your divorce.'

'Well, I wasn't. To be honest, I feel as if I've been let out of prison. The decree nisi should come through any day now.'

Liberty had been worried that Zac would contest the divorce, but because she was walking away from the marriage with only the money she had earned, he had let it go through. She guessed that he would have met someone else by now. Zac was not a man who could be on his own for long.

'Well, darling, enjoy it while it lasts because I doubt you'll stay single for long. And I imagine Cal and Angel know some very eligible young men who would love to meet a Hollywood star. Come and show Em.'

She also loved the dress and ignored all Liberty's protests that it was too short. 'For God's sake, if I had your figure, I'd dress like that all the time!' she declared, then added, 'So, Denys, do you know who is going to the party?' Denys invariably knew who had been invited to big events in the city.

She reeled off a list of footballers Liberty had never heard of, a couple of TV presenters, and several actors.

'Oh, and there's this absolutely gorgeous artist going. Cory Richardson, have you heard of him? He's made quite a name for himself painting various super-models and actors, and Angel in fact. I'm not sure if he's attached or single. But if he's single . . . well, I would be first in line. I met him at a charity dinner the other month, where he had donated one of his paintings for the auction. What a charmer! They don't make them like that any more.'

Liberty looked over at Em, who shook her head and put her finger to her lips. So, she was going to have a second chance to see Cory. But would he listen to anything she had to say? Not unless he'd had a massive change of heart. And she couldn't see how that was possible.

Denys had turned her attention to Em and didn't notice that Liberty had gone completely silent. She returned to the fitting room and took off the pink dress. Em knocked at the door and came in.

'Are you okay?' she asked.

'Yes . . . no. I don't know. How can I go to the party now?'

'Maybe he'll have calmed down and want to talk,' replied Em, ever the optimist.

'I doubt that very much. And I don't know if I could bear to see him with his wife again. They looked so happy together. What am I going to do, Em?'

'You're going to buy that dress for a start. And you are going to the party. Otherwise it's like you've got something to hide, and you haven't. Your ex-husband was the one to blame, not you. And you've got to tell Cory that, once and for all. But before that, you can give me your honest opinion about me in these dresses. I want something to blow Noah's mind.'

Liberty forced herself to stop thinking about Cory for a second. 'Of course. Start with the red one.'

Chapter 32

Brooke

In the week that followed Flynn barely spoke to Brooke. He seemed subdued, and rushed off after every class. To see Eve, she guessed. Well, good luck to them. But she felt hurt nevertheless. She had believed that they were getting closer and had come to enjoy talking to him, not even minding too much when he teased her. She missed their conversations, and she missed him. She wasn't so sure any more that she only saw him as a friend. It was just her luck to pick someone who was in love with someone else . . . .

She probably would have spent some nights brooding about him but Mila forced her to go to the gym every day after college. Brooke had unleashed the inner fitness fanatic in her. From hating the gym with a passion, Mila had now become obsessed. More than once Brooke would have far rather sneaked off home and crashed out in front of the TV, but she felt that she couldn't let Mila down.

One night they were finishing up with some stretches and Brooke was thinking longingly of a shower when

Mila nudged her and whispered, 'Hey, that guy has been here every single night that we have, and every single night he's checked you out. He's doing it now. Two o'clock.'

Of course Brooke looked the wrong way and saw an overweight middle-aged man, in a vest and shorts, with black hair sprouting from his back and shoulders, grunting with effort as he attempted to pick up some dumb-bells. *Perlease!* She might be single, but she wasn't desperate. She shot Mila a WTF look.

'Not him, you idiot. Him!' Throwing discretion to the wind Mila pointed at a dark-haired twenty-something guy, who smiled and waved and to Brooke's embarrassment walked over to them.

He looked as if he had barely broken sweat during his workout, whereas Brooke knew that her face was scarlet.

'Hi, I wondered if you would like to have a drink with me in the bar?' He looked at Mila. 'Both of you, of course. I'm Seb by the way.'

Okay, so he had nice manners, plus he was very good-looking with short dark-blond hair and hazel eyes. Also very nice teeth. He had the look of a younger Josh Duhamel, a Hollywood actor Brooke rather liked . . .

'Oh, I'm busy,' Mila replied. 'But I'm sure Brooke's free.'

Thanks for dropping me in it, Mila. Then again Seb seemed cute. And why the hell shouldn't she have a drink with him? No one else had shown any interest in her since she'd moved here, and a bit of male attention would certainly be welcome and make her feel that she still had something.

Half an hour later Brooke was sitting in the bar with

Seb, chatting over a smoothie and finding him very easy company. He was halfway through a degree in Marketing at Brighton Uni and was also making quite a good living as a model. His plan was to model for as long as he could and then open his own agency. She liked his ambition. Even better, he had been to LA and loved it – the climate, the vibe, the shopping, the restaurants, the beaches, the people. No hint of any judgment. At last! Someone who got it! And someone who could get her! And she was a hundred per cent certain that he wasn't gay from the looks he had been giving her. Serious eye contact, that could only mean one thing.

'So do you think you'll go back there?' he asked.

'You bet! As soon as I finish college and drama school here.'

'Good, you'll be here for a while then.' He paused. 'I would hate you to be leaving too soon. I'd really like to get to know you better.'

Okay, that was a little cheesy but Brooke was won over by the warm smile he gave her. What was wrong with being nice? He might not have Flynn's edge and wit, but Flynn was unavailable.

They arranged to meet the following week – Seb was going to be away until then – and Brooke went home feeling maybe life wasn't so bad after all. Seb was just the ego boost she'd needed.

Back home her mom was going through a pile of old photographs. She was sitting on the living-room floor with photos scattered everywhere.

'Mum gave me these the other night. I thought I'd sort them out and put them into an album,' Liberty told her. 'There are some beautiful ones of you.'

Brooke sat down next to her and started looking through the pictures. There were heaps of her as a baby and toddler, looking like the happiest child in the world, and masses of her with Liberty and Nina. She couldn't help feeling a little sad that there wasn't a single image of her dad.

She picked up a picture that showed her holding an ice cream, one of those whipped-up white ones with a flake that she would never allow herself to have now – far too many calories. Sitting next to her on the beach, laughing at her after she had managed to get ice cream all over her face, was a striking young man with blond hair and blue eyes.

'Who's this?' she held up the picture for Liberty to see.

Instantly her mom seemed to tense up. 'Oh, just someone I used to know.'

'Yeah, but who is he? He looks really nice.' Brooke noticed there were several more pictures of the young man with her as she flicked through the pile, and then she came across one of him with her mom. They were standing by the sea, arms round each other; Liberty was looking up at him and smiling and he was gazing at her. They looked completely, head over heels, in love. Brooke didn't think she had ever seen Liberty look at Zac like that.

Her mom practically snatched the photograph out of Brooke's hand and shoved it to the bottom of the pile, as if she couldn't bear to look at it.

'So, who is he?' Brooke repeated. 'You obviously really liked each other.'

'Someone who belongs in the past,' Liberty said, and began scooping up the photos and putting them into a plastic bag.

'Yeah, but how long did you see each other? What happened?'

Liberty was usually so easygoing that Brooke could

ask her anything, but now, without meeting her daughter's eye, she snapped, 'Nothing that I want to talk about. It was a summer romance; it didn't mean anything. Then I met Zac and moved to LA. End of story.'

Whoah! Liberty seemed seriously rattled. She managed to calm down enough to ask what Brooke fancied for supper: 'I could make a salade Niçoise.'

Brooke didn't want to be fobbed off so easily, but equally she didn't want to stress out her mom, who'd seemed genuinely upset by the questions.

'Fine by me.'

She was itching to go through the photos again to see if there were any more of the mystery guy, but Liberty took them with her and hid them away somewhere. Maybe she was thinking, out of sight, out of mind, but Brooke's curiosity was aroused now.

Over dinner Liberty asked her about college and what she'd been up to. It was a novelty, spending so much time with her mom, and Brooke had to admit that she liked it. It had been lonely at times at the LA house.

'I met this guy at the gym, Seb, he seems really nice. I might ask him to the party. It would be good to have a partner there. I don't want to be without a date at my eighteenth, that would be so tragic.'

'But I thought you'd go with Flynn.'

Where did that come from? '*Hello!* Flynn has a girlfriend.' She put on an English accent. 'A frightfully, frightfully posh girlfriend, who thinks that I'm not terribly classy and far too tanned. She's one of those English rose types.'

'Oh.' Liberty seemed surprised by the news. 'I thought—' She stopped.

'What?'

'I thought he really liked you when he came over that time. And I'm sure he was only helping out with the cooking to impress you. In fact, I'm a hundred per cent certain. He kept looking at you, and teasing you. Sure signs.'

'No way! He's always having a go at me for being such an LA airhead, and he hates LA. He criticises my clothes, my shoes, my accent, my attitude.' Brooke paused for a moment. 'Oh, I guess he was sweet when those women were so vile to me in the restaurant, and he told me I was a good actress. But no, Mom, he's not interested in me. Only as a friend.'

'Okay, if you say so.' Her mom actually smirked!

Brooke shook her head. She knew the truth about Flynn. And she didn't like the way her mom had managed to sidestep any questions about her own past. But Brooke had an ace up her sleeve – in the form of Nina. Her gran would know about the blond man, she was sure.

And so the following day, Brooke went round to Nina's after class. Her gran had been baking chocolate brownies and it was official, she made the best brownies *ever*. The whole house smelled deliciously of baking. Brooke was not going to be able to say no. Damn. It would mean extra time at the gym but resistance was futile . . .

Nina grinned at her as she sat at the kitchen table, drinking a mug of tea and tucking into one of the brownies.

'I can't believe you're drinking normal, regular tea and eating an actual brownie. What's got into you? Where's my LA princess? The girl who can only drink mineral water and thinks that sugar is the devil's work?'

Brooke rolled her eyes. 'You've worn me down by never having any herbal tea. And you know I absolutely have to eat your brownies!'

'Good, you could do with putting a bit of weight on.' Nina adopted a very bad American accent. 'Size zero is, like, so last season.'

'That's crap, Nina, you can never be too thin or too rich.'

'Don't you believe it. Men want women with curves, not some skeleton. How is your love life by the way? Your mom mentioned a boy at college, Flynn or something?'

Was nothing secret?

'Nothing's going on there. And actually, Nina, I wanted to ask you about Mom's.'

'Oh? I didn't think she was interested in seeing anyone at the moment, I thought she was doing the big *I want to be alone thing*. Even though, frankly, she's been doing that for the last God knows how many years, married to Zac. I've seen fridge freezers with more warmth than him. I don't know how she managed to stick it out for so long.'

Nina had never got on with Zac, who'd always kept out of her way when she was over for a visit.

'Come on, Nina, he's not that bad.' Brooke didn't know why she felt any loyalty to Zac, he'd hardly bothered to reply to her long emails other than to say everything was fine and he hoped that she was well. And this was someone she had spent nearly fourteen years of her life with . . . She wondered if he would even remember that it was her birthday soon.

'Anyway, let's not talk about him. I saw some of Mom's old photos and there was one of this good-looking blond guy she was seeing when I was about four. Mom tried to make out he wasn't important, but I got the feeling that wasn't true.'

She expected Nina to crack a joke, but unexpectedly she looked wistful. 'Oh, him.'

That seemed intriguing. 'So who was he?'

'Cory. The love of your mother's life, I think it's fair to say.'

WTF! Brooke had never even heard her mom mention him.

'And so what happened?'

'She met him when she was twenty-one and they spent the summer together.' Nina hesitated. 'I really think you should get your mum to tell you the rest herself. It's her story, not mine.'

Brooke thought of the way Liberty had snatched away the photos of Cory. It didn't seem likely that she would talk about him.

'So did she ever see him again? Where does he live?' Brooke was hungry for information. She suddenly felt as if there was this huge part of her mom's life that she knew nothing about.

'I've no idea. She never talks about him.' Nina smiled. 'She might do to you though. Ask her.'

'I did try and she completely blanked me. Said it was just a summer romance and it didn't mean anything. It didn't exactly sound like a brief affair, Nina.'

'No, it was definitely more than that.'

'So why did she end up marrying Zac?'

Nina shook her head. 'I can't answer any of these questions, sweetheart – only your mum can.'

Brooke pushed her plate away, suddenly not able to finish the brownie. She couldn't understand why her mom would have given up her great love and settled for second best. It didn't make sense to her.

'What's his surname? Maybe we could find out where he's living and put him back in touch with Mom again?' It seemed such a romantic idea, like something out of a play or film.

'We're talking fourteen years ago. You can't just

crash into someone's life like that. He's bound to be settled down and most likely has kids now.' Nina sighed. 'Sometimes, however painful it might seem, the past is best left alone.'

Brooke absolutely did not agree, but she could see that there was no point in telling Nina that so changed the subject to her party.

Chapter 33

Brooke's eighteenth birthday party was less than a month away and everyone at college who had been invited was hugely excited . . . everyone, except Mila, who shut down every time the subject was mentioned. Brooke guessed it was because she felt self-conscious about her body. And even though she was starting to lose weight from her regular gym sessions and by eating more healthily, she still dressed in shapeless, baggy clothes that did absolutely nothing for her. An intervention was needed, and Brooke knew just what to do. She invited Mila over for a girl's night in on Friday. Earlier she had arranged for a local boutique to send over a selection of dresses – the owner had been to school with her mom. Of course, once Harry got wind of the night, he begged to be included as well.

At first Mila was reluctant to take any part in the makeover. 'There's no point; nothing's going to make any difference. I'll still be the token fat girl in a sea of skinny beautiful people.'

Brooke exchanged eye rolls with Harry. This was going to be harder than she had anticipated. 'Look, just let me have a go at doing your make up. It's not a big deal, and if you don't like it, you can take it off.'

'Okay, but no posting any before and after pictures up on Facebook,' Mila warned.

'I swear that what happens in my bedroom, stays in my bedroom,' Brooke replied, wondering how she was going to get Mila to loosen up. Her friend was walking over to the dressing table as if she was on the way to her execution. It would have to be alcohol.

'Harry, stop reading *Heat* and go and get us a bottle of wine – ask my mom for some rosé.'

He sighed and threw the magazine down. 'I was in the middle of a very important decision – who do I prefer, Harry Styles or Max George? It's kind of cheeky boy versus naughty boy. Maybe I could have both. Ooh, I'd forgotten about the Beiber. I like him now he's gone a bit naughty, flashing his pants at everyone.'

'Wine,' Brooke repeated, knowing that Harry could go on indefinitely about those boys.

'Your wish is my command, mistress,' he declared, finally peeling himself off the bed.

'You've got beautiful skin,' Brooke told Mila truthfully as she began applying foundation. The more she had got to know Mila, the more she had come to realise how exceptionally pretty she was.

'I've certainly got a lot of it,' Mila replied. 'And so if I do lose weight, I'll just have folds of skin hanging down, like Elephant Woman. Still, on the plus side, I guess I could have my own website and charge people to have a look – my own private freak show – and that way save some money to go to college.'

It was typical of Mila to be so down on herself. Brooke tutted. Where was Harry with that bottle of wine? Didn't he realise that it was an emergency?

He reappeared clutching a bottle of rosé as Brooke

was getting to work on Mila's eyes, blending primer on to her eyelids before she applied the colour.

'Sorry, sweets! I got chatting to your mum, or Liberty as she said I could call her. Imagine . . . me, on first-name terms with a Hollywood star!'

'Ex-Hollywood star,' Brooke muttered. 'I don't think she'll ever act again in LA. My ex-stepdad will see to that.' Zac really did feel like her ex-stepdad – he had barely been in touch. It was as if he was divorced from Brooke as well. Thank God he and her mom had never had any kids, then it would have got even nastier . . .

'Well, it's a big old world out there. I'm sure she could get work wherever else she wanted.' Harry poured them each a large glass of wine and walked over to consider Brooke's handiwork. 'Not bad, princess. You rock as a make-up artist.'

'She's got her work cut out, trying to give me a makeover,' Mila muttered. 'It'll be her biggest challenge ever.'

Enough already! Brooke exchanged looks with Harry, who raised his eyebrows as if to say, *What can you do?* Well, not sit back and take this endless stream of negativity, that was for sure!

'Okay, we're going to have a rule that none of us can say anything negative about ourself and our life tonight. So I can't moan about missing LA, you can't bitch about your appearance, and Harry . . .'

'I never complain, I'm a constant ray of sunshine, haven't you noticed?' he piped up. 'I am one hundred per cent a glass half-full kind of guy.'

Actually, that was true. She had only ever heard him bitch about Eve, who frankly deserved it.

'Okay, well then, Harry can just be his lovely sunshine self.'

She finished working on Mila and allowed her to

look in the mirror. Brooke was rather proud of her handiwork. She had defined Mila's eyebrows and given them a great shape, and had emphasised her blue eyes with a smoky grey eyeshadow, flicks of black eyeliner and false lashes. Her skin looked flawless, under a shimmer of bronzer, and her lips were glossed a subtle red. Hmm, maybe if the acting didn't work out, Brooke could get a job as a make-up artist – that had to be better than waiting tables. Though she wouldn't get to see Flynn, and she had come to enjoy those times with him at the restaurant.

'What do you reckon?' she asked.

'Not bad,' Mila marvelled. 'If only I could have a new body as well—'

'No, no! We agreed, no negative comments. Harry, what do you think?'

'Love it. But, sweetie, you have got to do something about your hair.'

He was right. Mila's hair, peroxide blonde with two inches of black roots, was a mess.

'I know, I was going to bleach it again before the party.'

Ouch! It already looked to be in terrible condition. One more run in with the peroxide and Mila would be lucky if she had any hair left. 'Actually, my mom's booking a hairdresser for the day of the party, so they can do yours as well.' The old Brooke would have said up front and unapologetically that blonde was not for everyone, but now she found herself saying gently, not wanting to upset Mila, 'Maybe you should go darker – I think brunette would really suit you.'

'Yeah, I've been thinking that as well, but I can't afford to pay to have it done at the moment.'

'It's all paid for,' Brooke told her, again getting that buzz out of doing something for someone else. 'So

295

come on, now for the dresses.' She knew that this was the part that was likely to freak Mila out the most, as she never wore anything that showed off her figure, so she sent Harry downstairs to mix up some Strawberry Daiquiris. Her mom didn't mind if they had a little bit to drink at home. So long as no one got pissed and threw up on the carpets.

Mila remained sitting where she was, arms folded defensively.

'First of all I got you some Spanx.' Brooke threw a selection of packets on the bed. 'And before you try and make a negative comment, everyone wears them on the red carpet, and I mean *everyone* – from Gwyneth Paltrow to Katy Perry – and I wear them myself. So I'm going to see what Harry's up to while you get changed. Come down when you're ready. Oh, and help yourself to whatever shoes of mine you want.'

'Okay, thanks,' Mila said quietly.

Downstairs Harry was at work with the cocktail shaker, in between charming her mom with his anecdotes.

'How's it going?' he asked Brooke as she sat down at the marble breakfast bar.

'I'm not sure, I still think she might bail on us.'

'You've got her this far. I can really see that she's lost some weight from all your workouts at the gym, and at college she's been eating far more healthily. Usually she's, like, stuff it, I may as well eat whatever I want because it won't make any difference. But she's been going for salads and soups lately.' He looked over at Liberty. 'It's all your daughter's influence. She's been so lovely to Mila. A real friend.'

Liberty smiled. 'I know, and it's great.'

For once Brooke didn't even feel tempted to come out with a cynical putdown. It was a good feeling, knowing that she was doing something for someone else. She thought of how quickly she had dismissed Mila when she'd first met her, judging her entirely on her appearance, writing her off as the fat girl who could be of no interest to her, just because she didn't conform to Brooke's idea of what it was to look good. She was ashamed of her earlier attitude.

Twenty minutes and a cocktail later, Mila finally made an appearance. She had chosen a bright red halterneck dress, with a wide skirt and fitted waist. The Spanx had done their job of sucking everything in. She looked like a different person, a confident person. She actually walked differently, with her shoulders back and her head held high, rather than shuffling in, looking apologetic for even being there. Everyone was speechless as she stood in front of them.

'That bad, is it?' she asked, misinterpreting their silence. 'I thought so. You can put lipstick on a pig, but it's still a pig.' Her shoulders seemed to sag.

'No way!' Brooke rushed over to give her a hug. 'You look fantastic, I promise. Totally fantastic! Actually I'm kinda worried that you'll upstage me at my own party, which I don't think I can allow.'

'You really think I look okay?' Mila asked nervously.

'You look amazing,' Harry said, leaping off his chair and hugging her as well.

'Beautiful,' Liberty echoed. 'Like an old-school movie star.'

'And I'm getting the dress for you – my present, a thank you for making me so welcome here,' Brooke added. 'I think it's perfect for the party.' She could see Mila was about to protest and held up her hand. 'Really, I'm buying it and that's final.'

And then Mila managed a smile, a slight wobbly, tentative one at first that grew into a broad grin.

It ended up being one of the best nights Brooke had had in ages. Liberty went out to see a film with Em, leaving Brooke and her friends free to drink more cocktails and dance outrageously in the living room while singing along to the karaoke machine – Harry's suggestion naturally. It was practically impossible to wrestle him off the mic once he started. But they all managed to have a go. Harry belted out an Adele medley – it might be a while before Brooke wanted to hear 'Skyfall' again. She sang Rihanna's 'Umbrella' and Mila sang Gloria Gaynor's classic, 'I will Survive' – she was slightly flat, but the feeling was there. For the first time Brooke didn't think she would rather be anywhere else or with anyone else. It was brilliant hanging out with her new friends. And only having Flynn there as well would have made it perfect . . . though no doubt he would have been too cool to sing.

Midnight found the three of them stretched out on the sofas in their PJs, drinking hot chocolate. Something else she couldn't quite imagine Flynn doing, as he didn't seem like the kind of boy to wear PJs – she imagined him naked in bed or in boxers . . . phew! She should maybe stop imagining. Harry, of course, had a pair of red silk kimono-style PJs; Mila's were grey. That girl really needed to wear some other colours.

'How would you guys go about finding someone if you didn't have their second name?' Brooke had been meaning to ask this question all night. She had not forgotten about wanting to find out who her mom's great love was.

Instantly Harry and Mila were curious to know who she was talking about and she ended up telling them everything.

'Marco might know. He was at the restaurant when your mum was,' Harry suggested.

298

'Great idea! I didn't even think of that!' Brooke exclaimed.

'But, remember, this guy might not welcome you contacting him, if you do track him down,' Mila warned. 'Imagine how you would feel if you were dumped by the love of your life and then years later they contacted you again. And don't you think if they'd wanted to be in touch they would have been by now? It's so easy, with things like Facebook. There must be a reason why they haven't.'

But Brooke didn't want to hear that. To her it was a great romance and if her mom wasn't going to do anything about it, then she would. It was going to be her mission. She had helped Mila and she would help her mom.

In bed later that night, she actually constructed a whole fantasy about Cory and Mom back together and getting married. Brooke would be a bridesmaid in, say, a Stella McCartney number – her mom would be in ivory Vera Wang. She imagined a church wedding in a picturesque English village, then a reception in the grounds of a beautiful stately home. Her mom would make an emotional speech, and say, 'It's all thanks to my daughter that I've been reunited with the man I love. Brooke, we can never thank you enough.'

She went to sleep with the imagined applause and cheers from the other guests echoing in her head.

Chapter 34

Marco knew exactly who she was talking about when she asked him about Cory the following night at the restaurant. As he was clearly still feeling guilty for shouting at her the previous week, he was more than happy to tell Brooke all he knew, including the piece of prize information, Cory's second name: Richardson. He had been an American student, apparently, taking time out from his studies to travel, and one night had come into the restaurant with a group of friends.

'I swear it was love at first sight for the pair of them,' Marco said. 'Everyone could see. It was very romantic. Young love, first love.' He seemed quite wistful at the memory.

Brooke's excitement went up a gear, and she was itching to go off and Google Cory now she had his full name. But Marco hadn't finished. 'I think he lives near Brighton. I once saw him on the beach with his son. He didn't see me and I didn't say anything. Your mum left him very abruptly. I think he was heartbroken. I remember him coming in here trying to find her, but I had no idea where she had gone. I suppose she had her reasons for leaving him.'

All Brooke had taken in was the comment about the son. So Nina was right, he had moved on. She had been so caught up in the romantic story she hadn't considered that there would be other people involved. She suddenly felt dispirited. Her happy-ever-after scenario was fading before her eyes. Typical.

'He's a really respected artist now. You should tell your mum, she was always encouraging him to take that path. In fact, I think he's got an exhibition on at a gallery in Brighton at the moment.'

'Yeah, I will. Thanks, Marco.' She had no intention of telling Liberty. She wished she had never found out about Cory, who was obviously happily married with children. He was bound to have more than one son. In Brooke's head she gave him three children. He had everything that she would have wanted for her mom.

She felt subdued for the rest of the shift, though she tried not to show it in front of Mila and Flynn. She didn't want them asking any questions. Back home she couldn't resist Googling Cory Richardson when she was upstairs in her room. There were plenty of hits with his name and quite a few images, that showed him looking older but still as handsome as in the photographs she'd seen. Marco was right, he seemed to be a very successful artist and had painted a number of commissions for some very famous people. And from what she could gather, he lived just outside Brighton with his wife and son. At least there was only one child. God, she really hoped that her mom hadn't looked him up, though Brooke found it hard to believe that she wouldn't have. What did Nina say? The love of her life? Well, the love of her life was currently only a few miles away. How would it feel knowing that?

She promised herself that she wouldn't think about Cory any more, but the following day, when Liberty had gone to the gym, Brooke was once more drawn to Google him. She discovered where his exhibition was showing and decided on impulse to go and see it. She didn't exactly know why – maybe she thought there would be some kind of indication in his work that he still had feelings for her mom. Maybe she had been watching too many films where things like that happened. Either way, it was a beautiful day and she set off on her bike along the seafront. She was halfway there when she saw a familiar figure walking towards her. It was Flynn. She wondered what he was doing around here. As far as she knew Eve lived in a village just outside Brighton, in the opposite direction.

'Hi,' Brooke called out, coming to a halt and getting off her bike. Since their hug, she had experienced an outbreak of what could only be described as butterflies whenever she saw Flynn. It was temporary, she was sure. Once she'd been on the date with Seb, the butterflies would go back to their rightful place, but they were out in force now. Crazily so. Flynn was in a t-shirt and shorts, and looked seriously good.

'Hi, I was coming to see you. You were so quiet last night, I wanted to check that you were okay. So where are you off to?'

She wondered why he wasn't with Eve as they'd seemed to be joined at the hip for the last few weeks, but didn't say it. She wanted to get back to the banter they had shared, not throw up barriers.

'I'm fine, I was just tired last night. I'm going into Brighton to see an art exhibition, if you want to come?' She tried to make it sound casual but she knew that Flynn would be surprised as she had never expressed any interest in art.

'*Seriously?* You're not going shopping for more designer clothes? More crippling shoes? More

302

investment pieces? You're not going to have a spray tan or have your nails done or your hair? Or have the hairs waxed out of your nostrils?'

Brooke rolled her eyes. 'And to think I've missed seeing you.' Oops, she hadn't meant to say that. But Flynn didn't pick up on it.

'Okay, well, I'm up for the art. Why not?'

She pushed her bike as they continued to walk along the promenade, the seagulls wheeling over their heads, squawking loudly. It was good seeing Flynn, more than good. He made her feel alive.

'So how's it been going with that bloke?'

For a moment she didn't know who he could mean, as she was so caught up in thinking about him and wondering what he had been doing lately.

'The guy from the gym,' Flynn clarified, seeing her blank expression.

'Oh, Seb? We're meeting next week. He's been away on a course.'

'But you are going to see him again?'

Why all these questions? 'Yep. And before you say anything, he is definitely straight. I'm absolutely one hundred per cent certain of it.'

'How do you know? You don't exactly seem to be an expert in these things.' He grinned.

'Because he was the one who chatted me up, or whatever you Brits say, and the one giving me the eye from across the crowded gym. Gay men tend not to do that to girls . . . And how's Eve? Not been drinking any beer, I hope – it's *so* bloating. Didn't you know that?' She put on a posh English accent for the last comment.

'Very funny. She's fine.' He didn't seem to want to say anything else about his girlfriend and changed the subject to their drama project.

*

303

The exhibition was in Kensington Gardens, one of the narrow lanes, which was buzzing with shoppers. As they drew closer to the gallery, which was painted a chic grey, Brooke began to feel nervous. Perhaps it was a mistake to be digging into the past. It wasn't any of her business. But then she thought of her mom sacrificing her relationship with Cory and how she had reacted when Brooke questioned her. She needed to know if there was a picture that she could trace back to her mom, to know if Cory really did belong to the past.

She and Flynn paused outside and looked at the painting of the black female singer that dominated the window.

'I love that,' Flynn commented.

'Yeah, so do I.'

'Really?'

'Really. Did you think I would only like pictures of shoes and handbags?'

'Not exactly. Well, maybe.'

She swiped a punch at his arm. 'The trouble with you, Flynn, is that you're too quick to judge people. You should be more open to new experiences, like me.'

And before he could make a smart reply, she walked into the gallery.

There was no one in it, apart from the young red-headed woman working on her laptop behind the desk. She smiled at Flynn and Brooke then turned her attention back to her screen, probably realising that they weren't there to buy. Brooke walked slowly round the room, pausing to look at each painting. They were all striking, vivid works – some of individuals, a saxophonist, a dancer, a skateboarder, others scenes of urban life – a crowded bar where there was a couple sitting at a table, a hot day in a park, with people lying out on the grass. Disappointingly there wasn't a picture that reminded Brooke of her mom. Oh, well, maybe that wasn't surprising. It was all a long time ago.

The young woman glanced up at them again. 'Is there anything particular I can help you with?'

What Brooke really wanted to know was whether Cory was happily married, but that was hardly an appropriate question.

'I really like the bar scene,' she replied, gesturing at the painting. 'How much is it?'

'It's twenty-five.'

Brooke was pretty sure that she didn't mean pounds. Wow.

'Oh, that's slightly more than I can afford. I just wanted to get a present for my mom.'

'Sure. Well, why don't you take this leaflet about some of the artist's limited edition prints, which might be more in your price range.'

Brooke took the leaflet and thanked her and was all set to leave when a tall, blond man strode into the gallery. Cory Richardson himself, holding two takeaway coffees. Shit! She'd had no idea he would be here. She turned away and pretended to be looking at one of the paintings but all her attention was on what he was saying.

'Thought you might be in need of a caffeine fix, Daisy. How's it going?'

He had a pleasant voice, and still had an American accent.

'Really well, Cory, I've sold the dancer.'

'You have? That's fantastic. God! I should have bought a bottle of champagne to celebrate, never mind two lattes.'

He realised they weren't alone and turned to Flynn and Brooke. 'Sorry, you are being looked after, aren't you?'

305

'Yeah, my friend's admiring the bar scene,' Flynn replied. Damn – Brooke didn't want to draw any attention to herself.

Cory looked at her. 'You have good taste, that's one of my favourites.'

'Well, it's a little out of my price range, I'm only a student.'

'You could sell your handbags or your designer shoes,' Flynn whispered, 'I'm guessing they're worth a lot.'

Cory laughed. 'Don't you dare come between a woman and her accessories!' He seemed so open and warm, Brooke smiled at him. Then he seemed to do a double take as he looked at her. 'You seem very familiar, do I know you from somewhere? Perhaps the university? I sometimes do some guest lecturing there.'

He had given her the perfect get out, but should she tell him the truth? She thought of Nina urging her to leave the past alone, of her mom hiding the photographs away. She should say no. He was married with a son, she really should say no. But then she thought of Liberty, wasting all those years being married to Zac. She had to know if Cory still had feelings for her.

'Actually you do. But not from university. From a long time ago. About fourteen years.' She had everyone's full attention. For a moment Cory was speechless and then he spoke. 'I can only think that you must be Liberty's daughter. You have exactly the same eyes.'

She nodded. 'Yes, we've moved back to Brighton. My mom's getting divorced. I found an old photograph, and my mom and you looked so in love.' The words were tumbling out now. 'And I thought you should know that she's here.'

Something in Cory seemed to shut down as he said coldly, 'I know.'

Brooke winced at his tone. She didn't know what she had expected, but it wasn't this. 'Oh, well, aren't you going to see her?' she stammered. 'It seems like what you had between you was really special. A once-in-a-lifetime thing.'

'No. I don't want to see Liberty and I'm not going to see her. If you'll excuse me, I have work to do.'

When Brooke remained where she was, too shocked to come up with a reply, Flynn reached for her hand. 'Come on, we should go,' he said quietly. He led her out of the gallery, a gesture she was grateful for as she suddenly felt wobbly and on the verge of tears. She couldn't believe how badly that had turned out.

'Come on,' he said, 'we'll go and have a coffee, it's okay.' His being kind to her made it even worse.

'It's not okay!' Brooke burst out, oblivious to the shoppers looking at them as she stopped in the middle of the pavement. 'I've really upset him and I never intended that to happen. And I really thought he would want to know that my mom was here. Nina said that he was the love of Mom's life! Why won't he at least see her again? It seems so harsh, so final.' She couldn't make it tie in with the picture she had seen of Cory and her mom, gazing at each other lovingly all those years ago.

Flynn shook his head. 'I don't know, Brooke.'

She couldn't bear being surrounded by so many people, and in the end they got her bike and went and sat on the beach. She'd fully expected Flynn to give her a hard time for what she'd done, but he was calm and kind, told her not to blame herself, that she wasn't to know it would spark such an adverse reaction in Cory.

'Do you think he just said all that because he was shocked? D'you think maybe he'll change his mind?' She was obsessing now. She couldn't let this drop.

'I think you're going to have to leave it,' Flynn said gently. 'Whatever happened is between them.'

Brooke hunched her shoulders and stared out to sea. She could well and truly kiss goodbye to the fantasy of her mom being reunited with her great love.

'It's all my fault. If Mom hadn't had me, she would have been free to do what she wanted. It was having me that made her choose a life with Zac. She had a horrible marriage with him, I know she did.'

Flynn put his arm round her. 'Hey, that's not true. Your mum loves you, and she had her own reasons for making her choices. You can't blame yourself. Promise?'

He was gazing at her and suddenly, even upset as she was, she felt the rush of butterflies. His brown eyes were so warm; his lips were so, well, kissable. She held his gaze, unable to look away. Who was she kidding? She *really* liked him. She longed to bury her face in his shoulder, breathe in his scent.

The moment was ruined when Flynn's phone rang. Eve, of course, wanting to know where he was. Did she have some kind of inbuilt radar, able to detect whenever he was with another girl? Brooke picked up a handful of pebbles and threw them in turn at a piece of driftwood, trying to drown out Flynn's conversation.

'I'm really sorry,' he said, after he'd ended the call, 'but I've got to go. I'd completely forgotten that I was supposed to be having lunch with Eve and her family, it's her mum's birthday.' He pulled a face. 'They're all waiting for me in the restaurant. I got the dates wrong. Will you be okay?'

Not really, she wanted to say. *Not at all.* 'I'll be fine, thanks. At least I know now. Everyone was right. What my mom and Cory had belongs in the past.'

Chapter 35

Liberty

Liberty poured herself a large glass of white wine. It seemed the wrong thing to do after working out at the gym but she didn't really care. Seeing Cory again had pushed her into a dark place. She had been trying to put on a brave face, throwing herself into organising Brooke's party, buying a new dress for Angel's, but she couldn't stop thinking about the look of disdain on Cory's face as he'd told her to go. It felt as if it was burned into her consciousness. She would never forget it.

She glanced up as Brooke walked into the kitchen.

'Hi, honey, where have you been?' She forced herself to sound cheerful, even though she felt anything but.

'Just in town.' Her daughter seemed subdued too. She did that teenage thing of slumping at the kitchen table as if she didn't have the energy to sit up.

'Have you had lunch? I could make us poached eggs?'

Brooke shook her head. 'I'm not hungry.'

Liberty was about to launch into a speech about how

important it was to eat healthily and regularly when Brooke said, 'I need to tell you something.'

'Oh?' Liberty took a seat opposite her. Maybe it was something to do with Flynn. Liberty was convinced her daughter had a massive crush on him. At least that was one teenage boy she approved of.

'I went to see Cory Richardson,' Brooke blurted out.

Liberty was so stunned that for a moment she couldn't quite take in what her daughter had said. It was like having two parts of her life that she had always kept entirely separate collide.

But Brooke continued, 'I went to see him at the gallery. I wanted him to know that you had split up from Zac and moved here.'

'What on earth did you do that for?' Liberty exclaimed, leaping out of her chair. 'You had no right to do that! I wouldn't dream of interfering in your life!'

Brooke seemed taken aback by the strength of her reaction. 'Well, I know he's the love of your life! And you wasted all those years with Zac, and I wanted to help you.'

'No one can help me! I'm not some little project. Cory and I are finished; we were finished years ago. He's married with a son. He doesn't need silly little girls thinking that they can fix something that isn't even broken. Honestly, Brooke, I thought you had grown up since we've moved here, but you're still that spoiled girl who thinks that just because she wants things to be a certain way, then that will happen. Well, let me tell you, life isn't like that.' Liberty had gone too far but she couldn't stop the pent-up anger and hurt all coming out.

'I'm sorry. I did it for you,' Brooke managed to say. She was on the verge of tears, but Liberty still raged at her.

'Well, next time, don't fucking bother! I'm perfectly capable of sorting out my own relationships.'

At that Brooke grabbed her bag and ran out of the room. Liberty drained half the glass of wine. She heard the front door slam. It was just as well. Right now she needed some time out from her daughter.

But by nine o'clock she was getting worried. Her anger had passed and now she felt terrible for shouting at Brooke. She had called her daughter and texted her but received no reply, and she didn't know any of Brooke's friends' numbers. She paced around the house, unable to settle, clutching her mobile. She was just about to call Marco at the restaurant and see if he could give her Mila's number when her mobile rang. It was Nina.

'I've got Brooke with me. She's fine now. We've had a few tears but she's calmed down. D'you want to come over?'

Brooke refused to speak to Liberty when she walked into her mum's living room. She had her headphones on and was listening to music. She stared resolutely ahead, refusing to acknowledge her. Hardly surprising. Liberty knew she had some bridge-building to do.

'Give her a few minutes,' Nina advised. 'Come on, I'll make you a cup of tea, it looks like you need it.'

'I can't believe I shouted at her like that.' Liberty sat at the familiar oak table that had been in the house since she was little and still had the wonky letter B which Brooke had scratched into it when she was three, so proud of being able to form the letter that she wrote it everywhere. Now Liberty traced her fingers over it.

'Well, you did, and now you've just got to make things up. Maybe it's all for the best that it's out in the open. Secrets don't do anyone any good. So what are

311

you going to do about Cory? You've still got unfinished business, whatever he says.'

'I don't know, Mum.' She genuinely felt lost. All she wanted to do was make things up with Brooke. She drank her tea and then ventured into the living room.

'Can I sit down?' Liberty asked her daughter, gesturing at the space next to her on the sofa. A shrug was all she got from Brooke, who kept her headphones on.

'I'm really sorry I shouted at you. I understand why you did what you did. I reacted like that because I saw Cory last week and he made it clear that he didn't want to see me again. I guess I was taking all my hurt out on you.'

Now she had Brooke's attention. 'Really? He said that to you?'

'Yeah.' She tentatively reached out and rubbed Brooke's shoulder. 'It was a blow. But at least I know now. Please forgive me, Brooke.'

'Oh, Mom! That's so tragic,' she exclaimed, reaching out and hugging her.

'It's going to be okay,' Liberty said, hugely relieved that her daughter had forgiven her.

'Who needs men anyway?' Brooke said as she pulled away. 'They're all assholes.'

'Just because I swore at you, doesn't give you a free pass,' Liberty shot back.

'And enough of swearing off men, neither of you means it.' Nina had caught the comment as she walked into the room. 'And I definitely don't. And if you two have finally made up, you can bugger off. I'm expecting a gentleman caller.'

'Ooh! Who's that?' Brooke asked.

'He's called Chris and he's a chef. A man of few

words, but very good at other things, if you know what I mean.' Nina winked at them, to Brooke's outrage.

'TMI, Nina, TMI!'

But they were all laughing as Liberty and Brooke said goodbye.

Chapter 36

Brooke

After seeing Flynn on Sunday Brooke found that she couldn't stop thinking about him. Obsessing would be more accurate. She kept looking at his Facebook page and clicking through all his photographs. Eve had put up a picture of them both at the family lunch, smiling away for the camera. The beautiful, happy couple. Brooke felt a pang of longing for something that she couldn't have. She forced herself to click 'like' even though she definitely did not like, not one bit.

Oh, God! It was fucked up and hopeless but Flynn filled her thoughts. There was nothing she could do – there could be no campaign to attract him as there had been with Christian, she was going to have to deal with the fact that he was with Eve and out of reach. Besides, she didn't even think that she was his type of girl. And so Thursday night found her going out on the date with Seb, the guy from the gym, even though by now she had zero interest in him. She would far rather have stayed in and watched TV, so that didn't bode well.

He had booked a table at an Italian restaurant and from the moment Brooke sat down his conversation revolved around how many calories their respective meals contained and how her exercise regime was going. Yes, he was good-looking, but man, he was mind-numbingly boring! Why hadn't she realised this when she first met him? He could be used as a way of getting criminals to talk: lock Seb in the room with them and just let him drone on and on and the perps would confess all. Shit! They'd probably confess to things that they hadn't done – anything to avoid him listing the calorie content of every single food! Brooke could barely stifle the yawns that threatened to overwhelm her. If he didn't stop, she'd end up face down in her four-hundred-and-seventy-five-calorie mushroom risotto (though he said it might well be over five hundred). She had already nearly finished her large glass of white wine, which she now knew was over two hundred calories . . . but, God, she needed it to get her through this date . . . and she was going to need another at this rate.

'I can always do some personal training for you. It can make all the difference to your motivation and achieving your goals. And I'd give you a discount. Your mum too, if you like.'

Hmm, Brooke didn't like the way Seb's eyes lit up when he mentioned her mom . . . she wasn't sure if it was because he knew what Liberty looked like or whether he was thinking of the fee he could charge. And though she was working out how she could leave the meal early and never see him again, she was also keen to discourage any idea about him being her personal trainer.

'Oh, thanks so much for the offer, but I'm happy working out with my friend.'

'Oh, yeah, the curvy one. She's got quite a long way to go, hasn't she? I guess I could train you both. I'd have to make sure she didn't hold you back, though.'

She really didn't like Seb's dismissive tone when he talked about Mila. 'Like I said, I'm really happy with the way things are right now, I don't want to change anything.'

'So tell me more about LA – what are the current exercise crazes? The new diets? The States are always a couple of years ahead of us, aren't they? That's why I'd love to live out there, to feel like I was where things were happening.'

Brooke shrugged. Only a few weeks ago, she would have liked nothing more than to talk endlessly about LA. But nowadays she felt less and less like doing that. She was putting down roots here. LA was starting to feel like her past.

'To be honest, I don't know. I haven't kept up with them. My friend Kelly is really into Zumba, but that's big here now, isn't it? And sometimes we'd do the Roga class at Santa Monica Pier where you go running with a group and then have a session of yoga, looking out at the Pacific – that was cool.'

Seb seemed disappointed that she didn't have more to tell him. Clearly, she was not the girl he'd thought she was. He was silent for a few minutes, sipping his mineral water – he had refused wine, too calorific of course – apparently he only allowed himself alcohol one night a week. But he wasn't a man to be quiet for long.

'You look stunning in that dress,' he commented.

Brooke was wearing a cobalt blue skater-style dress that showed off her long tanned legs. 'Thanks.' Please don't let him say anything cheesy like she'd look stunning out of it . . . She wouldn't put it past him. He had the look of a man who might say panties.

'Yeah, you've got the perfect figure for it. My ex had one of those dresses.' Seb winced. 'In red. She kept wearing it, even when she was carrying too much weight. What is it with girls and food? When they're after you they keep fit and are slim, and the minute they get you, they pork out again and let themselves go.' He shook his head, as if he was very disappointed in and had been let down by the whole of womankind.

A new word, learned from Harry, sprang to mind – *tosser*. 'Yeah, but if you really like someone it shouldn't matter if they gain a few pounds here and there.' Brooke couldn't quite believe that she was saying this. Only a few months ago, the very thought of it would have been unimaginable to her. She had been so hung up on her appearance. She used to weigh herself every single day, obsess if she ever put on an ounce and then starve herself and exercise manically until she had lost it again. But since moving here she had stopped that cycle. She felt better, and honestly didn't think her weight had suffered from it. Clearly skipping meals was not good for you – now Brooke ate healthy food, three times a day, and allowed herself the odd treat.

'No, I don't agree. It's about respect. I'd respect any girlfriend of mine too much to put on weight, and I expect the same from her. Same goes for waxing.'

She couldn't have heard him right. 'I'm sorry?'

'You know, I keep it tidy down there – I have to because of my work and I expect my girlfriend to do the same.'

What the actual fuck! Did he really think that he was selling himself as a prospective boyfriend? Buff and waxed. Brooke had a vision of him weighing any girlfriend of his at the start of their relationship, and then regularly checking them to make sure they still

317

respected him by not putting on any weight. And monitoring their bikini line! She sincerely hoped that his last girlfriend had dumped him, but either way she was so much better off without him.

Somehow they got through the rest of dinner with Brooke inwardly vowing that she never wanted to see Seb again. She thought of the easy banter she shared with Flynn, the butterfly feeling he aroused in her, the sense of anticipation and excitement she got whenever she was around him. Being with Seb reminded her of the shallow, spoiled girl she had been, who had only cared about what she looked like and who would probably have found the conversation about calories enthralling.

She was dreading that Seb would ask her back to his place, or want to extend the evening with a drink, and was already planning her exit strategy. She had her excuses all lined up. She had terrible period pain, trapped wind, an urgent need to wax her bikini line. But, thank God, Seb said he had a really early start for a shoot.

Brooke was keen to say her goodbyes at the restaurant, but he insisted on walking her to the taxi rank. She couldn't help noticing that he spent most of the way there checking out his appearance in the shop windows they passed. He was as vain as Harry, but with none of his charm. Brooke was embarrassed that she had ever found him attractive. He made Christian seem like a decent guy . . . and that was saying something.

They were just passing All Saints when she noticed a familiar figure walking towards them. It was Flynn. He must have been working at the restaurant as he was in his waiter's uniform. His leather jacket was slung over his shoulder and he had never looked so handsome.

He grinned the moment he saw Brooke, and stopped

318

to speak to them. 'Out on the town while some of us have been working?'

If only he knew what hard work tonight had been! Frankly she would rather have been working a double shift waiting tables than spending any time with Seb, the giant tosser. Hell, she would rather have done the washing up all night and listened to Big Bruno singing Frank Sinatra songs, and he was a terrible singer, tone deaf, who murdered anything he sang.

She managed a smile and introduced Seb to Flynn.

Seb's first question summed up his character perfectly. 'So do you work out a lot then?'

'Nah, gyms are boring. I play football and I run and go swimming. That's enough, isn't it?'

'You think it's enough, but you're probably not working on specific muscle groups.'

'Yeah, well, I don't really have time for gyms.'

Who knows what other fascinating questions Seb had lined up for Flynn, but Brooke said that she *really* had to get a taxi, as she had a drama assessment first thing. She was certain that Flynn wore an ironic smile as he said goodbye. And so much for thinking that she would invite Seb to her party so she could have a partner for the night. She would rather be single than have to fake any kind of relationship with him.

She was just falling asleep when her phone beeped with a text message from Flynn. *Cheer up, we've all been on terrible dates, just put it down to experience. You were way too good for that gym bunny, even if he has worked all his muscle groups. xx*

She spent the next twenty minutes buzzing about the fact he had signed off with two kisses – surely that said they were more than friends? Oh, God! She *wished* it said that.

*

Mila and Harry wanted to know all the gory details the following day at college when they met up for coffee.

'It was a disaster,' Brooke told them. 'There was no chemistry between us at all. *Nada*. Nothing. *Rien!*'

'But Mila said he was so good-looking. What's going on with you, missy? It's about time you snagged yourself a hot English guy. One of us in this trio has to have a successful relationship.' That from Harry.

'Well, it's not going to be me. But I can deal with it. I'd rather be single than be with a jerk – however hot he is. Actually he wasn't even that hot, he kind of had a sweaty top lip, that grossed me out.' She then proceeded to tell them about Seb's outburst about his ex putting on weight and not keeping her bikini line in check, which had the pair of them in hysterics. In spite of feeling mortified that she had ever thought he was attractive, Brooke found herself joining in. The healing power of laugher, or something like that . . . Until Flynn turned up.

'What's so funny?'

Brooke wanted to warn her friends not to divulge the details, but of course Harry had to blab, even with her shooting him a pleading look. So much for solidarity. She folded her arms. Why was it her who always had to have her personal life raked over while she knew next to nothing about Flynn's relationship with Eve?

Flynn shook his head, and said in a mock-serious tone, 'So you were completely taken in by his looks and ripped abs? I'm disappointed in you, Brooke, I thought you had been on a journey of self-discovery since you'd moved here, that you'd left LA Brooke behind.' He sighed. 'We had all expected so much better of you. You have not been your highest self, have you?'

He was deliberately winding her up! She defiantly gave him the middle finger. 'Yeah, well, we all make mistakes, and I can admit that Seb was a big fat one.'

'Well, at least you didn't shag him, sweetie.' Harry, of course.

'Can you imagine? He probably has a mirror above his bed so he can watch himself perform,' Brooke replied, which set them all off giggling again, even Flynn.

'So I guess I'm going to be single for my eighteenth birthday party,' she declared. 'But so long as you guys are as well,' she pointed at Mila and Harry, 'then I can do it. Maybe I should ban people from bringing their partners. Or if they do bring them, there can be no PDAs. I'll have security guards going round and breaking up anything like that. It's my party, and if I'm not getting any action then no one is.' She looked meaningfully at Flynn.

'What? I don't do that kind of thing in public,' he protested.

'*Perlease!* You and Eve are repeat offenders,' Harry put in.

Flynn suddenly seemed awkward. 'Yeah, well, I'm not sure if Eve will be coming to the party. We had a row.'

'Oh?' Brooke asked, trying not to let on how interested she was in that piece of information.

But Flynn didn't say anything else and they all had to head off to their next class.

'*Please* let them have split up,' Harry whispered to Brooke as Flynn and Mila walked ahead. 'It's about time he realised what a bitch from hell she is.' He paused. 'And you know what I've been thinking – you and he would make the perfect couple. If he has to go out with a girl, then I would rather it was you above all others. At least that way I can get to find out what he's like in bed. You would owe me full disclosure. I take my pleasure any way I can in these lean times.'

'Harry, you're nuts!' Brooke exclaimed, certain that her cheeks were flaming bright red. 'And anyway, why do you even think Flynn would be interested in me?'

'Call it intuition, sweet pea. And you two have got that banter thing going on between you that only happens when two people really like each other. I can detect the chemistry between you.' He paused. 'And you're interested in him, aren't you?'

'Errr . . .' she stuttered.

'Yep, thought so.'

And before she could come up with a reply, he caught up with Mila and Flynn, leaving Brooke standing there, a mix of emotions bubbling up crazily inside her: excitement, hope, longing and the flutter of those butterflies. Oh brother, she just hoped that Harry could keep his thoughts to himself . . . but what were the chances? He was such a blabber.

Chapter 37

Liberty

'You look beautiful, Mom,' Brooke declared, from her vantage point on the bed, while Liberty sat at her dressing table getting ready for Angel and Cal Bailey's party.

'You think? I'm not so sure about this dress.' She stood up and considered herself in the full-length mirror. She was in the pink flared hem Hervé Léger bandage dress that Denys had picked out for her. 'You don't think it's too mutton?' She was aware that she was revealing a lot of flesh – the dress was strapless and was way above her knee. She hadn't dressed up since they'd moved back to Brighton, but lived in skinny jeans and t-shirts.

'Jeez! You're the youngest mom out of all my friends! How can it be mutton? What are you supposed to wear? A burqa?'

'It's just I'm so out of practice at going to these events.' Liberty hadn't told Brooke that Cory was going to be there. So many times she had thought about cancelling but it might be her only chance to see him and tell him about the letter. She couldn't hope to get any closure until she had done that. She picked up her silver Swarovski crystal clutch and checked she had everything in it that she'd need.

'Just go and have fun.' Her daughter sounded exactly like Em. 'Maybe you'll meet some handsome footballer and become a WAG or whatever they're called over here.'

'Hmm, let me think about that . . . No. I'm perfectly happy being single for the moment.' Several times over the last week Brooke had tried to bring up the subject of Cory, with varying degrees of subtlety, but Liberty had refused point blank to talk about him. She was very much hoping her daughter would forget about it soon, she didn't need the constant reminders. But some impulse made her open her jewellery case and reach for the dragonfly necklace.

'And what are you going to do tonight?' she asked, fastening the necklace.

'I'm seeing a film with the gang.'

'Flynn as well?'

'Yep – apparently Eve still isn't talking to him, which means he can come out and play with us.'

A car horn sounded from outside. 'Oh, that'll be Em and Noah.' Liberty blew Brooke a kiss. 'Promise I look okay?'

Brooke raised her eyebrows, smiled and said, 'I promise.'

Liberty was smiling to herself as she ran downstairs; it was so great hearing Brooke refer to her 'gang'. So what if she hadn't got a man in her life? Her daughter was happy and growing into a beautiful and well-balanced young woman. She was becoming everything that Liberty had wanted her to be.

*

Angel and Cal Bailey lived out in the countryside in a stunning Edwardian mansion set in over seventy acres of land, which was enough to accommodate Angel's horses, a swimming pool, hot tub, sauna and tennis courts, according to Em, who had all the inside info from Noah.

'Blimey, this is a bit posh,' the taxi driver exclaimed as they drew up to the imposing iron gates where two security personnel, dressed in black suits, with headsets and walkie talkies, were waiting to check people in.

'Are you lot famous or something then?' he continued. He peered at Em and Liberty.

'I'm not, she is,' Em pointed at her friend. But thankfully before he could launch into one of those 'What have I seen you in?' conversations, Noah paid the driver and they made a quick getaway.

The driveway up to the house was lined with flickering candles in ornate silver hurricane lamps. Now Liberty felt even more nervous. What would it be like seeing Cory again? Would she get the same hostile reaction?

Em linked her arm through Liberty's, sensing her nervousness. 'Come on, I need to get me some vintage champagne, but I can't eat too much or I'll burst out of my Spanx.' She looked very glam and pretty in an off-the-shoulder red Vivienne Westwood dress, and only slightly ruined the effect by trying to adjust her knicker line. Noah, who usually lived in faded jeans and t-shirts had scrubbed up well in a tux, but looked as if he'd prefer to be back in his jeans.

'Noah, does my bum look massive?' Em asked her husband. 'Is it going to cause an eclipse of the moon?'

'It looks great,' he said automatically. Clearly he'd been asked that question more than once.

Angel and Cal were having the party in a vast

marquee. Em laughed when she saw that it was white. 'I think Cal put his foot down about having a pink marquee again. Angel was allowed one for her thirtieth and he said she can't have another until her fortieth.'

When she saw Liberty's anxious expression, she said, 'Stop worrying. It will be good to see Cory again.'

Liberty didn't share her optimism but she followed her friend over to where Angel and Cal were greeting their guests. She reckoned Cal was in his late-thirties now and he was definitely one of those men who was getting better looking as he got older, with his olive skin, handsome face and jet black hair that was greying slightly at the sides. He didn't play football any more but he still had the physique of a sportsman. Angel was as beautiful as ever in a stunning silk chiffon coral gown with a frankly enormous diamond necklace round her neck.

As soon as she saw Liberty, she exclaimed, 'Oh, hiya! I'm so glad you could come, I've been meaning to invite you over for ages.'

The women exchanged kisses and then Liberty was introduced to Cal, who also gave her the obligatory air kiss. They chatted a little about how she was settling into Brighton, before the hosts had to go and talk to their other guests.

'Sorry. We'll catch up properly later. You know what these parties are like, you never get the chance to talk to the people you want to, you're always rushing around like a blue-arsed fly!'

Liberty and Em took a glass of champagne from the tray a waiter offered them, while Noah went off to track down a beer. He loathed champagne. Liberty scanned the marquee, which was by now full of guests. But there was no sign of Cory.

'Darling girls! How are you!' The blond, tanned

bombshell who was Jez appeared at their side. He seemed to have had his teeth whitened even more and they practically glowed in the subtle lighting. 'This is my husband, Rufus,' he declared proudly. Rufus was exactly as Liberty had imagined, a man of few, but well-chosen words, and clearly a complete sweetheart.

As they all chatted Liberty had an idea. She had promised Brooke to book a hairdresser for her eighteenth birthday party but hadn't yet got round to it. Jez would be perfect.

'Ooh, how adorable to work with some teenagers!' he exclaimed when she suggested it. 'Nowadays I'm all about the older woman. It'll be good for me to break out of my comfort zone.'

'Careful, you make it sound as though you work with OAPs rather than thirty-somethings!' Liberty teased. But she guessed that Jez was prone to exaggeration.

'I love the thirty-something lady. It's when they're most confident about who they are. Exactly like you, Liberty. You're a woman in your absolute prime. So, anyone here who catches your fancy?'

She shook her head. 'Nope.'

'Seriously? We should do a circuit of the room, like they did in the olden days. That dress is made to be shown off. And wouldn't you like to bag a footballer? Take one home and shag them, to prove that you've still got it?'

Rufus looked across at Liberty, and raised his eyebrows. 'You've met him before, so I guess you know what he's like.'

'Who's that then?' Angel joined them.

'Jez – you know how he speaks before he thinks,' Rufus said dryly.

'Yeah, he told me earlier that I was looking very mature. Bastard.' Angel glared at Jez.

'I meant sophisticated! It was only because, when I saw you the other day, you were wearing a hot pink towelling playsuit and looked a bit, well, how shall I put this? Like a slag.'

'I was only wearing it because I'd just had a spray tan! I wasn't on a fashion parade.'

Jez was about to come back with something else – Liberty could tell that he always had to have the last word – when Angel held up her hand and waved at someone to come over. 'There he is at last. I must introduce you two to each other.'

Liberty steeled herself. It was probably one of the unattractive but wealthy footballers. She didn't like to tell Angel that she found football completely over-rated. That was one thing she hadn't missed in LA, where soccer didn't have the same hold on the nation's heart. She plastered as sincere a smile as possible on her lip, which faded the instant the tall blond man joined the group. Oh God! She almost gasped as she stared into a familiar pair of bluer than blue eyes.

'Liberty, this is Cory Richardson. A very talented artist. I'll have to show you the amazing painting he did of me. Cory, this is Liberty Evans, a very talented actress – you've probably seen her on television.' Angel beamed at the pair of them, clearly pleased with her hostess routine. If only she knew . . .

Liberty waited for him to say that they knew each other; instead Cory, held out his hand to shake hers and said simply, 'Pleased to meet you.'

So he was going to play it like this. She had no choice but to shake his hand. And before Liberty got the chance to reply, he continued, 'I'm sorry, Angel, I've just had a call from my nanny. My son isn't very well, I'm going to have to leave.'

'It's nothing serious, is it?' she asked, concern showing on her beautiful face.

No, just an excuse, Liberty thought, staring down at her glass. She couldn't bear to see the look of indifference on Cory's face.

'I'm sure he'll be fine, but it's best I go. Thanks for a lovely party. Send my apologies to Cal, will you?'

And with that he was gone.

'That's such a pity,' Angel said regretfully, watching Cory weave his way through the party-goers. 'I really wanted to get you two together, I was sure you'd get on. I'll have to invite you both round for dinner. Don't worry, I promise Cal will do the cooking. Over ten years of marriage and I'm still rubbish in the kitchen. I can do a tomato sauce pasta and make an omelette.' She glanced at Liberty and seemed to realise that something was the matter. 'Are you okay? You look really pale?'

I feel as if my heart has been ripped out and trampled on. 'I'm fine. But why would you think that Cory and I would get on? He's married, isn't he?'

Liberty tried to sound blasé but was certain her voice was shaking.

'Oh, he's divorced. Over a year ago now. I think he's dated a couple of women since, but nothing serious. He's really gorgeous, don't you think?'

What did Liberty say to that?

Fortunately Jez piped up, 'He is a dreamboat! I mean, I don't usually go for blonds, being a natural blond myself—'

'In your dreams, Jez,' Angel interrupted. 'You can't even remember what your natural colour is, can you?'

'A bit like you then, madam. He's got a look of Ryan Gosling, a dash of Brad Pitt. Generally delish. And in black tie as well. I could just eat him up!

Sorry, Rufus. And he's a brilliant artist. And not at all a pale, sickly one, who looks as if he spends all his time inside breathing in paint fumes, but a healthy, prime specimen. Apparently he's a good footballer too and takes part in triathlons. Got to love a man with stamina.'

Liberty had hardly taken in a word of Jez's chatter because whether Cory was married or divorced made no difference to her. She had hoped that if he saw her again his reaction would be different, but his distant politeness felt even worse than his previous contempt. She just couldn't leave things like this. She gave Em her champagne glass and raced out of the marquee. She caught up with Cory as he was about to get into his car.

'Wait! Please, I have to talk to you.'

He turned to face her, surprised to see that she had followed him. 'Liberty, I thought I made myself clear, let's not go over it again.'

She was standing so close to him that it would have been easy to reach out and touch him. She *longed* to reach out and touch him.

'I wanted to say that I'm sorry Brooke came to see you. She's very young and got an idea in her head that we—'

'There is no we,' Cory cut across her. 'Look, this is all fucked up and weird. I hope I didn't upset your daughter, she's a beauty, looks just like you.' He made to get in the car.

And now Liberty did reach for his arm and grabbed it. He seemed to wince at the contact.

'Please, Liberty, I'm sure you had your reasons for what you did, but I can't go through this again. You need to stay away from me. What happened was a long time ago, my life's moved on.' And then he was sitting in the car, slamming the door, and she was watching as he drove away. Out of her life.

She was crying so hard that she was hardly aware that Em had joined her. Her friend put an arm round her.

'Come on, Libs. I'll take you home.'

'But what about the champagne and everything? It's your big night out.'

'I'm taking you home,' Em repeated.

Chapter 38

Brooke

Mila parked her car on the country lane and she and Brooke stared up at the manor house at the end of the driveway. It was an impressively large building built of beautiful honey-coloured stone and at any other time Brooke would have thought it was very stylish, straight out of a costume drama. But it was Cory's house, and all she could think was that the man living there had broken her mom's heart in the cruellest possible way.

'Are you sure you want to do this?' Mila asked. 'We could just drive off and you could maybe find out his email address and send him an email instead.'

Brooke's heart was thumping and she actually felt sick at the prospect of confronting Cory, but her voice was resolute when she spoke. 'Nope. I have to see him. My mom was in such a terrible state when she came back from that party. She finally told me the whole story about how *he* didn't turn up at the airport and left her standing there. Bastard!' Every time she thought of this it made her even angrier. And how dare Cory

332

have acted like the injured party when she saw him at the gallery? He was a manipulative bastard! There was no other word for him.

Mila had already heard her say this at least ten times already in the last two days, and it was a sign of true friendship that she replied, 'Total bastard,' with as much conviction as she had the first time.

Brooke took a deep breath. 'So, wish me luck because I'm going to do this thing.'

'D'you want me to come in with you?' Mila asked. 'A bit of moral support?'

'No, I have to do this on my own.'

Brooke walked up to the house, her legs wobbly with nerves. She had never done anything like this before, but she felt she had to stand up for her mom. Cory should realise what he had put her through and at least take some responsibility. But when she rang the doorbell there was no reply. Typical! The one thing she hadn't thought could happen. She had got herself so psyched up for the confrontation. She rang it again, but there was still no sign that anyone was in. Okay, she wasn't ready to give up yet. It was a beautiful afternoon; perhaps he was out in the back garden. Tentatively she walked round the house. He was obviously successful and had done very well for himself as the house was huge and set in beautiful grounds.

She breathed in the scent of honeysuckle and roses as she reached a back garden that was a riot of colour with summer flowers and a vivid green lawn. There was a trampoline, a swing and a slide. Hmm, she hoped she wouldn't run into his son, she'd forgotten about him. There was no sign of anyone there but at the very back of the garden she noticed a wooden summer house, which was bound to be a studio. Brooke stuck her shoulders back and marched over.

As she drew nearer she could hear music pouring out of the studio – the Black Eyed Peas,' 'Where Is the Love?' Good question, Cory. Here goes, she thought to herself as she walked through the open door. It was a large, airy room, painted white and flooded with light from the French windows to one side and the glass skylights above, canvases stacked against every available wall. And there in the middle of the room, standing at an easel, was Cory. He was completely absorbed in what he was doing and she almost lost her nerve and slipped away before he saw her. But no, she had got this far . . .

Brooke coughed quietly. 'Hi there.'

Cory spun round and nearly dropped his paintbrush. 'Jesus! You made me jump! I didn't hear you come in.' For a second he seemed almost friendly, but then he registered who it was and his expression hardened. 'You again. What are you doing here?'

His unfriendly tone made it easier for her to let rip. 'Well, I wanted you to know that you had no right to be so horrible to my mom at Angel's party. D'you have any idea how much you hurt her? You should really man up and face what you did.'

'Please, Brooke, you're meddling in things that really don't concern you. I'm sure your mum wouldn't have wanted you to come here.'

Brooke ignored him and carried on, 'Why didn't you meet her at the airport? You left her there and didn't even have the decency to call and tell her. You just let her assume you had changed your mind. She spent two hours phoning all the hospitals because she was terrified that you'd had an accident . . . until it finally dawned on her that you simply weren't coming. Imagine how that felt.'

Cory seemed shocked by what she'd said. 'That's

not what happened. She sent me an email saying she didn't want to see me any more.'

But before he could continue, a small boy suddenly came hurtling into the studio, calling out, 'Daddy, Daddy, Daddy! Can I have an ice cream?' He rushed over to his father who scooped him up in his arms, from where the child looked shyly over at Brooke. He had his father's blond hair and blue eyes, and at any other time she would have thought him adorable. But shit! Talk about bad timing. She could hardly say anything in front of his son, even if she did think that Cory was completely and utterly in the wrong.

'This is Brooke,' he said to the child. 'She came over to see some of my pictures. She's going now.'

Brooke held up her hand in a wave and managed a smile for the little boy, not wanting to traumatise him by seeming like a scary stranger. But she couldn't resist a parting shot to Cory as she left. 'You really are wrong about what happened. I don't know why you can't admit it.'

On her way out she passed a pretty young woman wearing shorts and a vest top and carrying a child's scooter. Cory's wife, she assumed. God! She was ridiculously young. She only looked a few years older than Brooke, if that. It confirmed her opinion that Cory was a cold-hearted bastard. Probably only a much younger woman would put up with him. Well, she was going to do all she could to encourage her mom to find someone else. She was far too good for Cory Richardson, and clearly always had been.

Later that day, Flynn, Harry and Mila came over and they sat on the beach drinking rosé wine and eating strawberries. It was a glorious afternoon, the sky a bold blue and the sea glittering in the sunshine. Brooke had

335

wanted her mom to join them, but she claimed she had a headache and had gone to bed. And meanwhile Cory was living his perfect life, with his perfect family . . . it made Brooke so mad and made her feel so helpless. She hated seeing her mom suffer like this. She had ranted all the way back in the car, to a very patient Mila, and had then repeated it all to Harry and Flynn.

They listened sympathetically and then Flynn said, 'Don't you think it's odd that Cory says your mum sent him an email? I mean, why wouldn't she have texted him? She must have had her phone with her at the airport and it would have been the quickest thing to do.'

'She didn't send any email!' Brooke exclaimed. 'For some fucked up reason, he's lying.'

'But why would he lie about that?' Flynn persisted. 'I don't get it.'

There was a pause and then Harry burst out excitedly, 'Maybe she *didn't* send the email. Someone else did, pretending to be her. Maybe they hacked into her email account.'

He looked at them, seemingly proud of his interpretation, and when they didn't respond, added, 'I know you're probably thinking that I've watched way too many movies, and I have a habit of confusing fiction with fact, but remember the phone-hacking story?'

He had a point.

'But why would anyone do that?' Brooke mused.

'Someone who didn't want Liberty and Cory to get together. Her husband, for instance?' Flynn replied. 'From what you've told us, it sounds as if he was really controlling of your mom. You said he hated her walking out on him and that he was going to stop her working in LA again – that is pretty extreme behaviour. Maybe he had found out that she was going to leave him at that time and decided to do something to stop it. It wouldn't be such a stretch for him to hack into her email account, would it? And he would have made sure that he covered his tracks by deleting the email he sent.'

'God! I don't know – I haven't even considered that – I just thought Cory had come up with this lie to make himself sound better.' Brooke suddenly felt a surge of excitement. This did sound plausible. And she really wouldn't put that kind of behaviour past Zac. She had always known that there was a dark side to him.

Then her hopes were dashed when Mila said quietly, 'But how would you ever prove that he did that? Zac's hardly likely to admit it, is he?'

'Bollocks!' Brooke came out with her new favourite expletive. 'Okay, back to square one.' She finished her wine. 'I could at least put it to my mom – find out if she ever worried that Zac spied on her.'

'Maybe you need to stop thinking about it for a while – do something to clear your head,' Flynn put in. She looked over at him, lying back on the picnic rug, arms behind his head, mirrored aviator shades on his face making him look even cooler. His t-shirt had ridden up, revealing a tantalising expanse of hard, flat abs. Yeah, what she'd really like to do was cuddle up next to him. Damn it! Of all the boys in Brighton, why, oh, why did she have to fall for him?

'Okay, I've got a challenge for you,' Flynn said, sitting up.

She really hoped he couldn't read her mind . . .

'How about going for a swim? You haven't been in the sea since you've lived here, have you? It should be a rite of passage for anyone moving to Brighton.'

'Like, der! Why would I go in that freezing cold,

337

probably dirty water? There isn't even any decent surf!' Brooke was appalled by the idea. Yes, the sun was shining, but it wasn't hot by her standards. She was wearing a hoodie and shorts and still had goose bumps from the sea breeze.

'It won't be so cold. Go on, I dare you,' Flynn taunted her. 'Or are you too much of a wimp? Do you need to wear your gold wet suit?'

Okay, that did it. She could never resist a challenge. Brooke stood up and began stripping down to her bikini. 'Last one in is a wuss . . . or what is it that Harry says? A big girl's blouse. Yeah, Flynn, you're a big girl's blouse – probably a pink one with a pussy bow.'

That was all the encouragement he needed to peel off his t-shirt. She tried not to stare at his bare chest and broad shoulders, but it required some effort to redirect her gaze at Harry and Mila, who remained sitting where they were, defiantly holding on to their wineglasses.

'And what about you two?'

Harry shook his head. 'You might want to take part in this macho, Bear Grylls-style posturing, but I do not. I only swim in the Caribbean.' He pronounced it like an American. 'Not that I've ever been, but one day I will.'

'Yep, I'm with Harry,' Mila added. 'We'll watch. And drink wine. Not that you'll be in for long, I reckon.'

'I can't believe what little faith you guys have in me!' Brooke declared. 'I expect it from Flynn, but you two?'

Harry shrugged. 'You're an LA princess, you're not going to last two minutes in the icy Channel.'

She looked over at Flynn. 'Ready?'

'Yeah, just let me dump my phone and wallet.'

But Brooke was already taking off and running towards the sea as fast as she could in flip-flops. Once at the shore she kicked off her shoes, took a deep breath and raced into the sea, wincing as her feet came into contact with the sharp pebbles. Her plan was to get straight in and swim but she just couldn't.

'It's freezing!' she squealed, waist-deep in water and feeling as if her body was going into shock from the cold.

Flynn came rushing in after her. Instead of hesitating as she had, he dived in and then swam effortlessly out to sea in a stylish front crawl. Naturally Flynn would be good at swimming – he seemed to be good at pretty much everything, she was starting to realise. Then he about turned and swam back towards Brooke, who was still wincing at the cold sea lapping against her.

'It's much better to get straight in. Honestly, after a few minutes you won't feel the cold.'

'What are you talking about? My teeth are chattering so much I can hardly speak. I'm going to get pneumonia and it's my birthday next week. I'll have to cancel and it'll be all your fault!'

From the beach Harry and Mila raised their glasses. 'It looks so lovely,' Harry called out, 'I'm so sorry we can't join you.'

Flynn didn't reply but swam up to Brooke. He put his arms round her waist, but there was no time to enjoy the contact as he lifted her up and . . . no! He wasn't going to do this, was he? Fuck! He was! She screamed as he raised her up and pitched her into the sea. She had the good sense to shut her mouth as she went under and then surfaced, spluttering with indignation. God, her hair was going to look beyond terrible! She smoothed it back, glared at Flynn and then turned her back on him and swam out to sea, willing her body to warm up as she sliced through the water. She did some fifty or so strokes then paused, treading water, and looking back at the beach. Flynn was swimming after her.

'See? I told you – it's refreshing, isn't it?'

'That's one way of describing it,' Brooke muttered. 'So, as you can see, I'm not a wimp.'

He grinned at her. 'No, you're not. You're full of surprises, Brooke, that's why I like you so much.'

Like as a friend, or like as something more? The thought sent a warm glow through her . . .

'So, I'll race you back – if you like I can give you a head start,' Flynn teased.

She was still so shaken up by the compliment, yes, an actual compliment from Flynn, that she struggled to keep up with him, but then she had a sudden burst of power and overtook him – not for nothing had she been surfing since the age of eight. From the beach Mila and Harry were whooping and cheering. 'Go, girlfriend! Go, Brooke!'

It was hard making an elegant exit out of the water when there was sharp, pointy shingle underfoot, rather than smooth white sand, but somehow Brooke clung on to her dignity.

Mila handed her a towel.

'You could have someone's eyes out with those,' Harry commented, gesturing at her nipples, that were visible through her red bikini top.

'The cold has that effect,' she retorted, wrapping herself up in the towel, and all three of them watched Flynn emerge from the sea. Brooke was sure she wasn't the only one who was transfixed by the sight of his wet shorts clinging to his thighs, lean hips, and, well – phew! Let's just say the cold didn't seem to have affected him in the way it did most men.

'Brooke! You won,' Harry declared. 'Girls win! Boys in the bin! Or something.'

Half an hour later she had showered and changed, as had Flynn. Because he hadn't got any spare clothes he was only wearing a towel and his t-shirt until his shorts dried in the tumble drier. It was disconcerting knowing that he was naked under the towel, which happened to be pink and didn't make him look any less manly.

She was expecting that Mila and Harry would stay and they would order in a takeaway, but Harry said he had an essay to finish and Mila said that she was going to go to the gym. Neither reason seemed plausible, especially when Harry winked at her when he said goodbye. And just in case his meaning wasn't clear enough, he whispered, 'Enjoy. And remember, I need to know *every* detail. You owe me.'

'So what do you fancy?' Flynn asked when she wandered back into the kitchen. He was leaning against the counter and checking on his phone for takeaways.

It was on the tip of Brooke's tongue to say, *You*. Instead she replied, 'Thai.'

'Sounds good. There's one here, take a look at the menu and I'll order.'

Their hands brushed as he passed her his phone, which immediately sent a flash of desire through Brooke.

'I'll just check if my mom wants something,' she said quickly. What was wrong with her? Her heart was beating so wildly and she was having such incredibly lustful thoughts about all the things she wanted to do with Flynn and to him . . . starting with ripping off that towel.

But that feeling went as soon as she knocked on her mom's bedroom door and discovered Liberty curled up in bed with the curtains drawn.

'Can I get you anything, Mom? I'm about to order some food in. Flynn's here.'

There was a muffled sniff from under the duvet and then, 'No, thanks, honey, I'm fine. I just need to sleep off this headache.'

Her mom didn't sound fine – she sounded as if she'd been crying.

'Are you sure? I could stay up here with you. We could watch a film together. I could tell Flynn to go.'

'Really, Brooke, I'll be fine.'

She hated leaving her mom in that state, but there was nothing she could do. Downstairs Flynn had put his shorts back on – just as well – and switched on the stereo. Alicia Keys, good choice.

'You like your R&B, don't you?' he commented, handing her a glass of wine.

'Yeah, through and through. My ex was into thrash metal, I should have known from the start that it was never going to work.'

He grinned. 'Nope, I can't exactly see you at one of those gigs.' He paused. 'How's your mum?'

'The same – she claims to have a headache. Broken heart more like.'

'So how about you contact Cory and tell him about the theory that someone hacked into her email?'

She thought of how angry and dismissive he had been yesterday. 'I think I'll pass on that. I don't think it will make any difference.'

'Don't look so sad, you've tried. Maybe it just isn't meant to be.'

It felt as if they were going round in circles. She couldn't talk about it any more. 'Yep. So shall we order? I'm starving.'

Despite worrying about her mom, Brooke had a great evening with Flynn. She loved spending time with him, loved the banter they shared, even more so now it was tinged with flirtation. Sure, it was bitter-sweet because she didn't know where she stood with him and there was always Eve in the background, and there were several moments when she wanted to ask what was happening between him and his ex (if she was his ex), but she didn't want to spoil things.

'So are you looking forward to your party?' he asked her towards the end of the night, when they were clearing up after dinner.

'Yeah – I was dreading it when I moved here, but now I think it's going to be good. Have you decided what you're going to wear?' She tried to block out the image of him in leather trousers that instantly came into her head. No question, Flynn would look seriously good in leather trousers and nothing else but leather trousers. FFS, this had to stop! The swim seemed to have unleashed her inner sex demon.

'It's going to be a surprise.'

'Hey, that's not fair! I've told you about the gold dress.'

'Well, you'll just have to wait and see.'

'I have ways of making you talk,' Brooke replied, and advanced towards him. 'I happen to know from Harry that you're really ticklish.'

'Don't believe everything Harry tells you, he's a compulsive liar and I swear I'm not.' But Flynn folded his arms together.

'Oh my God! I've found your fatal flaw! You act so cool and together, but it's all a big con trick!' Brooke pushed him against the wall and tried to inch her fingers under his arms. He was already laughing helplessly. But then the tables were turned on her as he grabbed her wrists.

'Seriously, Brooke, you have to stop!'

'Make me,' she teased him, 'I could do this all night. I'll film it and put it on YouTube. I'll get so many hits, it'll go viral.'

'No, you won't. You like me too much to humiliate me.'

'Oh? You sound very sure of yourself.'

'Yeah, I reckon you like me as much as I like you.' He was leaning closer to her; she could feel his warm breath against her face. Closer still, and his brown eyes were locked on hers. And then his lips brushed against hers, sending shockwaves through her. Closer still and the light touch became a kiss, his mouth soft on hers, a gentle kiss at first that blossomed into a deep, sexy, passionate kiss as he put his hands on her waist and pulled her against his body.

'Like' didn't even begin to cover the emotions he stirred up in her. She was crazy in lust with him, every part of her longing for his touch, tingling, burning, melting. She wanted him so much; it was breathtaking, mind-blowing. Every fantasy she had ever had about him gathered into one moment, here and now.

But suddenly she froze as she heard the unmistakable sound of her mom coming downstairs. They sprang apart guiltily just before Liberty walked into the room.

'Oh, hi, Flynn, I didn't realise you were still here.'

Liberty was dressed in her white silk robe. Her face was drained of colour and her eyes were red-rimmed from crying. She looked terrible.

'Shall I make you a cup of tea?' Brooke asked, tucking her hair behind her ear and hoping that her mom didn't notice her flushed and dishevelled appearance.

'Thanks, that would be lovely. Sorry, I didn't mean to interrupt your conversation.'

'It's fine. Actually I'd better go. I've got to get ready for the art trip – we're going to Berlin for a week and leaving tomorrow. 'Bye, Liberty, I hope you feel better soon.'

Flynn grabbed his jacket and headed for the front door and Brooke followed him, hoping that his hasty departure wasn't because he regretted what had just happened.

'So, I'll see you at the end of the week,' he said, ducking down and kissing her cheek. Her cheek! After what had just happened! That wasn't acceptable! But then he seemed to change his mind and kissed her on the lips, and kissed her and kissed her, and she was almost ready to suggest they sneaked upstairs to her bedroom . . .

'I wish I could stay,' Flynn murmured when they broke off for air.

'Will you text me when you're away?' She couldn't quite believe she had asked this. In the past she had always played it cool with boys, the ice maiden, who didn't need anything from them. But this was different . . . oh, God, this was so different.

'Of course I will.' And he kissed her again, then said regretfully, 'I really have to go. See you on Saturday.'

He left before she could ask him about Eve.

Chapter 39

Liberty

Liberty was determined to put what had happened with Cory out of her mind once and for all. The week-end had been a write-off, but she had to pull herself together because there was so much still to do for Brooke's birthday party and she wanted her daughter to have the most wonderful birthday ever, one that she would never forget.

On Wednesday evening Em came over to look at Brooke's party dress. The two friends sat in the living room, drinking wine and waiting for Brooke to make her grand entrance as she had wanted to model it for them. She'd been up in her room for ages. Liberty was about to tell her to get a move on when Brooke walked into the room. The sight of her in the stunning 1920s-style gold beaded and sequined dress silenced them. There in front of them was the most beautiful young woman, all long legs and slender arms . . .

'You look incredible,' Liberty exclaimed, with tears in her eyes. Her baby girl suddenly seemed all grown up. How had that happened?

'You really do, Brooke,' Em echoed.

'So why are you crying, Mom? Is it the wrong choice? Should I have gone for the green dress?'

'Of course not! It's just that you suddenly seem so grown up.'

'It's like that scene in *Mamma Mia!* when the Meryl Streep character sings that song to her daughter, "Slipping Through My Fingers." You know, the one about her daughter growing up and how she misses her,' Em put in. And then added, 'Oh, no, I think I'm going to cry as well!'

Brooke looked at the two of them, hands on her hips. 'You two need to toughen up, I'm not going anywhere yet. Concentrate, because I need your advice on how to do my hair.'

Liberty stood up. 'I know, I know, it just feels like one minute you were five and now you're about to turn eighteen. I'm sure you'll understand what I mean when you have children.' She smoothed back her daughter's hair. 'I'm thinking waves . . . that will look really stylish with the sequined headband. I'm sure Jez is a mean hand with the GHDs.'

'Okay. Sounds good. So long as it doesn't make my hair look too short.'

Liberty almost did a double take at her daughter agreeing with her so easily.

'You'll be the belle of the ball,' Em put in.

'I should bloody hope so! It is my bloody ball!' Brooke declared.

Liberty grinned; it was funny hearing her come out with typically English expressions in her full on LA accent. She liked this feisty new Brooke.

'So is Flynn coming on his own? Or is the evil Eve going to be putting in an appearance?' Liberty asked, and immediately wished she hadn't as Brooke frowned and sat on the sofa, arms folded.

'I don't know. He's been texting me from Berlin and he didn't mention her, but then Harry told me that she was on the same trip. I didn't even realise.'

'Don't worry, he really likes you,' Liberty replied, having that impulse to make everything okay for her daughter. But this wasn't like comforting her when she had fallen over as a little girl, or had a nightmare. It was a big bad world out there, and she was going to have to let Brooke make her own mistakes and go her own way. Much as she wanted to, Liberty couldn't wrap her up in cotton wool and protect her.

Brooke managed a smile. 'Anyway, he and Harry had an interesting theory about you.' She stopped and looked unsure if she should continue.

'Oh, yeah? What was that?'

'Okay, don't get mad, but after you got back from Angel's party and were so upset, I felt I had to do something. I know you told me not to after last time, but seriously, Mom, I had to.'

'Oh?'

Brooke took a deep breath. 'So I went to see Cory at his house and told him he was completely out of order, treating you like that.'

'Oh my God, Brooke, I can't believe you did that!'

'Wow, Brooke,' Em said, completely agog. 'That was brave of you. That's quite some kick-ass daughter you've got, Libs. I'm seriously impressed.'

'He claimed that you'd sent him some email saying that you didn't want to see him any more.'

'Of course I didn't do that! Why would he say that?'

'That's exactly what we all thought – sorry, I have

to 'fess up that I did tell the gang, but they're all really sympathetic. Anyway, Harry said what if someone hacked into your computer and sent the email pretending to be you? And the only person we could think who would ever do that would be . . .'

'Zac,' Liberty finished the sentence before her. 'I was always changing my password because I never trusted him. But I don't suppose it would have been that difficult to hack.' She sighed. 'It doesn't matter, though. Cory has no feelings for me any more. I can't blame him. Seeing him was a reality check.'

She changed the subject back to the party after that, but when Brooke left the room to get changed Em brought it up again.

'So what are you going to do? It's more than likely that Zac did send that email.' She sounded so hopeful and optimistic, as if Liberty could still do something that would make a difference to the situation.

'There's nothing I can do – and I could never prove it.' She smiled sadly. 'I know Brooke wants it to be my happy ever after, and it's so sweet of her, but life just isn't like that.'

But later, when she was lying in bed unable to sleep again, she went over and over the events of five years ago, trying to remember anything of significance in Zac's behaviour towards her when he'd returned from his trip. There was nothing she could think of, but then Zac was always very good at hiding his feelings and covering his tracks.

She sat up in bed and reached for her phone. There was no point in calling him, but there was always Tess. It was late-afternoon in LA, and she would still be in the office. Liberty selected her number.

Of course, first she had to get through Tess asking how she was and about life in the UK. Liberty had always got on well with Tess and knew she was upset about Zac basically blacklisting her in Hollywood.

Tess didn't even seem shocked when Liberty put the question about Zac hacking into her email.

'I don't know, Liberty, but it's certainly possible. I know he used to get regular updates from Ramon, your security guard, about what you were doing and who you were seeing, because one time I overheard them talking in the office. I'm sorry, maybe I should have warned you, but I figured you probably already knew and I didn't want to make things any more difficult for you.'

Any more difficult . . . .

'I know that Ramon doesn't work for him any longer, so it's maybe worth trying to track him down. Zac got rid of everyone when you left. It was like he was wiping the slate clean. Disconcerting, but he's always been like that. He's seeing someone else now, by the way. A young actress. Blonde, brown-eyed, as different from you as is possible.'

They ended the call by agreeing to stay in touch, though Liberty very much doubted that she would see Tess again – that part of her life was over. She tried the number she had for Ramon but it had been disconnected. He wasn't on Facebook and she didn't have an email address. He probably wouldn't even talk to her if she did track him down. She put her phone on the bedside table and sank back on the pillow. Brooke's theory about the hacked email changed nothing. Cory was still lost to her.

Chapter 40

Brooke

The first thing Brooke did when she woke up on Saturday morning was reach for her phone, ever hopeful that there would be a text from Flynn. Nothing. But it was still early. He had finally admitted yesterday in a message that Eve was on the trip and things were complicated between them and that he would explain when he saw Brooke. She didn't want there to be complications, she just wanted him not to be seeing Eve. That would be the best birthday present ever. She had been replaying that kiss over and over in her head. And she was certain it was a kiss that meant something.

Brooke put her phone back on the bedside table and noticed a small parcel, beautifully wrapped in blue-and-gold-patterned paper. It was a family tradition that her mom always sneaked a birthday present into her room while she was sleeping. It was funny. In the past she would have been desperate to know what was inside it, and whether it was one of the many expensive presents on her wish list. This year she'd had no idea what she wanted, and when her mom had asked, simply said, 'Surprise me'.

She pulled on her robe and padded downstairs, holding the present. Her mom was in the kitchen, hard at work making pancakes. Now this was a first. Usually it would have been Rosa making the pancakes to her own unique recipe that, as far as Brooke was concerned, produced the best pancakes in the world.

'Happy birthday!' Liberty exclaimed, immediately putting down the mixing bowl and hugging her daughter. Her hair, eyelashes and t-shirt were dusted in flour. It was fair to say that cooking did not come naturally to her.

'Did you like your present?'

'Oh, I haven't opened it yet.'

'Well, go on then!' Her mom darted back over to the cooker and looked anxiously at the frying pan. 'I so want these to be perfect! Rosa texted me the recipe. I've done a couple of practice batches and they worked out okay.'

Brooke was touched that she had gone to so much trouble. She sat down at the table to unwrap the present, and gasped. Wow! Her mom had given her a beautiful Hublot watch, in rose gold with diamonds. She had been asking for one of these since her thirteenth birthday. What a brat she had been . . . she wouldn't have appreciated it then. But she did now.

'Oh, Mom! You remembered! Thank you so, so much!'

Liberty planted a kiss on top of her head. 'You are so welcome. It's something special to mark your eighteenth. You've got other presents as well, but do you want to wait for Nina to come over before you open them?'

'Yeah, that would be cool – so long as you haven't

bought me too much and I get a lecture from her about being spoiled.' She was only half joking. The old Brooke wouldn't have cared less, but she didn't want to be thought of like that any more.

The pancakes, topped with blueberries, raspberries and strawberries, yoghurt and maple syrup, were very nearly as good as Rosa's, but Brooke told her mom they were even better. She went upstairs to shower and checked her phone again. Still nothing from Flynn, and he knew it was her birthday. She felt a pang of disappointment. All week since he had been away she had been filled with excitement at the thought of seeing him tonight, and now she was starting to feel a twist of anxiety that he might not come.

Just as she had finished getting dressed the doorbell rang.

'Can you get that, Brooke? I'm just about to get in the shower,' her mom called out.

She raced downstairs and opened the front door and then screamed in excitement because there, standing on the doorstep with her enormous Louis Vuitton purple-monogrammed suitcase by her side, was Kelly.

'Oh my God! Oh my God! I can't believe it!' Brooke exclaimed, hugging her friend. 'I had no idea you were coming. This is so awesome.'

'I know! I know! I was dying to tell you, but your mom said we should keep it a secret until your birthday. It was her idea and she paid for my flight and everything.'

The two girls had a brilliant couple of hours catching up on all their news. Brooke felt that Harry and Mila were true friends but nothing could beat spending time with her very best friend. Then Nina arrived with her birthday present – a pretty vintage-style photo frame that she had filled with pictures of Brooke, her mum and herself. 'The Evans women, in all their glory,' she declared. Liberty hadn't gone too mad besides buying the watch and flying Kelly over, and had bought her perfume, make up and a dress from All Saints.

Nina surveyed the pile of presents, admired the watch and commented approvingly, 'Just like the presents any eighteen-year-old girl would get. You really have changed, Brooke.'

She caught Kelly's eye and could only hope that Nina didn't know how much Hublot watches were . . .

At midday the party planners arrived to transform the living room and cinema room into a dance floor and chill-out area. Liberty banned Brooke from going anywhere near them, she wanted everything to be a surprise for her, so she and Kelly hung out upstairs. There was an almost tangible feeling of excitement in the house. Brooke had never had another birthday like it.

Mila and Harry arrived next. They had clubbed together and bought her a bright pink satchel bag that she had admired a few weeks ago when they had all been wandering through the Lanes, never imagining that they would buy it for her. It meant so much more to her than all the designer gifts she'd been showered with on other birthdays when she knew that money was no object. They sat on the balcony outside Brooke's bedroom eating sushi that the caterers had provided. Brooke had wanted to crack open a bottle of champagne but her mom had put her foot down, saying she needed to pace herself and she could have a drink at six.

At two there was a loud knock at the door and Jez, celebrity hairdresser, made his grand entrance. Meeting him was like coming face to face with a much older, more tanned, camper version of Harry (if that last part were possible). Introductions over, Harry immediately began interrogating Jez about his lifestyle in forensic detail.

'He's the me I am going to aspire to be,' Harry declared afterwards. 'He's got a fantastic career, a Range Rover, a house in Islington and an apartment in Brighton. He regularly eats out at Nobu, Scott's and The Ivy.'

'A Mini-me!' Jez exclaimed. 'That is adorable. But frankly none of it would be worth a damn if I didn't have the love of a good man in my life.'

'Oh, yeah – I missed out husband,' Harry replied. 'Where is he, by the way?'

'Downstairs with Liberty, being useful. He's one of those Action Men types who has to prove his strength on a daily basis, which is perfect because it means I don't ever have to take the bins out.'

'I think I'm going to be single for a while,' Harry mused, lying back on the bed. 'Lately I've only seemed to be attracted to straight men.'

Jez shook his head. 'That is a habit you have to break, it is ruinous to the spirit. Anyway, I have to get down to work! What needs doing?'

Kelly swished back her long glossy brunette hair, the result of hours and hours in the salon having extensions. Brooke knew that no one got to touch her hair except her favourite hairdresser.

'Kelly's good to go as she is,' Brooke replied. 'And I'd like a few blonde highlights at the front then my hair styled in waves.'

'Easy-peasy. Harry?'

'Just a blow dry.'

'No problem. And Mila?'

There was a pause and Brooke worried that she had got cold feet and would probably say she didn't want anything doing, but her friend replied, 'Um . . . I was thinking of going a little darker.'

Jez picked up a strand of her hair. 'I think ultimately you should go for brunette, but I can't achieve that in a day, so let's go a couple of shades darker. That will look fantastic with your lovely blue eyes.'

Brooke waited for Mila to come out with a self-deprecating comment but she didn't. Brooke felt like high-fiving Harry. Finally Mila was becoming more confident in herself.

While Jez was working his magic on Mila, Brooke and the others went and sat on the beach.

'It's so cool here,' Kelly said, taking in the view, 'I really love it.'

'Yeah, it's taken me some time, but I love it too,' Brooke replied. She reached for her phone again. Still nothing from Flynn. She'd given Kelly the full story, but not confessed to Harry about the kiss – somehow she had wanted to keep that to herself. It felt too precious to be picked over even by him.

'He'll text,' Harry told her, guessing who she was thinking of. 'I think their flight got in late last night.'

'I'm looking forward to meeting him,' Kelly replied. 'So long as you promise me that he's not like Christian?' She looked over at Harry. 'Our girl hasn't had the best track record when it comes to picking the right guys.'

'Flynn is gorgeous and the best guy you'll ever meet. No contest.' That from Harry.

'You do think he'll come tonight, don't you?' Brooke blurted out.

'He said he would, so he'll be here. He never plays games.'

'What about these complications with Eve he was talking about?'

'Their relationship has been rocky for ages, I reckon

356

it's over. And usually I would say that he would need a break after splitting from her, but not in this case. You and Flynn are perfect for each other.'

Brooke looked across at Harry, lounging in a pair of denim shorts and a turquoise shirt unbuttoned to get maximum rays. Was he telling the truth?

'You're not just saying that because it's my birthday, are you?'

'Nope, cross my heart.' He lifted his Prada glasses so she could see his eyes, and smiled at her. 'So stop looking so worried, he'll be here.' And then Jez called out from her balcony that it was Brooke's turn.

Jez was hugely entertaining, exactly as Brooke had thought he would be, swapping celebrity gossip with her – so much so that she almost forgot about her phone. But when it beeped with a message she shot out of her chair in her rush to get it, oblivious to the fact that Jez was halfway through folding in a foil. At last! A text from Flynn.

Happy Birthday Brooke. Things a bit difficult at the moment, but really hope I can see you later. x

Really hope? Not for definite? And by 'things' . . . he must mean Eve. What should she reply to that? Play it cool, say yeah, be great if you could come, understand if not. No. She didn't want to play it cool. She sat back in the chair, lost in her thoughts.

Really want to see you, Flynn. Have missed you. x And before she could change her mind, she pressed send.

'About a boy?' Jez asked. She guessed he must spend a lot of time listening to his clients talking about their love lives.

'Yeah, that obvious? I don't know if he's going to make the party tonight. He has issues with his ex, or not so ex. I don't know.'

'If he's worth anything, he'll be here. How could he not for beautiful you?'

And even though she simply didn't know, Brooke found herself smiling at Jez in the mirror.

The boys were banished from the room while Brooke, Mila and Kelly got ready for the party. Kelly was in charge of doing their make up as by now Brooke was too nervous and her hands kept shaking when she tried. There was a knock at the door and Liberty came in with a bottle of champagne and three glasses. She had dressed up as a sixties girl in a black-and-white checked dress and long white boots. She looked beautiful and sassy, and Brooke felt a rush of pride that she was her mom.

'Right, it's six o clock, you can have a drink and then come down and see what we've done.' She smiled at Brooke. 'Stop looking so worried, it's going to be the best party ever!'

Brooke managed a smile back. 'Yes. Thanks, Mom.'

Chapter 41

The champagne certainly helped with the nerves, which was good because Brooke hadn't had a reply from Flynn. She kept trying to tell herself that it didn't matter, but it did.

'Come on, Birthday Girl, I'm dying to see you in that dress!' Kelly exclaimed. She was dressed as Cleopatra, in a floaty white gown and gold headpiece, and looked drop-dead gorgeous. Mila was in the red fifties-style dress, her hair was now a softer honey-blonde, and Brooke would not have recognised her as the girl she first met two months ago.

Brooke took off the white towelling robe she'd been wearing most of the afternoon and stepped into the gold sequined gown. The material felt cool against her skin and the exquisitely made dress, that fitted perfectly, helped her feel as if she was getting into the part.

'Wow! You look amazing!' Kelly exclaimed as Brooke put on the matching gold hair band.

'D'you really think so?' she asked. The question had never seemed quite so important before. She had always been confident in her looks but tonight she wanted everything to be perfect.

Both friends smiled at her and Mila said, 'Beautiful. The golden girl.'

Downstairs her mom had pulled out all the stops. The house looked incredible, huge arrangements of flowers filling the air with the scent of lilies and freesias. Candles were flickering everywhere; pretty tea lights were arranged around fireplaces and windows. Everything looked so elegant and tasteful, but her mom hadn't been able to resist hanging up a huge pink banner with 'Happy 18th Birthday, Brooke' splashed across it. The living room was now the dance floor, and surrounded with pink and silver balloons. A mirror ball was spinning, casting discs of silver light against the walls and floor, and a DJ was set up, along with a stage for karaoke. The cinema room was now a chill-out space where there was going to be a fortune-teller, a magician, and a make-up artist to create temporary tattoos. Waiters were busy setting up food and drinks in the dining room. Liberty was looking anxiously at Brooke as she took her round. 'Well, what do you think?'

'It's brilliant, Mom! Thank you so much.' She didn't even stop and compare it with what might have been at Chateau Marmont. This felt so much more personal; her mom had chosen all her favourite things. It meant so much more to Brooke.

Harry, Jez and Rufus were sitting on the verandah, making inroads into a bottle of champagne. Harry whistled when she walked out. Well, Harry aka a blond Richard Gere. He'd gone for the *Officer and a Gentleman* look. Possibly Richard Gere's trousers hadn't been quite so figure-hugging and his jacket was buttoned up rather than being left artfully open to show off maximum chest, but those were minor details. Jez had changed into a dinner jacket and come as a sexy vampire complete with fangs and black-tinted contact lenses. But he'd kept the tan, so rather ruining the effect. Rufus made a very handsome Tom Cruise out of *Top Gun*.

Liberty had promised the neighbours that the party would be over by midnight, so guests started arriving from half past seven. Everyone had made a real effort with their costumes. There was an Indiana Jones, a Mad Hatter, two Dorothys, a Lara Croft, Minnie Mouse, Cruella de Vil, Captain Jack Sparrow, Austin Powers, a couple of zombies, vampires, and a pair of Ghostbusters. Back in LA everyone's costume would have been hired or bought from the best possible places, and would have rivalled the real thing. Brooke liked the fact that here so many guests' costumes looked home-made or put together from vintage or charity shops.

Every time the doorbell rang she kept hoping it would be Flynn, but it got later and later and there was still no sign of him. She had this hollow feeling of disappointment inside that she tried to block out by knocking back glasses of champagne and hitting the dance floor with her friends. Liberty had been determined that people weren't going to stand round the edges of the room while the music played so she had enlisted Jez and Harry – two natural-born entertainers – to get everyone up, but after dancing wildly for an hour Brooke was in need of a rest and she and Kelly wandered into the chill-out room.

'Why don't you get your fortune read?' Kelly commented.

'Okay, I will if you will.'

Brooke took a seat opposite the dark-haired fortune-teller, who was dressed in a long black evening dress with flowing sleeves and had perhaps OD'd on the purple eye make up. Brooke saw it as a bit of fun, but the woman – whose name was Marnie – was very serious as she got Brooke to shuffle the tarot cards and then hand them back to her. She dealt three out on the table, and even though Brooke didn't believe in it, she still felt a shiver of alarm when she saw one of the cards was the Hanged Man. Marnie smiled at her.

'There is no cause for concern. This is a good card, all about change and embracing change. And I think you have been through a big change yourself, haven't you?'

Well, that wasn't rocket science, she probably knew that Brooke had recently moved to the UK. Next card was the Lovers, which seemed more promising, and finally the Queen of Cups. As Marnie described the significance of each card, and how it related to her life, Brooke had a kind of parallel, so-what dialogue going on in her head. She was too busy wondering when Flynn was going to arrive. *If* Flynn was going to arrive . . . But then Marnie asked her to hold out her palm and looked intently at the lines.

'I see a man coming into your life.'

He'd bloody better hurry up, Brooke was tempted to reply.

'This man is strong but he has been hurt.'

Not by me . . .

'He is wondering what to do for the best. He is torn and conflicted, but he knows he has to act.' She closed her eyes and Brooke was tempted to mouth WTF at Kelly. This was so lame!

'I see blue eyes. Brown, no, blond hair.' Marnie opened her eyes again. 'He's on his way.'

Yeah, right, on his white charger . . . She hadn't expected Marnie to know about Flynn, but to get it so wrong was frankly disappointing. Brooke was just about to mutter a quick thank you and escape when she sensed that someone was behind her. She glanced round. There at last was Flynn, breathtakingly handsome in a black tuxedo. He had come as James Bond and he was definitely licensed to thrill, given the rush of butterflies Brooke experienced.

'Happy birthday, Brooke,' he said, thankfully not in a bad Sean Connery accent that would really have ruined the moment. Actually, he could have said it any way he wanted and it wouldn't have lessened the desire pulsing through her.

She stood up and said shyly, 'I thought you weren't going to come.'

'I wouldn't have missed it.' And he ducked down and kissed her lightly on the lips. The butterflies fluttered even more wildly.

Chapter 42

Liberty

Liberty and Em surreptitiously watched Brooke and Flynn on the dance floor. It was the first time Liberty had felt that she could relax with some champagne; she had been rushing around all day, overseeing everything.

'Look at them, Libs!' Em exclaimed. 'Dancing like love's young dream. Isn't it sweet?' Em made a very striking Catwoman in a black rubber suit, though she had been complaining about how hot she was. Noah was Batman and currently deep in conversation with Nina, who was the Queen of Hearts. Only Liberty's mum could have got away with that tight red corset at her age.

'Yes, she looks lit up from inside, doesn't she? I mean, she looked beautiful before he arrived, but now she has that extra glow.'

The party was going even better than Liberty had anticipated. All Brooke's college friends were so sweet and appreciative; they had none of that sense of entitlement that used to infuriate her in

364

some of Brooke's LA friends. The food was delicious, the music fantastic, and her daughter had never looked happier. All in all it was exactly how Liberty had wanted it to be. So much had happened to them both in the last couple of months and they'd had so much to adjust to. But not for a second did she regret leaving Zac and her acting career. Her new UK agent was hopeful that there would be some projects soon. In the meantime Liberty was happy to have this time with her daughter. It made up for all the times in the past when they'd barely seen each other. 'So she's sorted – we just need to fix you up,' Em said. 'Have you thought any more about contacting Cory again?'

Liberty shook her head. 'Nope, that ship has sailed.'

'I still think you should do something,' Em said stubbornly, adjusting her Catwoman mask.

'Well, I'm not going to,' Liberty replied, equally stubbornly. She watched as Flynn took Brooke's hand and the pair of them slipped out of the room.

'I'm going to check on the caterers. We're going to have mini fish and chips in an hour or so.'

Em curled her lip. 'Queen of Avoidance. Don't think I don't know what you're doing. And don't let me eat any fish and chips or I'll burst out of this suit! Not something that Anne Hathaway ever had reason to say.'

Liberty was halfway down the hall when the doorbell rang. Thinking it would be some late-arriving guests, she opened it. And did a double take, because standing there was Cory. For a moment they simply looked at each other.

'I know that this is the worst possible timing, but I had to see you,' he said quietly. There was no sign of the cold disdain she had seen in his expression at

Angel's party. His blue eyes were no longer like chips of ice, but flooded with warmth. She should reply that anything he had to say to her must wait until tomorrow, but she couldn't, she just couldn't.

The small office was the only room downstairs that hadn't been taken over by the party. Liberty stood by the desk, Cory by the door. He was still the most handsome man she had ever seen. A man now, not the boy he had been at nineteen, broad-shouldered and tall. He had lines round his blue eyes. Getting older suited him. She hardly dared breathe, feeling that this was going to be one of the most significant moments of her life. She waited for him to speak.

'You still wear the dragonfly necklace,' he finally said. 'I thought you would have got rid of it long ago.'

She instinctively reached up to touch it. 'Why would I do that? It was the only thing I had to remind me of you.'

'So why didn't you come with me? I understand why you left me the first time. I realise that I was too young. A boy. I didn't understand what I needed to do to support you and Brooke. I fucked up. But five years ago?' Now he didn't sound distant or disdainful as he had in the gallery. He was back to being the passionate Cory she remembered.

Liberty took a deep breath. 'I waited for you at the airport. You didn't come. I tried to call you but there was no reply. I thought you didn't want me.'

'So you didn't send the email? Brooke told me that.'

She shook her head. 'It must have been Zac. And I never received the letter you sent. He destroyed it. After he'd read it, of course.'

'All this time, I thought it was because you didn't want me.'

'I always wanted you,' Liberty said softly. She was

laying her heart on the line. If this was her only chance to tell Cory how she felt then she had to seize it. She was through with playing it safe. 'You're the only man I've ever loved.'

She waited for him to tell her that it was over between them as he had at the party. Instead he said, 'You really mean that?'

'I really do. I don't care what you think.' Liberty shook back her hair and looked straight at him, ready to take whatever he had to say. But Cory wasn't saying anything, he was walking straight towards her, putting his arms around her, drawing her close to him and kissing her, and she was kissing him in return. Hungry, passionate kisses took them back to where they had been. They were lost in their embrace until there was a knock at the door and Em's voice dragged them back to reality.

'Libs, are you in there? It's nearly time to cut the cake.'

They pulled apart. 'We need to talk,' Cory told her. 'After the party, will you come to my house?'

'It may be a while,' Liberty replied.

'I've waited all this time, I can wait a little longer.' Then he kissed her lightly on the neck and whispered, 'Just so you know, you're the only woman that I've loved. Still do.'

Chapter 43

Brooke

'You're not going to make me go in the sea again, are you?' Brooke asked as Flynn led her down the steps to the beach. 'Because I'm not bloody going in there. Do you know how long it took to make me look this good?'

'Nope, I just need to talk to you.' He took off his jacket and arranged it on the pebbles for her to sit down on. She turned to face him, waiting for him to speak, but then she didn't even know who made the first move but they were kissing and, oh, God, what a kiss it was. A gentle kiss that grew in intensity until it was a full on passionate, heart-stoppingly fantastic kiss. She slipped her hands under his shirt, caressing his skin. He seemed to shiver at her touch, which made her want to be so much bolder and do all the things she had been going to do with Christian but was now very glad that she hadn't. How could she ever have dismissed Flynn when she first met him? He was without question the most gorgeous, desirable boy she had ever, ever seen . . .

He was the first to break away. 'What have you done to me, Brooke?' he murmured.

'I could say the same to you,' she replied.

He ran his hands through his hair. 'I haven't been able to stop thinking about you since you turned up at the restaurant in those shorts, with that attitude.'

'I didn't have an attitude,' she protested, knowing perfectly well that she'd had one with a capital A.

He just smiled. She waited for him to tell her about Berlin and Eve. She had to know what was going on between them.

'So I guess I should tell you about Eve.'

'Is it still complicated?' she asked, willing him to say that it was OVER between them, in flashing neon lights.

He sighed, 'It's finished from my perspective. But Eve . . . You know that it's been on and off for the last year? At first it was her, and then it was me. And she couldn't handle that. When I split up with her she threatened to harm herself.'

'Oh my God!' Brooke never would have imagined that.

'She has a history of it apparently, I didn't know. So the reason I was so vague when I texted you from Berlin was because she was having a meltdown. When I told her it was over again, she seemed to take it really calmly and then she went into the bathroom and cut her wrists, not deep enough to do any serious damage, but you can imagine how the teachers freaked out and we had to take her to hospital. That's what I meant by complicated.'

'So what's happening now?'

'She knows it's over and I've told her parents. I should have told them before, but I thought I could help her. It turned out that I was the very last person who could.'

369

Brooke curled her arm round his. 'I'm so sorry. I thought you were really into her.'

'I was trying to be, because I was screwed up with worry about what she might do.' He rested his forehead against hers. 'You were like this ray of light coming into my life, showing me that it didn't have to be like that.'

'I feel the same way about you,' she whispered back.

The moment was shattered by the appearance of Catwoman on the path above them, yelling, 'Brooke! Come inside. You need to cut the cake.'

'Come on then, Birthday Girl,' Flynn said, leaping up and holding out his hand.

Inside the lights had been dimmed. The white chocolate birthday cake, exquisitely decorated with white chocolate roses, was taking pride of place on the dining-room table, with eighteen flickering candles on top. Immediately the guests broke into 'Happy Birthday' – the Stevie Wonder version, with Jez and Harry getting everyone clapping.

'Come on then, Brooke, time to make a wish,' Liberty said, smiling at her daughter.

She took a deep breath and exhaled, blowing out the candles in one go. *I want to be with Flynn and for my mom to be happy.*

The room erupted into cheers and clapping and when she turned round to look for her mom, she saw Cory standing next to her. The blue-eyed, blond man had arrived after all . . . just not for her. Her mouth opened in astonishment as Cory said, 'Happy birthday, Brooke. I'm sorry I've been so, well, obnoxious to you. I hope we can be friends. Again. You liked me when you were little and not just because I always bought you ice cream.'

'What's going on?' she asked in complete bewilderment.

'Your mom and I have got some talking to do. You were right. Would you mind if I took her away from the party now?'

He glanced over at Liberty, who laughed and said, 'Cory! I can't leave a houseful of eighteen-year-olds!'

'Course you bloody can!' Nina piped up. 'I'm staying here and no one messes with me.'

'And Catwoman's here and Batman, who else do you need?' Em added. 'So go.'

Liberty hugged Brooke. 'I'll see you in the morning.' And then she and Cory were walking out of the door, hand in hand.

Kelly appeared at Brooke's side. 'That fortune-teller is pretty shit hot – I'm going to have a session with her and she can tell me if Ray's the one.'

At midnight the gang were all sprawled on the sofas in the chill-out room, drinking hot chocolate (Nina had banned any more alcohol) and eating cake. 'Totes amazeballs!' Harry exclaimed. 'That might just win the prize for the most drama at the end of an eighteenth birthday party ever. I bet your mom was most worried about people throwing up, but you had a past love turn up and –' he glanced over at Flynn and Brooke '– a new one.'

'Yeah, so there were some good bits,' Flynn said, hugging Brooke.

'Some very good bits,' she replied.

'And Mila got a snog from a hot Ghostbuster. And Jez and Rufus said they would take me out clubbing in London. I'll get to be in the VIP area! Like a sleb!'

'Did you enjoy your party?' Flynn asked Brooke.

'It was the best,' she replied, and couldn't resist kissing him. Again.

'Oi! You two! Leave it out!' Harry shouted. 'What

371

did I say about PDAs! I'm going to start fining you two. I'll have enough money to get to the Caribbean for New Year at this rate. I can be one of those smug bastards strutting my stuff on the beach while the rest of you freeze your asses off back home. You'll be well jeal.'

'It'll be worth it,' Flynn replied, still with his arms round Brooke. 'So are you going to stay here? Or are you going to rush back to LA at the first opportunity?'

Brooke smiled at him. 'I'm happy here. I never thought I'd say it, but I am. LA will always be there. I want to stay right here.'

'My Brighton girl,' Flynn murmured, drawing her to him for another kiss and ignoring Harry, who was muttering that at this rate he'd be in the Caribbean next month . . .

Chapter 44

Liberty

They had talked non-stop on the journey back to Cory's, piecing together what must have happened five years ago. Apparently his phone had been stolen from his hotel room, just hours before he was due to meet her. They decided it must have been Ramon. He had dropped Cory and Liberty at the hotel. It wasn't such a stretch to imagine him telling Zac and then managing to get the phone lifted, so Cory wouldn't receive any of the messages from Liberty, wondering where he was.

It was after one a.m. by the time they arrived at the house. Liberty didn't think she had ever felt more wide awake in her life.

'Come on,' Cory said, taking her hand as she stepped out of the car. 'I've got something to show you.'

She expected him to take her inside the house; instead he led her round the side to the garden. There was a full moon, light enough for them to be able to see their way to his studio.

When he switched the light on she saw that the entire space was full of paintings of her. Paintings that

373

she didn't even know he had done of her. There were pictures of her when they'd first met, sunbathing on the beach, coming out of the water in her bikini, then lying in bed or sitting in Nina's garden with Brooke on her knee. Pictures of her after they'd met again in LA, when she looked older, more world-weary, standing in the art gallery not knowing her life was about to change.

'You kept all these?' she said in wonder.

'Of course I did. I could never sell them. They were all I had of you. And even though I could hardly ever bring myself to look at them, I had to know that they were there. I've been so good at sitting tight, going through the motions of life, being a good dad, working hard. But underneath it all was a constant need to see you again.'

The paintings felt like a declaration. He really did love her still; there could be no other explanation for him keeping them.

'You've no idea how I felt when you came into the gallery. I was so angry and hurt, and I wanted to lash out at you. But even as I did that, I was longing for you so badly.'

She reached out and lightly touched his face. 'We've hurt each other so much. Are we crazy to want to start it all again?'

He took her hand and kissed it. 'Probably. But I know why it didn't work between us the first time. I'm older now. Wiser. I'm never going to let you go again.' He grinned. 'Anyway, your daughter knows where I live, she'll hunt me down if I screw up.'

'She probably would,' Liberty agreed. 'Oh, God, do you think she's okay?'

'I'm sure she's fine. Seemed like that boy she was with was looking out for her.' Cory silenced any more of her worries with a kiss and murmured, 'We've got a lot of lost time to make up for.' He steered her towards the battered leather sofa, which she thought might have been in his flat all those years ago.

'Actually, can we go inside? It's freezing in here.'

'I promise it won't affect me,' Cory replied.

Of that Liberty was certain. She wound her arms round his neck. 'I'm sure it wouldn't, but let's go inside. We've got all night.'

'We've got the rest of our lives,' he replied, kissing her.

In the Name of Love

By Katie Price

On a sun drenched beach in Barbados, feisty sports presenter Charlie meets the irresistibly gorgeous Felipe Castillo. Instantly attracted to each other, they have a passionate affair, until he walks out, leaving her heartbroken.

It is only then that she discovers that Felipe is related to the Spanish royal family, is a brilliant rider and the lynchpin of the Spanish Eventing team.

But just when Charlie thinks she's managed to put her heartbreak behind her, Felipe returns, and she falls in love all over again. Soon they are the golden couple of sport, followed by the press wherever they go.

But as the pressure on the couple mounts, a dark shadow from Charlie's past comes back to haunt her.

'Glam, glitz, gorgeous people... so Jordan!' *Woman*

'A real insight into the celebrity world' *OK!*

'Brilliantly bitchy' *New!*

arrow books

ALSO AVAILABLE FROM ARROW

The Comeback Girl

By Katie Price

Once upon a time, Eden had it all; she was one of the most successful young singers in the UK, and the darling of the pop industry. Life couldn't have been better. But just two years after a sell-out tour, Eden is regarded as a has-been, better known for her drinking and the kiss-and-tell stories that a string of men have sold to the papers.

Desperate to get back in the big time, Eden begins recording a new album with songwriter Jack Steele, a man who drives her crazy for all the wrong reasons. But when she's asked to be a judge on the TV talent show *Band Ambition*, it's just the break she needs, and she's determined not to mess it up. So falling in love with Stevie, a contestant on the show, is probably not a very good idea. But Eden has always followed her heart, and she is sure that Stevie is 'the one'.

But is Eden setting herself up for another fall?

'Glam, glitz, gorgeous people . . . so Jordan!' *Woman*

'A real insight into the celebrity world' *OK!*

'Brilliantly bitchy' *New!*

arrow books

Angel

Katie Price

A sparkling and sexy tale of glamour modelling, romance and the treacherous promises of fame.

When Angel is discovered by a model agent, her life changes for ever. Young, beautiful and sexy, she seems destined for a successful career and, very quickly, the glitzy world of celebrity fame and riches becomes her new home.

But then she meets Mickey, the lead singer of a boy band, who is as irresistible as he is dangerous, and Angel realises that a rising star can just as quickly fall . . .

'The perfect sexy summer read' *heat*

'A page-turner . . . it is brilliant. Genuinely amusing and readable. This summer, every beach will be polka-dotted with its neon pink covers' *Evening Standard*

'The perfect post-modern fairy tale' *Glamour*

arrow books

THE POWER OF READING

Visit the Random House website and get connected with information on all our books and authors

EXTRACTS from our recently published books and selected backlist titles

COMPETITIONS AND PRIZE DRAWS Win signed books, audiobooks and more

AUTHOR EVENTS Find out which of our authors are on tour and where you can meet them

LATEST NEWS on bestsellers, awards and new publications

MINISITES with exclusive special features dedicated to our authors and their titles

READING GROUPS Reading guides, special features and all the information you need for your reading group

LISTEN to extracts from the latest audiobook publications

WATCH video clips of interviews and readings with our authors

RANDOM HOUSE INFORMATION including advice for writers, job vacancies and all your general queries answered

Come home to Random House

www.randomhouse.co.uk